Praise for *The Color of Distance* . . .

"An energetic and entertaining first-contact novel, complete with charming, strange, dangerous aliens and two intelligent, competent, imperfect heroines, one human, one not."

—Vonda N. McIntyre, author of *The Moon and the Sun*

"Intriguing."

—*Locus*

. . . and the award-winning *Virtual Girl* . . .

"Definitely not your usual girl-grows-up story. An entertaining and observant look at human beings from a computer's point of view. A diverting and highly promising first novel."

—*Locus*

"A promising debut novel with a decidedly different point of view."

—*Science Fiction Chronicle*

"A very good book in many ways and a superior first novel. Absorbing and suspenseful. It's worth your time and money to introduce yourself to Maggie. An engaging and believable character."

—*Aboriginal Science Fiction*

"A coming-of-age novel for the cyberpunk era . . . with a depth of compassion not found in most."

—*Denver Post*

"An excellent first novel. Grabs your attention and doesn't let go."

—*Kliatt*

"Steeped in tradition with a '90s sensibility, state-of-the-art technology, and a complexity of characterization reminiscent of Shelley. Thomson's robot isn't a generic automaton. She's real."

—*Minneapolis Star Tribune*

THROUGH ALIEN EYES

AMY THOMSON

ACE BOOKS, NEW YORK

THROUGH ALIEN EYES

An Ace Book / published by agreement with
the author

PRINTING HISTORY:
Ace trade paperback edition / July 1999

The Penguin Putnam Inc. World Wide Web site address is
http://www.penguinputnam.com

ISBN: 0-441-00617-5

ACE®
Ace Books are published by
The Berkley Publishing Group, a division of Penguin Putnam Inc.,
375 Hudson Street, New York, New York 10014.
ACE and the "A" design are trademarks belonging to
Penguin Putnam Inc.

PRINTED IN THE UNITED STATES OF AMERICA

10 9 8 7 6 5 4 3 2 1

For Rosalie the Wonder Cat

Literary mews, par excellence
1979–1998

ACKNOWLEDGMENTS

Although writing is a solitary endeavor, every writer has a support network that makes writing possible. My support network includes:

My husband, Edd Vick, who listened patiently to loony ideas, middle-of-the-night ramblings, and general maunderings-on concerning the book. He also slid sandwiches under the door when I forgot to eat, proofread manuscripts on short notice, and did far more than his fair share of the housework during the final slog through the manuscript.

My second readers:

Hugh Daniel, John Hecht, Ctein, Kim and Hank Graham, Rich Dutcher, Terry Garey, Laurie Edison, and Loren MacGregor. Their insight and feedback greatly improved the book.

And friends like:

Greg Bear, for thoughts on structure that helped me get where I needed to go.

T'om Seaman, who helped me understand some of the lessons Ukatonen needed to learn.

Anetta and Pekka Pirinen for help with the Finnish. Any mistakes are my fault, not theirs.

Steve Gallacci for help with terminology.

Howard Waldrop, for help with the solitaires and their kin. If you haven't read his excellent story, "The Ugly Chickens," you're missing a treat.

The members of the Feminist Cabal, for support, guidance, and their great sense of humor!

Don Maass, literary agent extraordinaire.

And to Ginjer Buchanan for editorial patience above and beyond the call of duty.

I also got help from the following people, who took the time to answer weird questions posed by a total stranger:

Skip Briggs of Weapons Safety, Inc., who answered some very unsettling questions about guns without batting an eyelash!

And to the personable and friendly staff of Turnbull Wine Cellars, Dutch Henry Winery, and Robert Mondavi Winery, who provided me with vital information about viticulture and oenology, and allowed me to sample some excellent wines! (Research can be hell!)

CHAPTER

1

Ukatonen looked out the window at his home world of Tiangi. It had
grown steadily smaller as the humans' sky raft sped through the starry, endless night. All the trees he had climbed, all the creatures he had ever
hunted, all the rivers he had swum in, were now contained in a cloud-
swathed blue crescent he could cover with his outstretched hand. It made
him feel very small and alone.

Moki's arm slid around his waist. Ukatonen looked down at the youngster, his skin brightening to pale blue with gladness. He was only a bami,
and a young one at that, but Moki was Ukatonen's last link with his home
world. Moki had been adopted by the human Eerin after she saved his life.
Ukatonen had made a formal judgment that Eerin could adopt the tinka,
brushing aside the objections of the elders of the village she was living in.
The adoption had worked out well; they had become exceptionally close.

When Eerin's people came to take her back to her home world, Moki
made it clear that he would either go with her or die. So Ukatonen had rendered a judgment that he and Moki would return to Earth with Eerin.
Since his life was forfeit if his judgment was wrong, the humans were
forced to take the two of them, or have the death of an enkar on their con-
sciences.

Now, looking at his world dwindling behind them, Ukatonen wondered if he had done the right thing. The ship, and these humans, were
stranger than he had imagined. Everything was bright, and smooth, and
bare. The air was dry and the ship was cold and very small. There was a
constant vibration underfoot and in his ears that masked the small sounds
he was used to. The people were either too friendly or seemed frightened

of him. He longed for the shady, concealing jungle of home, with its familiar smell of wet and rotting vegetation, and the distant sweet scent of flowers. The ship reeked of humans, and under that the dry smell of metal, the
waxy scent of plastic, and the sharp pungency of the substances used to
clean the ship. He was finding it very hard not to show how uneasy the
sterile environment of the ship made him feel.

Perhaps it would have been better for him to seek an honorable death.
But his people needed to know more about these humans, and it was his
duty as an enkar to learn everything he could.

Ukatonen looked up and saw Eerin watching him. Was that a look of
concern on her face? Even after four years of observing her, he had trouble
deciphering her alien features. It was even harder now that Eerin was
among her own people. She seemed like a stranger, her body concealed by
clothes, her skin the color of embarrassment, speaking the humans' noisy
sound speech. Even her name was different. The humans called her Juna,
or Dr. Saari.

Eerin came over to them and put her arm around Moki's shoulders.
The bami looked up at her, his skin flaring blue with happiness at her
touch.

"Are you all right?" Eerin asked.

Ukatonen's ears twitched at the sound of her words. Human sound
speech sounded like frogs in heat. It amazed him that intelligent creatures
actually communicated like that. If only Eerin could still speak properly.

"Tiangi looks so small from here." He spoke in the humans' skin
speech, which they called "writing." The human words appearing on his
chest were dark grey with sadness.

Eerin nodded. "Do you miss it much?"

"Everything's so strange here. So bright and dry and empty." He shook
his head. "I'll get used to it," he reassured her. He would have to. The journey from Tiangi to the humans' planet, Earth, would take more than four
months.

A trickle of grey anguish slid down his back. Four months in this barren, lifeless place! There were a few small trees and shrubs, planted in what
the humans called a garden, but none of them were big enough to climb
in, and only a few provided adequate cover. Well, Eerin had told him that
it was going to be difficult. He would find a way to adapt. He had to. He
was an enkar, and this was his duty. It was the only honorable thing to do.

*   *   *

Moki watched Ukatonen leave the gathering. He was worried about the enkar. Despite his brave talk, the enkar was finding it difficult to adapt. It was hard for Moki too; the ship was uncomfortably dry, cold, and cramped. But as long as his sitik was with him, even a place as strange as this could be home.

Because of their special status, enkar were expected to avoid close ties with others. Here on the humans' sky raft, only Eerin understood that. The other humans approached Ukatonen with an eager friendliness that stripped the enkar of the dignity and honor of his lonely status.

Moki looked up at Tiangi, dwindling on the screen. Soon, Eerin told him, the world he was born on would be just another spot of light like all the other stars in the sky. He found the idea frightening, but also strangely exciting. No other Tendu had ever gone this far. He and Ukatonen would be the first to see another world.

But right now Ukatonen needed the comforting presence of another Tendu, though his dignity would never allow him to admit it. Eerin, busy talking to one of the other humans, didn't even look up as Moki slipped away to find the enkar.

Juna stood watching the sparse crowd of people at the reception. The *Homa Darabi Maru* was running with a skeleton crew. Everyone else had been left behind on Tiangi. "Dr. Saari?" It was Commander Sussman, captain of the ship.

"Yes, Commander?"

"I was hoping to have a chance to get to know the Tendu. I've been so busy getting the ship underway that I haven't had the chance to talk to them."

Juna glanced around the room, looking for the small, long-limbed Tendu. They had slipped away again. Ukatonen had probably gone off somewhere to brood, and Moki, concerned about the enkar, had followed him.

"I'm afraid that they've slipped out of the room, Commander. They're not used to shipboard life just yet, and I think the reception was a little overwhelming." Her lips tightened in momentary exasperation. It was considered very poor form to snub the captain of the ship, especially at a formal reception like this.

Guilt replaced her irritation. Ukatonen was here because of her. If she had not adopted Moki, Ukatonen would not be here. But then, neither would Moki, and she couldn't imagine life without her irrepressible bami.

She shook her head. She could not change the past. The present was all that mattered now. She apologized to the commander, and went to find her two wayward aliens.

Moki found the enkar in the garden. He held his arms out, spurs upward, asking to link with Ukatonen. Here on this sterile, barren ship, their world dwindling behind them, Moki needed the comfort of allu-a as much as the enkar did, and it would not violate his dignity to admit it.

"Let's go to our cabin," Ukatonen said. "It's too open out here. The humans will see us."

Moki nodded. Allu-a made the humans uneasy, so they had to link in private. A yellow flicker of irritation forked down Moki's back. Everything about them seemed to make the humans uneasy. He hated the restrictions their discomfort burdened him with.

They left the garden and threaded the long, bright maze of passageways with their brilliant white walls and sharp corners, their feet silent on the soft beige carpet. The empty hallways made Moki nervous. He kept expecting something to jump out at him from behind one of the myriad identical doors that lined the hallways. His nervousness was the result of long years as a tinka with no sitik to protect him from predators. The reflexes of that vulnerable time came back to him here in the bare corridors of the humans' sky raft.

They passed several humans, who looked away uncomfortably. Something about them embarrassed the humans. Yet only a few of the humans on Tiangi had responded like that. What were they doing wrong?

At last they reached their cabin. The door slid open with a sound like the hiss of an angry ganuna. Still, Moki felt profoundly relieved when the door hissed shut behind them. This cold, dry, alien room was the only spot on the ship where they could truly be themselves. The two of them sat on one of the strange, flat beds provided by the humans. Moki stretched out his arms, spurs upward. Ukatonen grasped Moki's forearms. Their spurs pierced each other's skin and they plunged into the inner metabolic world of tastes, smells, and emotions that was allu-a.

As always, Moki marveled at the power of Ukatonen's presence. Linking with Ukatonen was like being swept along by a rain-swollen river. Despite his power, Ukatonen controlled the link with the delicate precision of a mitamit building her mating web. Moki drifted, letting the comfort of the enkar's presence carry him along. Ukatonen's presence enfolded Moki, and Moki let his sour loneliness and bitter frustration wash into the link, where the power of the enkar's presence swept it away.

Moki reached out to Ukatonen, trying to release the fear and loneliness that the enkar kept hidden. Ukatonen pushed him away. Moki relaxed immediately, emitting shame and embarrassment at his presumption. The swiftness and contrition of Moki's apology amused Ukatonen. Even if he hadn't gotten Ukatonen to relax his rigid emotional control, Moki had at least alleviated the enkar's dark and lonely mood.

They lingered well past the point of emotional equilibrium. Neither wanted to leave the familiar haven of allu-a for the alien world outside. At last Moki began to tire, and Ukatonen broke the link with a bittersweet tinge of regret.

The door hissed open and Juna climbed down the spiral staircase to the garden. The garden was silent and empty, the bright sun lights shining down on the motionless plants. Everyone not on duty was at the reception. She felt vaguely guilty, slipping away like this.

Well, if they weren't in the garden, they were probably in their cabin. She headed down the carpeted hallways until she reached their cabin. Opening the door, she peeked inside. Ukatonen and Moki were seated on the bed, lost in allu-a.

Juna sat on the cabin's second bed and watched the two aliens. She had been so busy dealing with the details of getting them settled and preparing for orbit that she had been able to link with the Tendu only once. And the Survey had prohibited allu-a. It was a regulation that came from Earth, based on the report she had made four and a half years ago, when she was first marooned on Tiangi. She had barely known the Tendu then, and linking was still a strange and frightening invasion.

The regulation was stupid, but no one on this side of the jump gate had the authority to countermand it, so Juna had decided to ignore the rule. Moki had a deep physiological need to link with her. If he could not engage in allu-a with his sitik, he would become apathetic and depressed, and eventually die.

She sighed, wishing she was linked with the Tendu. Their skins were a calm, neutral celadon, reflecting their inward preoccupation. Seated, with their long limbs folded, they looked strangely childlike. The spidery, graceful Tendu had made her feel huge and awkward when she was on Tiangi. Here on the ship, they seemed somehow diminished. Ukatonen, who was one of the tallest Tendu she had ever met, barely came up to her chin, and Moki was nearly a foot shorter than that.

Those first few weeks had been a brutal time. The filters on her environment suit had failed and she was dying of anaphylactic shock when the aliens found her. She had awakened in a strange, leathery cocoon, halfway up a tree. Her skin was wet and slimy, and changed color in response to her emotions.

The Tendu thought she was some strange new animal, and had treated her as such until she learned to communicate with them. Even after that it had been hard. She had to learn to eat raw meat, and sleep in a pile of rotting leaves, and struggle to understand the Tendu's primitive, harsh lives. The loneliness, strangeness and isolation had nearly unhinged her.

Ukatonen and Moki were suffering the same dislocation and loneliness that she had felt on Tiangi. She did everything she could to help them, but it was up to them to adapt to life among her people. Unlike her, however, they had chosen to leave their people. And they had each other for company. Most important of all, they had allu-a to help ease their loneliness.

Allu-a was the bond that held the Tendu culture together. Linking cemented the bond between bami and sitik; it drew villages into a harmonious, coherent whole; and helped the enkar resolve disputes. After four and a half years on Tiangi, she had learned to treasure the intense level of intimacy that came with linking. The formal, distant life she had lived in the Survey seemed sterile and lonely now.

She missed her life on Tiangi nearly as much as the two Tendu did. But she also missed being among humans again, and she fiercely missed her family. Her brother Toivo's spine had been crushed in a spinball accident, leaving him paralyzed. She had to see Toivo, and try to help him. And so they were all here, on their way to Earth. She hoped she had done the right thing. Unlike the enkar, she had to live with her mistakes.

With a sudden, deep inhalation, Ukatonen opened his eyes and sat up, unclasping Moki's arms. Moki awoke a moment later. They looked better. The link must have gone well.

"Hello, Eerin," Moki said, reaching out and brushing her cheek with his knuckles. "It was a good link. I'm sorry that you weren't with us."

"I wish I had been," she told them. "I came to see how you were doing. I'm concerned about you, en," she said to Ukatonen. "You seem unhappy."

Ukatonen nodded, a gesture he had learned from her. "It is a difficult thing to watch your world growing small enough to hold in the palm of your hand."

"Are you sure that this is what you want to do?" Juna asked. "It's not too late to turn the ship around and go back."

"Eerin, when have I ever gone back on my word?" Ukatonen said. "You warned me that it would be difficult, but I will learn to live among your people as you learned to live among mine."

Juna nodded. She hadn't really expected him to change his mind. Going back would mean a loss of honor so profound that he would have had to kill himself. Still she had to remind him that the option existed.

"Then what can I do to help you adapt?"

Ukatonen shook his head. "Nothing. Everything must happen in here," he said gesturing at himself with a long, graceful hand.

"And Moki, what about you?" Juna asked.

Moki rippled amusement. "You are my sitik," he replied. "Your home is my home, your life is my life. Every day you teach me more about how to live among your people. All I need is time, and useful work to do. Though perhaps our cabin could be warmer," he suggested, "and perhaps more—" he paused, searching for the correct word—"water in the air."

"Humidity," Juna told him. "The word is humidity." She traced the letters on his arm, showing him how it was spelled. The word flared on his chest several times as he memorized it. Ukatonen practiced the word along with Moki.

"I'll let the environmental technicians know. And I'll ask the Life Support people if they'll let you help them in the garden."

Waves of blue coursed over Moki's body. "Thank you, siti," he said.

"I can't promise anything, and if you are allowed to help, you must do exactly what the gardeners tell you to." Moki nodded eagerly, and four horizontal bars flickered across Ukatonen's chest in acknowledgment. "We look forward to learning the gardeners' atwa," the enkar told her. "It will be good to be of use."

Juna smiled and was about to reply, when she heard them paging her over the ship's public address system.

She swore in Amharic, the language of her mother. "I'm late for the staff meeting!"

At least I have a good reason for being late, she thought as she headed out the door at a run.

"Welcome, Dr. Saari," Commander Sussman said as Juna took the last remaining seat. "Let's begin, shall we?"

Juna listened as the ship's divisions delivered their reports. It was a good, well-run ship, there were only a couple of minor problems, quickly solved. At last it was her turn.

"By now most of you have met Ukatonen and Moki," she said. "Hopefully you've had time to read through my preliminary report on the Tendu." She was greeted with mostly blank looks.

"I'm afraid that getting the ship under way has taken up all of the crew's time, Dr. Saari," the first mate told her apologetically. "But the crew is interested in the aliens, and will read the report as soon as they can. Perhaps you can summarize the details for us."

Juna glanced at Commander Sussman, who nodded. "If you would be so kind, Dr. Saari. I'm sure the staff would appreciate it."

"It is easy to underestimate the Tendu," Juna began. "Their culture seems quite primitive at first glance, but they have been stable and at peace for many millenia. Their medical and biological sciences surpass our own in many respects. I was dying of anaphylactic shock in the forest when the Tendu found me. They created a symbiotic skin that protected me from the deadly allergens on the planet, and made it possible for me to speak Tendu skin speech. Because of the Tendu's help, I am the first human to survive on the surface of a living alien world without an environment suit." Juna paused a moment to let the implications of that sink in before going on.

"Moki and Ukatonen are highly intelligent, and moderately fluent in Standard. They can understand you if you use simple language and speak slowly and clearly. The Tendu language is visual. They "speak" in color and pattern. They also display emotions as color. Red is anger, orange is fear, turquoise is pleasure, and so on. There's a complete listing in my report.

"When they're speaking Standard, the Tendu spell the words out on their skin. If you have trouble communicating, try writing out what you are saying. Sometimes that helps. Their name for me is Eerin," she said, writing out both the Standard spelling and the skin speech glyph.

"Ukatonen, the taller of the two, is an enkar. The enkar are the closest thing the Tendu have to a ruling body, though there is no formal government as such. Mostly the enkar visit villages and help solve problems. Each enkar's word is law, and if an enkar's formal judgment goes wrong, that enkar is expected to commit suicide. Ukatonen is almost a thousand years old, and highly respected among his people. He is accustomed to a high degree of respect, and should be treated with great politeness. Think of him as visiting royalty.

"The smaller one is my adopted son, Moki. He is about thirty-four years old. When I met him, he was a tinka, or juvenile, living in a village on the coast. I saved his life, and as a consequence, wound up adopting him. Ukatonen performed the physical transformation that made him into a bami, or sub-adult, and we've been together ever since. He is every bit as much my son as any child born of my body would be."

Juna felt a fierce, protective pride as she remembered the joy of their presences merging during Moki's first awakening as a bami. That moment of bonding had been the most profound rapport she had ever experienced. His delight and amazement at his own awareness had lifted her out of her loneliness and isolation. Caring for him had helped her make a place for herself among the Tendu.

"Dr. Saari, is it true that the Tendu eat their young?" one of the women in Life Support asked her.

The question jarred Juna from her reminiscences. Of all the differences between the Tendu and humans, that had been the hardest for her to accept. It was even harder to explain it to others, who didn't have her understanding of the Tendu culture.

"Each year, a female Tendu lays hundreds of eggs, producing far more young than the land can support," Juna told her. "The surplus tadpoles form a major source of protein for the Tendu during the rainy season.

"It seems harsh to us, but at that point in their life cycle, the tadpoles are barely aware of anything except food. If all of their offspring survived, Tiangi would be awash in Tendu."

"Doesn't it bother you?" the woman asked.

"Yes, it does," Juna confessed, "but this is the way that the Tendu have ordered their society for longer than we have had history. We have no right to tell them how to live their lives."

"Could you explain a little more about the bond between yourself and Moki?" Commander Sussman asked.

"The relationship between a bami and a sitik is not the same as the one between a human parent and child. A bami can survive quite well on its own. The task of a sitik is to prepare the bami for adulthood, to create a wise elder who is well-schooled in the ways of its village. Once the bami is mature, its sitik either dies or leaves the village and becomes a hermit or an enkar. The bonding process involves a physiological link between the sitik and its bami. Without frequent linking, the bami loses its will to live. If a sitik dies before its bami is mature, the bami will die as well. Moki had to come with me, because otherwise he would have died. Ukatonen came along to help with Moki, and to learn more about us."

She paused, and a forest of hands rose in the air. She glanced at Commander Sussman, and the commander gave a fractional shake of her head.

"Most of your questions about the Tendu are answered in my report," Juna said. "The important thing to remember is that Moki and Ukatonen are in a strange place, very far away from home. They feel lost and alone. It's going to take some time for them to adjust. I have a few requests that I would like to make on their behalf.

"The Tendu are finding their cabin too cold and too dry. Can Life Support do anything about this? They're also homesick for greenery. Could they help out in the garden? Contact with living things would help make them feel more at home on board ship."

The head of the Life Support division spoke. "As I recall, we set the controls for their cabin as high as they could go, given the conditions in the rest of the ship, but I'll see what we can do about making things a little warmer. And we'd be glad to have more help in the garden."

"There's a couple of portable humidifiers in the infirmary," Dr. Caisson volunteered. "And we might have a small heater as well."

"Thank you, Louise," the commander said. She turned to the head of Life Support. "Maria, could you raise the ambient temperature and humidity of the rest of the ship as well? I'd like Ukatonen and Moki to feel more comfortable throughout the ship. I'm sure we can all manage to cope with a more tropical environment for the sake of our guests."

Everyone smiled. Survey ships were generally on the cold side, something everyone complained about.

"Thank you, Commander," Juna said. "That will be very helpful." Not only would the Tendu be more comfortable, but the crew would have a reason to be grateful to them.

The commander continued. "I also want everyone on board to access Dr. Saari's report on the Tendu. They are going to be our shipmates for several months; I think we should make an effort to understand them. Are there any more questions?"

"Dr. Saari, the Tendu's inability to speak may cause some communications problems, especially when we get back home. How can we solve this?" It was Dr. Maass, one of the two Alien Contact specialists sent along to help with the Tendu.

Juna suppressed a surge of resentment. She didn't need any help with the Tendu, and if she did, an Alien Contact specialist was the last person she'd turn to. A-C people tended to be extremely long on theory and very short on practical experience. Most of them resented her because she was a biologist, not a trained A-C specialist.

"That's a good question, Don," she replied. "I'm afraid I don't know yet. The A-C team will need to discuss that." She smiled at him, hoping her hostility didn't show.

"Dr. Saari?" a voice spoke up hesitantly. It was the head of the Maintenance staff, a shy, mousy woman whose name Juna kept forgetting. "Some of my crew have mentioned that they would feel more comfortable if the Tendu wore clothing."

"Thank you, Jeanne," Don said, "That's just the kind of feedback we need. It helps to know what makes people on board ship feel uncomfortable about the Tendu. That way, we'll have some idea what problems people on Earth will have with Moki and Ukatonen. Not," he said, seeing Juna sitting forward, about to interrupt, "that I think we need to turn the Tendu into imitation humans, but I think that Ukatonen and Moki need and want to know what bothers us."

Juna sat back, pleased and relieved. Perhaps she could work with this A-C specialist after all. "You're right, Dr. Maass, we should schedule some feedback sessions with the ship's crew, in order to help us prepare the Tendu for Earth."

"That's a very good idea, Dr. Saari," Commander Sussman agreed. "You and Dr. Maass and the Tendu should discuss this and present something at our next staff meeting. Are their any more pressing questions?" She looked around, but no one spoke up. "In that case, thank you all for a good and useful meeting." The commander gathered her papers together and stood.

Dr. Maass came up to Juna as she was leaving the meeting.

"I wanted to thank you for backing me up in there," he said.

Juna shrugged, "It was a good idea. I'm glad you suggested it. I appreciate your help. It must be hard for you, having to leave Tiangi to escort us to Earth."

He shook his head. "Jen and I volunteered to come with you."

"You left a whole world full of Tendu behind, just to study two Tendu?" Juna asked in surprise.

"Two Tendu, and you, Dr. Saari. You're the one who made contact. You know things that none of the A-C specs on Tiangi know. I wanted the chance to learn from you."

"You're very kind, Dr. Maass, but the Tendu did most of the work," Juna told him.

"I've watched you with the Tendu," he said. "When you're with them, you change—you become almost a Tendu yourself. I think that's what enabled you to succeed."

"Perhaps," Juna said. She looked down, embarrassed by his praise. "But it isn't easy."

"Real contact never is," he replied.

She looked up again, meeting his eyes. "No, it isn't."

Juna sat in the cafeteria, a cup of vile Survey coffee cooling slowly in front of her. The meeting had gone well. The crew seemed willing to accept the aliens. And Don had surprised her with his interest in her ability to work with the Tendu. That was encouraging, but Ukatonen was already in a decline, and Moki was worried. How was she going to help them adapt to life on board ship?

"Hey, Juna!"

Startled out of her brown study, Juna looked up. It was her lover, Bruce Bowles, a technician with the Survey. Juna had fallen in love with him on Tiangi. She smiled, slipped her fingers through his, and kissed him.

"You looked like you were going to stare a hole through that bulkhead.

Is Moki all right?" he asked, sitting beside her. Bruce was fond of the little Tendu and tended to worry about him.

Juna shook her head. "Actually, it's Ukatonen I'm worried about now. He's depressed, homesick. I can't blame him, really. It's a big change for them. I miss Tiangi too."

Bruce's hand tightened on her shoulder. "I know," he said, "but you're home now, Juna. You're back among your own people again."

Juna nodded, but she remembered how connected she felt, living among the Tendu. Even though she was among her own people, she missed that sense of belonging.

"Earth to Juna, can you read me?" Bruce said.

"What?" Juna said, coming out of her reverie.

"You looked a million miles away."

Juna smiled ruefully. "I'm sorry Bruce." She looked down at her cold cup of bitter coffee. "Let's go somewhere quiet. I can't hear myself think." It was a feeble excuse. The galley, between shifts, was almost empty.

"My place or yours?" Bruce said, taking her hand.

Juna looked up at him, "Yours, I think. Less chance of being interrupted."

Juna rested her head against Bruce's shoulder, feeling the sweet relaxation that followed good sex. Being with Bruce was good, but it would never take the place of allu-a. Linking seemed to satisfy a different desire than sex, less urgent perhaps, but no less important to her now. She could live without allu-a, she supposed, but it would be like losing the ability to see the color blue. She was glad that the two Tendu had come with her. It would have been impossible to give up both Tiangi and linking.

Ukatonen slowed to a walk just before the entrance, letting Moki hurry on ahead. They were late for their first day of work, but it would not do for an enkar to be seen hurrying. The humans could wait a moment or two longer. His ears flattened back against his head and his skin paled to beige in disgust as he thought of the humans' obsession with clocks. Imagine living your life under the command of a dead thing! A cloud of olive-grey resignation passed over his skin. It was yet another thing to get used to.

The door to the garden hissed open as Moki approached it, and Ukatonen's nostrils flared wide at the welcome scent of green growing things and freshly dug soil. His skin flared turquoise with pleasure at the smell. This was the only living place on the whole ship. Even the hydroponic area, where most of the fresh food was grown, seemed eerie and mechanical; the plants' growth was forced and artificial. Here, things grew at their own pace, in soil, not a chemical solution. Ukatonen felt himself relax as he walked through the door.

The humans were already at work. The gardeners straightened up and stared as the Tendu came in. Ukatonen could sense the humans' discomfort at their presence. Several of them glanced away. Human emotions were still very hard for him to read. Were they embarrassed, angry, frightened? What were he and Moki doing to cause the humans this continual uneasiness?

One of the humans, a female, her hair shot through with the silver threads that marked an elder, set down her tools and stepped forward, her arm extended in greeting. She seemed more self-possessed than the others, but Ukatonen thought he detected traces of the same awkwardness, more carefully concealed.

"You must be the Tendu," she said. "My name is Giselle."

Ukatonen nodded. "How is it spelled?" he asked.

She wiped her hands on her trousers, pulled out a pad of paper, and wrote her name on it. Moki peered over her arm to see what she was writing.

"Thank you, Giselle," the enkar responded, spelling out the words on his skin. "My name is Ukatonen, and this is Moki. Thank you for showing us the gardening atwa. We are honored to learn from you."

"You're welcome. I'm honored to be teaching you," she replied with a smile. She picked up a tray of soil containing small plants. The plants had wide dark green leaves dappled with small white spots that looked like little stars. "This way," she said beckoning them forward with a movement of her head.

She led them over to a patch of churned-up ground. It smelled rich and full of humus and nutrients, much more fertile than the red jungle soil that Ukatonen was used to. It was more like the soil they made for the dry season treetop plantings, compounded of mud and refuse from the bottom of a na tree, mixed with composted leaves and some coarse river sand. He stuck a spur into it, and nodded. "It's good soil," he said.

"We compost most of our waste and put it back into the soil," Giselle told him.

"I would like to see how that is done sometime," Ukatonen said.

Giselle shrugged. "Compost is compost. If you really want to see it, I'll show you the recycling facility sometime."

"Thank you, I'd be honored," Ukatonen said.

"Sure," Giselle returned. "Now, here's what you do."

She neatly transplanted one of the plants with a small metal tool, explaining what she was doing as she worked. Ukatonen's ears lifted and clouds of pink and lavender crossed his body in surprise and relief. He had done this before, every dry season.

"What kind of plants are these?" Moki asked Giselle.

She smiled, "They're melon plants. It's a variety called Moon and Stars. It's one of my favorites. Not only does it produce delicious fruit, but it's pretty as well."

Ukatonen's ears lifted. "You grow plants because they look pretty?" he asked.

"Of course," she said "Otherwise we would just be raising crops. We want this area to look beautiful, but it's nice if we can grow some fresh food here as well. Gardening is all about growing plants in arrangements that are beautiful to look at, nice to smell, or even pleasant to touch."

Giselle ran her hand along the branch of a small shrub, releasing a sharp and pungent aroma. She held her hand out to Moki. "Here, smell."

Moki sniffed her hand. Ukatonen could see the nictitating membranes flick over his eyes as he did so. It was a good smell, but powerful. Giselle didn't realize how overpoweringly strong the smell was to a Tendu.

"It's rosemary," Giselle explained. "We use it in cooking to add flavor to food, but it also smells wonderful." She knelt beside a silvery grey plant, and stroked one of its leaves. "Feel this," she told Ukatonen.

He reached down and felt one of the plant's soft, furry leaves.

"We call this plant lamb's ears, because the leaves feel as woolly and soft as the ears of a lamb."

"Oh. So how does it taste?" he asked.

"It's not edible," she said. "We grow it because it looks pretty and feels nice."

Ukatonen shook his head in puzzlement. It seemed a very strange reason to grow plants. Perhaps plants on Earth were uglier than those on Tiangi and needed more help to look nice.

Moki picked up a plant and a trowel.

"How far apart should they go?" Moki asked. Giselle showed him, and the two Tendu began gently easing the plants into the soil. The gardener watched them for a few minutes.

"You've done this before."

"During the dry season, we build platforms in the trees, put soil on them, and grow food plants. In the rainy season the platform rots away and the dirt is washed onto the ground, where it nourishes the soil of the forest. Some trees have roots on their branches that we weave together to make the platforms. They draw nourishment from the soil we put on them," Ukatonen told her.

"I didn't realize that the Tendu farmed."

"Only during the dry season," Ukatonen said.

"I hope you'll tell me more about it, when we have the time."

"Of course, I'd be glad to," Ukatonen replied.

Giselle thanked him, and left them to their work.

It was a satisfying task. The soil, rich and moist, was a pleasure to work in. The plants would prosper. Moki touched his arm and Ukatonen looked up. A small pink animal wriggled in his palm. Except for the color, it looked much like a yetilye, an orange worm that ate decaying leaf matter and tiny soil organisms. The yetilye aerated the soil and fertilized it with their droppings.

"What is it?"

Ukatonen stuck a spur into it. It had the distinctive metabolic profile of an Earth animal. "I don't know. Ask Giselle what it is."

The creature was called an earthworm, and it did much the same thing as a yetilye.

Moki described the yetilye to Giselle. "Why is the earthworm so much like it?" he asked.

"That's a good question. It's probably because the two creatures live in the soil and eat pretty much the same thing, even though they're on two different planets."

"Ah," Ukatonen said. "They occupy the same ecological niche."

"Yes, they do," Giselle said, her eyebrows lifting. "Certain kinds of animals seem to occur over and over again on other living worlds. There is a large oceanic predator called a shark on Earth. A similar predator occupying a similar niche seems to turn up in every suitable ocean. The details of the skeleton, skin, and organs vary, but they are all much the same shape. Even their teeth are similar. I understand that the oceanic Survey team caught several sharklike animals on Tiangi. There are pictures in the Survey report. Perhaps you could identify them sometime."

"I would be glad to try, but first we must finish planting the Moon and Stars," the enkar said with a ripple of amusement.

Giselle grinned at his joke. "And once that's done, we need to do some weeding," she said, patting him on the shoulder. Ukatonen stiffened at the familiarity of this gesture, and he saw Giselle draw back.

"I'm sorry," she said. "I forgot myself."

"It's all right," Ukatonen assured her. "You humans do the same thing when we touch you."

Giselle looked embarrassed.

"It's all right," Ukatonen said again. "We just have to learn to get used to each other."

She smiled. "I forgot because I like you," she explained.

"I know," Ukatonen told her. "Thank you. You honor me."

Giselle met his gaze. "You honor me as well," she replied.

They finished transplanting and joined the rest of the crew at their weeding. Giselle teamed each of them up with another gardener to show them which plants were weeds. Ukatonen's partner seemed stiff and embarrassed, mumbling instructions so that Ukatonen had to strain to hear. The earlier pleasure he felt was gone. Instead, he mulled over his partner's discomfort. What caused it? Could he make the man feel more at ease?

Ukatonen set down his trowel, got up, and walked over to where Giselle knelt, also weeding. He touched her on the shoulder. Giselle sat back on her heels, "Yes, what is it, Ukatonen?"

He squatted beside her, "Why do Moki and I make everyone so uncomfortable? Are we doing something to offend them?" he asked, keeping his words small and private.

"It's nothing you're doing, Ukatonen." Giselle said. "They're just not used to working with people who have no clothes on."

"But your people didn't act like this back on Tiangi."

"Ukatonen, on Tiangi you were dealing almost entirely with Alien Contact personnel. They're trained to accept cultural differences. Besides, your nudity probably seemed more natural in your own environment. Here on the ship it's more noticeable. They'll get over it eventually."

Ukatonen thanked Giselle, and returned to his work, deep in thought. Giselle had dismissed the problem, but Ukatonen could not. Their nudity posed a serious barrier to harmony with the humans. Perhaps Eerin could help them come up with a solution.

"How did you like it?" Juna asked as she met Moki and Ukatonen after their gardening shift.

"It was fun!" Moki told her. "I learned a lot. And I got to play with an earthworm!"

"And you?" she asked Ukatonen, whose skin was muted and cloudy.

"Oh, the gardening atwa went well enough," Ukatonen told her, "but I have discovered a problem. Perhaps you could help me bring harmony to this situation."

"What is it?"

Ukatonen told her what Giselle had said.

"Well, what do you want to do about it?" Juna asked when he was finished.

"I don't know. Perhaps it might be better to wear clothes, but we can't talk if we're all covered up."

"You don't need to wear a lot of clothes, Ukatonen. Maybe we can rig you a pair of shorts." She glanced at her watch. "We've got about three hours before dinner. Let's go see what the fabricator can spin for us."

The fabricator took the Tendu's measurements in a quick flicker of light, and a couple of queries. Juna reassured the fabricator that the measurements were correct. Then, with help and comments from Moki and Ukatonen, she began designing some clothing for them. At last they arrived at a design that made them all happy, a pair of loose shorts with a brief kilt-like skirt over them. It provided modesty and freedom of movement, while leaving the torso bare so that the Tendu could communicate freely.

Juna pressed the button, and the fabricator hummed quietly for about fifteen minutes. Then, with a faintly triumphant-sounding beep, the first pair appeared. She helped Ukatonen put them on. He peered down at the shorts. They needed to be a couple of inches longer, and a bit tighter in the seat, and looser at the waist, but for a first try, it was pretty good. Juna showed him the mirror, and watched as the enkar regarded himself. She had dreaded the idea of Tendu dressed up like humans, but this outfit had a faintly alien air to it that she liked.

"Well?" she asked. "Do you like them? Are they comfortable?"

Ukatonen shrugged. "Will this reassure the humans?"

"It should."

"Then they're fine."

She adjusted the fit on the computer, and then told the fabricator to make another pair. These fit perfectly. Then she made a pair for Moki, who donned them eagerly. He was very proud of them. "Can we make them in different colors, like your clothes?" he asked.

Juna smiled. "Of course we can, but right now it's time to eat. Let me adjust the fit a bit, and then we'll go show off your new clothes at dinner."

The clothing, minimal as it was, made a surprising difference in the crews' attitude toward the Tendu. People began talking to them. Moki became the center of a cluster of human friends wherever he went. Ukatonen made acquaintances more slowly and tentatively, but Giselle and several other members of the Life Support team befriended him, despite his enkarish reserve.

Moki was extremely excited with his new clothes. He made dozens of them in brilliant colors and patterns until Juna, concerned that he would deplete the fabricator's fiber supply, put a stop to it.

Ukatonen made only a few pairs, mostly in neutral shades of green. They soon became rumpled, giving him the air of an absent-minded alien professor. Juna smiled at the thought. The stereotype fit him. He tended to ignore everything that wasn't alive. It would be a problem for him on Earth. She imagined Ukatonen crossing a busy street, oblivious to the lumbering buses, trolleys, and delivery trucks, and winced. One problem was solved, but there was still a lot of work to do.

She slipped out of bed, careful not to wake Bruce, padded across the cabin to her computer and entered a reminder to discuss this fresh worry with Don and Jennifer at their next meeting.

She looked over her notes. Her list of things to discuss with them was already several pages long. How could they possibly teach the Tendu everything they needed to know before reaching Earth? She shut down the computer, and slipped back into bed.

Bruce slid his arm around her, and she snuggled against the warmth of his body. The next thing to work on, really, was smoothing out communication between humans and the Tendu. Juna stared up at the ceiling, her mind churning with problems and plans. Her Tendu-enhanced night vision bothered her on wakeful nights. Her cabin seemed too bright to let her rest. She got up and put a towel against the bottom of the door, blocking out the light filtering in from the companionway, and returned to bed, settling against Bruce's warmth again. The Tendu's problems would have to wait until morning. She needed some sleep.

Ukatonen lay awake, marveling at how much difference wearing a length of cloth around his hips had made to the humans. But now that the humans were coming up to talk to him, his use of skin speech Standard got in the way. It got in Moki's way too, though the friendly little bami managed to transcend the problem.

Eerin told him that the humans would get used to their skin speech. But Giselle had said the same thing about clothes, and yet they had made a big difference to the humans. If a small thing like that change made such a difference, surely speaking sound speech would help even more.

But the Tendu's throats couldn't make human sounds. It would be easy to alter Moki's throat. Working on himself would be harder, especially since he would be working on the passage that supplied his lungs with air. A misstep could cost him his life, and Moki needed him. He could not die now.

He tried, softly, to speak human speech, just to see how close he could come. The result sounded like nothing he'd ever heard a human say.

"Are you all right, en?" Moki asked. "What is it?"

"I was trying to make sound speech, like the humans. It would be easier to reach harmony with the humans if we could talk the way they do."

"I've tried to speak like the humans too, but my throat isn't shaped right," Moki said. "Can you imagine how surprised Eerin would be to hear us using sound speech?" Glowing laughter rippled over the bami's body.

Ukatonen laughed with the bami. "It would be fun to surprise her. But I can't work on myself alone."

"I can monitor you while you do the deep work on yourself, en," Moki said, his words as solemn as the glowing nighttime skin speech could be. "You have taught me well."

"You have been a good student," Ukatonen told him, "but are you willing to assume responsibility for my life?"

Moki's skin darkened as he considered it. "If you think I am good enough, en."

"Then we will start in the morning, after we've slept and eaten well."

"Yes, en," Moki replied. "And thank you."

"Go to sleep now, little one. We have a lot to do tomorrow."

Moki's eyes slid closed, though Ukatonen could tell from the bami's breathing that he was wrestling with the burden that Ukatonen had just laid on him. He reached over and let a couple of drops fall from his spurs onto the bami's skin. Moki's breathing slowed as the sleeping potion took effect.

Ukatonen lay awake a few minutes longer, thinking through what needed to be done. He looked over at Moki, his face illumined by the wash of light leaking in under the door. This link would demand all of the bami's skill at allu-a. He hoped that Moki would not fail him.

Moki awoke to the realization that Ukatonen's life would depend on his skill at allu-a today. Was he up to the task? He had monitored Ukatonen before, when he was doing deep work, but Ukatonen would be working on himself today, and that was always risky.

Ukatonen woke, and the two of them showered, luxuriating in the all-too-brief warmth and humidity. The humans had made the ship much more comfortable, but it was still too cold and dry.

Eerin knocked on the door as they were basking in the steam produced by the shower. They pulled on their clothes and went with her to breakfast.

"You're eating a lot today. What's up?" Eerin asked.

"I was showing Moki some linking techniques last night," Ukatonen told her. "We were very hungry when we woke up this morning."

Moki's ears lifted at Ukatonen's tale. The enkar glanced at him, and he lowered his ears and focused on finishing his breakfast.

Eerin nodded. "Next time you can get something to eat from the galley; there's someone on duty all through the night."

"Thank you," Ukatonen said.

"Don and Jennifer want to discuss ways to improve your communication skills. Can you meet with us on Tuesday afternoon, after lunch?"

Ukatonen nodded. "Of course. We'll be there."

They finished their breakfast, and hurried to their cabin.

"I'd like to be speaking sound speech by that meeting," Ukatonen said as they settled themselves on his bed.

"But en, that's only three days from now! How can we learn to speak sound speech that quickly?"

"We only need to speak well enough to let them know that we are capable of using sound speech. But we must not waste time discussing this. We must begin now, and work well and swiftly."

The enkar held out his hands and they linked.

Ukatonen's presence surged into Moki. The enkar did a quick physical exam and then settled down to work. Moki's windpipe tingled as Ukatonen began reshaping it. That done, Ukatonen moved on to alter Moki's palate and thicken his tongue. When he was done, Ukatonen examined his work, and then broke the link.

"Try some sound speech," Ukatonen suggested. "Think of how Eerin's throat feels when she speaks."

Moki concentrated, remembering the movements of Juna's lips and tongue from the few times she had spoken during a link.

"Huuwoo! Hoo ah oo?" Moki said, his voice sounding buzzy and flat. He bit his tongue on the last syllable.

Moki shook his head. "It didn't work," he said in skin speech.

"It was almost recognizable. Keep trying. Eerin told me once that it can take years for a young human to learn to speak. You did very well for your first try."

"Perhaps the computer knows something about how humans learn to talk," Moki suggested.

Ukatonen hesitated. He disliked working with the computer. It seemed wrong that a nonliving machine should hold so much knowledge. But the computer was a human thing, and he needed to learn about it. And it would not be good for Moki to see his discomfort. He was an enkar, after all.

"Let's see what we can find," Ukatonen said, forcing his dislike out of his mind.

Moki woke the computer. After fifteen minutes of careful searching, he downloaded several useful articles. They picked their way through them, pausing often, and getting explanations from the computer. Then Moki began practicing phonemes, while Ukatonen coached him. By lunch time, Moki had learned to pronounce several consonants, and was able to differentiate between most of the vowels. His voice still sounded buzzy and flat.

"You're doing well," Ukatonen told him, as they got ready for lunch.

"Ah hobe zzo," Moki replied aloud. "Izz harr."

Ukatonen brushed his shoulder reassuringly. "I know, but you're learning quickly."

"I miss hunting," Moki complained in skin speech, as they joined the queue of humans waiting for lunch. "The food is all right, but getting it is really boring. No wonder humans had to make so many different machines. They needed something to do with their time."

A ripple of amusement coursed down Ukatonen's back. "Perhaps, little one, but remember, one of those machines made that clothing you're so proud of."

Moki's ears flattened against his head. "Yes, en," he said, his words dark brown with embarrassment.

Ukatonen brushed his shoulder. "Learning to live with the humans is difficult. But this trip is about more than just being with your sitik. You are here to learn about your sitik's people. Someday you will help the Tendu and the humans achieve harmony."

"Yes, en," Moki replied, his words a contrite shade of greyish brown. Inwardly he cringed at the responsibility that Ukatonen expected him to assume. He loved Eerin, and he wanted there to be harmony between humans and Tendu, but they were so different. How could such a thing be possible?

Eerin and Bruce waved them over as they emerged from the food line. Eerin was explaining the fine points of the life cycle of the gauware tree to Dr. Maass and Jennifer when the two Tendu joined them at the table.

Moki glanced up at Bruce, who was listening to the discussion. He looked bored. It was a small disharmony, but it troubled Moki, because he could not fix it. He touched Bruce on the shoulder.

"What is it, Moki?"

Moki spoke in small, private speech on his forearm, "Ukatonen and I need your help on something. It's a secret, though. We want to surprise Eerin and the others when we meet with Don and Jennifer on Tuesday. Do you promise not to tell?"

"What is it?" Bruce asked.

"We want to speak like humans," Moki told him, "but we need your help. Can you come to our cabin after lunch?"

Bruce nodded. "I'll be there at two o'clock."

He arrived with typical human promptness. This human habit of punctuality was certainly convenient when you didn't have much time, Moki thought. Humans always seemed to be in a hurry. Perhaps it was because they didn't live as long as the Tendu.

"What do you want me to do?" Bruce asked.

"We need to link with you," Ukatonen told him. "I need to compare your vocal anatomy to Moki's and see if I need to make any corrections."

"I could get in trouble," Bruce protested. "It's against regs to link with you. I could be court-martialed and drummed out of the service."

"I'm sorry, Bruce," Ukatonen said. "We shouldn't have asked this of you. Forgive us."

Bruce shrugged, then looked up. "You know, I've always wondered what it was like for Juna. What were you going to do to me?"

"We won't do anything to you in the link. I just want to check my work," Ukatonen reassured him. "We'll be monitoring you, and if you get scared or overwhelmed, we'll stop."

Bruce looked thoughtful for a minute, "You promise you won't do anything to me?"

"You have my word as an enkar," Ukatonen reassured him.

"Well, this was going to be my last trip out, anyway. I may never have another chance. Let's do it."

They pushed the beds together and sat in a circle. Moki showed Bruce how to hold his arms.

"It'll sting a little bit when the spurs pierce your skin," he warned.

Bruce nodded. "Go ahead. I'm ready."

Moki could feel Bruce's fear and anxiety as he entered the link. He and Ukatonen waited while Bruce got his bearings. Then Ukatonen slowly and gently began infiltrating the link with calmness and a sense of well-being. The enkar waited until Bruce was deeply relaxed, then set to work. Moki could feel Ukatonen working on his throat, thickening his new vocal chords, changing the shape of his palate, and enlarging the resonating chambers in his sinuses. He followed Ukatonen's work closely. Soon he would have to monitor Ukatonen as the enkar worked on himself.

Ukatonen broke the link, and asked Moki to talk.

"Iz bedder," Moki told him aloud. His voice was smoother-sounding now, less buzzy and more resonant.

Ukatonen nodded, "Now me," he said, holding out his arms for a link.

"Are you sure, en?"

"You can do this, Moki. Just stay calm and focused."

Moki gripped Ukatonen's arms and the two of them plunged into the link. Ukatonen worked swiftly and well on his own sinuses, tongue, and palate. Then, he began altering his vocal chords. This was the dangerous part. Gradually, he reshaped the flaps of tissue, making them longer and wider. He was nearly finished when one of his newly enlarged vocal chords slid across the other, effectively blocking the airway. It opened as he breathed out, but flapped shut again as he inhaled.

Moki immediately began feeding the enkar as much oxygen as he could through his allu, breathing deeply and hard while Ukatonen worked feverishly to reopen his throat. At last Moki intervened, forcing an opening that undid all of Ukatonen's work but opened the enkar's airway. Air began flowing back into his lungs. The crisis was over.

Ukatonen rested for a moment. Then he methodically repaired his vocal chords. There was one terrifying moment when the enkar's throat almost closed again, but much to Moki's relief Ukatonen managed to stop it without his intervention. After that, everything went smoothly, but it seemed to Moki as though an eternity passed before Ukatonen broke the link.

"You did well, Moki," Ukatonen told him in skin speech. "I was proud of you for keeping your head."

Moki shook his head. "Thank you, en. I'm sorry that I made you redo your work."

"If you hadn't acted when you did," Ukatonen said, "I would have died."

Moki shrugged. "I'm glad we're done."

Ukatonen rippled agreement. "We may have to make some small adjustments, but nothing as major as that one."

"Are you all right?" Bruce asked. "Your breathing went all funny for a couple of moments. I was starting to get worried."

"Ahm ohkeh," Ukatonen said aloud. " 'An oo unnersand mmmee?"

"I'm okay. Can you understand me?" Bruce repeated.

Ukatonen nodded and tried again. The words were clearer this time.

"That's pretty good!" Bruce said encouragingly.

"It's a beginning," the enkar said in standard skin speech. "With your help we will improve quickly."

Moki and Ukatonen had a quick snack of fruit juice and sugar. Then, their reserves replenished, they linked with Bruce. They had him speak while they monitored his lips, tongue, and throat.

"Now you try it," Bruce said after they broke the link.

"Hello, how are you?" the two Tendu chorused.

Bruce laughed, "You sound exactly like me."

"Thank you," Ukatonen said aloud. "You were our"—he paused, searching for the word—"the thing you use to make copies of a shape," he continued in Standard skin speech.

"Template," Bruce supplied. "I was your template."

"Tem—temblate, tempuhlate," Ukatonen repeated. "You say it now, Moki," he encouraged in skin speech.

Moki got it on the second try.

"Very good," Bruce told them. "You need more practice, but by the time of the meeting on Tuesday you should be able to talk well enough to be understood." He grinned. "I wish I could be there to see the look on Juna's face when she hears you."

Juna, Moki, and Ukatonen filed into the meeting room. Juna noticed that Moki looked unusually excited about something, but just as she was about to question him, Don and Jennifer arrived.

"I'm sorry we're late," Don said. "It took us a bit longer than I expected to find the necessary reports."

"That's all right," Juna assured him, pleased that for once she and the Tendu were on time and the others a bit late.

"We need to prepare Moki and Ukatonen for life among humanity," she said when everyone was settled. "The first thing we should do is list the potential problems that they might encounter when we arrive, and then decide which are the most serious."

"Well," Don said, "we've already dealt with the problem of nudity. I think our next problem is communication. We need to make it easier for people to understand Moki and Ukatonen when they use written Standard skin speech."

"No, you won'd. Moki and I are learning do speak like you," Ukatonen said.

"I'm sorry, what did you—" Juna began, and then stopped as she realized that Ukatonen had just spoken aloud.

Don and Jennifer were staring open-mouthed at the enkar.

"You can talk!" Juna exclaimed. "How—"

"We linked," Moki explained, also speaking aloud. Pink lightning flickers of excitement cut across blue and green ripples of laughter on Moki's skin. He was clearly enjoying his surprise. "Ukadonen changed me; then I helped Ukadonen change. Bruce helped us learn do puh-puhro—" Juna watched him struggle with a difficult word.

"Bruce showed uz how do zay de words," Ukatonen explained.

"Moki, Ukatonen, this is amazing. I guess we've solved your communication problems."

"We need help," Moki said. "We don'd know many words."

"Perhaps Bruce could continue helping us," Ukatonen suggested in skin speech. "We enjoyed working with him."

"That's a good idea," Juna said. She was pleased that they'd found something for Bruce to do. She had noticed that he was becoming bored and restless lately. A shared task like this might help their relationship last until they reached Earth. Juna sighed inwardly. She longed for something more permanent than these shipboard relationships.

". . . perhaps we might want someone with a little more experience in linguistics or speech therapy," Dr. Maass was saying. This was no time to be daydreaming, Juna told herself sternly. Her first responsibility was to Moki and Ukatonen.

"That won't be necessary, Dr. Maass," Ukatonen replied falling back into skin speech. "All we require is a native speaker of Standard to provide a template for our own speech."

"There's no point in worrying about this unless we have a competent speech therapist on board," Juna pointed out.

"I studied and trained as a speech therapist," Jennifer said. She lowered her eyes, blushing. "I was planning on using it as a fallback career if I couldn't find a job in my major. I'd be happy to work with Crewman Bowles and the Tendu to help smooth out any vocal irregularities or other difficulties."

"It wouldn't hurt to have someone with some formal training helping out," Juna said.

"Would you be willing to link with us?" Ukatonen asked. "By feeling how you speak, we can learn faster."

"I-I can't. It's against regulations," Jennifer said, looking at Dr. Maass.

"No one on board ship is allowed to link with the Tendu," Dr. Maass explained. "Even Juna is forbidden to link with you." He sighed and looked up at Ukatonen and Moki. "I know it makes things a lot more difficult. I wish the regulations weren't so rigid. Perhaps you can convince them to change the rules when we reach Earth, but for now"—he held up his hands in a gesture of helplessness—"those are the rules, and I'm afraid that we have to abide by them."

Juna frowned at the ceiling. *I'm getting very tired of the Survey's fondness for rules*, she thought sourly.

"I don't understand," Ukatonen said. "If none of you agree with this prohibition on linking, why do you obey it?"

"Because that's what the Survey says we're supposed to do," Dr. Maass told him. "That's what the rules are."

"Who made those rules?" Moki asked.

"They came from the central Survey office, on Earth." Dr. Maass replied. "They were part of our original mission orders."

"So you are following rules made by people who have never been to our planet or met any of my people," Ukatonen said.

Dr. Maass nodded.

"The enkar are trusted to make their decisions based on the situation at hand. Why do your people do things so differently?" Ukatonen demanded.

Juna glanced down at the table. "The Survey is based on a military pattern, where control and command are centralized. It's easier to make rapid decisions involving large numbers of people that way. In this case, the Survey hierarchy and, I suppose, the Security Council are more concerned with matters of intelligence and security. They're afraid of you."

"Why?" Ukatonen asked.

"Because you're different. Because you're strange, and because of this." She held her arms out as though for allu-a.

"They're afraid of linking?" Moki asked.

"Not of linking, Moki, but of what you can do with it. The potential of allu-a is tremendous. It frightens them." She shrugged. "It frightens me, too, a little bit, and I know and trust you. They know linking changes people. They're afraid to trust people who have linked."

"But that's crazy!" Moki exclaimed, puzzled. "You're still you, even after years of linking."

"No, Moki, I'm not," she told him. "I'm a different person after all my time with the Tendu. Allu-a was a part of that change, a big part. I'm no threat to the security of humanity, but I do think differently than I did before. Because I've changed, the Survey isn't sure they can trust me. But they still need me. Without me, there is no link between our people. Without me, there is no trust."

Ukatonen reached out and brushed her hand affectionately with his knuckles. "You are wrong, Eerin," he told her. "It takes two people to trust. There is no trust without us." He looked at Dr. Maass and Jennifer. "Jennifer may help us without linking, but it will take us many months to learn to speak properly if we are not allowed to link. We do not have that time to waste."

With that, Ukatonen rose and headed for the door, followed by Moki. Juna went with them. There was nothing more to say. All of them knew that the Survey's protocols were worse than useless. Don and Jennifer had made their token protest, and that would be the end of it. The real Survey brass back on Earth would not be nearly so easy to deal with.

Much to Ukatonen's relief, Don and Jennifer avoided noticing Bruce's linking with the two Tendu. Jennifer spent several hours each day drilling the two of them on pronunciation, projection, and tonality.

Initially, Ukatonen doubted that Jennifer would be any help at all, but he soon realized her suggestions were useful. Gradually, their voices acquired depth and resonance, and their pronunciation became more accurate. In addition, their voices began to reflect their personalities. Each day Moki sounded more like an inquisitive, mischievous, and lighthearted child. Ukatonen's voice acquired authority and dignity.

There was still an alien timbre to their voices. They would never be mistaken for human. It bothered him at first. Ukatonen had wanted to sound completely human, but Jennifer and Eerin convinced him that sounding different made their voices more memorable and distinctive.

In the three months it took to reach the jump point, the two Tendu learned to be comfortable with speaking aloud. The crew made a game of teaching them new words. Moki complained that his head was going to burst. Even Ukatonen felt inundated by the flood of words, though he hid it well.

He was grateful for the language lessons, though. They distracted him from the toll that the monotonous and barren environment of the ship was taking on him. He was grateful when the jump day arrived. It meant that there were only a couple of months more to go before they got to Earth.

"I'm looking forward to the jump," Ukatonen remarked to Moki. "It will be good to be moving toward Earth instead of away from Tiangi." Regret fluttered over his skin like windblown mist. "I need a world around me again. The garden is nice, but it isn't enough."

Each day the ship seemed smaller, colder, and more barren. The bright lights hurt his eyes and the dry air clawed at his lungs. He longed for greenness and moisture and a sense of concealment. Some days it was all he could do to leave the warm, moist den of his bed and face another day in this sterile environment.

Moki nodded agreement. "I want to feel the wind on my skin again. It's been so long," he said, his skin blue-grey with yearning.

"There's still two and a half more months to go," Ukatonen reminded him. "I will be glad when we finally get off this dead ship and feel living air on our skins again."

Eerin stuck her head in the door. "Commander Sussman tells me that we're going to have to strap in for the jump in about forty minutes. We should go to the lounge now. Is all your stuff secured?"

Moki told her it was. They had spent the morning making sure that every loose item in their cabin was stowed safely in locked drawers. Eerin double-checked everything.

"Okay," she said. "Let's go."

Ukatonen hauled himself up off the bed and followed Moki to the observation deck for a last look at Tiangi. Every day it seemed harder to find the energy to leave his cabin. It wasn't a physical ailment; he was just losing interest in his surroundings.

When they reached the observation deck, they saw that the protective shielding on the aft window had been lifted back, revealing a sky strewn with hard, untwinkling stars. Their sun was a bright bead of light set against the blackness, larger than the other stars but still impossibly distant.

"There," Eerin said, pointing. "There's Tiangi. The blue star, to the right of your sun."

Ukatonen followed her pointing finger. His world was a bright blue speck of light, lost among the millions of stars. He felt awed by how far he had come.

"Who could believe that so big a world as ours could be so tiny, just a spot of light?" Ukatonen murmured. He looked away from the window, overwhelmed by sudden sadness.

Moki touched him on the shoulder. "Who could believe that the universe is so large?" he said. "And that there is so much in it still to learn?"

Ukatonen looked down at Moki and nodded. "You're right," he agreed, looking back out the window. But in his heart, there was no optimism. There was only the desperate need to get off the ship and onto a living world again.

He stood looking at the window full of bright stars for another long moment, longing for the warmth and familiarity of home. Then the massive shielding slid over the window like the closing of a giant eye, and it was time to strap in for the jump.

C H A P T E R

2

The alarm beeped insistently. Ukatonen slowly opened his eyes and rolled over, his skin a pale, cloudy yellow. It was time to get up. Time for another day of fussing over that inadequate garden, one more day of forcing his brain to learn more human sound speech. It all seemed so meaningless. He reached a long arm out and fumbled with the clock until it stopped beeping, then tossed the thing across the room, and rolled over and went back to sleep, grateful that Moki was spending the night in Eerin's cabin.

"En?" It was Moki. "Wake up, en, it's past noon, en."

"I'm tired, Moki. Go away."

"But, en, you've been asleep since right after dinner last night."

"And I'm not ready to get up yet," Ukatonen replied. "Go away and let me rest." He pulled the covers up over his head and went back to sleep. He barely heard the door hiss shut as Moki left the room.

"Ukatonen?" Eerin said. "I brought you some soup, en. You should eat. Please, en, wake up and eat something."

Ukatonen hauled himself upright and took the steaming bowl of hot soup. Soup was one of the humans' better inventions. It made him feel warm, and the steam of it eased his tortured sinuses. He drank it down, slurping up the noodles.

"Thank you," he said, handing Eerin the bowl and sliding under the covers again.

"It's my pleasure, en," Eerin told him. "Would you like the doctor to come and look at you."

"I'm not sick," Ukatonen told her. "I'm just tired. I don't want to get up."

"Forgive me, en, but I think it's more than that. I think you're depressed."

Ukatonen shrugged and looked away. "I'm tired of being too dry and too cold. I'm tired of everyone shoving words into my ears. I'm tired of making do with that tiny garden. I've been pushing myself ever since we left Tiangi. We'll be arriving at Earth in another couple of weeks. I need some time to rest before then."

"All right, en," Eerin said. "But Moki's been worrying over you all day. I'm worried that he's fretting himself into a decline."

"He's your bami, Eerin. Link with him. Cheer him up."

"Yes, en," she said. "I will leave you to rest." She picked up the bowl, and the door slid shut behind her as she left.

Ukatonen's eyes slid closed again. It was good to rest, here in this warm, dark room where he could pretend that he was safe on Tiangi again. He would get up when he was ready, and not before.

The door hissed shut behind Juna as she emerged from Ukatonen's cabin, a worried look on her face.

"How is Ukatonen, Dr. Saari?" Commander Sussman asked. She had been waiting outside the cabin with Bruce and Don and Jennifer.

"He's no better," Juna told them. "And Moki's been worrying himself into a frazzle over the last week." She looked up at the commander. "He feels responsible for Ukatonen's depression. If it wasn't for him, Ukatonen wouldn't be here." She shook her head. "I'm glad we're docking in two more days. They've got to get off the ship."

"Juna," Commander Sussman said, "I just got word that the Survey intends to quarantine the ship and all its crew until we can prove that the Tendu do not pose a threat." The commander looked furious.

Juna swore in Amharic. "Why are they doing this? No one on board ship has been ill. Dr. Caisson's only had to bandage a few scrapes, and set one broken arm." She slumped against the wall, her arms crossed over her chest.

"I know," the commander said. "Louise tells me that this is one of the most boring trips she's ever been on. There haven't even been any colds."

"When will they let us out?" Jennifer asked.

The commander's expression was bleak. "They're not saying."

"This is crazy!" Juna protested. "They've known we were coming for over two months. Why are they pulling this now?"

"I don't know, Juna," the commander replied.

"Ukatonen's almost stopped eating, and Moki's losing weight as well. I'm worried that the Tendu are going to die while the Survey bureaucracy sits on its hands. This is no way to treat the first alien envoys to Earth!"

"It's also no way to treat the rest of the crew," the commander declared. "Everyone wants to go home. The Survey hasn't even let our families know that we've arrived."

Juna felt her own despair welling up inside her. She was aching to see her family.

"So what do we do?" she asked, looking up. "How do we convince the Survey to release us from quarantine?"

"Perhaps after we dock, Moki and Ukatonen can convince the Survey that they don't pose a threat," the commander suggested.

"Commander, Ukatonen is so depressed he can barely move and Moki's not much better. We have no way to prove that this is a psychosomatic illness."

"It will be hard," Commander Sussman admitted, "but Dr. Caisson says she'll do everything in her power to break this quarantine. Louise used to be a researcher for the Center for Contagious Diseases. Hopefully she can convince them that Moki and Ukatonen aren't a danger to humans. At least they'll be allowing us to contact our families once we've docked. There will be a lot of security on the link out," she cautioned. "You may find your calls disrupted if you breach security."

"Thank you, Commander," Juna said. "The chance to talk to my family means a lot to me." Tears pricked at the backs of her eyelids as she thought about seeing her father, her aunt, and her brother again, even over a secured comm unit.

"I wish I could take credit for it," the commander said. "It's a concession to the crew. The Survey wants to keep the union out of this mess." She caught herself. "I'm going to do everything possible to fight this quarantine."

"I know you will, Commander, and thank you."

"I only wish I had better news, Juna. I promise you that I'm going to fight this as hard as I can. But if the Tendu don't show some signs of improvement . . ." The commander left the rest unsaid.

"I'll do what I can," Juna assured her.

*   *   *

Juna managed to get Ukatonen and Moki out of bed to watch the docking. They sat in the observation lounge and watched the looming space station draw closer. There was a sudden jarring, and a deep rumble as the ship's docking probes linked with the station's. Then there was a queasy moment as the ship's gravity matched that of the station's.

"Well, we're here," Juna announced.

Moki's ears spread wide, then drooped, Ukatonen glanced up briefly, then returned to studying the floor.

A few minutes later, Juna was summoned to the captain's conference room.

"I think you should come with me," she told the Tendu. "It's probably about the quarantine."

Moki took her hand. They waited while Ukatonen got up with agonizing slowness and shuffled along with them to the meeting. He looked old, Juna thought. Old and sick and tired. The last Tendu she had seen who looked this frail had been Ilto, just before he killed himself. She closed her eyes in pain, and pushed the memory away.

Commander Sussman and Dr. Caisson were sitting with three e-suited figures around the conference table. She rose as they came in.

"Dr. Saari, thank you for coming," she said. "This is Dr. Daniel Nyere, head epidemiologist of the Center for Contagious Diseases; Chief Officer Gabriella Martinez, the administrator in charge of Broumas Station; and Ambassador-General Iago Joven, the United Planets ambassador at large."

Juna nodded to each of the anonymous, white-suited figures. They had rolled out some impressive brass for the occasion. The fluorescent lighting made it difficult to see their faces through their faceplates.

"This is Ukatonen, an enkar of the Three Rivers Council of the Tendu, here on behalf of his people, and this is my adopted son, Moki," Juna told them.

The white suits nodded at the Tendu, and the Tendu nodded back.

"Dr. Saari, could you please enlighten us as to the nature of the Tendu's illness?" one of them asked.

"I am suffering from a malady that we refer to as greensickness," Ukatonen said.

"I see, and is it contagious?"

"It is what you call psychosomatic. I am out of harmony with the world. I've spent too long on this ship, out of touch with the natural world.

It has made me sick. Releasing us from quarantine will help us recover," Ukatonen explained.

Exhausted by the effort of making this speech, the enkar slumped back in his chair. Moki touched his arm, ears spread wide, ochre with concern.

"What has Dr. Caisson found?" Dr. Nyere asked Commander Sussman.

"Louise?" the Commander prompted.

Dr. Caisson rose to speak. "I've found nothing. No detectable viruses, no antibodies, and their intestinal flora have not infected any of our test animals. Commander Sussman has included a copy of my report in your briefing folder. I believe you'll find I've been quite thorough."

"We'll want to check her results and run some tests of our own," Nyere told Sussman.

"Of course, Dr. Nyere," Commander Sussman agreed. "How soon do you think you can finish your tests?"

"We should have some preliminary results in about four days, and our final results in a week."

"And the quarantine? I have a ship full of people who all want to get home as soon as possible. And there's the health of the Tendu to be considered as well."

"We're not sure when the quarantine will be lifted," Ambassador Joven told the commander. "I'm afraid that it's out of our hands."

"Then whose hands is it in?" Juna inquired. "There's absolutely no evidence that the Tendu are contagious. No human on board this ship has died or gotten sick. Meanwhile, the first representatives of an alien race ever to visit Earth are growing weaker and more depressed with each passing day. If you keep them cooped up in this ship much longer, Ukatonen may die. What are you proposing to do about this?"

"We'll do what we can," Ambassador Joven assured her. "I understand your concerns, Dr. Saari, but we have to take into account the safety of the entire human race."

"But—" Juna began. Ukatonen laid a hand on her wrist.

"Ambassador Joven, before coming here, Moki and I agreed to abide by your Alien Contact Protocols. Neither of us would injure a human. We bring nothing but goodwill and a desire for harmony between our two people. How can I convince you that we mean no harm?"

"I appreciate your position, Mr. Ukatonen," Ambassador Joven said. "I will pass along what you have said to my superiors. I'm sure they will take your expression of friendship and goodwill into consideration."

That, Juna thought, was one of the most hollow reassurances she'd ever heard.

"Ambassador Joven," she asked, "who is in charge of lifting the quarantine?"

"That will be a joint decision between the Center for Contagious Diseases and the Interstellar Survey Department, with input from the Department of Defense."

"I see. Thank you, Ambassador Joven," Juna said. These officials had no real authority to free them. She looked down at the bland grey plasteel table, fighting back her anger and frustration.

When the meeting let out, Juna and the others accompanied the e-suited officials to the airlock.

"Thank you for coming," Commander Sussman said as she shook hands. "On behalf of the entire crew, I urge you to lift this quarantine as soon as possible. Not only do we all want to go home, but we're also concerned about the Tendu."

"Thank you for your hospitality, Commander," Ambassador Joven said. "Dr. Saari, Mr. Ukatonen, Moki, Dr. Caisson, it's been very nice meeting you. We'll be publicly announcing your arrival in a few more hours. After that, you will be able to contact your families."

"Thank you, Ambassador," Juna said, her eyes stinging with tears of longing.

The airlock opened, and Juna found herself peering into it, straining for a glimpse of the outside, though she knew that all there was to see was the closed and locked door to the outside. She looked around and saw that the others were doing the same. Then the inner door swung closed. Juna heard a heavy clunk as the locks were dogged home, the hiss of evacuating air, and the rush of water, as the decontamination cycle started on the other side of the airlock.

"Well," she said, feeling the sound of the closing door settle like a weight on her soul. "Let's go sit in the garden until I can call my family."

Ukatonen, Eerin, and Moki settled themselves in the midst of the circle of sunflowers and bean vines that the gardeners had planted especially for the Tendu. The sunflowers were more than two meters high, with huge, platelike leaves. The bean vines, growing up the sunflowers' sturdy stems surrounded them with a curtain of living foliage.

Ukatonen lay flat on his stomach, barely aware of the others. His eyes were closed and his nose brushed the lower leaves of a bean vine, inhaling the scents of earth and growing plants in an attempt to feed the starving place inside. He longed for the wet warmth of the jungles of Tiangi, for the rich, familiar smells of thousands of different plants, animals, and insects growing, breeding, and being eaten by each other. The smell of the rain forest was rich with the smell of life. The smell of this tame garden was as thin and empty as the humans' clear cold tap water.

The emptiness inside Ukatonen had grown until there was no room for food or pleasure, and barely room for allu-a. He felt like a seed rattling around inside a sun-bleached gourd. In a strong wind he would crumple up and blow away, but there weren't even any breezes here, only an endless sameness surrounded by a universe full of nothing at all. Even this tiny scrap of a garden couldn't rescue him from the sterile monotony that had overtaken his spirit. He felt as though he was about to fade away entirely. His eyes slid shut, and he slipped back into the welcome oblivion of sleep.

Juna sat down at her comm unit, her mouth dry with fear. She glanced down at Moki. What if her family didn't like him? She had left Ukatonen sleeping in the garden. This introduction would be complicated enough. They could meet Ukatonen later. She smoothed her hands against her pant legs, took a sip of water, and punched in the comm address for her father's house.

The round, pleasant face of her aunt Anetta appeared on the screen, "Hello, Ad Astra Vin—Oh!" Anetta's blue eyes widened in amazement as she recognized Juna.

"Hei, Netta-Täti, olen palata?"

"Oh, my god! Oh, my god! It's Juna!" Anetta exclaimed. She started to run away, then stopped and turned back to the comm screen. "I'll go let everyone know you're here!"

Juna felt giddy with joy at seeing Aunt Netta again. She squeezed Moki's shoulder, wishing she could link with him, and share the full intensity of her joy.

Then her nephew, Danan, was there. "Juna-Täti! Juna-Täti! You're back!"

"*Hei*, Danan," she began, then saw her father striding into the comm's viewfield. "*Isi!*"

He looked older, his face more creased, his hair whiter than she remembered, but healthy and happy. "*Hei, tytär*," he said, throwing an arm around Danan's shoulders, drawing him closer as he sat down to speak with her. "You look almost like a teenager again," her father teased. "I expected you to look like—" He broke off awkwardly, not wanting to bring up her transformation.

"Ukatonen changed me back again," Juna told him. "You'll meet him later." She drew Moki into the comm's viewfield. "This is Moki, *Isi*, he's my adopted son."

"Hello," Moki said. "it's good to meet you." A flicker of pale orange nervousness forked like lightning down the bami's back. Juna touched him lightly, reassuringly, on the shoulder.

Her father looked from Juna to Moki and back again for a long moment. Juna's heart caught in her throat. She should have waited, should have broken the news more gently. . . .

Then her father's seamed face broke into a wide smile. "*Hei, tyttärenpoika.* Welcome to the family. *Puhutteko suomea?*"

Sudden relief brought tears. Her father had just referred to Moki as his grandson. He was willing to accept him as part of the family.

Moki looked up at her, purple with puzzlement.

"He wants to know if you speak Finnish," she translated, wiping away the tears.

Moki's ears lifted, and he shook his head.

"Well, then," her father said, "we'll teach you."

"When are you coming home?" Danan asked.

"First they have to let us out of quarantine. I don't know when they'll do that," she told them, shaking her head. "They're worried about the Tendu. Ukatonen and Moki aren't well, but it's more like a case of severe homesickness. There really isn't any reason to keep us here. The Tendu don't have anything contagious, and none of the humans have been sick." The security telltale at the top of her screen was blinking, warning her that her words were being cut off.

"Juna? Can you hear us?" her father asked. "Is everything all right?"

Juna pressed the Acknowledge key and the security telltale stopped blinking. "I'm sorry, *Isi*—there was a problem with the comm at my end. Can you hear me?"

Her family nodded.

"Hopefully, they'll let us out in a few days. So, tell me, how is everyone?" Juna asked, steering the conversation away from dangerous ground.

Anetta, Danan, and her father fell all over themselves telling her the news. Juna's fame had brought reporters to the vineyard. The subsequent coverage had increased interest in the winery, and sales were booming, helped by several extremely good years.

"We bought another ten hectares just spinward of Toivo's place, and we've still got enough in the bank to send Danan to the best college in the system!" her father told her proudly.

Juna smiled. There had been so many years of struggle; at last the family was prosperous.

"And Toivo? How is he?"

A shadow crossed her father's face. "Not so good, dear. He tried to kill himself last March. We stopped him, but he moved to one of those zero-gee colonies a few months later."

Juna glanced at Danan, who was looking stony and determined. Clearly he missed his father very much.

"You talk to him, dear. Maybe you can get him to come back," her aunt told her.

Tears welled up in Juna's eyes. "I'll try, Netta, I'll try."

"Harvest starts next month. I hope you can make it," her father said. "We can't wait to see you and your little one. What was his name again?"

"Moki, *Isi*, his name is Moki," Juna reminded him.

"Bring Moki, and the other one." Juna heard the question in his voice.

"Ukatonen, *Isi*."

"Bring Ukatonen, too, but most importantly, bring yourself." Her father reached out and touched the viewscreen. "We've missed you so much."

"I'll come, *Isukki*," she said. "We'll all come. Thank you." She reached out and touched her father's fingers on the screen. "We'll come as soon as we can. Goodbye."

Juna's eyes were brimming with tears as she broke the connection. Her father, Anetta, and Danan were all right, and they were looking forward to meeting the Tendu. But there was still Toivo to worry about. She wiped her tears of joy away and keyed in the comm address for him with a heavy heart.

The comm rang several times, followed by the familiar ascending chime that signaled a recorded message. Toivo's face appeared on the screen. He looked at least a decade older than Juna remembered; his face seemed thinner, more haggard, tired and cynical.

His message was ordinary enough, but his voice sounded harsh and bitter. A descending chime prompted her to record her own message.

"Hello, brother," she said in Amharic, which had been their private language since their time together in a refugee camp. "I'm back. I heard about the accident and I want to talk to you about it. Danan, Father, and Netta send their love. They want you to come back. I want to see you too. Please come for a few days at least."

Juna turned off the comm program, leaned back, and closed her eyes. Moki touched her shoulder. She looked up at him. He held out his arms in the wordless gesture for linking.

"We should find Ukatonen first," Juna said.

"He's probably still in the garden," Moki told her.

"Let's go check on him."

They found the enkar sleeping in the garden. They sat in the sunflower circle, and watched him sleep.

"Moki, what are we going to do about Ukatonen?"

"I don't know, siti. What can we do?"

Juna shook her head, feeling the crushing weight of responsibility on her shoulders. "I wish I knew, bai. I wish I knew."

Moki wandered the corridors of the ship. It was two hours before first watch, and the ship was quiet. Worry woke him, and the desire to think through his worries kept him awake. He entered the dimly lit garden, crept into the living shelter of beans and sunflowers, and curled up there to think.

Ukatonen was getting worse. He moved as slowly as a morra during the few hours of the day he managed to stay awake. Coaxing and time in the garden did nothing to bring the enkar back to life. If only they could get off this ship, and go to Eerin's family. Eerin had told him that there were trees there, some big enough to climb. He closed his eyes and thought wistfully of the huge rain forest giants he had lived in. You could go all the way from the seashore to the mountains without ever touching the ground. He missed hunting, missed the smell of green in his nostrils, and the shimmer of birdsong and animal calls in his ears so loud and constant that it was almost as palpable as the trees themselves, and the warm breezes heavy with moisture after a rainfall. . . .

He sat up, shaking his head irritably. He was getting as bad as Ukatonen, and if that happened he would be no help at all.

Juna buttoned up her dress uniform jacket. It had been a hell of a week. Morale was declining and tempers were getting short. A fistfight broke out in the galley. There were several incidents of drunkenness severe enough to warrant confining the offenders to quarters. One belligerent drunk had to be locked up in the brig. The Tendu weren't the only ones suffering from their confinement. Juna looked herself over in the mirror. She was being especially careful of her appearance these days. Looking slovenly would only add to the morale problems aboard ship. She tucked a stray tuft of hair behind one ear, picked up her files, and set off for the weekly staff meeting.

Commander Sussman looked tired. Her eyes were puffy and blood-shot. "I'm sorry to report that there has been no change in our quarantine status," she said. "My sources tell me there's a huge debate raging among the Survey hierarchy about what to do with the Tendu. I have a feeling they're going to keep us in quarantine until they reach a consensus."

"That could be a life sentence!" Dr. Caisson protested.

"I know," the commander said. "I've filed protests with the Survey and with the union, but I doubt it'll do any good."

"We're going to start running out of supplies soon," Lieutenant Murphy warned.

Commander Sussman nodded. "I'll speak to Chief Officer Martinez about resupplying the ship from Broumas Station."

"We're also running low on fresh vegetables," Murphy added. "We're planting fresh stuff as fast as we can, but it'll be at least six weeks before the new crops will be ready to eat. We hadn't planned on needing produce after we arrived."

The commander rubbed her forehead. "I'll see if there's anything Chief Officer Martinez can do about that as well."

"I've already had to patch up three or four people who've been fighting. I don't know how much longer the crew is going to be able to take this," Dr. Caisson said.

"We all want to get off this ship," Commander Sussman said sharply, then looked apologetic. "I'm sorry, Louise, I just got word that my mother's had another stroke. They're not sure how much longer she has left.

"The union says that they're fighting the quarantine, but they can't override Survey security. Now, is there any more urgent business?" the commander asked, returning to her usual brisk tone of command.

There were no replies.

"I suggest that you keep the crew as busy as possible; it'll help keep them out of trouble. I know how hard this is on all of you, and I appreciate everything you're doing to keep up the crew's morale. I want to assure you once more that I'm doing everything in my power to lift the quarantine. Thank you."

With that, the meeting broke up. Juna waited until the staff officers had all expressed their sympathy to the commander for her mother's illness.

"Commander Sussman," she said. "I'm sorry to hear about your mother. Is there anything I can do to help?"

The commander shook her head. "You could figure out a way to get us off this ship," she replied with a wry smile.

"I'll work on it, Commander," Juna said.

Ukatonen sat in the garden. Finding the strength to get out of bed had taken all his will power. But being here was no better than being in the cabin. The cold and lifeless ship still surrounded him. There was no escaping it, not even in the shelter of his own mind. Even with his eyes closed in the midst of the garden, the dryness, the plastic and metal and sweaty human smell of it filled his nostrils. The deep bone-throbbing hum of the life-support system and the rush of the air in the ventilators clamored in his ears and under his feet.

It was all too much for him to carry any longer. It was time to let go. Slowly, painfully, he got up. He needed to find Moki and tell him of his decision.

"He's done what?" Juna exclaimed, when Moki told her what the enkar had done.

"He's gone to sleep until they let us out of here," Moki repeated. "I'll be feeding him through my spurs."

"Where is he?" Juna demanded. How could he leave her alone to cope with all of this?

"In the garden, siti. In the middle of the sunflowers."

"Take me there," Juna said.

Ukatonen was lying curled in the center of the sunflower circle, covered by a thin layer of dead leaves. Crouching beside him, Juna brushed the leaves away from his face. His color was good but his breathing and pulse were very slow.

"En? En? Wake up, en!" Eerin said, gently shaking his shoulder. "Are you all right?"

Ukatonen's eyes slid open. "There is nothing more that I can do to help, so I am going to go to sleep now," he said in skin speech. "Moki knows how to take care of me. He'll feed me and make sure that I don't dry out. Do not worry. I will be perfectly safe. Wake me when we get out of quarantine."

With that, his eyes closed and his breathing slowed as he slipped back into unconsciousness. Juna sat back on her heels, furious at Ukatonen for abandoning her.

Moki hesitantly touched her elbow. "What do we do now, siti?"

"We need to tell Commander Sussman, and I want Dr. Caisson to examine him."

"But he's not sick," Moki said. "He's just gone to sleep for a while."

"It doesn't matter, bai. Commander Sussman will want the doctor to look at him anyway."

Dr. Caisson folded her probe and put it in her pocket. "He's unconscious. His heart rate and breathing are extremely slow but otherwise strong and regular. If he were human, I'd say he was in a very deep sleep, possibly even a coma. I'd like to attach him to a monitor, if I may. I have a portable one that will work out here."

Juna nodded. "Of course, Doctor. Is he going to be all right?"

"I don't know what's normal for his species," Dr. Caisson said uncertainly. "It sounds like a voluntary state, though, and you said the little one isn't worried. We can only hope that we get out of quarantine soon, and that this state doesn't cause him any permanent damage."

"I'll have to report this to the officials in charge of the quarantine," Commander Sussman said. "It's bound to affect our chances of getting out of here. I only wish I knew whether it will affect them for better or worse."

Juna sat slumped in her desk chair with the lights dimmed, thinking things over. Her family had once had an old irrigation pump that seized up at the slightest provocation. Juna, who had been in charge of irrigating the section served by that pump, had to kick the pump until it ground into motion again.

The Survey still refused to explain or clarify the reasons the ship was in quarantine. Now Ukatonen had retreated into hibernation. The situation was well and truly stuck. The question was where and how to deliver a good swift kick to get things moving.

She couldn't do much imprisoned on the ship. She needed to find someone outside who could get things unstuck for her, someone who could do the serious digging needed to ferret out the people behind the Survey's ruling, and someone with the clout to expose what was going on.

She turned on the computer and set to work.

"Bruce, do you know anyone on the ship who can help me get around the security system on the comm channel?" Juna asked.

Bruce rolled over onto his side, and looked down at her, his face pale and moonlike in the darkness.

"Juna, are you crazy? You could flush your whole career out the airlock trying a stunt like that."

"I'm the only one that Ukatonen and Moki will work with. The Survey can't fire me." Juna sat up in bed. "Going through official channels hasn't gotten us out of this situation. If the Survey won't listen when we ask them politely, it's time to get in their face. It's time to do an end run around the bureaucracy. The Tendu are headline news, but people are only hearing what the Survey chooses to release. We need to get our side of the story out."

"It's risky, Juna," Bruce warned. "This whole thing could blow up in our faces."

"The Survey could sit on us for years if we let them," she pointed out.

"I know a computer tech who might be able to help," Bruce admitted.

"Thank you," Juna said.

Bruce shrugged. "I was planning on quitting after this trip. I've nearly made my nest egg and the Survey is no place for people who want to raise a family."

Juna looked down. Her own marriage hadn't survived the long Survey missions. The worst part about coming home again was realizing how much she envied her brother and the big, wonderful family he had married into. It was impossible, of course. She had the entire future of Tendu-Human relations resting on her shoulders. There was simply no time for any more family than she already had.

She kissed Bruce gently on the cheek. "I hope that whoever you settle down with brings you happiness," she told him.

Bruce enfolded one of her hands in his. "Thank you, Juna. That means a lot to me."

Juna smiled despite the sudden stab of longing in her heart. "I'm glad," she said. "I should go. Moki's waiting for me."

"I'll let you know if I find someone willing to help," Bruce told her.

Juna nodded her thanks as she started to dress, unable to speak past the sudden lump in her throat. She dressed quickly, fleeing the hungers that Bruce had stirred up. In the safe privacy of her cabin, she threw herself down on the bed and gave in to pent-up tears of loneliness.

A soft touch on her shoulder interrupted her. It was Moki. Wiping her eyes, Juna sat up.

"What's the matter, siti?" Moki asked.

Juna forced a thin smile. "I'm just tired, bai."

Moki sat beside her on the bed and held out his spurs. They linked. Juna relaxed in the bami's gentle presence. She might never have children of her own, but she had Moki. She floated in Moki's love and caring, letting her own love for him rise up and flow out of her until they drifted in a dark, silent pool of warmth and safety. The two of them rested there, savoring the harmony of allu-a for a while, before emerging from the link. Juna opened her eyes and sat up. Her pain and loneliness had been eased for the moment, though she knew it would return again.

"Thank you, Moki. I feel much better."

He touched her arm. "What is the matter, siti? This is a human sadness; allu-a cannot wash it away. Please explain it to me."

"Oh, bai," Juna said, taking Moki's slender hands in hers, "you are a good bami, but this is an old sadness. Nothing can be done about it."

"Please tell me what it is anyway, siti."

Juna closed her eyes and rubbed her face with her hands.

"Sometimes—" She paused, unsure of how to go on. "Sometimes I wish I was married and had family and a child of my own. It has nothing to do with you, Moki, please understand that. In fact you make things easier, because in so many ways you fill the need I have for a child. I was married once, to a nice family, but it didn't last. I was away too much. Eventually, they divorced me."

She sighed sadly, remembering how lost and alone she had felt then. Her father had taken her back, had been glad to see her. She had moped around the house, avoiding Toivo, who was surrounded by his happy family and bursting with pride over his newborn son, Danan. As soon as she could, Juna fled back into space. Two years later, the pain had diminished, and she spent most of her next leave getting to know Danan, who was a boisterous toddler. Toivo's family, busy with two more youngsters and a new spouse, was grateful to Juna for looking after him. Her six months of leave had been over too quickly. Danan cried when she left, and, much to her surprise, had flung himself into her arms with a joyful bellow when she returned two and a half years later. He showed her over the whole farm, his treasures, and his hiding places. It was like being a child again. She had missed him keenly during her years away.

"Why don't you just go ahead and have a baby?" Moki asked.

"A human baby isn't like a Tendu bami," Juna explained. "They're completely helpless. They need constant supervision and care for the first several years of their lives. It's very difficult to do alone. You need people to help you. That's why we have families. Besides, I can't have a baby all by myself. I need to have sex with someone to get pregnant."

"You're having sex with Bruce. Is he going to make you pregnant?"

Juna wasn't in the mood to discuss complex issues like contraception and population control. "No," she said. "I've taken steps to keep from getting pregnant. Actually, I'm much more worried about getting off this ship and going home again. I'm sad that I don't have a baby, but I'll get over it. I always have before. I appreciate your worrying about it, but this is not a problem you need to solve."

"Forgive me, siti," Moki said, deepening to brown in shame, his delicate, fanlike ears drooping.

"Oh, Moki," Juna said, putting her arm around him, "it's all right. You were trying to help, and you have. Thank you, bai."

Moki brightened at her praise.

"I have some work to do now. Why don't you check on Ukatonen?"

Obedient as always, Moki left her to her work. Juna smiled a little sadly. He was more independent than a human child. Sometimes she wished that he needed her more. He slipped out of her grasp like a breeze floating out through an open window.

Juna sighed and woke her computer. She scanned the newsnet files, downloading all the articles she could find on the Tendu. The popular response to the Tendu was divided into two camps. There was the fear camp, which immediately began trying to determine what kind of a threat the Tendu posed. And there was the somewhat smaller, but no less avid, awe camp, which spoke of how the Tendu had come to heal the human race, and exalted them as noble savages. Several of the gushier articles gave Juna the giggles; the rest just made her feel vaguely queasy.

A small group of net reporters held the middle ground, dispensing informative and objective articles about the Tendu. They were, most of them, cautiously optimistic, but were waiting for further details.

Among the latter group of reporters, Analin Goudrian's work stood out. She had a deeper insight than most of the other journalists, and the glimmerings of a sense of humor filtered through the objective prose. She seemed genuinely interested and curious about the Tendu for themselves, not in terms of what they meant to humanity. Juna created a file of her stories to look through the next morning, shut down the computer, and went to bed.

The next morning, before breakfast, she read through Goudrian's story file, then downloaded as much background material as she could about the reporter. Goudrian was in her thirties, only four years younger than Juna. Juna could not help smiling back at the slender, dark-haired reporter's photograph. She was from the Nederlands, in northern Europe, which was a good sign. Juna had always admired the Dutch people's history of tolerance. Goudrian had been a stringer for WorldNet for six years. Before that, she'd had several vastly different jobs, ranging from Ecorps worker to tour guide to net gofer. She had graduated from the University of Amsterdam with advanced degrees in anthropology and cultural preservation. That explained a great deal. Anthropologists, unlike the Alien Contact people, actually got some practice in their discipline.

Juna realized that she had made up her mind. She copied out the background information on Goudrian and headed off for a well-earned breakfast.

"How's it going?" Bruce asked.

"I'm about ready to contact someone," Juna said.

"I'll let my friend know," Bruce told her.

After breakfast, Juna found Moki sitting beside the pile of moist leaves that concealed Ukatonen's sleeping form. She told the bami about her plans, and showed him her file on the reporter. Moki read it over, his skin a pensive dark blue.

"What do you think, bai?" she said when he was done reading.

Moki studied Goudrian's photograph carefully. "She looks like a nice human, siti. But you are my sitik. You must find the best way to get us off this ship."

Juna squatted down beside the bami. "I know, but this is risky. I could get us quarantined here forever by contacting this woman. I have only a little control over what kind of story she chooses to tell, and even less control over whether this works." She glanced down at Ukatonen's leaf-shrouded form. "I wish Ukatonen was awake."

Moki laid a hand on her arm. "What is making you hesitate, siti?"

Juna sighed. "I don't want to make things worse. I don't want to fail."

"It is your decision, siti," Moki said. "But I think there is little you can do to make this situation worse."

"I know, bai," Juna replied with a rueful smile. "I know." She stood, brushing a few stray leaves off her uniform. "You're right. Things can't get much worse than this," she said with sudden resolve. "I'll do it as soon as Bruce can get us a comm line out."

"It's all right to go ahead and call your aunt Analin," Bruce told her two mornings later at breakfast.

"But—" Juna began, then realized what he was saying. "Thank you," she said, squeezing his hand. "Do I have to do anything special?"

"No, my friend fixed it so that the security system cuts out when you talk to her. Just get us all off of this ship."

"I'll do what I can," Juna promised, her stomach tightening. She managed to force down a couple more bites of her breakfast roll, then grabbed a glass of juice and headed for her cabin. Moki followed her.

Juna sat down at the computer, turned it on, and before she lost her nerve, typed in Analin Goudrian's comm code. Moki, sensing his sitik's nervousness, brushed her shoulder and rippled encouragement at her.

She sat there while the comm rang.

It was answered by a video. A message in Dutch, and then in Standard, said: "Greetings, this is Analin Goudrian, I can't answer the comm now, please leave a message." Juna noticed that she pronounced her name "Howdrian" with a soft *H* sound rather than a hard *G*.

"Hello, Ms. Goudrian? This is Dr. Juna Saari."

"Dr. Saari, please hold while I page Ms. Goudrian," the comm told her. "She would prefer to speak with you directly."

Analin was awakened by a priority-one page. Someone in the headlines wanted to speak with her. She forced herself out of bed and stumbled to the comm unit, raking her fingers through her hair. Her eyes widened and she swore incredulously in Dutch when she saw the caller's name blinking on the comm screen.

She sat down, took a deep breath and let it out, and told the comm to open a link to her caller.

"Hello, Dr. Saari. It's good to meet you. I'm afraid you caught me at the tail end of a nap," she said. Dr. Saari looked much younger than she had expected, but the face peering over the explorer's shoulder was undeniably that of an alien, so this was no hoax.

Analin's face creased in a broad smile of wonder. "Or perhaps I am still dreaming. Is that a Tendu looking over your shoulder?"

"This is my adopted son, Moki," Dr. Saari said. Despite her dark skin, Dr. Saari had a faint Scandinavian accent, and Analin remembered that her father was Finnish.

"I'm pleased and honored to meet you, Moki," Analin said to the alien. The alien was smaller than she'd anticipated, fine-boned and spidery, like one of those long-armed monkeys in the zoo. "Congratulations on your release from quarantine. I had not heard—"

"We're still on board the *Homa Darabi Maru*. The quarantine has not been lifted. Officially we're not supposed to be talking to you," Dr. Saari said. She peered over her shoulder as though afraid of being overheard.

A surge of excitement tightened Analin's throat. This was a major story. "I see. Then we should get right to the point. To what do I owe the honor of this phone call?"

Dr. Saari began to explain, and after a couple of sentences Analin stopped her. "This is important. Have I your permission to record this conversation? It will be kept confidential, unless you agree to its release."

Dr. Saari nodded, and Analin pressed the Record, and the little microphone telltale began blinking in the upper left-hand corner.

Dr. Saari explained their dilemma, with Moki occasionally adding a detail or an observation. The reporter listened with growing excitement, so caught up in the story that she forgot to ask questions. The Survey was holding the entire crew of a starship prisoner, on the increasingly flimsy excuse that the Tendu represented a health threat. According to Juna Saari, the quarantine was slowly killing the Tendu. Who was behind this quarantine? And more importantly, could she find independent proof of Dr. Saari's claims?

"All right," she said when Dr. Saari had finished. "What do you want me to do?"

Juna Saari shrugged her shoulders. "I was hoping that some publicity would force the Survey to let us go."

Analin kept her face neutral. Dr. Saari clearly had not dealt much with politics or politicians. But then, she was a Survey researcher. She had spent most of her life on the frontiers of known space. Why should she know? And clearly no one in the Survey was lifting a finger to help her. Analin suddenly felt very angry.

"Dr. Saari—Juna—what you're proposing to do is very risky. You understand that, yes?"

Dr. Saari nodded. She looked scared, but then she was risking her career, her reputation, everything, by making this call.

"Why did you call me?" Analin asked. "There are reporters who have given the Tendu much more positive coverage."

Dr. Saari rolled her eyes. "Most of it was pretty awful. The other journalists were reporting what they wanted to be true. You reported only what you knew to be true. That's what made me think I could trust you."

Analin glanced down in sudden embarrassment. "Thank you, I'll have to work pretty hard to live up to your impression of my work."

"Then you will help us?" Moki said. He turned the most remarkable shade of blue. It was almost magical, watching his skin change color like that.

"Of course I'll help you. It's a very important story, Moki. I'm lucky that you asked me to tell it."

She looked at Juna Saari. "The trick will be finding proof to back up your claims. Let me do a little digging, and see what I can find out. Can you call me back in about twelve hours?"

Juna nodded.

"Good," Goudrian said. "I'll want an exclusive follow-up interview after you're released from quarantine. Will that be all right?"

"Of course."

"And can you get me a copy of the medical officer's report on the Tendu?"

"I'll download that now. Is there anything else you can think of?"

"Not yet," Analin said. "But probably later, after I know more. Thank you, Dr. Saari, for trusting me with this. I'll do my best to find out who's behind this."

Dr. Saari nodded. "I appreciate that, and so does Moki."

Analin nodded and signed off. She sat back, feeling limp and tired. This was the story of the year, and a total stranger had just handed it to her on a plate. She got up, shaking her head, and headed for the shower. She had a lot of work to do.

Juna glanced at the clock on the screen before signing off. They had talked for over two hours! No wonder she was so tired. She stood up and stretched. What she needed was a good hot bath to soak out all the kinks in her muscles.

"I'm going to take a bath in the *osento*," she told Moki. "Would you like to join me?"

"I think I'll go to the garden instead," Moki said. "Giselle needs some help planting out a crop of lettuce transplants and I need to check on Uka-tonen." He laid a reassuring hand on her arm. "I liked the reporter, siti. I think we can trust her."

Juna felt some of the tension leave her. "Thank you, bai."

Moki's skin flared turquoise with pleasure at the implied compliment. "Let's link after lunch."

"Thank you, Moki, I'd like that," Juna said. She brushed his shoulder with her knuckles, and went off to the baths.

She let herself drift in the warm water, thinking over the morning's conversation. Suddenly her head bumped up against something. She opened her eyes. It was Bruce.

"Hello there," she said with a smile. "Are the baths closed for maintenance?"

"No, should they be?"

Juna turned in the water, stood up, and kissed him in answer.

"Yes, I think the baths do need a little maintenance," Bruce said. "I'll go put the sign out." He pulled her hips close against his and kissed her again. "Be back in a minute."

Juna waited in the quiet steamy dusk of the baths. With so few people aboard ship, the baths weren't very crowded, and it had become the custom to close them off for couples during the quiet midmorning and midafternoon hours. She had been pleased to find the *osento* open and empty, and even more pleased that Bruce had joined her.

Bruce slipped back into the water. Juna pushed off and met him in the middle of the bath.

"I ran into Moki in the garden. He told me you were in here," Bruce said as she slid into his arms.

"I see. So this isn't just a coincidence, then."

"Not really, no."

"Good." Juna said, and kissed him. They slid down, letting the dark, warm water embrace them.

Afterwards, they floated side by side.

"How did your conversation go?" Bruce asked.

"She wanted to do some research. I'm supposed to call her back tonight." Juna paused, staring up at the dark ceiling, thinking over her conversation with the reporter. "I like her, but I don't know what that means. I don't know if I can trust her. I don't know if she's on our side, and even if she is, I don't know if this scheme is going to work."

Bruce smoothed his hand along her back. "Juna, the Survey's going to keep us here until hell freezes over. Yes, what you're doing is risky, but doing nothing's far worse."

Juna let out a deep breath, letting the water close over her. She lay in the water, feeling her heart beat. It reminded her of allu-a, and it comforted her. She surfaced, letting the water skim her mane of dark, frizzy hair away from her face. It was getting long enough to be unruly. She needed to get it cut.

"I hope I've done the right thing," Juna said. "If I were an enkar, and this blew up in my face, I'd be honor-bound to kill myself."

"Then I'm glad you're not an enkar."

"So am I," she said. "So am I."

Analin emerged from the shower, fixed herself a pot of strong coffee, and set to work. She dug through story files and declassified archive reports on the Tendu, assembling a more complete history of the aliens. The deeper she dug, the less sense the quarantine made. There was no health-related evidence to support the quarantine. The only deaths on Tiangi were the members of Juna's Survey team. According to Dr. Saari's report, they had died of anaphylactic shock from inhaling airborne alien proteins when their suit filters failed. Despite extensive testing by both Survey teams, there had been no cross-infection of Earth organisms by Tendu pathogens or parasites.

Analin leaned back in her chair, and frowned at the computer screen. So what was the real reason behind this quarantine? She got up and fixed herself breakfast, and then started making some phone calls. Her first call was to her best contact within the Survey, an old friend from college.

"Per! How are you?" Analin said, when she finally got through to him. She let the string of pleasantries and reminiscences run on for a few minutes. It really was good to catch up with Per.

Then Analin pounced.

"Per, according to the official news, the Tendu are in quarantine pending a medical examination to determine whether they are carriers of any contagious diseases. But I've heard from a reliable source that there's no scientific basis for those concerns. Apparently the Survey is holding the Tendu and the crew of the *Homa Darabi Maru* prisoner for political reasons. What do you know about this?"

Per's eyes widened at the question. Analin exulted inwardly; she had struck a nerve. "Where did you hear a thing like that?" he asked, after a silence that was too long to be innocent, yet not quite long enough to be overtly suspicious.

"Let's just say that the source was reputable enough to make it worth checking out. I thought that perhaps you might know who could shed a little light on the situation."

Per smiled. "You should contact our Public Information Bureau for information on that, Analin. Here, let me give you their comm number." He typed it onto the screen and Analin dutifully copied the number into her address book. Meanwhile, Per was rubbing the left side of his nose, a code that indicated he would contact her later, on an unmonitored line. He had her anonymous-source address, so the whole transaction would stay off the official record.

They chatted pleasantly for a few more moments. Per invited her over to see his vegetable garden. The tomatoes in his greenhouse were really big. Then he signed off.

Analin poured another cup of coffee. Per hated tomatoes, and didn't garden, so the news he had for her had to be really important. She made a few more calls, while waiting for Per's message, but most of her other sources either professed to know nothing at all, or simply didn't speak to her. That was odd. Usually they would at least speculate a little. Someone had told them not to talk about the Tendu or the quarantine. But who? And more importantly, why?

She paced through her tiny, cluttered apartment, waiting for the message from Per to come in. What the hell was going on? She was about to call the Survey's Information Bureau, just to get their official version, when Per's message arrived.

"There's some serious power behind the quarantine. Even the head office is running scared. The rumor is that someone is using the CCD to keep the Tendu bottled up on that ship, but you didn't hear this from me." He spoke hastily, as though afraid that he was going to be overheard. "Be careful, 'Lin," he said as he reached forward to end the message.

Analin pushed back from the comm and stared at the blank screen. Per knew she could take care of herself, so he was warning her that this could be serious. She should move someplace safe before she did any more digging. Despite her caution, a frisson of excitement fluttered in her stomach. She bustled around her apartment, packing.

Into one large trunk she carefully packed all the keepsakes and records that she didn't want anyone to destroy or read. She threw her travel clothes into a backpack, backed up her comp, then did a high-security reformat and rewrite on the memory, erasing every shred of information, and writing over it with meaningless data. She carefully disassembled one lamp that had a hidden compartment in it, and left it lying on the dining room table. A thorough search would trash her apartment, but perhaps she could convince them that there was nothing here to search for. She had cleaned up after several such searches before, and she didn't want to have to do it again.

She was almost finished packing when Dr. Saari called back.

Analin told her what she had learned so far.

"At least Survey isn't behind this," Juna said when she was done. "That's something. Thank you."

"Call me at the same time in two days," Analin said. "I should know a lot more by then." She glanced past Juna to Moki. "I'm doing everything I can to get you out as soon as possible."

"Thank you," Moki said. "I appreciate what you're doing for us, Ms. Goudrian."

"Please, call me Analin," she said. "And it is my pleasure. I never thought I would get to meet you, even over the comm."

Analin shook her head in wonder after they signed off. These two had handed her the story of the year, and yet they were grateful to her!

She turned the comm off, and packed the last few items. Then she put the trunk and a laundry bag full of pillows and dirty clothes onto her luggage cart, swung on her backpack, and left. She shipped the trunk via slow freight to her uncle in Canada, with instructions to contact her when it arrived. The pillows got dropped off at the laundry, where they would be safe from searchers with knives. She was still finding feathers from the last time someone searched her place. Then she tightened the straps on her backpack, and headed for the train station.

She spent the night hopping around Frankfurt, calling her contacts in the CCD. Then, around four in the morning, she took the train to Paris, and checked her messages in an all-night net café. One of her CCD contacts came through with a name: General Alice Burnham. On the train to Lyon, she did some digging. She got off the train in Dijon, and caught a train to Bern. In Bern, she contacted a net pirate she knew about from a friend.

He was a burly man with a grizzled red beard, who went by the name Morgan. They met in a café.

"Are you Morgan?"

"You Goudrian?" he asked.

She nodded. "Yes, Brinker sent me."

Morgan drained the last of his thick Turkish coffee. "Were you fol-lowed?" he asked.

"Not that I could see, but—" She spread her hands and shrugged. "The world's a big place, yes?"

"Come on, then," he said. He motioned to the big, bald-headed man with the enormous black handlebar mustache behind the counter. The man nodded and opened a door at the back of the café. Analin went through onto a landing at the top of a dark staircase. Morgan took her hand, and they carefully descended the dark stairs and went through a door that opened onto a parking garage.

Morgan tossed a ring of keys to the attendant. "Trieste, I think, tell Milán to send me a red Gavotte this time. And call Ian and tell him to meet us at the Erdbeere."

"That way." he told Analin, gesturing at a door. They went through the door to another garage, and then through a maze of hallways, garages, and basements, emerging finally in the lobby of a seedy apartment building. They left the building, and got into a waiting cab.

"What do you need?" he asked her, as they settled back into the cab.

"Traceless shielding on this comm unit for a few days."

"Why not get another number?"

"I'm expecting an important call on it tomorrow evening."

He nodded. "We'll forward it through one of our tracer mazes. It'll look like you're calling from Brazil."

"I also need a dossier on General Burnham, security head of the Space Service, including as much classified material about her connections with the CCD as you can find. And a good night's sleep somewhere safe."

"O.K.," Morgan said, "but it will cost you."

"I know. How much?"

"Fifteen thousand Swiss credits."

Analin shook her head. "Too much. Five thousand."

"May I remind you that you're in no position to bargain. Burnham's a difficult target."

"I thought you were a professional," Analin said, lifting her chin defi-antly. She didn't have fifteen thousand credits. Eleven would wipe her out, but this story would earn it back several times over.

"One of the best," he said. "That's what you're paying for. Twelve thousand."

"Six."

"Ten."

"Seven."

"This problem intrigues me. I'll go as low as eight and a half."

"Eight and a half," she agreed after a moment's hesitation. It was a good price, for what he was offering, but it would not do to appear too eager. "But I get one more follow-up report."

"All right," he said. They linked wrist comps, typed in their access codes, and completed the transaction. The money would remain in escrow until Analin confirmed that the work had been done.

The deal made, Morgan leaned forward and said something in Swiss to the driver about a hotel. The cab turned and sped to an anonymous-looking pension.

"I'll be back in eight hours with a preliminary report," Morgan told her when she was safely in her room. "Sleep well."

Analin nodded. As soon as he was gone, she shucked her clothes, showered, climbed into bed, and let sleep take her.

She was awakened by a knock on the door. Groggily, she got up, shrugged on the rumpled clothes she'd cast off the night before, and peered out the security peephole. It was Morgan, carrying a paper bag and a fat manila envelope.

She opened the door.

"Breakfast, and your report, Ms. Goudrian. May I say that it is utterly fascinating reading?" Morgan announced as he strode in. He set the paper bag down on the table and took out a breakfast pie and a large container of coffee. The smell of hot pastry made Analin's mouth water. It had been twelve hours since her last meal. She glanced from the envelope to the breakfast pie and coffee, torn between hunger and her desire to read the report.

"I'll summarize the contents of the report while you eat," Morgan said. "Your General Burnham is a most interesting person. She's a hard-line Expansionist, and a professional paranoid. She's part of a clique of highly placed Expansionists in the Space Service. Burnham has official ties to HumanSpace, and the Terraforming Foundation. Unofficially, she has ties to several pronatalist groups including a couple with terrorist leanings."

Analin nodded. "And her ties to the CCD?" she asked, taking another bite of breakfast.

"There's a Dr. Koro, who heads the Expansionist clique at the CCD. Their affiliations have a significant overlap. Koro's comm logs show a significant increase in calls from Burnham over the last two months, beginning about the time the *Homa Darabi Maru* came through the jump gate."

"I see." Analin pushed aside her food and flipped through the report. There was a lot there; it would take a couple of hours to study it.

"Your inquiries have stirred up a hornet's nest," Morgan told her. "Burnham's people are looking for you."

Analin shrugged. "That's why I'm here. Are they coming close?"

"You ditched them in Dijon. It'll take them a while to go through the train station's security-camera files. By tomorrow, they'll know you came to Bern.

"By tomorrow, I'll be somewhere else," Analin said. "I've done this sort of thing before." She held out her wrist comp to signal the completion of their transaction.

But before she left, she needed to start work on the article she would post on the Web. She went over Burnham's dossier, pulling out the evidence she needed. Then she dove back into the net, digging out more information on the CCD and Dr. Koro. All she needed were a few more quotes from Juna and Moki and she would be ready to file. She shook her head, marveling at the stroke of good fortune that had moved Juna to contact her instead of some other net reporter.

Juna sat back, mulling over what Analin had just told them.

"Analin, why don't the Expansionists like us?" Moki asked.

"They have nothing against you or Ukatonen specifically," Analin told him. "They're isolationists, and the idea of aliens out there scares them. They want the universe to themselves."

"But why are they afraid of us?" Moki asked.

"Because you're not human," Juna explained. "Because you're different." She turned back to the comm screen. "What are the Expansionists saying about the Tendu?" she asked Analin.

"About what you would expect. The Tendu are dangerous, and they may be diseased. They're also spreading horror stories about how the Tendu turned you into something grotesque and deformed."

"Hasn't the Survey let them know that Ukatonen changed me back?" Juna asked.

"The Survey hasn't said much at all about you or the Tendu, aside from the fact that you're here and that you're in quarantine."

"This whole thing is so silly," Juna complained. "The Tendu aren't dangerous. In fact, they can help us a great deal. Their skill at healing can advance our own medical knowledge. Their knowledge of ecosystems could help us restore Earth's environment and speed up the terraforming of Mars and Terra Nova. With their help, we could explore living worlds without an environment suit, perhaps even colonize them. But first, the Tendu and humanity need to get to know each other, to learn what we can do for each other. We can't accomplish that trapped up here in quarantine."

Analin smiled. "That was well said, Juna. May I quote you on that?"

Juna shrugged, embarrassed and flattered. "Sure, if it will help you get us out of here."

"I hope so," Analin said. "I should have my article finished and on-line in a few more hours."

Juna swallowed, her throat suddenly dry with nervousness. This had passed beyond her control now. "Oh," she managed to say.

Analin leaned forward, toward the comm screen. "Juna, I'm on your side. They're illegally holding you prisoner. Besides, I'm looking forward to that exclusive interview. I can't get that until you're off that ship. There are no guarantees that what I write will spring you, but at the very least it should cause a major scandal. Burnham and the others will be too busy covering their tracks to keep you and the Tendu bottled up much longer."

Juna felt hopeful for the first time in weeks. "Thank you, Analin. I know you'll do your best."

Analin nodded, suddenly shy. "Check this address in two hours. I'll have a copy of the story there for you to download. The article should be on the net in four hours."

"Good luck," Juna said.

"Thanks," Analin replied.

Analin was as good as her word. The file was waiting for Juna two hours later.

"Dear Juna and Moki," it began.

"Here is the story. I hope it helps spring you. I'm sorry I'm not available for you to talk to. Given the sensitivity of this news, I think it's better for me to be a moving target for a few days. Good luck!—Analin Goudrian"

Aliens Held Hostage to Expansionist Paranoia

INN-Nederlands—Sources within the Survey administration say that General Burnham and a clique of Expansionists in high positions are responsible for the prolonged quarantine of the Tendu on board the *Homa Darabi Maru*, despite the fact that there is no apparent reason to keep them there.

According to Dr. Juna Saari, the Survey researcher who first discovered the Tendu, none of the crew has been sick since the Tendu came on board. This is corroborated by the Chief Medical Officer of the *Homa Darabi Maru*, Dr. Louise Caisson, who previously served as a researcher at the Center for Contagious Diseases on Luna.

Despite their freedom from contagious diseases, the Tendu's health has been impacted by the prolonged quarantine.

"The Tendu are suffering from what they refer to as greensickness," Dr. Saari said, during a recent interview. "Essentially, it's a form of depression caused by their isolation in the artificial setting of this spaceship. The Tendu need a natural environment. Without it they become depressed and stop eating. Although greensickness is not contagious, it has made the Tendu severely ill, and could even kill them. Ukatonen has been so severely affected that he has gone into a coma."

The CCD confirms that there has been no illness among the crew of the *Homa Darabi Maru*. When asked why the entire crew remained confined, the CCD and the Survey both said that "significant security concerns prevent the release of the passengers and crew of the *Homa Darabi Maru* from quarantine."

General Alice Burnham, an arch-conservative Expansionist, has the command authority to release the Tendu and the crew of the ship from quarantine. However, the Expansionists have taken a very strong stand against the Tendu, and sources within the Survey accuse General Burnham of keeping the Tendu in quarantine for political reasons. General Burnham refused to comment on whether her political opinions have influenced her decision to keep the Tendu in quarantine. When asked when the Tendu and the crew of the *Homa Darabi Maru* would be released, the general said, "That is entirely up to Dr. Koro of the CCD. When he approves a release from quarantine, then I will act upon it."

Dr. Koro, who could not be reached for comment, is also involved in a number of Expansionist organizations. He is on the board of directors of the Space Frontiers Foundation, and is a member of HumanSpace, as well as the Terraforming Foundation.

According to Dr. Saari, "The Tendu aren't dangerous. In fact, they can help us a great deal. Their skill at healing can advance our own medical knowledge. Their knowledge of ecosystems could help us restore Earth's environment and speed up the terraforming of Mars and Terra Nova. With their help, we could explore living worlds without an environment suit, perhaps even colonize them. But first, the Tendu and humanity need to get to know each other, to learn what we can do for each other. We can't accomplish that trapped up here in quarantine."

The Interstellar Space Explorers and Workers Union said that they had received several appeals from the crew of the *Homa Darabi Maru*, but that Survey security had assured them the quarantine was necessary. "If these allegations are true, then the union will have no choice but to take quick and decisive action against the Survey," said Mark Manning, president of ISEWU.

"Well," Juna commented, "I think it's a good article."

"I don't understand, siti," Moki said. "Why can General Burnham keep us here?"

"Because the people in charge gave her the authority to do so, bai. If we're lucky, this article will embarrass her so much that she has to release us."

"Will she decide to die?" Moki asked.

"No, bai, she's not an enkar."

"Then why is she running things?"

"Because the people in charge trusted her to do a good job."

"Are they enkar? Will they die?"

"No bai. It doesn't work like that here."

Juna had tried several times to explain human politics and the concept of democracy to the Tendu, but they always ended up bewildered. "All the humans get together and decide who will run things. This process is known as an election."

"But none of them are enkar?"

"No, bai. We have no enkar. If they do a bad job, we don't elect them again."

Moki shook his head. "How can you trust them?"

Juna shrugged. "We don't, bai. We watch them all the time, to make sure they don't make mistakes. Analin is one of the people whose atwa it is to watch our leaders, and to tell us when a mistake is made. That is why she is helping us now."

"It seems like a bad way to run things."

"Perhaps, bai, but it works for us."

"Dr. Saari, I just received an irate call from General Burnham's office. They claim that you breached security. There's also been an inquiry from the union, based on statements that they claim you made. Would you please explain this?" Commander Sussman said.

Juna handed her a printout of Analin's article. "This will explain everything, Commander."

The commander read the article, her face carefully impassive.

"My," she said when she was finished. She stood, both hands resting on her desk, her blue eyes fixed on Juna. "What the hell were you thinking of, Dr. Saari?"

"You wanted me to figure out some way of getting us off this ship," Juna said. "This is what I came up with."

"You defined that suggestion pretty broadly."

"Yes, ma'am, I did."

"I'm going to log an official reprimand on your record. By rights, I should have you thrown in the brig, but given the circumstances I'd say that being stuck in quarantine is discipline enough."

"Yes, ma'am. I apologize, ma'am."

"You've taken an awful risk. You know that you could wind up court-martialed for this?"

"Yes, ma'am, I know that. And, Commander Sussman, I want to formally state that this was entirely my own idea. No one on board helped me in any way."

"Of course," the commander said skeptically. "However, that will not save my ass or the ass of anyone who was supposed to have the power to stop you. I don't know if you thought of that before you launched this crazy scheme of yours."

Juna stared at the floor, her face hot with shame. "No, ma'am, I did not."

"Thank you, Dr. Saari. That is all I have to say to you at this time," Commander Sussman said stiffly. "Dismissed."

The Survey shut down all the comm channels. Only the commander could call out or receive calls. Morale plummeted. Some of the crew began pointedly avoiding Juna and Moki.

Five days later, Commander Sussman called a general meeting of the entire crew.

"Due to the controversy surrounding the recent news report about the quarantine, the union has expressed concerns about conditions aboard ship," she began, carefully avoiding Juna's gaze. "An inspection team from the union will be coming aboard tomorrow. We are expected to assist them in their investigation."

A murmur of excitement passed through the assembled crew. Juna's heart soared like a white-winged bird. Analin had come through for them. This was their chance to get out of quarantine!

Sussman waited until the murmuring died down. "We've been through some pretty difficult times these past few weeks. I'm sure many of you have statements to make to the union representatives. I want to remind you that all claims made to the union must be provable. Rumors and opinions will only weaken our case. If any of you have any formal protests to file, please get your proof ready to present.

"I want to thank all of you for your very hard work. The ship looks as if it was newly commissioned. While I haven't done any inspection of your personal quarters, I expect they'll look as good as the rest of the ship."

The crew smiled good-naturedly at the commander's veiled order.

"If any of you have any questions about how to file a protest, you should ask your union shop-stewards. Any other questions should be directed to your staff officers. Thank you all very much for your patience and hard work during this quarantine. I'm proud of you." She gave them a stiffly correct military salute. "Dismissed."

As Juna filed out with Moki, Dr. Caisson intercepted her.

"The commander would like a word with you in her office, if you have a moment."

"Thank you, Doctor, please tell her that I will be there."

Commander Sussman stood as Juna came into her office. "Congratulations, Dr. Saari. That article stirred up quite a controversy. I've been catching all kinds of official hell for this." The commander frowned ruefully.

"I'm sorry," Juna apologized.

"I'm not," Commander Sussman said bluntly. "This is my ship and my crew, and we've been treated very badly for the sake of the Expansionists' political convenience. This quarantine was absolutely inexcusable. I hope the union kicks the Survey's ass." She paused, smiling ironically. "I didn't invite you here for a tirade, Doctor. I wanted to apologize for losing my temper last week."

Juna shrugged. "I'm sorry you were involved. I took an inexcusable risk with you and your crew."

"Well, it got results," Sussman admitted. "Have you given any thought to what you're going to say to the union officials?"

"I don't really know what they're going to ask," Juna replied.

"They're probably going to focus much of their attention on you and the aliens. Legally, I can't advise you on what to say, but I do urge you to be prepared to make the best case you can. If this doesn't work—"

Juna nodded. "There's a lot at stake. I'll do my best, ma'am, for you and all the crew, as well as for the Tendu."

The commander looked straight at her. For a moment, her mask slipped, and Juna could see the toll that this quarantine had taken on her.

"Thank you, Juna. Let's hope this works."

Juna was there with Moki, Commander Sussman, Dr. Caisson, and First Mate Vargo when the e-suited inspection team came aboard with their security escort.

The leader of the team approached Juna, hand outstretched in greeting. "Dr. Saari, I presume? I'm Mark Manning, president of ISEWU," he said, shaking her hand. "It's an honor to meet you. And is this Moki?" Manning sounded hoarse and a bit out of breath.

Juna nodded and introduced him to her bami. She watched as Manning turned to greet the ship's officers. The president of the union had come for this inspection. They must be taking this very seriously indeed.

The introductions over, Manning turned to Sussman.

"Commander Sussman, before we interview the crew we'd like to see the ship, and speak with your medical officer."

"Of course, Mr. Manning. This way please."

They showed Manning and the other union representatives around the ship. Manning watched attentively and occasionally murmured remarks into his suit recorder.

"Dr. Caisson, I understand that you used to work at the Center for Contagious Diseases."

"Yes, Mr. Manning. I was the head researcher in their xenomicrobiology department, before requesting a posting here on the *Homa Darabi*. I wanted a chance to conduct more research in the field."

"Louise's experience in xenobiology was one of the reasons that we were selected to go to Tiangi," Commander Sussman explained.

"I see. That's very interesting. And since the Tendu arrived, there's been no illness on board ship?"

"None at all. We followed careful decontamination procedures, and there were very few pathogens on board when we left Earth. There were a few colds on the way out, but nothing at all on the way back."

"Mm-mhm. I see. Would it be possible to meet the other Tendu now?" he asked.

"Of course, Mr. Sussman," Juna said. "This way."

The group followed Juna into the garden where Ukatonen was sleeping, hooked up to an array of beeping medical monitors.

"This is a voluntary state?" Manning asked Moki.

"He decided to go to sleep and wait until we were let out of the ship," Moki agreed.

"He's all right otherwise?"

Moki nodded. "He just needs to be some place with trees and plants."

"Dr. Caisson," Manning asked, "have you found any organic cause for Ukatonen's condition?"

"No," the medical officer replied. "I've been monitoring Ukatonen ever since he went to sleep. I ran extensive blood tests, and aside from being a bit underweight, he seems healthy. He is in quite a remarkable state. His entire metabolism is running much slower than usual, but otherwise he appears normal. His brain seems to be deeply asleep. Moki feeds him and filters wastes out of his system via his spurs. If we could replicate this state of stasis, we could drastically cut the cost of space travel. We wouldn't need to feed and amuse our passengers. Think what it would mean for transporting colonists to Terra Nova, or even Mars."

"Are you sure that you're not an Expansionist, Dr. Caisson?"

The doctor raised her eyebrows. "I'm not paranoid or bigoted enough to be an Expansionist," she replied.

Juna saw Commander Sussman smile at that remark.

"I see," Manning said once again. "Well, I'm convinced that there's nothing wrong with the Tendu."

He reached up and undogged his helmet.

"What are you doing!" the security escort shouted, reaching for Manning as he lifted his helmet off and shook loose his lion's mane of fiery red hair.

"Violating quarantine," Manning said in an amused tone of voice. "I'd let go of my arm if I were you. Roughing up the president of ISEWU wouldn't be a good idea. The crew of the *Homa Darabi Maru* needs an on-site union observer to ensure that their rights aren't being violated. Given the situation, it wouldn't be right to ask a subordinate to risk violating quarantine, so I'm volunteering for the job."

Juna's eyebrows rose in astonishment and admiration.

Manning coughed several times, "And if this unreasonable quarantine is not lifted within five days, I will go on a hunger strike," he continued in his reasonable, slightly breathless tone of voice, as though he were explaining this to a small child. "If the quarantine continues for more than ten days, I will urge all our union members to show solidarity with their fellow workers aboard the *Homa Darabi Maru* by declaring a general strike."

Matters moved fairly quickly after that. Manning had brought along a small portable IR transmitter that he rigged to the ship's antenna. He began broadcasting the union's demands and taking part in the negotiations for their release from quarantine. Communications were restored to the ship as a whole within hours of Manning's violation of quarantine.

Juna was besieged by requests for interviews from the press. She issued a brief statement, explaining the situation, reassuring people that the Tendu posed no health risk, and pleading for a quick release from quarantine. When she was done recording her statement, Moki touched her arm.

"Siti, can I say something to your people? I know that Ukatonen would want to if he was awake."

Juna smiled. "Thank you, Moki. That would be wonderful."

Moki stood in front of the recording camera. "Hello," he said, speaking simultaneously in formal Tendu skin speech and verbal Standard. "My name is Moki, and I am a Tendu. I greet you on behalf of my people, and for Ukatonen, who cannot speak to you today. His sickness is nothing that affects humans. He will be well as soon as we are in a natural environment. We're looking forward to seeing your world and learning more about you. We hope that the Tendu and the humans achieve harmony together. Thank you."

Watching her bami, Juna felt a surge of pride. He was a little awkward, but he spoke with the undeniable authority of someone who spoke from the heart. His words would help ease people's fear of the Tendu.

"Was it okay?" Moki asked when the camera was turned off.

"It was fine," Juna assured him. "Just fine."

"You did well, both of you," said someone at Juna's side.

She looked up. It was Mr. Manning.

"Thank you," Juna said. "And thanks for the risk you took, breaking quarantine."

"It wasn't much of a risk. No one was sick," Manning said with a shrug. He sat down and took out an inhaler. "Excuse me, but I have bad lungs. Decompression burn. My suit got torn by flying debris while I was trying to patch a badly holed habitat. At least I got the hole patched."

"You take a lot of risks," Juna remarked.

"Somebody's got to," he said, looking at her levelly. "Otherwise everyone who works out in space would get screwed. The union went to bat for me when I got injured. I'm just carrying on the tradition."

"Well," Juna said, feeling a little awkward in the face of such commitment. "I wish it wasn't necessary. If I'd stayed on Tiangi instead of coming home . . . " She left the rest unsaid.

"Juna, this is the Expansionists' fault, not yours. It should be over soon," Manning reassured her. "Thanks to Ms. Goudrian, the media is all over Burnham and the Survey. Burnham can't take that kind of pressure, not in the middle of the appropriations debate. It's a pity," he noted, glancing down at his stomach. "I was kind of looking forward to a hunger strike. I need to lose some weight."

"Can I see what's wrong with your lungs?" Moki asked, when the technicians had left them alone in the room.

"All the damage is inside, Moki. There's nothing to see."

"That wasn't what he meant," Juna explained. "He wants to link with you, and see if he can heal your lungs."

"Do you think he can?"

"The Tendu can do a lot. But there's no guarantee. And linking can be overwhelming and a little frightening if you're not used to it."

Manning hesitated.

"You don't have to decide now," Juna said.

"Do you really think Moki can heal me?" he asked again.

"When we were negotiating with the Tendu one of our negotiators had a massive heart attack, out in the middle of the jungle. The Tendu saved his life. The doctors who examined the man after the Tendu healed him, said that his heart was as healthy as that of a twenty-year-old. I've seen Tendu regrow severed limbs. And then there was what they did to me."

"But Moki is just a child," Manning pointed out. "Does he have the experience to do this?"

"Moki is thirty-four years old. And he's been learning from one of the best healers on Tiangi."

"And Juna will be monitoring me," Moki added.

"I've felt like a fish out of water every day for the last ten years," Manning said, looking thoughtfully down at Moki. "And if you say that he can heal me, then I'm willing to try it. What do I do?"

"Roll up your sleeves, and hold out your arms," Juna directed.

Moki pulled his chair a little closer to Manning, and grasped his outstretched arm. Juna grasped Moki's other arm.

They linked. Juna could taste the flat acidity of insufficiently oxygenated blood, felt the leathery scars of decompression burn on the inside of Manning's lungs. She felt the bright, tart taste of Manning's fear, and enfolded him in reassurance. When he was calm again, Moki set to work clearing away the scarring that kept Manning's lungs from fully expanding. Then he triggered the growth of fresh new tissue in the damaged parts of his lungs. That done, the bami scanned the rest of Manning's body for more subtle damage.

Moki had learned a lot from Ukatonen. He tired much less easily now than he had back on Tiangi. He managed to repair a damaged shoulder joint and cleared most of the plaque from the inside of Manning's major arteries before Juna broke the link. She would have to tell Ukatonen how much Moki had improved.

Manning awoke. Cautiously, he took a breath, then another, deeper one. "It doesn't hurt!" he said wonderingly. "I can take a deep breath and it doesn't hurt!" His voice sounded smoother, all traces of the previous hoarseness gone.

"Your lungs will improve as more new tissue grows back," Moki told him. "It'll take a week or so before it's done. Eat lots of meat and vegetables. Get plenty of sleep. Your body will be working hard."

Manning took Moki's hand in his. "Thank you."

"Thank you for trying to get us out of here," the Tendu said.

"It's my job," Manning replied.

"And healing is part of what I do," Moki said. "We have achieved harmony."

Manning returned to the negotiations with a vigor and energy that amazed his opponents. A day later, word came that the quarantine would be lifted the next day. Joy swept through the ship. The crew cheered, embraced one another, and then hurried off to pack.

Ukatonen was swimming deep below the surface of the sea, the waters dark and murky. The faint shadows of fish flickered away from him as he swam. The water was thick with the taste of life. He swam through a curtain of millions of tiny plants and animals, living, breeding, dying, and being born. It was cold and dark, but reassuring to be surrounded by so much life, even here in the depths.

Suddenly a brilliant beam of light cut down through the water, and he was surrounded by the sweet taste of joy. A presence swam with him, a familiar one. He turned and followed it up, up out of the depths into the sunlit shallows. As the dream grew brighter, he recognized the presence. It was Moki. He emerged from the link, opening his eyes.

He remembered where he was, and why he was asleep.

"The quarantine?"

"They're letting us out tomorrow."

Leaf mold flaked and crumbled off Ukatonen's body as he slowly sat up, still a little dazed from so much sleep.

"Here, en." Moki handed him a hot bowl of soup. "Eat this, it will help."

He could feel himself settling back into consciousness as he ate the soup, as though he had been shattered and the soup was gluing him back together.

Finished, he handed the bowl to Moki and stood, brushing away as much of the remaining leaf mold as he could. He washed off the rest underneath a hose, oblivious of the stares of the humans. Then, still wet, he climbed into a pair of shorts and followed Moki back to their cabin.

Eerin had prepared a feast of fresh vegetables, fruit, and even some raw fish and chicken, all arranged on clean, fresh leaves from the garden. There was also a small gourd filled with Earth honey. It was clear that she had taken pains to make the meal as much like a Tendu feast as she could. While he ate, they told him everything that had happened while he was asleep.

After the meal, Ukatonen went out for a final walk around the ship. It was awash in celebration as the humans said goodbye to each other. He felt a little lonely as he watched the humans rejoice in their hard-won freedom. They were celebrating a homecoming, and he was leaving for an unknown world.

A yellow flicker of irritation forked down the inside of Ukatonen's arm. He was an enkar; he should be used to leave-takings. After all, he had spent hundreds of years traveling from one place to another. The handful of years he would spend here would be barely an eyeblink. Yet he had already been overwhelmed by the humans' difference. Even Moki, a mere bami, had dealt with the changes better than he had. If he hadn't gotten greensick, the humans would not have had the excuse to keep them locked up in here. Ukatonen turned deep brown with shame as he thought of how weak he had been on the journey here. He would have to do better from here on out, he told himself.

Moki touched him on the arm. He looked down. The bami held his spurs out, requesting a link. Ukatonen looked at the crowd of humans laughing and talking with each other in the lounge. "Let's go to the garden," he said in skin speech. "It's quieter there."

The garden was deserted except for a couple of humans who were more intent on each other than their surroundings. The garden looked a little tired. Many of the plants they had grown were going to seed, or had gotten lank and tired-looking. The sunflowers in the circle were going dry and brown as the seeds in their big flower heads ripened.

"It'll be good to see real trees again," Moki said.

Ukatonen nodded, and they sat in silence a while longer, taking comfort in each other and the garden. It was easier to take comfort here now that Ukatonen knew they would be leaving it behind.

"I'll miss this place," Moki remarked. "We worked hard here."

"There will be other places," Ukatonen told him. "You have done good work here, and it is time to move on. That is one of the things you'll have to learn in order to become a good enkar."

"An enkar? En, I am much too young for such things."

"Nevertheless, someday you will become one. I allowed Eerin to adopt you for a reason. We need to understand the humans, and that is your job. You must pay attention to the humans, Moki. You must come to understand them so well that they do not surprise you. One day humans will be your atwa. You will be responsible to them and for them. They must be brought into harmony."

"I can't do that, en. Humans are not like the Tendu. Besides, there are many humans, and I am only one person. I cannot change them all."

"If the humans and the Tendu do not achieve harmony, both will suffer," Ukatonen informed him. He touched Moki on the shoulder. "And you are not alone. The other enkar will help you. But we need to know more about the humans before we can bring them into harmony. That is why we are here. That is why Eerin is your sitik." He looked directly into Moki's golden eyes. "You must never forget that. One day you will be an enkar, and then nothing must matter to you but the good of the Tendu. Do you understand?"

"Yes, en, I understand," Moki said in formal skin speech. He held his arms out for allu-a.

Ukatonen grasped Moki's forearms and they linked. The bami's presence was muddy and roiling with doubt. Ukatonen enfolded him with reassurance and approval. Moki's turmoil gradually eased, and they achieved a harmonious equilibrium, though Ukatonen could still sense the faint muddy tinge of doubt remaining in Moki.

It was no matter, the bami would learn. Already Moki had the makings of an exceptional elder. With Ukatonen's guidance, Moki would then become an outstanding enkar. All that was needed was time and patience, and Moki would find his way as surely as a stream finds its way to the ocean.

Moki breathed deeply and regularly, his body at rest. Outwardly he seemed sound asleep, but he was awake, and deeply troubled by Ukatonen's words. It disturbed him to see his future laid out so neatly by someone else. He was coming to prefer the humans' way of letting each person decide their own future.

Besides, he didn't think that it was possible to bring the humans into harmony with the Tendu, and even if he could, he wasn't sure that he should. He liked the humans the way they were.

Juna lay awake beside Bruce, too excited to sleep. Tomorrow she would be off the ship, and free. Then life would get complicated. She knew that she should be organizing some kind of diplomatic mission for the Tendu, and dealing with the requests for interviews and research that had already begun pouring in, but first she needed to see her family. First thing tomorrow she would put in for leave. It was nearly harvest time and they would need her. And then there was Toivo . . . Juna pulled the sheet a little higher, and turned onto her side, trying to quell her rising emotions.

Tomorrow, she told herself firmly. *Get some sleep and think about all of this tomorrow.* She slid closer to Bruce, savoring his warmth. Though it was clear that they were too different to make a lasting pair, he had been good company. Good in bed, too, she thought with a smile. She would miss him. She slid into sleep, amid a haze of fond memories.

CHAPTER

3

Ukatonen stood with Moki and Eerin as the doors of the airlock swung open. A man in an ensign's uniform led a group of six other humans wearing privates' uniforms through the airlock. Ukatonen found uniforms oddly comforting. They carried meaning, like skin speech. It was easy to tell the status of the people wearing them. If all humans wore uniforms, his life would be a great deal easier.

"The airlock is ready for departure, Commander."

"Thank you, Ensign, the crew is ready to disembark," Commander Sussman replied. Though she was trying to hide it behind a mask of formality, Sussman's joy at their release from quarantine was obvious. Watching her, Ukatonen understood that Commander Sussman was as constrained by her rank as an enkar. He wished he had understood that earlier, he could have learned so much from her.

The ensign turned to Eerin and the Tendu. "Dr. Saari, the press is waiting to speak to you. If you and the Tendu will come with me?"

Eerin nodded. "Thank you, Ensign."

Ukatonen picked up his small duffle bag. The crew of the *Homa Darabi Maru* cheered as the security escort ushered the three of them off the ship. They went down the long, brightly lit tunnel of the airlock and then onto a metal walkway that overlooked an enormous room with high ceilings and bright lights. Huge machines moved immense metal boxes around. The air rang with the whine of machinery and the heavy clang of metal. The smell of metal and hot oil was strong enough to taste.

"It's the cargo bay," Eerin shouted over the noisy machines. "This is where the ships are loaded and unloaded."

Moki stared down in fascination at the enormous machines, his skin roiling with excitement and awe. Ukatonen felt small and exposed, like a tinka in a clearing.

He was relieved when they passed through another airlock, then down a long corridor, and out into a wide, brilliantly lit atrium. It was a huge room, full of humans. Towering over the crowd was an enormous tree. Long streamers of vines and aerial roots trailed from its branches down to the ground. Ukatonen stopped dead, all pretense at nonchalance forgotten. Under the wet-bird smell of the assembled humans, Ukatonen could smell the rich green aliveness of the tree. The rest of the room ceased to exist for him as he headed for the tree, aching to feel bark beneath his hands and feet again.

Analin stood by a pillar off to the side of the room, watching the surging press corps jockey for good camera angles on the riser under the tree. It was nice, for once, not to have to be part of that milling scrum. Instead, she kept her eyes and her head-mounted video camera trained on the double doors where Dr. Saari and the Tendu would enter the room. Analin was more interested in the aliens' entrance than the press interview. She would have her own exclusive interview with the three of them later.

So she was one of the first to see Juna and the aliens as they came in the door, flanked by their security escort. The group stopped as they came in, giving Analin a moment to look at them.

What surprised her most was how small they were. The Tendu were tiny, barely coming up to the chest of their brawny escort. Their long, gangly limbs looked spidery and fragile. Juna, despite her humanity, seemed to partake of that same fine-boned fragility. She was small, barely five feet tall, but she carried herself with the pride and poise of a queen. Her features were striking, delicate yet determined. She had the narrow, straight nose, wide solemn eyes, and arching eyebrows of an Ethiopian, but her skin was lighter, coffee with a hint of cream.

The Tendu's skins flared a sudden surprising hot pink as the lights of the assembled cameras flickered explosively over them, recording their images for the NetNews teams. The noise of the crowd swelled as reporters spoke into microphones. But the aliens were looking beyond the reporters.

Analin followed their gaze with her eyes. They were looking at the giant tree behind the riser. In that moment, the Tendu ran for the tree. The security escort moved to stop them, but the aliens were already beyond their reach, racing up into the tree's massive branches with the quick fluidity of squirrels. The Tendu reached the upper branches and paused a moment, their skins turning the clear, startling blue of a summer sky, and then began leaping and swinging from branch to branch, hot-pink lightning flickering over their brilliant blue bodies.

The still pictures and her comm conversations with the Tendu had not prepared her for their nonhuman grace and agility. In the trees, their awkward gangliness vanished. They were beautiful in motion. She could have watched them for hours.

Dr. Saari strode up to the riser, and with a thunderous clatter plucked the microphone from its stand. She turned off the microphone, and stuck it in her pocket. Then she swung up into the crotch of the giant tree with the same fluid skill as the Tendu, except that her movements had a familiar human quality. She pulled the microphone out of her pocket, switched it on, and tapped it to get the attention of the rapt and wondering press corps.

"Hello," she said, then waited until most of the cameras and microphones were trained on her. "Hello, I'm Dr. Juna Saari," she began, "and these are the Tendu. It's been a long time since Moki and Ukatonen have seen a tree big enough to climb in, so you'll have to excuse them if they're a bit distracted."

At the sound of her voice, Moki and Ukatonen turned a darker, more somber shade of blue, and swung down to settle next to her on a branch, bright pink flickers of lightning still coursing down their bodies. Juna introduced the Tendu, then thanked the crew of the *Homa Darabi Maru*, Mark Manning, the union, and the Survey for their help in expediting their release from quarantine. Then she handed the microphone to Ukatonen.

"Hello," he said, then paused in surprise at hearing his own voice magnified by the public address speakers. "Hello, my name is Ukatonen. I am an enkar of the Three Rivers Council from the planet of Tiangi. I have come to learn more about your people so that we can learn to be in harmony with each other. I hope you will be patient and kind teachers. Thank you." He spoke simultaneously in human Standard and in the Tendu visual language. How beautiful and strange their language was! The camera lenses whirred and spun as they focused in on him.

He handed the microphone back to Juna. Analin saw him cast a longing look up at the treetops.

Juna shook her head, and handed the microphone to Moki.

"Hello," he said, clearly repeating what he had heard Juna and Ukatonen say. "I am Moki. Dr. Saari is my sitik. You would say that I am her adopted son. Thank you for letting us out of quarantine and giving us a chance to climb this wonderful tree."

The reporters began shouting their names. Juna looked momentarily a little overwhelmed and frightened at the sudden clamor. Analin wondered where the Survey's press flacks were. They should be up there, helping Juna out.

"You," Juna said, pointing to a woman in purple down near the front. Analin winced as she recognized the enormous trademark beehive of Fay Tsui from one of the Asian music Tri-D channels. Recognizing Tsui first was an insult to all the serious journalists from the major networks. Why the hell wasn't anybody up there with Juna?

"Dr. Saari, do you have any comment to make about your long stay in quarantine?"

Analin relaxed. At least Tsui asked an intelligent question. Maybe there really was a brain under all that hair.

"Yes, we're glad to be out."

Analin smiled. Juna had given them a good response.

"What's it like being back on Earth?" another reporter shouted.

"I don't know. I'll tell you when we get there." It was an old joke, but it got a laugh.

The press corps shouted more questions at Juna. She fielded them as well as she could, occasionally handing one off to the Tendu. She was handling herself well. If someone had sent her out here alone to make her look like a fool, they had failed. Although Juna was new to this, she had a great deal of grace and poise, and an instinctive ability to dodge difficult questions. None of the reporters managed to bulldoze her into answering a question that she wanted to avoid.

While Juna and Ukatonen were preoccupied with the reporters, the little one, Moki, climbed into the higher branches of the tree, and began swinging from branch to branch. The questions stopped as the cameras started tracking him. Analin smothered a grin. Moki was stealing the show.

Juna used the distraction to bring the press conference to a close. Moki and Ukatonen followed her out of the large hall with many longing looks back at the tree. Their escort fended off the reporters who tried to follow them as they led Juna and the Tendu into a security elevator. At least the security people were doing their jobs. As the doors slid closed, the reporters pulled out their comm units and began filing stories.

Analin got herself a cup of coffee and a pastry at a corridor-side café. She watched the reporters hustling by, their comm units pressed to their ears, and smiled. How nice not to have to rush to a deadline, she reflected. She sipped her coffee, savoring the moment. When enough time had passed for Juna to have gotten settled, Analin picked up her comm and dialed her number.

Juna answered the call. "Analin! It's good to see you! Where are you?"

"I'm here on Broumas station. Are you up for that interview?"

"Of course," Juna said. "We were just about to find a quiet spot with some trees to climb."

"Why don't you meet me in the West Atrium Park? It has some lovely big trees, and it's just a couple of blocks from the shuttle stop. It'll be nice and quiet at this time of day. Can you be there in twenty minutes?"

"Sure!" Juna said. "We'll see you there."

Analin slid a healthy tip under her coffee cup, shrugged on her backpack, and headed for the elevators.

She got off the shuttle at the West Atrium station, with its colorful tile murals, and wandered into the park. Big banyan trees arched over her, their fibrous roots dangling down. Some of them had grown all the way to the ground, thickening into muscular-looking mottled grey pillars. She wandered between them, wondering where Juna and the aliens were.

There was a rustling in the branches overhead. Dead leaves pattered to the floor around her. She looked up but saw nothing. Then one of the Tendu leaped to the ground, startling her.

"Hello, Analin!"

"Moki?" Analin asked uncertainly.

He nodded. "Juna and Ukatonen are this way."

She followed him through the grey pillars of the banyan trees to the enormous central trunk.

"Juna said this would be the easiest route up," Moki told her.

Analin stared up into the branches. "Um, I'm not much of a climber, Moki."

"It's a really easy climb. I'll carry your equipment for you," he offered.

"I see," Analin said, resigning herself to the ordeal.

Moki slung her heavy satchel of recording and video gear over his shoulder as though it weighed almost nothing. Then he helped Analin up into the tree.

As long as you didn't look down, it was an easy climb. The branches were broad, and sloped upward at a gentle incline. Moki had to steady her a time or two, but otherwise she was fine. Juna and Ukatonen were settled in a spot where the tree branched and rebranched, splitting into several large, level branches that offered a number of comfortable places to sit.

Moki sat next to Juna. Several brilliant patterns kaleidoscoped across his skin. Juna smiled, and brushed his shoulder with the backs of her fingers, the strange gesture clearly conveying her fondness for the alien youngster. Moki's skin flared blue, and then settled to a cool shade of celadon.

Juna greeted Analin warmly. "Thank you for climbing up here. It's been such a long time since the Tendu have had the chance to climb a tree. Besides, we won't be disturbed here. People never think to look up."

Analin settled herself against an upright branch. "It was a good idea," she said. "Thank you."

"I was surprised when you called. I didn't see you at the press conference."

"I was watching from the back. I knew I was going to get an exclusive interview with you, so I let the others ask the questions."

Juna made a rueful grimace. "That press conference was a disaster," she said. "It was completely out of control."

"I thought you handled a difficult situation rather well," Analin said. "Didn't the Survey send anyone along to help out?"

"Just the security escort," Juna said.

Analin shook her head. "Either they're really disorganized, or someone was hoping you'd make a fool of yourself. Don't worry, you were fine," she reassured Juna. "Was this your first press conference?"

Juna nodded. "I hope I never have to do another one," Juna admitted.

"You're famous, yes?" Analin said. "You must get used to them. It will get easier."

Juna shook her head. "I don't know the first thing about dealing with reporters."

"Juna, you need a press secretary, a professional who knows how to handle the press."

"Would you do it?"

"Me?" Analin said, amazed. "B-but I'm just a journalist. I don't have any experience as a press secretary."

"You know the ropes," Juna said, "and you like the Tendu without being silly about it. It would mean spending a lot of time traveling, though. And you'd have to work with Ukatonen and Moki, to teach them how to behave in front of the cameras."

"I'll think it over," Analin said, hiding her excitement at the opportunity she was being offered. "But I promised the editor of the *Times* NetNews an exclusive interview with you and the Tendu. I need to do that before I consider any job offers." She took out her video cameras and recorder, and started to set them up.

The interview went well. It was easy to draw Juna out. Soon she was entwined in reminiscences of her time among the Tendu. Ukatonen and especially Moki, helped fill in her account with explanations and details of village life, and life among the enkar. Analin forgot she was doing an interview, and listened raptly, until her computer chimed, signaling that its memory was full. She checked the clock on the computer and realized that they'd been talking for over two hours. Her behind had grown numb from prolonged contact with the unyielding tree limb. Only then did she remember that this was not a lengthy chat with an old friend.

"Well, I hope I said something useful amid all that chatter," Juna said, suddenly awkward.

Analin smiled. "Juna, I could write a book from what the three of you told me tonight."

"Oh," Juna said, with a fleeting look of concern. Analin could tell that she was worrying that she'd said too much.

"But I won't," Analin reassured her. "I only have time to edit this interview for the net. Then I'll be too busy being your press secretary."

She looked up, eyes wide. "Really? You'll do it?"

She nodded. "Juna, you're offering me the chance of a lifetime." She shook her head ruefully. "I hope I'm up to the job. You're a very hot property." Analin crumpled her comp up and tossed it in her knapsack. "Of course," she added mischievously, "I do have to get down from this tree without breaking my leg before I can take the job."

It was good to be off the ship, Ukatonen reflected, though this place was not that much of an improvement. At least there were trees to climb, and new things to do. There were many people, each of them as full of questions as a river is full of water. They all wanted to know about the Tendu and about Tiangi. After a while, the river of questions seemed to flow back into itself, repeating and repeating the same questions over and over. He lost interest in the endless questions.

But General Burnham's hostility continued to puzzle him. Why had she fought so hard to keep them on the ship? According to Juna and Analin, she represented a group of humans who were afraid of the Tendu. The idea seemed ludicrous. Their world was far away across an ocean of nothingness and stars. The Tendu could not come here without the humans and their sky rafts. He shook his head, deeply purple in his puzzlement.

"Analin," he said, at the end of yet another long day of interviews, "I want to talk to General Burnham. Is that possible?"

Analin looked at him, her brows raised in what Ukatonen was coming to recognize as surprise.

"Why?"

"I do not want her to be afraid. And I want to understand her. Is it possible to speak with her?"

"It is, but I am not sure that it is wise."

"Perhaps not," Ukatonen admitted, "but it does seem to be necessary."

"Ukatonen, she does not mean you well," Eerin warned him.

"I understand. She kept us prisoner on board ship. She is afraid of us. But perhaps if she knew us, she would not be afraid."

"But if she is your enemy, Ukatonen, the more she knows about you, the more opportunity she has to hurt you," Analin pointed out.

"Perhaps, Analin, but I must try to reach harmony with her."

"That will be hard, en," Eerin put in. "And you must be cautious. First we must know more about her."

"That, at least, is easy," Analin said. She unzipped her backpack, and took out a thick envelope. "This is a dossier on General Burnham that I had prepared when I was working on the quarantine story. It is quite thorough."

"I see," Eerin said. "Thank you, Analin. It will be a big help."

Eerin went over the general's file with Ukatonen, but almost everything in it seemed incomprehensible to the enkar. It only reminded him of how much he had to learn about humans.

At last, after most of an evening spent in explanations that clarified nothing, Ukatonen looked up at Eerin. "I think it's time I called the general up and talked to her. There is nothing more I can learn from this file."

"Are you sure, en?"

Ukatonen nodded.

"Then we will call her tomorrow morning, before our first interview."

The next morning, Ukatonen sat down at the computer, the comm number for General Burnham emblazoned on one arm in Standard skin speech. He closed his eyes for a minute, thinking over what he was about to do. Burnham's background was a confusing blur to him, but he could tell that the humans were scared of her. She held the responsibility for many humans in her hands, but not kindly. Best to think of the general as the leader of a pack of predators, he decided. He had to try and reassure her that he and his people were not a threat to humans or their territory. It would be hard—she was already afraid of the Tendu—but he had to try to understand her, to make her less afraid of him, to reach harmony with her.

He opened his eyes and looked up at the others.

"I'm ready," he said, and keyed in the comm sequence.

"General Burnham's office, may I help—" The man's eyes widened as he saw Ukatonen.

"That's her secretary," Analin whispered.

"Good morning. I am Ukatonen. I would like to speak to General Burnham. Is she busy?"

"Um-ah . . . please hold," the secretary said. The screen went dark. The word "holding" flashed on the screen in blue. Ukatonen glanced up and saw that Eerin and Analin were both smiling.

"He's flustered," Analin said. "That's good."

The screen lit up again. The secretary was back, looking a bit calmer. "May I ask the purpose of your call?"

"I wish to speak to the general," Ukatonen said.

The secretary glanced sideways, then back at the screen. "Yes, but why?"

"See how he keeps looking away? The general is there in the room with him, listening to what you're saying," Analin whispered. She was standing off to one side, out of range of the comm unit's camera.

"Thank you," Ukatonen said to Analin in skin speech, the words flowing across his back. To the secretary he replied, "I was hoping that she could explain why the Expansionists seem to be afraid of my people."

"I see," said the secretary, hesitating. He looked sideways again, clearly listening to someone off-screen. "The general will speak to you now."

There was a pause, and then the screen switched to another office. General Burnham was seated behind a desk. Ukatonen recognized her from her photograph. Her face was soft and round, but there were hard lines in it.

"Good morning, General Burnham," Ukatonen said.

"Good morning. I understand you wish a lesson in politics?"

"I wish to understand humans better, yes," Ukatonen said. "I do not understand the nature of the Expansionists' concerns about the Tendu. I was hoping that you could enlighten me, so that we could reach harmony in this matter. It is not good that there is fear between us."

"I am in the military, Ukatonen," General Burnham told him. "It is my duty to protect humanity from outside threats. You and the other alien showed up without warning. It is natural for me and those who believe as I do, to urge caution. If you had waited, Earth would have extended an invitation."

"And Eerin would have had to choose between her family and her child."

"Who?" General Burnham asked.

"It is our name for Dr. Saari," Ukatonen explained.

"I see," she said. "Dr. Saari's decision to adopt an alien child was a flagrant violation of our Contact Protocols. Choosing between the child and her family was a consequence of that decision," General Burnham said. She sounded angry. It was time to back down, Ukatonen realized, but he could not let Eerin's difficult choice go undefended.

"Our decision to come with her was a consequence of that choice also. It seemed to us to be the least harmful course. We cannot cross the great emptiness without your ships, General. There are only two of us, and Moki is not yet an elder."

"But he's not exactly a child, either," General Burnham replied.

"Not as you understand it, but Moki needs Dr. Saari as much as a human child needs its mother, perhaps more. We came with Dr. Saari so that she could see her family without deserting her bami. We agreed to abide by your Contact Protocols, General Burnham. You have the word of an enkar that we will cause harm to no one."

"I have heard that, yes," Burnham admitted. "But I do not know how much you can be trusted. Remember," she said, "it is my duty to protect humanity. We must be wary."

"My promise to abide by the protocols was a formal judgment. If I fail, I must kill myself," Ukatonen explained. This woman was as hard and seamless as the shell of a purra. There was no way in past her defenses.

"I understand that," Burnham said, "but your people are still unknown to us."

"As humans are to the Tendu. You possess more knowledge of us than we do of you. That is the other reason I am here, General. I wish to understand your people. How can I gain your trust? How can we reach harmony?"

Burnham shook her head. "Trust is not my job," she said. "Caution is. Thank you for calling."

Ukatonen inclined his head, "Thank you for speaking with me, General. I have learned much." He felt a hollow sadness in his stomach at the general's hostility. How could a person live in the world and think this way? How had she grown to be like this?

The general frowned, as though regretting even this short conversation. "Goodbye," she said, and reached to touch the disconnect button.

Ukatonen stared at the blank screen for a moment, then shut down the computer. He took a long deep breath and let it out again.

"*So hard,*" he remarked to himself in skin speech. Aloud, he wondered, "Why is she like that? She must be very sad and lonely."

"There are many humans like her," Eerin told him. "Trust is not easy for us, en. We have fought among ourselves for so long. Remember how long it took me to learn to trust you."

Ukatonen nodded. "I do not think that she trusts anyone," he said. He felt as though he had stared too long at the empty ocean of space. How empty the general must be, barricaded within the walls of her suspicion.

Moki watched the blur of people coming and going. They all wanted to talk to Eerin about the Tendu. Some of them were important people from the Survey, which was somehow part of Juna's atwa. The rest of them were from the press. Moki was still trying to understand what the "press" was. As far as he could determine, it was an atwa that involved telling people what was going on. But the people in the press atwa preferred to talk to Eerin or Ukatonen. They ignored him, or talked to him as though he had trouble understanding them.

Moki and Ukatonen weren't supposed to go out without Eerin or Analin, so they spent most of the day watching the Tri-V or listening to Analin and Eerin talk about them. It was fun at first, seeing themselves on the Tri-V, but they only showed the same few pictures and words. He and Ukatonen only got to climb trees when no one was around, and it was always the same few trees.

"When are we going to meet your family, siti?" Moki asked.

"I don't know, Moki. My request for leave hasn't been approved yet. The Survey wants us to go to one of their research stations where they can study you. The press wants to interview us, and I just want to go home."

"Then we should go home," Ukatonen said.

"If only it were that simple," Juna replied. "I can't go until the Survey tells me I can."

"Everyone else from the ship has gone on leave," Ukatonen said. "Why are we still here?"

Juna shrugged. "They don't know what to do with us, I think. There are lots of different departments who want to study us."

Moki's ears folded tight against his head. "Please excuse my lack of patience, siti, but I'm tired of watching people talk to you about us."

"No, bai, you've been very patient. I've just been thoughtless. Tomorrow we're going to cancel all our appointments and go explore the space station. The world isn't going to fall apart if we take the day off."

Juna watched Moki and Ukatonen swinging through the branches, their skins alive with blue and green flickers of alien laughter, and her worries lifted for a moment. She had needed this break as badly as the Tendu.

She felt tired and bloated. The stress of the last few days was getting to her. She longed to be up there with Moki and Ukatonen, but she couldn't muster the energy to join them. But just watching the Tendu playing was enough to lift her spirits.

"Hello, Dr. Saari."

Juna looked up. It was the union president, Mark Manning.

"Analin told me I might find you here," he said. "May I join you?"

"Of course," Juna said, and he sat down beside her on the bench.

"I wanted to thank Moki again for all he's done. I feel like a new person. It's like a miracle."

Juna smiled proudly. "For them, such things are normal. For us . . ." She shrugged. "Even now, they still amaze me."

Manning nodded. They sat for a while without saying anything, watching Ukatonen and Moki leap like gibbons from branch to branch, their skins a riot of blue happiness and pink excitement.

"I was a little surprised to hear that you were still on the station," Manning said at last. "I had expected you to be with your family."

"I would be, but my leave hasn't come through yet. I think the Survey's too busy fighting over what to do with me." Juna ran her fingers through her hair. "It's been five-and-a-half years since I last saw my family. I want to go home." She looked at the pebbled concrete floor, fighting back a surge of emotion.

"Analin tells me they sent you out all by yourself for that press conference. Even the Survey isn't usually that bad. Someone's being petty in the home office," Manning said. "They should have assigned someone to take care of you."

"I'd rather have Analin than some Survey PR flack. Analin likes the Tendu, and they like her. She lets me decide what I want to say. And she works for me, so there's no conflict of interest." Juna was silent for a while, watching Moki and Ukatonen swing back and forth between the same two trees. It suddenly reminded her of caged tigers in the zoo. "I just want to see my family," she said.

"Let me see what I can do for you," Manning offered. "I think I can shake your leave loose. They shouldn't be allowed to get away with this kind of harassment."

Manning was as good as his word. Two days later, Juna's leave was approved. Amazingly enough, there were no problems with taking the Tendu along. Clearly they were still protected by the volume of publicity surrounding their imprisonment in quarantine. Juna and the Tendu boarded the very next shuttle for Berry Station. Analin would follow in a couple of weeks.

The shuttle trip to Berry Station took several hours, most of it in zero-g. There had been a few seconds of zero-g on the *Homa Darabi Maru*, but they had been securely strapped in then. Fortunately the shuttle was empty, and the Tendu were able to zoom around the cabin, ricocheting from viewport to viewport, their skins awash with flickering colors. Juna joined them for a while, until a sudden wave of queasiness sent her to her seat. She must be more exhausted than she realized; she hadn't been spacesick since she was a small child. She settled back into her seat and let sleep carry her away.

She was awakened by the announcement directing passengers to strap in for arrival. Moki and Ukatonen came back to their seats. As the familiar bulk of her home station loomed into view on the forward viewscreen, Juna felt a sudden pang of anxiety. Her family had been nice enough on the comm, but how would they react to the aliens face to face? Especially now, with the harvest in full swing. And then there was Toivo. Her father had told her that Toivo had come to help with the harvest, but he refused to talk to Juna on the comm.

"He's changed," Aunt Netta had said, worry written on her face. "He's pulled into himself. He reminds me of how your father acted after he brought you back from the camp."

Juna remembered that time. Her father had found them in the refugee camp in Germany. Juna had seen him talking to a relief worker, and pushed her way through the crowd. He picked her up and held her. Juna hung on as though she would never let go.

"You're so thin!" he had exclaimed. "Where's your mother?"

Juna had lifted her head from his chest and just looked at her father, unable to find the words to tell him that her mother was dead. Finally she and Toivo had led him to the graveyard, to the mass grave where she had been buried.

A light had gone out of him when he realized what Juna was trying to tell him. He sat on the muddy earth and wept like a child. Juna had watched, terrified by the depth of his grief.

"I'm sorry, *Isukki*," she had said, resting her hand on his head. It was all her fault. She should have saved her mother, taken better care of her, not let her die. Her aunt Netta, the only other member of her father's family to make it safely out of war-torn Finland, came to live with them on Berry Station. Her father spent months wandering around like a ghost. The whole family had seemed like walking shadows. Juna closed her eyes in pain at the thought of Toivo acting like that.

The jarring of the ship against the lock of the space station shook her out of her reverie. With a heavy, solid clang, the docking mechanisms engaged. They were home.

Moki touched her arm. "Are you all right?"

Juna smiled weakly and patted Moki's hand. "Yes, it's just nerves." She unfastened the safety strap, and pushed herself toward the door. They would be in free fall until they reached the elevators that would take them down to the inspection station.

A figure in a wheelchair was waiting for them when they emerged from the agricultural inspection station. It took Juna a second to recognize who it was.

"Toivo! How did you get up here?" she cried. She dropped her things and bounded over to hug him, moving lightly in the half gravity of this level of the station. She stopped a few steps away, uncertain how to hug someone in a wheelchair.

"Hello, older sister," he said in Amharic as he reached up from his chair to enfold her in an embrace. "Kiroko was working security downstairs. She let me come up to meet you."

He looked older, Juna realized, older than she expected him to, and there was a hard-bitten edge of defiant bitterness that was apparent even through his gladness at seeing her again. She looked at his wheelchair and a torrent of fear, anger, and love surged through her. She wanted to tear that chair apart with her bare hands, and raise him up on two good legs. His shoes, she noticed, were smooth and unlined from lack of use.

Fighting back her conflicting emotions, she knelt down beside Toivo so that they were eye to eye. "How are you?" she asked.

"Shorter," he said. "But my feet don't get tired."

He glanced past her at the Tendu.

"Moki, Ukatonen, this is my brother, Toivo."

Moki stuck out his hand, "I'm honored to meet you, brother of my sitik." Moki was only a little taller than her brother, seated as he was in the wheelchair.

Toivo reached out and took Moki's hand.

"Good to meet you, Moki," he said.

"Moki is my adopted son," Juna told him.

"I know," Tovio said. "Welcome to the family, Moki."

"And this is Ukatonen," Juna said.

Ukatonen extended his hand. "I'm honored to meet you, Toivo. Juna has told us so much about you and the rest of your family. I'm glad that we are finally here. I've wanted to see what a human family was like for a long time."

"Welcome to the zoo," Toivo said dryly, shaking the enkar's hand. "C'mon, Juna, let's get your bags." He wiped his hand on his pants leg.

Juna smiled. It took a while to get used to the cool moistness of the Tendu's touch.

"How is everyone?" she asked in Amharic, as they headed for the elevator. Toivo's chair moved easily in the half-gravity.

"Busy with the harvest," he replied in the same language.

"The harvest, is it going well?"

"Bumper crop this year. Weather Control optimized for wine grapes this season. Dad bought two more vats this summer, getting ready for the new vineyard. We'll fill all the vats and have grapes left over, if we can get them in. Wermuth's buying the surplus this year. He has the vat space. We've already sold him ten tons of chardonnay grapes. He'll take some merlot, and a bit of cabernet as well."

The elevator doors opened, and they got in. The hammered copper paneling on the elevator walls had recently been polished, and it shone. Surrounded by the rich, textured gleam of the copper, Juna knew she was home. The copper panels were a common, recurring theme in Berry Station's public architecture, courtesy of a rich vein of copper ore that the station's builders had discovered as they were hollowing out the asteroid that became the station's outer shell.

"Sounds like the winery's doing well," Juna said as the elevator started to descend. A riffle of excitement stirred in Juna's stomach as the increasing gravity pulled at her. They were almost home.

Toivo shrugged. "We need a good year. Dad shelled out a lot for doctors when I got hurt. Labor's tight, though. We need more pickers."

"I brought two more helpers," Juna said. "Moki and Ukatonen are pretty hard workers. The sun'll be a problem for them, though."

He looked up at her, brown and familiar as no one else in the world was, and he smiled.

"We've got hats," he said, referring to their father's collection of tractor hats. Poking fun at the collection was an old family joke.

Juna was suddenly overwhelmed with happiness. Wheelchair or not, Toivo was still himself. Drawn and sadder, perhaps, but still her brother. She was home. She reached down and squeezed his shoulder.

"It's good to be back, little brother," she said.

Toivo nodded. "With you here, it's home again."

Juna touched his cheek with the back of her hand, tears welling in her eyes.

The elevator doors opened onto the stone-floored concourse of the shuttle terminal. A boy stood there, waiting for them.

"*Hei*, Juna-*Tāti!*"

"Danan!" Juna called. She dropped her bags and ran to embrace him. He was a beautiful boy, on the verge of becoming a handsome adolescent, with his creamy-tan skin, and large, solemn eyes that were the clear, intense green of a freshly sliced lime.

"How did you get so big!" she exclaimed, tousling his curly chestnut hair.

"He's taking after his mother in that," Toivo said, wheeling up to them, with the larger of her two bags on his lap. "And he eats like a horse."

Moki, Ukatonen, this is my nephew, Danan. He's Toivo's son."

"I'm Moki, and this is Ukatonen," Moki said.

"You're the one my aunt adopted, aren't you?" Danan asked Moki as he lifted Juna's bag from his father's lap.

Moki nodded.

"Then I suppose we're cousins."

Moki looked at Juna questioningly.

"I suppose you are," Juna said, grateful for Danan's easy acceptance of the aliens.

"I've never had a cousin before," Danan remarked.

"Neither have I," Moki replied as they emerged from the station. Moki looked up and stopped dead, bright pink with surprise. Ukatonen nearly fell over him, as he too looked upward.

Juna smiled. The station arched above them, a quilt of green and brown that made up both land and sky, delineated by the bright glare of the sun windows, brilliant lines of light running the length of the satellite. The far wall of this segment was barely visible in the distance. Beyond that wall were four other segments, each a kilometer long. It was an old design, very space-inefficient, but the view was spectacular.

"It takes some getting used to, doesn't it?" Juna said.

Ukatonen nodded. "Why doesn't it all fall down?"

Juna started to explain about centrifugal force as they followed Toivo out to the waiting truck. Danan opened the door on the passenger side for his father.

"He's driving his old man around now," Toivo told Juna.

"What kind of machine is that?" Moki asked, gesturing with his chin at the pickup.

"It's a truck. We use it to carry people and stuff around. On the farm we mostly use horses, but this is easier for going to market."

"How does it work?" Moki asked.

"I'll show you sometime," Danan offered. "Right now, we've got to get back to the farm. We're pretty busy."

"Juna told us you were harvesting grapes," Moki said.

"That's right."

"I've never seen a grape. What are they like?"

Danan grinned. "Don't worry, you'll get to see a lot of them over the next few days."

"Better get back to the farm," Toivo said. "Be needing the truck this afternoon."

Juna climbed into the back of the truck. Danan handed the bags up to her, lifting even her heaviest duffle by himself. The Tendu swung over the side of the truck and into the back with athletic grace. Danan helped Toivo lift out of his chair, and into the cab of the truck, then carefully buckled his father into the seat with a solicitousness that Juna found heartbreaking to watch. Danan folded the chair with practiced ease and handed it up to her.

Juna hesitated for a moment before taking it. Then, doing her best to hide her dislike of the thing, she grabbed hold of the chair and lifted it into the truck. The chair was surprisingly lightweight; she had expected it to be heavier. She stowed it in the front of the truck bed, then nodded to Danan, who had been watching her from the back window of the cab.

Juna settled herself against the side of the truck as it started up. She was home at last, and as always, her homecoming held pain as well as joy. The home she returned to was never the one that she had left. She had been gone twice as long as usual, and the changes were amazing. Danan had shot up from a pudgy child to a lanky youth on the verge of puberty. And Toivo had been transformed from a strong, happy, prosperous young farmer to a bitter cripple on the verge of a premature middle age. He looked ten years older than she did.

They were passing the Jadav family farm, with its neat rows of fruit trees, tall hop vines, and the stubble of the barley fields. The Jadav brothers and their wife were out with a work crew, picking apples. As the truck approached, they set down their baskets and ran to the fence, shouting a welcome. Danan slowed the truck, so that Juna could say hello. Mrs. Jadav, her stomach bulging with pregnancy, handed her a basket.

"Fresh apples, for you and your family," she said, glancing sidelong at the Tendu. Her two sons climbed the fence and stared openly at Ukatonen and Moki.

"Thank you, Sumitra! And congratulations on your pregnancy! You were just starting to show with the first one when I left."

"Then you haven't met my sons. This one is Dayal, and the little one is Devi. And this one will be a girl! It'll be nice to have a little company in the family," she said, beaming proudly at her two husbands and their sons.

"You'll have to come by and meet Moki and Ukatonen," Juna said. "And thanks for the apples!" she called as the truck sped up. She and the Tendu waved at the Jadav family as they faded into the distance. Moki took an apple from the basket and bit into it. He flushed turquoise with delight.

"It's good!" he declared, handing one to Ukatonen. "Try one, en!"

Juna picked an apple out of the basket, polished it against her thigh, and bit into it. It was sweet and still warm from the sun. Juice ran down her chin. The Jadavs' fruit sold for premium prices in cislunar space. Back on Broumas Station, this apple would have sold for five credits, almost enough to buy a used comm unit. The Jadavs' beer cost ten credits, and was only available at certain upscale bars. A bottle of their pear cider was even harder to find, costing almost as much as a mid-priced bottle of wine.

Farming in space was expensive, but there were no losses due to disease or pests, and you could optimize the weather for your crop. Here on Berry Station, they specialized in high-value crops that cost a lot to haul up out of a gravity well. There were a lot of wineries and breweries here, as well as orchards and truck farms. They supplied a lot of smaller stations with premium fruit and produce, some fresh, and some flash frozen. They were required by their charter to grow a certain amount of grain as well. Some, like the Jadavs, turned most of their barley into beer, others fed it to animals, raised out on the high-g outer level, where they put on muscle faster. There was still a healthy surplus that was shipped out to the stations for human consumption. It wasn't as profitable as the higher value crops, but the price supports made it worthwhile.

Life was good here on Berry. Looking up at the station arching over her head, Juna wondered why she had ever left. But she had felt trapped and bored here, and wanted to travel far, and see alien suns rise on distant worlds. Now all she wanted was to stay home. She was tired of traveling, tired of coping with a strange universe.

The truck hit a pothole, jolting her from her worries, and throwing Ukatonen forward onto their luggage. Moki looked worried for a moment.

"Are you all right, en?" Juna asked.

Ukatonen nodded.

"The harvest traffic is a bit rough on the roads," she explained, raising her voice so they could hear her over the puttering of the truck's hydrogen engine. "There'll be a few more potholes, so you should be prepared for them."

Ukatonen settled himself more firmly into place.

They were passing the Swensen place. Hanging from the porch was a big hand-painted banner that said WELCOME BACK JUNA. Juna smiled and blinked back sudden tears. Lena Swensen had probably painted that. And gotten it hung, even in the midst of harvest. She could see the Swensens' crew out in the back orchard, picking apples. She recognized Lars and his two brothers from their shocks of red hair. They waved at the distant truck. Juna waved back.

It was like that at all the places they passed. People working near the road stopped and ran to the fence to say hello and stare at Moki and Ukatonen. They handed Juna bags filled with produce, or preserves, or fresh-baked bread. The Tendu shook hands, waved, and shouted greetings. It felt rather like a one-truck parade.

Finally, they turned spinward at the Uenos' farm, where tall, spreading paulownia trees arched across the road. They passed the Diversity Plot, a band of forest that stretched all the way around the circumference of the inner level of the station. Moki and Ukatonen sat up, their ears wide and quivering, their skins pink with excitement. Juna smiled. She had been looking forward to their reaction. Moki turned to her, purple with curiosity.

"Yes, you can climb the trees. But you should wait until we get settled. Then I'll show you the forest."

The Tendu stared at the forest as it faded into the distance, like thirsty travelers gazing longingly at an oasis.

The truck left behind the paulownias and passed under a stately row of ginkgo trees. Juna's heart rose as she saw the slender, graceful gingkoes, their dancing fishtailed leaves just turning to gold. Beyond the trees, rows of vines heavy with grapes stretched away into the distance. They had entered her father's land. She craned her neck for a glimpse of the farmhouse she grew up in.

Then they were passing through the gate, and down the long, cypress-lined driveway. Danan slowed as they pulled up to the house. Juna vaulted out of the truck and bounded up the steps before Danan had stopped the truck.

"*Isi!* Netta *Täti!*"

"They're out back, Juna!" her brother called.

Juna rushed through the house, and out the back door, then stopped in surprise. There, out in the tree-shaded yard, was a big table spread with a huge buffet. Her father was there, and her aunt, and half a dozen old family friends.

"Surprise! Welcome home!" they shouted.

Her father rose from his chair, a little more stiffly than he had before, Juna noted with a trace of sadness. "*Hei, tytär,*" he said, spreading his arms. "Welcome home!"

Juna ran to his arms, tears flooding her eyes. "Oh, *Isi!*" she said. "It's good to be home, but who's harvesting the grapes?" she asked, looking around.

"We can spare a couple of hours to welcome you back. Toivo's family sent some people to help out. There's just the last of the merlot, and that's going over to Wermuth."

The truck rounded the side of the house. Ukatonen and Moki lifted

Toivo's wheelchair over the side. Danan unfolded it, and helped his father out of the truck.

"Was she surprised?" Danan asked as they came in the gate. "We were going to pull around back, but Juna jumped out of the truck before we could stop her."

"It was a wonderful surprise!" Juna said, ruffling Danan's curly chestnut hair affectionately.

"Welcome home, Juna," her aunt Anetta said, coming up to her niece and enfolding her in a warm, soft embrace. Juna could smell Netta's familiar lavender perfume. It reminded her of all the times her aunt had been there to comfort her in the difficult years after her mother died. Fresh tears welled in Juna's eyes.

"Thank you, Netta. I can't believe I'm actually here. I've missed you all so much," she said, wiping the tears from her face.

She glanced up from the circle of her family, and saw Moki and Ukatonen looking on, pale purple with uncertainty.

"*Isi*, Netta, everyone, this is my adopted son, Moki, and my friend Ukatonen." She beckoned to them, and put her arm around Moki.

There was a long, uncertain silence.

"*Hei*, Moki, Ukatonen, welcome to our home," her father said, a little too heartily. Aunt Netta shook hands with Ukatonen, looking a little startled at the cool wetness of his touch.

"Juna told us you make good apple pie, Netta *Täti*," Moki said. "Do you have some? It sounds delicious."

Everyone laughed at that, and soon the party was rolling again. Anetta cut the bami a big wedge of pie. "Here you go," she said.

Moki took a forkful and popped it into his mouth. His skin flared turquoise with delight. "It's good! Here, Ukatonen, try some." He handed the plate to the enkar.

Ukatonen was equally pleased. "That was wonderful," he told Anetta, turning the same happy shade of blue as Moki.

Anetta smiled. "Here, let me cut you a slice of your own, Ukatonen."

"A small slice, please. There's so much here I've never eaten before."

Anetta's eyebrows rose. "Then let me help you fill your plates." She took charge of Moki and Ukatonen, giving them a taste of everything, watching to see what they liked. Juna smiled in relief. The two Tendu had clearly won over her aunt. It was an important step in their acceptance by her family.

Juna looked around at the familiar faces of her family, the small tree-shaded yard, and the massive, comforting presence of the house with its massive, laser-cut stone walls, and deep-bosomed porch. A fleeting breeze stirred her hair, and shifted the branches of the big chestnut trees. She took a deep breath, smelling the dusty sun-warmed earth, the hay and manure smells of the barn, the dusty, fruity smell of ripening grapes. It smelled even richer and deeper than she remembered. Home. She was home at last.

Moki watched Eerin with her family. It was uncanny, seeing so many other people with Eerin's face. Her father was pink-skinned and white-haired, but Moki could see Eerin's distinctive cheekbones echoed in the faces of her father, and her aunt. Eerin and her brother were even more alike, with their brown skin, long straight noses, thin eyebrows, and big eyes. Toivo was stockier, and his face was leaner, more like his father's, but despite these differences, Eerin and Toivo were startlingly alike.

The family smelled the same, too. Even Aunt Anetta, under that strange, nose-twisting scent, smelled like Eerin. They seemed as alike as a litter of gudda pups. Moki found it simultaneously confusing and reassuring to be surrounded by so many people who smelled like his sitik.

He watched them clustering around Eerin. She looked so happy, there among her relatives. It made him glad, but he also felt a bit excluded by their closeness.

"*Hei*, Moki," Danan said, touching him on the shoulder. "I need to drive the truck out to the field. You want to come with me? I can show you around the farm on the way back."

"Thank you, Danan, I'd like that," Moki replied.

He touched Ukatonen on the shoulder. "Danan is going to show me around the farm, en," he told him in skin speech.

Ukatonen flickered assent.

"Okay," Moki said. "Let's go."

"That's really solar, the way you make pictures on your skin. How do you do it?" Danan asked.

"That's skin speech," he told Danan. "It's how we Tendu talk."

Danan opened the door of the truck and got in. Moki started to climb into the back of the truck.

"*Hei*, Moki, come sit up here, with me," Danan said, sticking his head out of the truck.

Moki climbed through the open window into the front seat.

Danan laughed. "Moki, you're weird."

Blue and green ripples of laughter slid over Moki's skin. "Of course," he replied. "I'm a Tendu."

They drove past a big building called a barn, where something called horses were kept, then another big building, the winery, where grapes were made into wine. Then they drove out into a big field with rows of plants draped over wires that were supported by tall metal frameworks. The vines were heavy with dark purple-black clusters of berries. Moki felt sorry for the plants, they seemed so confined.

"Those are the grapevines," Danan informed him. "Those metal pipes are part of the irrigation system. We feed the drip lines off them during the summer. If it's a cold rotation, we put tall sprinkler heads on top, to keep the plants from freezing."

Moki nodded. He only understood bits and pieces of Danan's explanation. He had seen irrigation equipment before, on the ship, but he didn't understand how it kept plants warm. And why would you need to, anyway?

"How does the truck work?" Moki asked, hoping to get onto familiar ground. Machinery fascinated him, and he had forever been pestering the crew of the *Homa Darabi* to explain things to him.

"That's kind of complicated," Danan replied. "There's an engine that runs on—that is, eats—hydrogen. It makes the power that turns the wheels. I'll show you sometime. We'll have to service the truck after the harvest."

"Is there a fuel cell?" Moki asked. Most of the things on the ship that used hydrogen ran on fuel cells. He didn't understand how a fuel cell worked, really, but he understood what they did.

"Kind of," Danan said.

Up ahead, there were people in the fields, and some kind of machine with two large animals tied to it. Danan pulled the truck up to the machine, got out, and handed the keys to a woman sitting on top of the machine.

"Hi, Danan, how's Juna?" the woman asked.

"Just fine," Danan said. "She looks really good."

"You see the aliens?"

Danan nodded. "Hey Moki, come on out and meet one of my mothers."

Moki climbed out of the truck. "Hello," he said a bit hesitantly, wondering how Danan could have more than one mother. "It's good to meet you."

"Hello Moki. I'm Astrid Fortunati," the woman said. "How do you like it here?"

"It's much nicer than the *Homa Darabi Maru* and Broumas Station," he said. "There's more room, and lots of big trees."

"Well, I'm glad you like our home," Danan's mother told him. "We're nearly done loading the wagon. If you want to wait for a few minutes, I can give you a ride back to the barn."

"What kind of animals are those?" Moki asked, pointing at the big brown creatures tied to the wagon.

"They're horses, Moki. The brown one's Herman and the blue roan is Dusty," Astrid explained. "Danan, why don't you introduce him to the horses while we finish loading the wagon?"

"They're so big!" Moki said as they drew close to the horses. "Is it safe to get so close?"

"Sure. They're real gentle." Danan reached over and rummaged in the wagon, pulling out a handful of long orange carrots. "You can give Dusty a carrot. He really likes them. Here, I'll feed Herman so you know how it's done."

Danan broke off a piece of carrot and held it out flat on his palm. The big brown horse reached out with its long nose and gently took the carrot from his hand. There was a crunching sound as the big animal's massive teeth ground the carrot to pulp.

"What's that metal thing in the horse's mouth?" Moki asked.

"That's a bit. It's how you control a horse's speed and direction." The other horse, whose coat had a grey frosting the color of regret in Tendu skin speech, nudged Danan with his big nose. Danan smiled. "See, Dusty wants a carrot too." He broke off a piece of carrot and handed it to Moki. "Here, you give him one."

Danan showed Moki how to hold his hand out. Moki cautiously reached out and gave Dusty a carrot. The horse's big nose was surprisingly soft and gentle as it nuzzled Moki's palm. The carrot was gone in a moment. Dusty breathed out a huge, warm puff of air, and nudged him with his nose, asking for another carrot. The horse had a reassuring smell of fermenting vegetation that reminded Moki faintly of the jungles of home. He fed the big animal another piece of carrot.

Danan stroked Herman's nose, then reached up and scratched the horse behind the ears under the complex arrangement of straps the horse wore on his head. Even the humans' animals seemed to wear clothes. "There, Herman. Good horse. You like that, don't you?" Danan crooned as the horse's head drooped, and his eyelids half closed.

"Does he talk?" Moki asked.

Danan laughed, and Dusty jerked awake. "No, Moki. Horses don't talk, but they like being talked to, and they respond to your tone of voice. They're easily startled, and a scared horse is a dangerous horse. You don't want to sneak up on a horse, especially from the rear. If they're startled, they tend to kick. But most of the time, horses're very calm, especially if they've been well treated and properly trained."

"Danan, Moki, we're ready to go," Astrid called.

"How can you have more than one mother?" Moki asked as they headed for the wagon.

"Astrid's not my biological mother, she's just one of the other mothers in our family. She takes care of us kids, though. My real mother, the one who had me, is up at the house with Toivo. I'll introduce you to her when we get back."

"Oh," Moki said, "she's like an elder in the same village."

"No, she's part of my family."

Moki turned purple in puzzlement. "I don't understand."

Astrid, who had been listening to this conversation laughed gently. "Go easy on him, Danan. Moki just got here, and it's going to take him some time to figure it all out." She picked up the reins, shook them, and made a clicking sound with her tongue. Dusty and Herman started to move, and Moki realized that the horses were pulling the wagon forward. His ears lifted and he turned deep fuchsia in amazement.

"What is it, Moki?" Astrid asked.

"The wagon! The horses are moving it!"

Astrid smiled. "That's one of the things that horses do for us, Moki. They pull loads for us, and carry us around on their backs, and they're good company. Before Juna found you, humanity's only other friends were animals."

Moki's ears widened again in surprise. Animals as friends. Danan had talked to Dusty as though he were a friend, even though the horse couldn't understand him. He shook his head in puzzlement. There had been tame animals in Narmolom and Lyanan, but they weren't friends. Humans had some strange ideas.

"But you eat animals," Moki said, confused. "How can you eat them if they're your friends?"

"It's kind of complicated," Astrid said. "Maybe you should ask Juna to explain it to you."

Danan pulled a cluster of grapes from one of the flats piled in the back of the wagon, and handed it to him. The grapes were warm from the sun and richly fragrant.

"Here, Moki, try some grapes," he said.

Moki put one in his mouth. The skin was tart and astringent on his tongue, until he bit into it, and then sweet juice burst into his mouth. There was a hard seed in the middle that tasted bitter, and he spit it into his hand.

"Oh! It's good! It's wonderful!" Moki exclaimed, turning turquoise. He ate another one.

"I think he likes them," Astrid said with an amused grin.

"Why do you make wine out of something that tastes this good? Why not just eat the grapes?"

Astrid smiled. "We like the taste of the wine, and we like getting a little drunk off the alcohol in the wine. And the wine will keep for years. The grapes last for only a few days."

"What is 'drunk'?"

"The alcohol in the wine relaxes us, and reduces our inhibitions," Astrid explained. "In moderation, the sensation can be pleasurable."

"But the alcohol is a poison," Moki said. "One of the reasons I don't like wine is that it's so much work to filter out the alcohol."

"Juna lets you drink wine?" Danan asked.

"I didn't ask her. I just saw everyone else with some, and tried it. It didn't taste very good," he said, going beige with distaste.

Astrid laughed. "Oh Moki, I'm glad you're here. I like you."

Moki turned blue with pleasure. "Thank you," he replied. "I like you, too."

Moki ate grapes all the way back to the barn. Danan kept hopping off the wagon and picking new and different varieties for him to sample. They were all grapes, but each variety had startlingly different flavors.

"So many flavors from just one kind of plant," Moki observed wonderingly. "So different, yet all the same."

"Those vines are the product of thousands of years of careful breeding," Astrid explained.

Moki's ears lifted wide. They had accomplished remarkable things in such a short time. And they did it without spurs to sample the genetic taste of a plant. "That's amazing," he said.

Astrid drove the wagon through the broad doors of the barn and into the cool dimness of the winery, where other workers began unloading pallets of grapes.

Moki was very thirsty, and his skin felt tight and dry after so much time out in the hot, dry vineyard. A long, shallow tub full of water stood just outside the door. He climbed into it, sending a cascade of water flooding over the sides. He closed his eyes and savored the moist coolness of the water on his skin.

"Moki, what are you doing?"

He opened his eyes. Danan and Astrid were looking down at him, their faces puzzled.

"My skin was drying out," he told them.

"But that's the horse trough," Danan said. "The water isn't very clean, and besides, it isn't good for the goldfish." He held out his hand. Cupped in his palm was a small, plump fish, bright orange in color. "He was pushed out with all the water."

Moki got out of the trough and helped Danan rescue the rest of the struggling fishes and return them to the water.

"They're awfully small," he observed as Danan turned on the water tap to refill the trough. "Are they good to eat?"

"We don't eat goldfish, Moki. We put them in the trough because they eat the algae, and they look pretty. Look at that one," he said, pointing to a particularly plump and awkward-looking fish with long trailing fins and huge, bubblelike cheek pouches. "Isn't he weird? The Uenos gave that one to us. They raise goldfish and ornamental carp. I helped clean out their ponds last summer. They gave us a bunch of different goldfish for our horse troughs."

"Don't those cheek pouches kind of slow him down?" Moki asked, wondering how such an awkward creature could survive.

"Yes, but it doesn't matter. There's nothing here that could eat him. He's a pet. It's his job to swim around in a tank and look pretty." Danan reached up and turned off the water.

"Come on, let's go back to the house and get something to drink. Netta *Täti* made some lemonade this morning. You'll like lemonade!"

Ukatonen watched Moki drive off with Danan. He felt a twinge of envy at the bami's ability to win the humans over. It was partly due to the humans' perception of Moki as a child, but the bami was naturally curious and outgoing. After centuries as an enkar, Ukatonen's reserve was an ingrained part of his personality. Besides, the constantly shifting gravity on the trip over had left him feeling disoriented, which only increased his habitual reticence.

A tall blond woman approached him. "This must be a lot for you to get used to," she said with a graceful gesture that took in the people sitting and chatting, as well as the arc of the space station. "I'm Selena, Danan's mother."

"You are married to Toivo?" Ukatonen inquired.

"Yes. We're a dyad in the same group marriage, a branch of the Fortunati family. Danan is my biological son."

"I see," Ukatonen said. "What is a dyad?"

"We're a monogamous couple within the larger family of our group marriage. My primary relationship is with Toivo; he's Danan's father."

"So a group marriage is like a village?"

Selena shrugged. "I don't know. What is a Tendu village like?"

"A village is a group of Tendu who share the same territory, and live in the same tree or school in the same waters. They are rarely genetically related."

"We're more closely linked than a village, then. Our branch of the family has twenty-two adults and eight children. We share child care and household chores and pool our child-rights in order to have more children."

"I'm afraid that I still don't understand how the child-right system works. Could you explain it to me?"

"The regulations are complicated, but basically, we're trying to reduce the population on Earth, keep it stable on the stations, and allow it to grow slowly on the Moon, Mars, and eventually, on Terra Nova. So, on Earth and the stations, each person has three-fourths of a child-right. On the Moon and Mars, where there's room to expand, you get a bigger child-right, one full child-right per person on the Moon, and one and one-half of a child-right on Mars. When you get married, you pool your child-rights, which enables you to have one child. You can either sell the remaining fractional child-right, or purchase half a child-right in order to have a second child. If you're part of a group marriage, you can pool the family's child-rights. For example, a group marriage of four people can have three children without having to buy any extra child-rights."

"How do you decide who gets the third child?"

"That depends," Selena said. "There are all kinds of group marriages, and each one has different ways of assigning children." She looked over at Eerin and Toivo talking earnestly in one corner of the yard, and her smile disappeared. "Toivo and I were planning to have a second child. But then he got hurt, and he can't—" Her voice caught for a moment. "We can't have any more children," she finished quietly. Ukatonen realized that she was on the edge of tears.

"I'm sorry. Is there something I can do to help?" Ukatonen asked. Humans were so fragile. They lived their lives on the edge of disaster. The Tendu were vulnerable to accident and injury too, but they either chose to die or recovered in a matter of days. There was nothing like this lifelong helplessness among his people. How could the humans stand such misery?

He looked over at Eerin's brother, surrounded by his family. He was laughing at something someone said. His life had been torn apart, and yet, he could still laugh. Humans, for all their physical weakness, could be very strong. He had seen that strength in Eerin. Where did it come from?

Selena touched his hand. "Ukatonen, I—"

But she was interrupted by Eerin's aunt Anetta, who wanted to introduce Ukatonen to some neighbors, and the moment passed.

Moki and Danan came back, and the three of them sat in the shade and drank big glasses of tart, sweet lemonade as the light grew more mellow, then began to dim. The light had the warm golden color of late afternoon, and sunset, but the strange double shadows cast by the trees and the people never grew any longer. It was eerie. As the light reddened and dimmed toward sunset, the guests left, one by one, until only the family was left.

*   *   *

Juna said goodbye to the last group of guests, and then sat down on a stone bench near Toivo.

"Toivo, why don't you keep your sister company while we finish clearing up?" Anetta suggested.

"Sure, Netta," Toivo replied. A quick, resentful frown passed across his face almost too quickly to be seen.

"Is it hard being stuck in that chair?" Juna asked in Amharic.

Toivo looked grim. "It's been more than a year since the accident, and I still can't get used to it. Even in zero-gee it was hard, dragging all this useless flesh around."

"Toivo—" Juna began, then paused, uncertain how he would react to what she wanted to tell him. "You know that Ukatonen is one of the Tendu's finest healers. Please, let him look at you. He may be able to help you walk again."

Toivo took one of her hands, and enfolded it in both of his. "Big sister, I know that you mean well, but the best doctors in the system have done everything they can. My spinal cord wasn't just severed; they could have fixed that. Six inches of my spine was crushed by the impact. My pelvis was shattered, and my legs were broken in half-a-dozen places. They haven't healed right. Even if my spine was repaired, I couldn't walk again. I'm in this chair for the rest of my life."

"Toivo," Juna persisted, "I've seen the Tendu do amazing things. You've seen the pictures of how they transformed me. Please, Toivo, let him look at you."

"Juna, it hurts too much to hope anymore."

"Toivo, don't turn your back on this. It will only take a few minutes. I wouldn't ask you if I didn't believe it was going to work." She grasped his hands and gazed directly into his eyes. "Please, Toivo. We've come all this long way because we wanted to help you walk again. At least let him try."

Ukatonen and Moki had come up while they were speaking. Ukatonen touched Toivo on the shoulder. "Your sister is right. What we do is different than what human doctors do. I believe that we can help you, if you'll let us, but I won't know until I look."

Toivo was silent for a long time, his face carefully expressionless, his eyes guarded. Juna waited, afraid to hope.

"All right," he said, looking up at them. "I guess it's worth a try. What do I do?"

Ukatonen sat down next to Eerin on the rough cool stone bench.

"Come closer," Ukatonen told Toivo. "Put your arms out like this," he said, showing Toivo how to place his arms for linking. He pierced Toivo's skin with his spurs, and entered the link.

Toivo's body was so much like that of his sister's that for a brief, confusing moment, Ukatonen thought he had somehow entered Eerin's body. If he had seen a group of villagers this closely related, he would have taken drastic action, possibly even resettling the villagers. But this close genetic relatedness was normal for humans, though he recoiled at the idea.

Although they resembled each other physically, the emotional flavor of Toivo's presence was very different. Toivo's injury had wounded him emotionally as well as physically. Everything was flavored with the bitter astringency of deep depression. Where there should have been hope, there was only a slow, pungent fear. What sustained Toivo in the face of such profound despair?

Such deep, pervading sadness could easily drag the healer down into the same emotional morass as the patient. He gently adjusted Toivo's emotional chemistry to lighten his despair. Toivo, enfolded in the deep reassurance of Ukatonen's presence, didn't seem to notice the shift in his mood.

Ukatonen turned his attention to Toivo's injuries, tracing the healed breaks on his shoulder, collarbone, an arm, and several ribs. Most had healed cleanly, but there were a couple of breaks that needed work. Then he moved down Toivo's back, tracing the spinal column. There was a severed nerve just above the break. Ukatonen teased the frayed fibers together, feeling the bright, tart taste as nerve impulses began to spark across the healed break. He encouraged the nerves to branch and grow toward each other again. There was a sharp upward spike of sweet hope as Toivo sensed the new nerve connection. The intensity of it made even Ukatonen's rock-solid control waver for a moment.

He waited until Toivo's emotional storm subsided. Then the enkar moved into the strange, subdued world below the break in Toivo's spinal column. It was like swimming down into dark, stagnant water. It was strange to feel the cells doing their work and the blood moving through the veins without the bright aliveness of the nerves. It was hard to navigate;

even the solid mineral presence of the bones was uncertain. Toivo's pelvis was like a broken gourd. Ukatonen groped his way down past the distorted pelvis to the crookedly healed femurs, and the shattered knees. Past that, there was one cleanly healed break on the left tibia, and a couple of rougher breaks on the other leg. Several broken bones in Toivo's right foot completed the catalog of damage. Ukatonen made his way back up to where the nerves were functioning, then broke the link, emerging from Toivo's damaged body with a feeling of profound relief.

It would take an incredible amount of work to bring Eerin's brother back into harmony. The work would be disquieting, and difficult, but he had never repaired anyone this badly damaged. The challenge pulled at him. He might never have another chance to perform a healing like this. Would Eerin's brother let him try?

"I can feel my back again!" Toivo said as he awoke from the link. "I actually felt you bring it back to life!"

"Yes, I repaired a severed nerve," Ukatonen explained.

"Can you heal him?" Eerin asked. Toivo's jubilant face became a still, impassive mask as he waited for Ukatonen's answer.

"It will be difficult," Ukatonen said. "And we may not be able to fully restore you, Toivo, but I think you will be able to walk again."

"Really?" Toivo asked. He looked doubtful, as though he was afraid to trust this good news.

"The damage is extensive," Ukatonen cautioned. "It will take some time."

"Will I be in much pain?" Toivo asked.

Ukatonen turned purple and spread his ears wide in amazement. "Why would you be in pain?" he asked.

"Toivo, it will be just like what he did today, only more so," Eerin explained. "You may feel an occasional twinge, but nothing more. Ukatonen is very good at this. It will not hurt."

"When can we start?"

"I'm a bit tired, and in need of a bath and a meal. Would it be possible to wait until after dinner?"

Toivo laughed, his brown face creasing around the eyes. "I wasn't expecting to start so soon!"

"Why wait?" Ukatonen said.

"Come on, let's go tell *Isi* and Netta-*Tāti*!" Eerin said, standing. "They'll be ecstatic at the news."

The days quickly fell into a pattern. Ukatonen woke, ate a big breakfast with Moki, Eerin, and her family. Then he went back to Toivo's room with Moki and Eerin to work on healing Toivo. Toivo was staying with them while the Tendu healed him. They worked from the bottom up, straightening and strengthening Toivo's poorly knitted foot and leg bones, then rebuilding the shattered pelvis and vertebrae.

Toivo remained in a coma during much of this work, allowing most of his metabolic energy to be channeled into healing. Ukatonen and Moki nourished him through their spurs, and filtered out the wastes from his body. Members of the Fortunati family took turns watching over him, though there was little to do except watch him breathe. Ukatonen found himself strangely moved by their patience, and the depth of their solicitude.

After the healing session, the enkar, Moki, and Eerin ate another quick meal. Then they donned shirts and wide-brimmed straw hats, and joined the family in the vineyard. The three of them picked grapes until the sun became too intense for them to bear. Then Moki and Ukatonen retreated to the cool shade of the forest. In the evening there was dinner, and afterwards they would check on Toivo to see how he was doing. After that, they would sit up with the family, reading, talking, or watching Tri-V.

Anetta, overhearing a discussion about Toivo's progress at breakfast one morning, suggested that the Tendu take mineral supplements to help out. Ukatonen tried some, and found, to his delight, that the increased availability of bone-building minerals would speed up the work considerably. He and Moki began taking them by the handful at meals, and passing them along to Toivo through their allu. It was an idea that the enkar would have to take back to Tiangi. Surely there was some way they could make their own supplements to help speed healing.

It took nearly eight days to finish piecing Toivo's pelvis together. At the end of that time, they had picked all but the late-harvest Riesling grapes. Ukatonen was concerned about Eerin. The healing on top of the hard work of harvest, had left her weak and exhausted. She was in danger of getting sick.

"We'll take a break for the next few days," Ukatonen announced.

"We're all tired, and I want to give Toivo's bones some time to strengthen before we go on. Can your father spare us for a few days?"

Juna nodded. "Right now, he's busy with fermentation and racking. We'd just be in the way. Weather Control has scheduled some hard frosts in a couple of weeks, and then we'll be picking the late harvest grapes, after they've been sweetened by the frost."

"Good," Ukatonen told her. "You need to eat well and rest. I have let you give too much of yourself to this healing."

"I doubt you could have stopped me," Juna said. "This is my brother we're working on, and I want to do everything I can to make him better."

"Rest then, so you will have more to give your brother when we begin again."

Juna woke late the next morning. She lay there, grateful for the chance to rest. Every day it had gotten harder to get out of bed, and the strange nausea that had plagued her on the trip over had returned. A day in bed would be lovely.

She spent the rest of the day in bed, reading, and eating, and awoke the next morning awash in nausea. She barely made it to the toilet in time to throw up. Something was very definitely wrong. Normally, she would ask the Tendu to find the problem, but they were still tired from healing Toivo.

Besides, Juna thought with a smile, it would be a good excuse to see Dr. Engle. She could drop by on her way in to pick up Analin at the shuttle terminal. Juna had seen Dr. Engle briefly at the party, but he had been called away to see a patient, and they hadn't gotten a chance to talk. He had been her doctor ever since she was a child.

Juna remembered how gentle Dr. Engle had been with her and with Toivo, after her father rescued her from the camps. He had come and sat with her, and talked of his own childhood. He had lost a beloved little sister to the wave of resistant typhoid that had swept through Miami during the unsuccessful Secession revolt in the waning years of the Slump. He understood her guilt, and guided her gently out of the swamp of grief she had been mired in.

In her teens, Dr. Engle had let her help out in the office, greeting patients, peering through microscopes, and studying anatomy and physiology in his old textbooks. His kindness had sparked Juna's interest in biology, and started her down the path that led eventually to her degree in xenobiology and the Survey. She suspected that he'd always been disappointed that she hadn't become a doctor.

She thought of her brother's face, brown as a chrysalis in the cocoon of his bed, his bones knitting as he slept. She had become a healer of sorts. It was an irony that Dr. Engle would appreciate.

"Juna!" Howard Engle exclaimed. "It's good to see you!"

He threw his arms wide and enfolded her in a big hug. As always, Juna was surprised by how small he seemed in person. In her childhood memories, he loomed over her. Now she was a couple of inches taller than he was.

"It's good to see you too," Juna told him.

He held her out at arm's length and looked her over. "You look great!" he said. "I guess the Tendu took really good care of you."

"It was pretty hard at first, but once I got used to it—" She shrugged.

"How's your family?" he asked, taking her hand.

"They're fine."

"Your brother? How is he?"

"His spirits are good. I think he's happy to see me. He's staying up at the house until the end of harvest. You should come by and see him. And I want you to get to know the Tendu. You'd like them, especially Ukatonen."

"I'll do that," he said, patting her hand. "Now, what brought you to see me?"

Juna described her symptoms.

"Hmm. Do you feel puffy? Breasts sore?"

Juna nodded.

"Well, I'll have to run a couple of tests." He got up and started rummaging through a cabinet. "So, what are your plans now that you're back? You going to settle down? Start a family?"

"I'd love to, but I can't. The Tendu need me, and I just don't have the time."

He sighed and shook his head. "You're getting along in years, Juna. You don't have that much more time."

"I know. I guess I'm just going to have to get used to the idea of never having children. I should start thinking about what to do with my child-right." Sudden tears of longing filled her eyes, and she found herself overwhelmed by sadness.

Dr. Engle rubbed her back, and handed her a tissue. "There," he murmured. "There."

"I'm sorry," she said as her sobs subsided. "I don't know what came over me." The outburst had startled her; she felt shaky and uncertain.

"You okay now?"

Juna nodded.

"Good." He handed her a plastic cup. "I need a specimen. Go pee."

Juna did so. He took the specimen, and dipped a small strip of paper in it.

"Hmm," he commented and took another strip of paper and dipped it in the urine."

"Well?" Juna said.

"I'd hang onto that child-right if I were you, Juna. You're pregnant."

"I'm what?" Juna exclaimed in amazement.

"You're pregnant. You've got a baby in there. According to the test, you're somewhere between five to six weeks along."

"That's impossible. I can't be pregnant," Juna insisted. "How could I possibly be pregnant? You gave me the contraceptive shot yourself, in this very office."

"You haven't done anything to undo that shot?" Dr. Engle asked.

"How could I?" Juna said. "I've been on board a Survey ship for the last six months. Before that I was on another planet, living among—" She paused as the realization hit her. "*Farradabenge!*" she swore in Amharic. "The Tendu!"

The Tendu must have done something to reverse the contraceptive shot. But when? She racked her brain, trying to remember when it was done. She shook her head. For all she knew, Ilto had done it when they first rescued her. Anito, or Ukatonen, or any one of the dozens of Tendu she had linked with could have undone her contraceptive shot without her realizing it. Even Moki could have done it. He had known that she wanted a baby. But he would never do something like that without telling her.

"Juna, what are you talking about?"

"The Tendu. They must have done this."

"Juna, are you saying that the Tendu got you pregnant? That's not biologically possible, even if you did have—" He stopped, and to her amazement, blushed.

Juna followed his train of thought, and laughed. "No they didn't make me pregnant. One of them must have reversed my contraception. But my partner must have gotten the shot too. I mean, doesn't everyone get them nowadays?"

"That depends," Dr. Engle said. "Where was he from?"

"He grew up on Cummings Station. His family was part of a religious commune."

"Hmm. There was a fairly strong pro-natalist sentiment on Cummings back then. Boys in the colonies weren't required to get the contraceptive shot until about twenty-five years ago. It's possible that your partner didn't get an anti-fertility shot. Given the fact that you're pregnant, I'd say it was extremely likely."

She looked up at the doctor. "I should have known, after all they did to me. I should have had my status checked."

He took her hand in his and held it firmly. "Juna, don't blame yourself. You did nothing wrong. If anything, the fault is with the Survey doctors. They're the ones who should have checked your contraceptive status." He paused. "What's important is what you're going to do now."

Juna sighed. "This is all so unexpected. I-I need to think it over."

Dr. Engle nodded. "I understand." He got up and paced, his chin tucked into his chest. "But there are legal ramifications. I'm supposed to contact Population Control immediately when I discover an illegal pregnancy."

Juna opened her mouth to protest, but the doctor held up his hand, forestalling her comments.

"I know, I know," he said. "You didn't mean to get pregnant—it was truly an accident, rare as that is these days. The difficulty will be getting the Pop Con people to believe you. It's going to be a major scandal." He stood, hands behind his back, bearded chin tucked, thinking hard.

"I could take care of it now, and not report it. There'd be some bleeding and cramping, worse than a normal period. I'd need to keep an eye on you, but it would be over in a day."

"You mean kill the baby?" she asked. The realization felt like a kick in the stomach. She folded her arms protectively over her stomach. "No. I mean I—" She stopped, wordless, and started to cry again. She was pregnant. She had wanted a child so much and now here it was, and it was impossible. She had no idea what to do.

Dr. Engle patted her on the back, but the tears continued to flow.

"I'm sorry, I—" she sobbed. "This is so sudden. I don't know what to do."

"Juna," he said, squatting down, and gently pulling her hands away from her face, and looking directly up at her. "Go home, think it over tonight. Call me in the morning."

"But the Pop Con—"

He shook his head. "In your case, it can wait a day. Call me tomorrow, when you've thought it over." He took her hands in his again. "I wouldn't do this for anyone else, Juna. I'm trusting you not to do anything foolish."

Juna nodded, dried her tears, washed her face with the warm towel that he gave her, and headed home. It was a good thing that Dusty knew the way. Juna sat in the cart in a stupor, staring unseeingly at the horse's rear end. A baby. A baby of her own. The idea made fountains of joy erupt inside her. She was no longer alone.

But the practicalities. It was impossible. How could she manage a bami *and* a baby? What about maternity leave?

At least she could afford the child-right—she had years of back pay stacked up in her account, enough to make her moderately wealthy. But she was unmarried. It would be much harder to raise a child all alone. And then there was Bruce. How would he feel about this? She liked him, but she couldn't imagine being married to him.

"Oh, god," she muttered, rubbing her forehead. There was so much to think about. She let the horse walk on, her mind churning with possibilities and potential problems. Suddenly she realized that they were standing in the driveway in front of the barn. Dusty was switching his tail and looking back at her, ears forward in puzzlement. She had absolutely no idea how long she'd been sitting there, lost in thought.

"I'm sorry, Dusty," she said with a rueful smile as she climbed to the ground. "Let's get you rubbed down and turned out into the paddock."

Ukatonen came out of the house as she began unharnessing the horse.

"Let me do that," Ukatonen said. "You should be resting."

"I'm pregnant," she told Ukatonen. "I'm going to have a baby."

"That's why you should be resting," Ukatonen pointed out.

"You knew?" Juna said, startled. "Why didn't you tell me?"

"You didn't know?" he said, turning fuchsia in amazement.

She shook her head, "I wasn't expecting it. I had a contraceptive shot to keep me from getting pregnant. It got undone on Tiangi without my knowing it."

"I see," Ukatonen said. "You were fertile when I met you. So it must have been Ilto or Anito who did it."

"What am I going to do, Ukatonen? I can't have a baby!"

"Why not?" he said.

"I'm all alone! There's no one to help!"

"I don't understand. How can you be alone? There's your family, and you have us as well."

"Ukatonen, a baby needs almost constant supervision for years. We'll be traveling all the time. A baby would get in the way. And then there's Moki. A bami doesn't have to share its sitik with anyone. How is he going to feel about a baby?"

"He's fascinated by your family, Juna. He sees how much you love Toivo. I think he'd like to have a sibling of his own that he could love like that."

Juna shook her head. "It's so complicated. There will be trouble when it gets out."

Ukatonen turned purple in puzzlement. "I don't understand. Why is this?"

"Ukatonen, I'm pregnant with an unlicensed child. Among our people, it is not allowed. I told you a little bit about Population Control, didn't I?"

"Yes, I remember. The number of children that your people can have is limited. The rest seemed rather confusing."

"Well, you're supposed to get formal permission to have a child. You fill out an application, and Pop Con checks that you have enough child-rights, and then they send you to a doctor to turn off your contraception. Then you start trying to get pregnant. In my case, one of the Tendu undid my contraception. I got pregnant by accident. That never happens among my people. People will think that I did this on purpose." She shook her head. "It's going to be a mess."

"I could undo the pregnancy," Ukatonen offered.

"No," Juna said. "I mean, I don't know whether or not to keep the baby. I want to. I want to very much, but it will be so difficult." She rubbed her face with her hands and got up to unharness the horse.

"You should be resting," he told her.

"As soon as I'm finished with this."

"Sit down. Let me do it."

"But—"

"You can tell me what to do. I need to learn."

Dusty eyed Ukatonen curiously, ears forward, nostrils spread wide.

"What do I do first?"

"First you need to introduce yourself to the horse," Juna told him. She got up, and took Dusty's head. "I'll need to help," she insisted. "There's a can of treats just under the seat. Open it up and hand me a couple."

Juna told him how to unharness the horse and rub him down. Dusty sniffed Ukatonen over anxiously at first, but he settled down quickly under the enkar's kind, firm handling.

"He likes you."

Ukatonen shrugged. "I've dealt with animals for a long time," he said.

When Dusty was unharnessed, they led him out to the paddock, and watched as the horse ambled over to an open mesh bag of hay hanging from the fence and started to eat.

"Oh, Ukatonen. What am I going to do?" Juna said as she watched Dusty eat. She felt overwhelmed.

"For now, rest, eat," Ukatonen said. "You must take care of yourself and the young one."

Juna shook her head. "There's so much to worry about." Just then Danan drove up with a truckload of supplies, and Juna remembered that she was supposed to collect Analin at the terminal. "Oh my god! Analin! I forgot to pick her up."

"It's all right," Ukatonen told her. "Danan and I will go and get her. You should rest," he said. "If you wish, I'll help you fall asleep," he said, holding out his arms. "You'll think better after a good nap."

Eerin looked at him. For once Ukatonen could see the strain on her face. "Thank you, en. I appreciate it."

Moki was out in the barn with Danan, helping clean and oil Herman's bridle when Ukatonen came in to talk to him.

"Your sitik has just found out that she is pregnant," Ukatonen said in skin speech.

Moki's ears lifted. "You mean she didn't know about the baby?" he asked, pink with surprise. "How could that be!" He had been puzzled by his sitik's failure to speak about the baby, but now he understood why she had said nothing.

"You know how body-blind humans are," Ukatonen reminded him. "And without her allu, she cannot sense what her body is doing anymore. Besides, she's had a lot on her mind, these last few weeks."

"I wish she had her allu again," Moki said wistfully. "Our linking isn't as close as it was on Tiangi."

Ukatonen brushed his shoulder in sympathy. "I wish I could make it easier for you."

Moki shrugged. "She's my sitik. Without her, I wouldn't be alive now. Besides, there are compensations. We are here, seeing things that no Tendu has ever seen. And I will be the first Tendu to have a sister. That will be interesting."

"I'm glad you're pleased about the baby. But Eerin's very frightened and confused. She may decide not to keep the child. You must help her understand how you feel."

Moki looked solemn. "I will do what I can, en."

"You must reassure Eerin," Ukatonen told him. "It would be good if she kept the baby. We would learn a great deal about humans from watching one grow up. And we can help teach it about the Tendu."

"I should go to Eerin now," Moki said.

"In a while," Ukatonen said. "She's asleep now. But she forgot to pick up Analin, so you and Danan should go and meet her at the shuttle station."

Moki nodded. "Danan?" he said, speaking in human sound speech. "Something's come up, and Juna couldn't pick up Analin. Can we go out to the shuttle station and get her in the truck?"

"Sure," Danan said. "*Isoisi* isn't going to need it for another couple of hours. Is Juna-*Täti* all right, Ukatonen? I saw you help her up to her room and she looked kind of upset."

"She just needs to rest for a bit," the enkar said. "You'd better hurry. Analin's shuttle will be here in twenty minutes."

"Okay, let me grab the keys and we'll be on our way!" Danan said.

Juna awoke to find Moki perched like a gargoyle on the footboard of the bed, watching her.

"Hello, bai," she said.

"Hello, siti," Moki replied. "Are you feeling better?"

Juna sat up in bed. "Yes, I am."

"Ukatonen told me that you just found out about the baby. I'm looking forward to helping you raise it. I've never had a sister before."

"Moki it's not that easy—" Juna began and then stopped as his words sank in. "It's a girl?" she asked

Moki nodded. "Yes. A sister." He left his precarious perch and came and sat on the edge of the bed. "You will not be alone, siti. Ukatonen and I will help you."

Juna shook her head and laid a hand on her belly. "This is an unlicensed child. There will be trouble. It will tie us down, and make it harder for me to show you what my people are like."

"Siti, every day we are here we learn more about what your people are like. Besides, watching the baby will teach us how humans learn to be humans."

He was right, Juna realized, but building diplomatic bridges was crucial for the Tendu right now. "Yes, bai, you're absolutely right, but as an enkar, Ukatonen needs to meet the humans who run things. I can't help him do that with a baby under my arm."

"Don't important people like babies?" Moki asked.

"I suppose they do, but babies are a distraction during diplomatic functions."

"What about your family?" Moki asked. "Won't they help?"

"*Isi* and Anetta are getting old, bai. They will not be alive for many more years. And Toivo has a family of his own. It isn't fair for me to ask them to help with the baby."

"Still, they love you, siti. You should talk to them about it."

There was a knock on the door.

"I'll get that," Moki told her as she got up out of bed. Juna pulled on her robe as Analin came in.

"Analin! I'm so sorry! I meant to pick you up, but—"

"It's all right. Moki and Danan came and got me. What's the matter? Are you sick?"

Juna scrubbed at her forehead. "Not exactly. I'm pregnant with an unlicensed child. I just found out a few hours ago. It was such a shock that I forgot to come pick you up."

"How did it happen?" Analin asked.

Juna explained the situation.

"I see," Analin said when she was done. "You're in a pickle, aren't you? What are you going to do?"

"I don't know. I'd like to keep the baby, but it's so complicated. I haven't told anyone yet, except for the Tendu. I don't know how my family is going to take it. Or the Pop Con authorities."

"You have enough money for a child-right, yes?"

"There's plenty of money," Juna said. "It's everything else that I'm worried about. How can I raise a child all by myself? It isn't fair to the child. And then there's the Tendu, and the Survey. How can I fulfill my responsibilities to them?"

"Take one thing at a time, Juna," Analin urged. "You can afford a child. You want a child. Now you need to plan your life so that you can have a child."

"But—" Juna protested.

"Talk to your family, Juna. See what they can do for you. Despite everything, they are your family."

"But what about Population Control?"

"Let me handle them," Analin offered. "I'll find you a good lawyer. You tell your family."

"Tell your family what?"

Juna and Analin looked up, startled.

"Isi!" Juna said. "Come in, sit down."

Her father settled himself on the bed. "Okay, what is it?"

Juna told him what had happened.

"You're having a baby? Juna that's wonderful!"

"I don't know if I'll get to have the baby, Isi."

"If you need help buying a child-right, I'm happy to help."

"Isi, it's not the money. I can afford the child-right. It's—" She shook her head. "How can I have a baby all by myself, Isi? It's not fair to the child. And I don't want to bring the scandal of having an unlicensed child down on our family."

"Juna," her father said, "you know that Netta and I could care less about a scandal. That's not important." He grasped her hand in his weathered, rough one, and looked into her eyes. "Do you want this baby?"

Juna remembered Toivo's finger curling around hers as a newborn, how much she had loved him, and how much she wanted a child of her own to love, to watch it grow.

She blinked back the tears. "Yes, Isukki, I do."

"You know, Mariam and I were going through some hard times when you were born. We were barely managing to make ends meet up here. Our families were back down on Earth. There was no one but the neighbors to help us. But we wanted a family, and so we went ahead and had you. It wasn't a perfect time, but we did it anyway. Even in those difficult times, you were a gift. You taught us so much, you brought us closer to all our neighbors. Go ahead, *tytär*. You'll have all of our love and support. Somehow, we'll help you make it work."

Moki touched her shoulder. "Ukatonen and I will help as well."

"Thank you," Juna whispered, overcome with emotion. "Thank you all." Tears were trickling down her cheeks, despite her best efforts to stop them.

Her father fished out a big handkerchief and handed it to her.

"There now, *tytär*. Dry your tears. Don't worry. Between us all, it will work out. Now, Moki, let's get Analin settled while Juna freshens up."

He ushered Analin and Moki out of the room, leaving Juna alone.

Juna smiled. She wasn't alone now, she thought, resting a hand on her stomach. She wasn't going to be alone for the next eight months, or for all the years after that.

"Hello, daughter," she said. "Welcome and love."

Juna sat in Dr. Engle's office, twisting her hands together nervously.

"You should notify the Population Control officials. I've decided to keep the baby."

"Are you absolutely sure, Juna?" he asked, his gaze intent and piercing.

Juna swallowed hard, and nodded, meeting his gaze. "Yes, I'm sure. I've already contacted a broker about purchasing the fractional child-right I'll need. My family has agreed to provide the emotional and physical support that I'll need during pregnancy and afterward. My father is willing to sign a statement to that effect. I've also contacted a lawyer to defend me if they file criminal charges."

"Good girl," the doctor told her. "I'm glad to see you're ready for this. Pop Con isn't going to be easy on you. They never are. As your doctor, I'm willing to back you up on this. You're too far along to have gotten pregnant anywhere but aboard ship. Have you contacted the father yet?"

Juna shook her head. "I tried, but he's traveling, and he instructed the comm not to forward any messages. I don't know how to get in touch with his family." She rubbed her forehead worriedly. This wasn't going to be easy for Bruce. Pop Con tended to be particularly hard on fathers. "My lawyer is trying to find him."

"I see." Dr. Engle looked up at her, a pained expression on his face. "I'll call Population Control now. You should contact your lawyer as soon as I've made the call."

"She's standing by," Juna said. "I'll wait in the reception room while you make the call."

"I'm sorry, Juna."

Juna turned, her hand on the door. "It's okay. I know you have to do this."

Moki and Ukatonen sat with her as they waited for the sheriff to come. Moki went orange with fear each time the door opened. Finally Sheriff Hiller arrived.

"Hello, Toni," Juna said.

"Juna, I'm afraid that I have a warrant for your arrest from the Population Control Board." Toni's stocky, powerful body was hunched over, as though she was trying to shrink from this task.

"I understand." Juna held her hands out to be cuffed. Being arrested by someone she had gone to school with was a very strange experience.

"Don't be silly, Juna, I'm not going to cuff you," the sheriff said. She glanced at the two aliens. "These must be the Tendu."

Juna nodded. "This is Ukatonen, and this is Moki, my adopted son."

"I see," Toni said. "Well, Moki, I'm going to have to take your mother away for a while. You can come and visit her in the brig later this afternoon."

"You'll take good care of her?" Moki asked.

"Of course I will," Sheriff Hiller reassured him. "She'll be out in a few days."

The brig was spartan, and had a feeling of disuse, but Toni made her as comfortable as possible.

"It's been six months since we had anyone in here. A couple of transient laborers got drunk and started a fight over at the Gonzaleses' place. I threw them in separate cells, let them sleep it off, and kicked them off the station."

"Well at least I've given you something to do," Juna said with a smile. She wasn't surprised by the jail's lack of occupants. Most of the people who came here to pick, plant, or weed came for a paid break from the small, cramped stations they lived on. Morale was generally pretty high, and fights were rare.

Being in jail didn't feel entirely real. It was as though she were on some kind of school field trip and had somehow gotten left behind.

"It feels strange locking you up, Juna," Sheriff Hiller said as she slid the cell door closed with a heavy rumbling thud. "Is it true? Did those aliens get you pregnant?"

Juna stared at Toni incredulously for a second or two, teetering on the edge of anger. Then the silliness of the situation struck her and she laughed. "No, Toni. The Tendu didn't get me pregnant. They undid my contraception without my knowledge. They didn't know what they were doing at the time. The father was entirely too human," she said with a rueful grin. "This really was an accidental pregnancy, rare as that is these days."

"Oh," the sheriff said, straightening in relief. "I'm sorry. It did sound kind of crazy."

Juna shook her head, and shivered. "Can you turn the heat up a bit?" she asked. "I feel kind of cold."

The sheriff nodded. "Shock. It happens sometimes. You've been through a lot today. I'll get you an extra blanket and nudge the heat up a bit. Get under the covers and warm up." She padded down the hall and shut the door behind her, leaving Juna alone in her cell. Juna climbed into the narrow bunk, pulling the covers up over her head. Gradually her shivering eased and she fell soundly asleep.

C H A P T E R

4

Juna was awakened by the rumble of her cell door opening. She sat up, rubbing her eyes sleepily.

"Your lawyer's here to see you," Sheriff Hiller told her.

"Thank you, Toni," Juna said. Her mouth tasted sour and gummy, and her hair looked like a half-collapsed haystack. She combed her fingers through it and tried to look awake.

The sheriff escorted a slender, olive-skinned, dark-eyed older woman into the cell. The woman was elegantly dressed in a tailored silk suit that made Juna feel even more rumpled and frowzy.

"Dr. Saari, my name is Sohelia Gheisar. Your press secretary asked me to represent you." Her voice had the clear, musical precision of someone from Persia or India.

"Hello," Juna said, trying to make her brain function through a thick fudge of sleep. "Thank you for taking my case."

"I seem to have caught you sleeping. Why don't you take a few minutes to get yourself together before we go over your case."

Juna nodded gratefully, and shuffled over to the sink. She dampened a corner of the small jail-issue washcloth and ran it over her face.

"Here," the lawyer said, handing her toothpaste, a toothbrush, and a hairbrush.

"Thank you," Juna said. She bent over and brushed her hair out into a full lion's mane, then straightened, and brushed it back from her face. She still needed a haircut. She tucked in her shirt and peered into the wavy steel mirror, grateful for the lack of detail that it showed. At least she felt more awake. Filling a plastic cup with water, she sat down on the bunk across from her lawyer.

"How much did Analin tell you?"

"That you're pregnant illegally and you need my help. She said that the aliens had somehow reversed your contraception. I told her that I would get the rest of the details from you. I must say it sounds like an interesting case."

"I'm afraid so," Juna agreed ruefully.

"Why don't you tell me about it?" Sohelia said, taking out a recorder and switching it on.

Juna explained what had happened. Then, when she was finished with her explanation, the lawyer went over it all again in minute detail, taking down names and dates.

"Well," Sohelia said, switching off her recorder. "It is an interesting case. Clearly you are the victim of the Survey's negligence."

"I am?" Juna said, surprised. She had been too busy worrying about whether to keep the baby to give much thought to blaming anyone.

"The Survey should have checked to make sure that your contraception was intact. A contraceptive test is a standard part of any physical exam in many places. I don't know why they didn't perform one, especially given the radical physical transformation you underwent. The Tendu could have done almost anything to you. I'll have to subpoena your records from the Survey. Will you give me permission to do so?"

"Of course, Counselor," Juna said.

"Good. I'll need to talk to your doctor. You said his name is Engle?"

"Yes, it is. He's been my doctor since I was a small child. He gave me my contraceptive vaccination when I turned thirteen."

"Good. That will be extremely helpful."

"Counselor, what about Bruce—I mean, the baby's father?"

"We're still trying to find Mr. Bowles. Apparently he's gone scuba diving somewhere in the Indian Ocean. I only hope that we find him before the Pop Con officials do. They're not too easy on population violators in that part of the world."

"I see," Juna said. Her feelings about Bruce were decidedly mixed right now. She was angry at him for getting her pregnant, and simultaneously terrified that he might somehow take the baby away from her. And a very small, shameful part of her wanted to cling to him for help and guidance.

"What about custody issues?" she asked.

"Juna, I think that's a problem for later."

"I need to talk about it now," Juna said. "I didn't plan for this child. It was an accident, but now that I have her, I want more than anything to keep her. I don't want Bruce, or anyone else, to take her away from me."

"I understand, Juna, and I'll support you in that. Since you have agreed to pay for the additional child-right, your custody position is very strong, but Bruce has rights in this matter too. Until we find out what he wants, there's very little we can do."

Juna looked down at the grey plasteel floor. "I see," she said, then looked up at the lawyer. "How much longer will I be here?"

"I'm going to try to get you released on bail as soon as possible. The arraignment is tomorrow. You should be released a few hours later."

A weight lifted from Juna's shoulders. "Thank you, Sohelia."

"Remember now, that's a hope, not a promise," the lawyer said, standing and gathering her papers. "Everything depends on the judge."

"I understand," Juna said, feeling her giddy relief settle again. "I know you'll do your best."

Counselor Gheisar smiled. "I always try to."

She pressed a buzzer to summon the sheriff. Toni came and let her out. With a rumble and a clang, the door shut and Juna was alone again.

The press had somehow gotten onto the station, and they were waiting for her in front of the small administrative building that did double duty as a courthouse. Sheriff Hiller escorted Juna through the surging, shouting crowd of reporters, like a small burly tugboat pulling a heavy load in high seas. Juna did her best to ignore the reporters, choosing instead to nod a greeting to the two strapping red-headed Swensen boys who let her and the sheriff in.

The door closed behind them, cutting off the clamor of the crowd. Juna let out the breath she hadn't even realized she'd been holding. Counselor Gheisar handed her a hairbrush and a mirror as the Swensens locked the doors against the crowd of reporters.

"I'm sorry about this, Toni," Juna apologized.

Sheriff Hiller shrugged. "We closed the spaceport as soon as we could, but this lot got in on the same shuttle as the judge. They're all supposed to leave on the next shuttle, but that isn't until this evening. I'm afraid we're stuck with them until then."

"Well," said the judge after listening to the charges, and to the testimony of several old family friends on Juna's excellent character. "In the ten years I've served on the bench in this circuit, I've never known Howard Engle to be mistaken on a question of character, and your other witnesses have been equally impressive. I'm going to release you with only the minimum required bond of ten thousand credits, which your father has agreed to post. You are dismissed on your own recognizance until the date of the hearing."

He banged his gavel and climbed down from the bench. Toni and counselor Gheisar led Juna out of the courtroom, followed by her family and Analin Goudrian.

"Is there anything you need back at the jail?" Toni asked.

Juna shook her head. Her lawyer had her clothes.

"Well, then, you're free to go."

"Thank you, Toni. If I ever have to be arrested again, I hope you're the one who does it."

"Do me a favor," Toni told her, "don't stick me with this job again." She squeezed Juna's shoulder. "Keep out of trouble, okay?"

"I'll do my best, Toni," Juna said with a smile.

"You should make a statement to the press," Analin urged her. "Otherwise they'll be all over you at the farm."

"Analin's managed to keep them away from us so far," her father said, "but they've pestered the neighbors pretty badly. It's worse than when word first came out about the Tendu."

"I've had to deputize almost a dozen people just to deal with these reporters," Sheriff Hiller complained. "I'll be glad when the shuttle gets here."

"Analin, why don't we announce a press conference at the shuttle station?" Juna said. "Once we're through, Sheriff Hiller can keep them there until it's time to leave. Then they won't be bothering the neighbors in the middle of harvest."

"It might work, if we can schedule it correctly."

"I could provide transport to the shuttle terminal," Sheriff Hiller offered. "My grandfather is the local historian. He'd be happy to say a word or two about the station."

Juna met Toni's eye, and the sheriff winked at her. Juna fought back a laugh. Grandpa Hiller's long-windedness was notorious. Listening to him rattle on was almost more punishment than the reporters deserved.

"That's very thoughtful of you, Sheriff," Analin said.

The sheriff shrugged. "They're tying up the roads. It'll help ease congestion."

Clearly Grandpa Hiller had outdone himself. The reporters looked slightly dazed when they got off the bus at the press conference. It took ten minutes for them to recover enough to begin asking really probing questions, and Analin was able to bring the press conference to a close after a few more minutes. One of the deputies dropped Juna at home, and she slipped quietly upstairs and gratefully into bed, even though it was only the middle of the afternoon. She was so sleepy lately. She felt like a bear, slipping in and out of hibernation.

She was awakened around dusk by a comm call.

"Good evening, Dr. Saari, I'm Counselor Tatiana Konstantin, from the Survey's legal department. As you know, the Survey is most concerned about the situation that you are in, and we are doing everything in our power to help you. We've arranged for the charges to be dropped as soon as your pregnancy is terminated."

Juna felt the rising hope in her fall away at the lawyer's last words. She clutched the edge of the table and took a deep breath, reining in her anger. "There seems to be some misunderstanding here. I'm planning on keeping the baby."

"I see," the woman said, obviously surprised. "You realize that you are not allowed on active duty while you are pregnant?"

"That clause in my contract refers only to space travel and hazardous duty."

"Your duties with the Tendu will require considerable travel."

"Then I guess we're both in a bind, aren't we?" Juna said. "We'll have to work out a compromise that will enable me to continue to work for the Survey."

"That may be quite difficult, Dr. Saari."

"I understand that," Juna replied, "but Moki and Ukatonen need my help and support, and I can best help them by remaining in the Survey." She smiled inwardly. The Survey wasn't the only one who could deal in veiled threats. "It would be a shame if I was forced to retire because the Survey was unable to work around the needs of me and my child."

"I see. We will need to reconsider our position in this matter."

"Yes, we will," Juna said. "The Tendu and I need to have a say in the Survey's plans for us."

"I'm sure we'll take your needs into account, Dr. Saari."

"How can you do that if we're not included in the decision-making process?" Juna demanded.

"I'm sure we'll discuss your request, Dr. Saari," the woman said. "I'll talk to the director, and set up a meeting with you after your leave is up."

"Thank you," Juna said, doing her best to sound grateful. "We look forward to discussing our plans with you."

"You're welcome, Dr. Saari," she said, and signed off.

Juna sat back with a weary sigh, rubbing her forehead. She was bone-weary. Even though she had just wrung a concession from the intransigent Survey bureaucrats, it did not feel like a victory.

There was a knock on the door.

"Come in."

It was Anetta, carrying a tray laden with food.

"You've had a long hard day, dear, so I brought your dinner up on a tray. I made you pea soup. When you're done with that, there's roast chicken and spanakopeta," she said, setting the tray down on the desk.

"Thank you, *Täti*." Juna said gratefully. She really was too tired to go downstairs to eat.

"I remember when I was pregnant with my first." Her aunt paused a moment, her eyes shadowed, remembering her family, lost in the war. In that moment she looked truly, frighteningly old. "I was so tired I could hardly move for the first couple of months. And you've had a very hard day."

"Netta-*Täti*, do you think I'm being selfish?"

"Selfish, Juna? Why on earth would you think that?"

"For having this child, all by myself, without planning it. I ask myself why I want a child, and nothing comes back. All I know is that I want this child. Maybe it's for all the wrong reasons."

Anetta reached out and took Juna's hands. "When I was young, surprise children happened a lot more often. A lot of women stopped the pregnancy, and for them it was a difficult choice, but the right one. But some women wanted to keep their children, and somehow they made room for them, even when it was hard. Juna, you want that child. Don't let anyone talk you out of it. You have all of us behind you, and we'll make it all work out somehow. It won't be easy—children never are. But most worthwhile things are difficult."

"Thank you, Netta."

Anetta reached down and hugged her. "You're like a daughter to me, Juna."

Juna looked at her aunt's kind face, seamed by time. She had helped fill the hole left in Juna's life by the death of her mother. "You helped bring me back to life after the camps, *Täti*," she said. "I was so afraid for so long."

"We helped each other, Juna. That was a bad time for us all. Some days I thought the cloud would never leave us. It was like that when Toivo was hurt, too. Your father—" She shook her head. "I thought your father was going to go crazy. Then Toivo pulled out of it. The doctors performed miracles, but it was Toivo's stubborn spirit that made the difference. He just refused to die. Then, when he found how bad it was, it was your father and Selena who wouldn't let go of him, who made him live."

"I wish I'd been here when Toivo was injured," Juna said regretfully. "The worst part was knowing he was hurt, and not being able to do anything."

"But you brought the Tendu and their miracles, and soon he'll walk again. He hasn't been this happy since the accident. And that baby will be another miracle," she said. "You've given us so much, *veljentytär*." She stood. "Now, eat your dinner before it gets cold."

"Yes, *Täti* Netta," Juna said with a smile. She dug into her soup with sudden enthusiasm. She was still scared and uncertain about her future, but at least she wasn't alone.

It took nearly a week to find Bruce, and then two more days to get him out of the backwater jail he was imprisoned in. Juna was settling into bed when the comm chimed.

"Juna, it's for you," her father called from the foot of the stairs. "I think it's Bruce. I'll transfer it upstairs to your comm."

Juna padded to the door, pulling on a robe as she went. "Thanks *Isi*," she called down. "I'll get it."

She switched on the comm. Bruce's face appeared. He looked rumpled and peevish.

"Hello, Bruce," she said.

"Have you got any idea how bad a time I've been having?"

"I'm sorry, Bruce."

"That's easy for you to say, isn't it? You didn't have to spend a week in a stinking Mauritanian jail."

"Bruce, we got you out as quickly as we could," Juna told him.

"I wouldn't have had to go through all this if it hadn't been for you. First I was stuck on that damned ship— Now this."

Juna took a deep breath and pushed away her pain and anger at Bruce's sudden, surprising hostility.

"It was an accident, Bruce. The Tendu undid my contraception without my knowledge. They had no idea what they were doing, and I didn't know I could get pregnant." She considered pointing out that she would never have gotten pregnant if he had gotten his shot too, but that would only make matters worse.

"And now you want me to give up part of my child-rights so that you can have the baby."

"Bruce—" Juna began. "I don't want to take your child-rights away. I'm not out to get you. I think you should get a good night's sleep, and think things over tomorrow morning. I'd like you to come up here, meet my family, and talk the situation over. It's your child too, Bruce, and I want what's best for all of us. You, me, and our daughter."

"A daughter?" Bruce said. "You mean—It's a girl?" His angry expression was replaced by sudden amazement.

"So the Tendu tell me."

"A girl," he said and shook his head. "A girl," he repeated somewhat more quietly. "I'll be damned."

He was pleased. Juna felt her own fear and anger vanish. Perhaps now he would be willing to talk.

"When do you want me to come up?" he asked.

"As soon as it's convenient."

"I'll see what I can do, and then call you. What's the time difference?" he asked.

"We're plus 3 GMT," she told him.

"Oh jeez. I woke you up," Bruce said, looking embarrassed.

"Not quite," she said. "It's all right. Let me know when you're coming up." She felt herself relax with relief at his sudden shift in mood. Maybe she could work things out with him after all.

"Okay," he said. "I'll see you as soon as I can." He shook his head again. "A girl. I'll be damned," he muttered as he reached for the disconnect button.

Juna and Counselor Gheisar picked Bruce up at the shuttle station.

"Well," he said tightly after Juna had introduced him to her lawyer. "I guess you've got me surrounded."

Juna winced inwardly. She wished Analin was here. She would have found some clever way to defuse the tension, but Analin had gone back to Earth, where she could work more directly with the major news organizations.

"Bruce, it's not like that," Juna protested. "Sohelia wants to find out what the Pop Con people have said and done, so that we can build the best case to keep our child."

"I see. Perhaps I should have brought my lawyer as well."

"If you'd like," Sohelia broke in, "you can ask him to come up or have him present by comm link during our discussions. I'll need to speak with him, anyway."

"That would be good," Bruce said.

"Your lawyer is Bernard Frishberg, I believe? I've worked with him before. He's good."

"Thanks," Bruce replied. "He should be. He costs the earth."

"With a little luck, the Survey will wind up paying your legal fees. After all it was their negligence that caused this pregnancy."

"So Bernie says." Bruce sounded dubious.

"Moki is looking forward to seeing you, Bruce," Juna interjected, to change the subject. "He's busy helping my nephew repair the grape crusher. Moki's still crazy about machines," she added, smiling fondly. "He misses you."

"It'll be good to see him again. How's Ukatonen?" Bruce asked, clearly relieved at the change of subject.

"Much better. They both perked up as soon as they got here. They've been a big help around the farm, and with the new vineyards we've put in we need all the help we can get. Ukatonen's developed a real liking for the

farm horses. My father's asked him to help train a pair of colts to harness."
According to her father, Ukatonen had a gift for working with horses.

"You seem happy to be home," Bruce noted. He sounded a bit wistful.

"I am," Juna agreed. "I think living with the Tendu made me appreciate my family more."

"I guess after four years of living in a tree with aliens, it would be nice to be home."

"No," Juna said. "That's not what I meant." She paused, trying to find the words that would bridge the gap of understanding that lay between them. "The Tendu were together so much. No one was ever alone. It was hard at first, living in everyone's pocket, but gradually I became part of the community, even though I was an alien and a stranger. I felt more alone on the ship coming back than I did living among the Tendu. They made me realize how much strength I could draw from being a part of a community."

Bruce looked uncomfortable. "I think you've been spending too much time with the aliens and not enough time with your own people," he told her. "You need to remember that you're home now, Juna, among human beings."

His words saddened Juna. She realized that she was seeing an aspect of his personality that she had refused to acknowledge on board ship. If only she could make him understand how much her time with the Tendu meant to her, how deeply it had changed her.

"Bruce, I wouldn't change what happened to me on Tiangi. The Tendu taught me so much. I can't imagine my life without the Tendu in it."

"Juna, I—" Bruce began, "You shouldn't—Dammit Juna, I don't want my daughter raised by aliens!"

She placed one hand protectively on her stomach, and took a deep breath, pushing away her fear that he would take the baby away.

"Bruce," she said gently, "I'll be her mother, not Ukatonen, not Moki. I want to marry into a family that will love her as much as I will. Ukatonen and Moki will be part of her life, but she'll also be surrounded by humans."

"Then marry me, Juna. We can make it work—you'll see."

She felt a wave of sadness wash over her. She couldn't marry Bruce, not after what he had said about the Tendu.

"I'm honored that you would ask me, Bruce. It's very kind of you to offer, but we're too different. It wouldn't work."

She hoped that she had turned him down gently enough. If he got angry at her, he might make things even more difficult.

"But, Juna, the child needs a father!" he exclaimed.

"Bruce, the child needs a family, a happy one, not two people married to each other out of obligation."

"And what about me, what about my rights?" he demanded.

"That's one of the reasons you're here, to help settle the custody issues," Sohelia pointed out. "I don't expect any final agreement to come out of this, but perhaps we can find out what each of you wants, and start to outline some kind of settlement. However, you two may be arguing over something that will never happen. Pop Con could force Juna to end the pregnancy. I'm going to do everything in my power to prevent that," the lawyer continued, "but until the hearing, custody is a moot point. If you want this child to live, you must work together to make that happen."

They drove on in sullen silence until they passed the Ueno place. "We're nearly home," Juna said, trying to break the mood. "I hope you're hungry. My aunt's making a big dinner for us. She's a wonderful cook."

"Actually, I'm starved," Bruce admitted. "I don't eat much when I'm shuttling between stations. All those gravity changes do strange things to my stomach."

Sohelia nodded sympathetically. "Mine, too."

"I guess I got used to shifting gravity, growing up here," Juna remarked. "They sent us to school out on the outer rim, where the gravity is heavier, so our bones would be strong. After the first month, I hardly noticed the change anymore."

Juna turned in at the gate to her family's farm. "Here we are."

Bruce looked out the window at the solid-looking stone house. "I expected something a little more spartan."

"The house was built by the first colonists, a group of Reform Amish," Juna explained. "The Amish had big families, so they built big. And they built to last. The stone was left over from building the station. Most of the original houses are made of it. It was the cheapest building material they had."

"It's a nice place," Bruce said.

"Thank you," Juna replied. She stopped in front of the house, and pulled Bruce's bag out of the back of the truck. Anetta came out on the porch, wiping her hands on a dishtowel, and nodding at Sohelia as the lawyer went inside.

"So you're the father of my new niece!" Anetta said when Juna had introduced them.

"Well, I suppose I am," Bruce acknowledged, looking suddenly embarrassed.

Just then, Moki came out of the barn. "Bruce!" he shouted, and broke into a run. He took his bag. "Bruce! I'm going to have a sister! Isn't that great!"

"Moki, why don't you help Bruce get settled, and show him around the farm?" Juna suggested, relieved to be passing Bruce along to someone else for a while. "I'll go help Anetta in the kitchen."

"Okay," Moki said. "Danan and I got the crusher put back together. It runs much better now."

"Good for you!" Juna said. "You're turning into a real mechanic." She smiled. Moki was sounding more like Danan every day. Sometimes he sounded deceptively like a ten-year-old boy.

Bruce followed Moki around the farm. Moki clearly liked the vineyard, and was intrigued by the winery, with its tall steel vats, and the crushing and bottling machines, as well as the small, immaculately clean lab for testing the wine. But it was clear that the little alien was even more excited by the prospect of having a sister. Listening to him made Bruce's blood run cold.

How could this alien child blithely assume such a close relationship to his daughter? And how could Juna and her family allow it? It all seemed deeply, profoundly wrong to Bruce. Finally, he excused himself and retreated to his room on the pretext that he needed to wash up before dinner. He winced as he lay down on the bed. The bruises from the beating he had received during his arrest were still tender. He closed his eyes, shutting out the high-ceilinged room, and tried to remember how he had gotten himself into this situation.

Juna had seemed improbably beautiful when he had first seen her on Tiangi. Brilliant colors and patterns flickered and slid across her naked body like some strange light-show. Walking in the forest with her was like stepping into Eden. She was graceful and completely at home in the alien forests of Tiangi. Then she had cried in his arms like an abandoned child.

He had been touched by her loneliness and vulnerability, and flattered that someone as famous as she was would be drawn to him.

She remained beautiful after the aliens had given her back her original creamy brown skin. But on board ship she had gotten more and more wrapped up with the aliens and their problems. The final frantic flurry of sex during the quarantine had been exciting, but he had been secretly relieved to have the relationship end. Only, now, it wasn't over.

At first he'd thought the arrest was a joke, some kind of mistake. He had argued with the police, and instead of reasoning with him, they hit him with their rubber truncheons, threw him in their hot, filthy jail. He swallowed against the tightness in his throat as he remembered the smell of the place. And here he was, his life turned inside out by a woman he thought he had said goodbye to.

Dinner was long and tense. The food was good, the wine was excellent, but it was all ashes in his mouth. Juna's father, Teuvo, tried to draw him out, but Bruce felt too nervous and out of place to talk. Instead he worried about what he was going to say at the upcoming meeting.

At last the dessert plates were empty. Bruce pushed away from the table with a sense of guilty relief.

"Mr. Bowles," Juna's lawyer said, consulting her watch, "it's nearly time to call Bernie Frishberg for our conference. Is there anything you need before we start."

Bruce shook his head. "We might as well get it over with," he said.

"You can use the library," Juna's father offered. "It's very private."

Bruce followed the others into the library. He felt like a condemned man being led to the firing squad. At least, he thought sourly, it was a handsome room, lined with books. One whole set of shelves was devoted to technical books on winemaking and grape-growing. They looked well-thumbed. There was a low table in the middle of the room with comfortable chairs set around it. But the comfort and dignity of the room did nothing to quell his worries as he sat down and set up his comm unit.

"Well," Counselor Gheisar said when they were all settled and Bruce's lawyer was listening in on the comm link, "Juna has expressed an interest in trying to work out the custody issues with your desires in mind, Mr. Bowles. But in order to do that, we need to know what you want."

Bruce took a deep breath and leaned forward. "Before all this happened, I was planning on getting on with the rest of my life, hoping to get married. I've worked for years to get enough money to afford a second child. I don't want to lose my child-rights." Anger surged as he spoke.

"Bruce, I—" Juna began.

"And now you've involved me in this scandal, I'm going to have to spend all my savings on legal fees." All his plans were in ruins because Juna hadn't thought to have her contraception checked.

"Bruce, don't worry, the Survey is clearly negligent. They'll wind up paying the court costs on this one," Bernie said reassuringly. Bruce's lips tightened. He would believe that when it happened.

"Juna intends to pay for the fractional child-right," her lawyer told him. "You'll still be able to afford a second child."

Bruce nodded grudgingly. It was the least she could do.

"What are your feelings about custody?" Counselor Gheisar asked.

Bruce looked down at the worn rag rug that covered the floor. This was the hardest question to answer. "It bothers me to know that the child is going to be raised with the aliens. I mean, I like Moki and Ukatonen well enough," he said, glancing up at Juna's lawyer, "but I don't want them looking after a child of mine. Juna's all alone. What kind of mother can she be, without support? And she has the aliens to take care of. That's a pretty demanding job. I don't want my daughter raised in a situation like that."

"Do you want custody?" Sohelia asked him.

Bruce looked at Juna, who was watching him, her dark eyes intent on his face. He dropped his gaze to the rug. This was going to be hard enough to say without looking at her. "I think the whole thing is a bad idea," he said quietly. "I don't think Juna should have the baby."

"Bruce, I—" Juna began again, but her lawyer laid a cautionary hand on her arm.

"You've brought up some very genuine concerns," Counselor Gheisar said. "First, the matter of money. You are not being asked to give up any of your child-rights. Juna has agreed to buy the remaining fraction of a child-right that she needs on the open market. Second, as Bernie pointed out, the Survey will very likely pay all legal fees and fines. They should have checked to see if her contraception was still intact, and they're clearly negligent under current law. They're responsible for Juna's becoming pregnant."

Gheisar stood. "The matter of custody is a good deal more complex. As an unmarried man whose child-rights are not involved, you have very little say in the custody of the child. Juna would be well within her rights to never allow you any access to her child at all. Instead, she has agreed to allow very liberal visitation rights. As far as your other reservations are concerned, Juna has the support of her family, and of her brother's family. They will help her raise the child. It's not a marriage, perhaps, but it is a family, and a solid one."

"Bernie, what do you think?" Bruce asked, appealing to his lawyer for support.

"Basically, Counselor Gheisar is correct. Juna is being extremely generous here. Custody is a long shot. You have some options, but they're expensive and time-consuming. If you like, we can discuss them later."

Bruce examined the carpet again. There was no easy way out of this. He raged inwardly at the situation.

"This brings us to the matter of the Tendu," Counselor Gheisar continued, "Why, exactly, do you object to them?"

"Because Moki is planning on being my daughter's brother! It isn't right, it isn't natural! It can't be good for the child!" Bruce exploded, venting his frustration.

"Bruce, I don't understand," Juna said. "You like Moki. Why don't you want him around our daughter?"

"I don't trust the Tendu," Bruce replied, scowling. Juna and her lawyer were herding him into a very small corral, and there wasn't a damned thing he could do about it. Why couldn't Juna let go of the baby? She already had fame, money, and the Tendu. Wasn't that enough? Why was she dragging him through this?

"Bruce, I've known Moki and Ukatonen for years," Juna told him. "I've trusted them with my life. I wouldn't go through with this if I thought that the Tendu would harm our daughter."

"But Juna, they eat their young!" Bruce blurted out. "How can you let them near a baby!"

Juna's eyes widened in surprise. "Ukatonen and Moki understand the difference between a human baby and a Tendu tadpole. If you don't believe me, we can call them in and ask them!"

"That's an excellent idea, Juna," Counselor Gheisar said. "I can't think of a better way to deal with this question. Please, go ahead."

Bruce glared at her lawyer as Juna went to the door and called the Tendu in. The aliens came in and sat down, deep purple with curiosity.

"Go ahead," she told Bruce. "Ask them."

Bruce stared at the floor, embarrassed and angry at being put on the spot like this. He mumbled a curse under his breath.

"What did you say, Bruce?" Moki asked.

"Are you—" he began, then shook his head. "You called them in here, you ask them," he said, looking up at Juna.

"Bruce is concerned that you might eat the baby," Juna said.

Ukatonen's ears spread wide, and he turned a deep purple in puzzlement. Moki sat up indignantly, a lightning fork of red anger flickering across his chest.

"Why would we do a thing like that?" he demanded. "Why would I eat my own sister?"

Ukatonen touched Moki on the shoulder, and said something in skin speech. Bruce couldn't follow what he was saying with the rudimentary skin speech he had picked up from them on the ship. Ukatonen stood, drawing himself up proudly. Suddenly the alien seemed like the largest person in the room, even though he didn't even come up to Bruce's shoulder.

"I am an enkar of the Three Rivers Council," Ukatonen declared. "I am about to render a formal judgment. As Eerin knows, my life is forfeit if this judgment is wrong. I say that no Tendu will harm Eerin's daughter."

He relaxed his formal pose, yet still seemed to dominate the room.

"We promised, when we came here, that we would abide by the Contact Protocols," Ukatonen continued. "Eating a human child would be a clear violation of those protocols." Bruce recognized the amusement that flickered across the alien's chest, and his lips tightened in anger.

The amusement vanished as the alien turned to speak to Bruce. "Eerin's child is important to both our people. By growing up with Moki and myself, she will learn about the Tendu. When she is grown, Eerin's daughter will help provide a link between our two peoples. There is too much to gain for us to want to hurt her."

"Eerin's daughter this, Eerin's daughter that," Bruce complained. "She's my daughter too. I want her to be a normal, happy little girl, not some half-alien thing I can't understand! I don't want her to grow up to be an alien. I don't want to sacrifice her on the altar of alien diplomacy! She's just a little girl who isn't even born yet!"

"Bruce!" his lawyer cautioned. "That's enough."

"We don't want to turn her into a Tendu, Bruce," Ukatonen told him. "We want her to be a human with a deeper understanding of the Tendu. We will help Eerin raise her, but she will be Eerin's child, and if Eerin does as good a job with her daughter as she has with Moki, then I think the child will be exceptional."

Bruce looked down at the carpet once again, unable to find words that would express the dread he felt. They wouldn't listen, anyway.

Juna's lawyer began gathering up her notes.

"Perhaps we should all get a good night's sleep and think things over," she suggested. "We've gotten a good idea of how everyone feels, and that's an important first step. Now we need to arrive at an agreement that we can all live with. We can work on that tomorrow.

"Bruce, we all realize that you're hesitant about the child being raised around aliens, but the Tendu seem to care about her, and mean her no harm. Also, you should be aware that Juna is being extremely generous. She's offering you liberal visitation rights, and carrying the financial burden of bearing and raising this child herself, freeing you to marry as you wish.

"Juna, you understand that Bruce has deep misgivings about the way you wish to raise your child. You need to think about how to reassure him that your daughter will have a normal childhood. Now, go," Sohelia said, making shooing motions with her hands. "Go and think things over."

As Bruce left the meeting, he saw Moki glance at him and turn away, his skin clouded with grey.

"Damn," Bruce muttered under his breath. He had not wanted to hurt the little alien's feelings. He headed upstairs to his room with a heavy heart. It had been a very long, hard day.

Moki walked out onto the front porch and stood in the darkness for a few moments, his skin a smoky roil of grey and purple. Bruce liked him. Why was he so afraid that he would hurt the baby?

Moki stood on the porch until the cold made him feel sluggish and dull. The cold numbed his body, but did nothing to erase the hurt he felt. With a slow ripple of sadness, he turned and went back into the house and all the troubles it contained.

He went into the kitchen to brew a cup of peppermint tea. He liked the warmth and reassurance of tea, and the sweet, pungent scent reminded him of the smell of fresh aka leaves. He huddled in front of the stove, waiting for the water to boil.

"*Hei, pikkuinen,* what are you doing?" It was Eerin's father.

"Making some tea, *Isoisi,*" he said, using the Finnish word for Grandfather. "Would you like some?"

"You look cold, Moki. Go sit by the heater and warm yourself. I'll make the tea. Let me guess, you want peppermint, right?"

"Yes, *Isoisi,*" Moki said, "but I should do it. You are an elder, after all, and the father of my sitik."

Teuvo smiled. "It's all right, Moki, I may be an elder, but I'm not so ancient that I can't make a mug of tea for my daughter's bami. Besides, Juna just stalked up to her room without saying a word, and I want to hear about what went on in the library."

"Now," he prompted when they were settled near the heater in the living room, "tell me what happened."

Moki told him about Bruce's fears for the child.

"I don't understand, *Isoisi,* I thought he was my friend. I thought he liked me. Why is he afraid to let me help Juna with her baby?"

Teuvo stared into his mug of tea. "Many humans are afraid of what's different, Moki. When I married Juna's mother, Mariam, both our families were extremely upset."

"Why?" Moki asked, puzzled.

"Mariam's skin was even darker than Juna's, and my skin, as you can see, is light. She and I came from very different people. Our families were afraid of how different we were from each other. They wanted their children to marry someone like them.

"To be honest, it was hard at first. There were some terrible arguments." Teuvo smiled, remembering. "Sometimes I think the only reason we stayed together was because we couldn't understand each other's insults. But there were good times too, lots of them. When she died, I felt like I'd lost my other half." He paused for a moment, his gaze turned inward, lost in remembrance.

"Most of our relatives forgave us when Juna was born," Teuvo continued. "It's amazing how grandchildren can bring a family together again. Our children and grandchildren are very precious to us.

"I've had some misgivings about you and Ukatonen and the child," he admitted. "But I know Juna better than Bruce does, and I trust her judgment. If she's willing to trust you and Ukatonen, then you must be worthy of that trust."

"You honor me. I will try to be a good brother to your grandchild," Moki told Teuvo. He spoke as formally as he could, given the limitations of human sound speech.

Juna's father chuckled. "Of course you will, *pojanpoika*, of course you will."

"But what about Bruce?" Moki asked. "How can I achieve harmony with him?"

Teuvo shook his head, "I don't know, Moki. You should talk to him, but he may not be as interested in harmony as you are. There may be no solution to this problem, Moki. But if there is, I'm sure you will find it."

Ukatonen turned up the heat on his warmsuit. It was deadly cold this morning. In the shadow of the barn, the ground was covered with a thin white coating. He took off one of his gloves and touched a stone covered with the white stuff. The rime coating the stone burned with cold, but disappeared when he touched it, leaving only a dark wet spot on the rock where his finger had been. Ukatonen sniffed his finger, smelling nothing but moisture. He shoved his hand back into his glove, grateful for the heated glove's warmth. His whole body felt suddenly warmer, as though he had stepped into a warm room. He stood, feeling his hand slowly stop aching from the cold.

"What is this white stuff, Teuvo?" he asked Juna's father, who was watching him.

"It's frost, frozen water vapor. It settles onto the ground on cold nights. It'll be gone as soon as it warms up a bit."

"It will get warmer, then?" Ukatonen asked. He felt smothered inside the muffling warmsuit. While wearing it, he was restricted to human speech, or to small private words on his face, but in the cold, his skin became sluggish and unresponsive to his thoughts. He pulled his hood more closely around his face, leaving only his eyes and muzzle exposed to the numbing, burning cold.

Teuvo laughed, his breath becoming a white cloud in the cold air. "Of course it will. The pickers are already out in the vineyard, picking the grapes before they thaw for *eiswein*. I'll have to go and oversee the crushing in about an hour. But for now"—he held up a pair of halters—"we have a little time to train the colts. They'll be full of ginger this morning!"

"Ginger?" Ukatonen said, trying to put a questioning inflection into his voice.

"The cold will make them frisky and full of energy."

"You mammals!" Ukatonen said reprovingly. "No sensible creature would live in a climate like this."

"Come on, then, Mr. Cold-blood. A little work will warm you up."

Ukatonen followed Juna's father out to the relative warmth of the sun-lit paddock. Helping Eerin unharness her horse had aroused his curiosity about the massive but gentle animals. They were so big, and yet so amazingly gentle and eager to please. Teuvo had noticed Ukatonen watching the horses, and had invited him to help work with them.

He enjoyed working with the horses. Teuvo seemed to think that he had a real gift for it, but it was just like taming pets at home, only easier. It helped that the horses had a real sweet-tooth, and weren't afraid of him, but the rest was just patience and timing. Once you understood that they were herd animals, and hated being alone, the rest was easy.

Teuvo was the master of the horse atwa. He moved with the sureness of long practice around the flighty young colts. They were training these two colts to be light draft and riding horses for the Fortunati family, in exchange for help with the harvest. The colts had come up from the outer ring of the station, where the higher gravity helped them put on bone and muscle. According to Teuvo, horses raised in the outer ring were ready to ride four months earlier than horses on Earth.

Teuvo stood at the gate and gave a loud whistle. The horses trotted up, ears forward, eager for their treats, and for company. Ukatonen haltered the animals and led them to the smaller fenced ring to work with them.

"Today," Teuvo said, "we're going to work them on the lunge line to take the edge off, then start working them together as a team."

The morning went well, the horses moving sweetly through their paces. At first they were skittish, but Teuvo and Ukatonen spoke soothingly, doling out treats with a liberal hand, and the colts soon settled down. Then it was a matter of walking the paired horses over carefully spaced poles on the ground to encourage them to synchronize their strides. Ukatonen led the colts, while Teuvo followed along behind, holding the long harness reins and giving commands. Soon they were moving in perfect unison.

The day's training completed, Ukatonen and Teuvo unharnessed the horses, rubbed them down, and turned them loose in the paddock. Leaning against a metal fence rail, they watched the young horses settle down to graze.

"We did good work today, Ukatonen," Teuvo said. "I've never seen two horses learn to move together that quickly. Look at them now. They're even grazing in sync."

Ukatonen nodded, watching the two horses eating in precisely the same rhythm.

"You linked with them, didn't you?" Teuvo asked.

"I synchronized their body rhythms while I was leading them," Ukatonen told him. "It is a thing my people do when they need to work together. It will wear off in an hour or two."

Teuvo shrugged. "It's a little spooky, watching them. Do you think it'll make a difference tomorrow?"

"We will both find out. This is a new thing. I've never tried it before. I won't do it again, if you don't want me to."

"Just tell me first."

They stood silently together watching the horses.

"I wish they weren't going back to the outer level after we've finished with the harvest," Teuvo said with a regretful grimace. "It's so much more convenient working with them here. And I'm getting too old to deal with the gravity out there."

"I don't understand getting old, Teuvo. What's it like?"

Teuvo looked at him, one white eyebrow raised. "From what Juna tells me, you know a lot more about it than I do."

"We grow older but we do not"—Ukatonen paused, searching for the right word—"age as you do. Our bodies do not wear out. Unless we are unlucky, we get to tell our bodies when to die. Here it is your bodies that tell you when you will die. What is that like for you?"

"Our lives have a rhythm to them, Ukatonen. At first we are young and active—our lives are full of exploration and discovery. Then we mature, and have children. Then we get old. We have some time to enjoy the fruits of our lives, and watch our children and grandchildren grow up. There's nearly ninety years of experience inside this head. That's a lot of good memories. I like being able to look back on a broad sweep of time. Soon it'll be time to let go, let the next generation come up to take my place."

He sighed. "But as nice as all that sounds, I don't want to die yet, Uka-tonen. I like the life that I have. I built this vineyard, planted those grapes. Now it's doing well, and I want to enjoy that. I want to see what happens to my children and grandchildren. I'm not ready to leave yet, but I know that no matter what, my body is going to continue to decline.

"To tell the truth, growing old is mostly unpleasant. Everything hurts. You get tired more easily. Every time you forget something, you wonder whether your mind is going." He sighed again. "That's what I worry about most, you know, my body keeping on going while my mind is gone. Though the other option, having an intact mind while my body doesn't work, is pretty bad too. I don't want to wind up like—" He paused.

"Toivo?" Ukatonen prompted.

Teuvo nodded and looked down at the ground. Ukatonen watched him, wishing he understood human expressions as well as Moki did. Clearly Teuvo was saddened by his son's injury, but he sensed that there was more to it than that.

"There were times when I wanted Toivo to die," Teuvo confessed. "I actually wanted my own son to die."

"I don't understand you humans," the enkar said. "A Tendu crippled beyond healing would have chosen death. Why do you humans try so hard to live?"

"I think you said it yourself, Ukatonen. The Tendu choose when to die, and we humans have death forced on us. As a result, we cling to life, even when it is easier and sometimes better to die. Toivo did try to kill himself once. We managed to save him."

"Why?"

"When Toivo was injured, we didn't know if Juna was still alive. I thought that Toivo was the only child I had left," he said. "Besides, there wasn't much time for thinking about it when we found him. We got him to the hospital immediately." Teuvo looked back at the horses, still grazing in sync. "After he got out of the hospital, he left for the zero-gee satellite. Being here broke his heart, I think. Every day he was reminded of all the things he couldn't do anymore. I'm still amazed that he came back to see Juna. I guess he hadn't said goodbye to her yet."

They stood silently in the morning light, watching the horses.

"How soon will Toivo be well again?" Teuvo asked.

"We'll be done with our work in a week or so. It would be faster if Juna weren't pregnant, but we have to be careful about the baby. After we're done, then Toivo will have to learn to use his body again. That could take months."

"Could I—?" Teuvo began.

"Yes, Teuvo?" Ukatonen prompted.

"I wanted to know what it was like. Linking, I mean. Perhaps I could help when Juna gets tired?"

"Thank you," Ukatonen said, "We'd be honored to have your help. It will make the work go much faster."

They gathered up the bucket of treats and the lead rope and headed back to the barn.

"I'm worried about Moki," Teuvo remarked as they put their gear away in the tack room. "He wants to try to work things out with Bruce, to 'achieve harmony' as he puts it. I don't think he understands how irrational we humans can be when it comes to our children. I'm afraid that he's going to get hurt. Keep an eye on him, please."

"I'll try," Ukatonen promised. "I would like to achieve harmony with Bruce, too, but I will keep your words in mind when we speak to him. Tell me, what would be the best way to approach this?"

"To be honest," Teuvo admitted, "I don't think you can work this one out, Ukatonen. Bruce has made up his mind that this is a bad idea. If I thought I could stop Moki from interfering, I would, but he's such a determined youngster."

Under the muffling confinement of his warm suit, Ukatonen rippled amusement. "Determination is what Moki's best at," he agreed, remembering the little one's dogged pursuit of Eerin through the forest, determined to either be adopted or die.

"Well, Ukatonen, enough playing with horses. It's time to get back to work," Teuvo said, clapping him on the shoulder. "Same time tomorrow, eh? and we'll see how well those two work together."

Ukatonen nodded, a pale blue flicker of affection appearing on his skin as he watched Teuvo head to the winery.

Moki didn't have a chance to talk to Bruce until after lunch, when he went out for a walk.

"Can I show you the forest?" Moki asked. "It's beautiful, and very quiet. I think you'd like it."

Bruce accepted, and the two of them walked in silence through the vineyards and the orchards. The leaves on the trees and vines were bright red and yellow, as though the plants were angry at the cold weather. Moki mentioned this to Bruce, and he smiled and shook his head.

"You say the damnedest things, Moki. What makes you think they're angry?"

"Yellow and red are the colors for irritation and anger," Moki explained. "If the trees were Tendu, that's what they'd be feeling." He looked up at Bruce. "What makes you think I would harm your daughter?"

Bruce let out a long sigh, and stopped walking. "Moki, I've just spent all morning going over this with Juna and that damned lawyer of hers. I came out here to get away from all of that shit for a while."

Moki turned contritely tan all over. "I'm sorry, Bruce, but it's important for me to understand what you're thinking. I don't want to be out of harmony with a friend."

"Moki, I—Dammit Moki, if it weren't for the Tendu, I wouldn't be in this mess!"

"That's true," Moki observed, "and if it weren't for Juna, I would be dead. We can't change the past, Bruce, we can only live with what is. Adopting me has made my sitik's life more difficult. Even so simple a thing as having a child is a struggle for her now. That shames me, because a bami is supposed to make a sitik's life easier. But we care about each other, and that helps."

"If Juna cared about me, she wouldn't be putting me through this!"

"But if you cared more about Eerin, perhaps you would understand why she is doing this," Moki replied. "Eerin wants this child with her whole heart. She was willing to be put in a cage for this child. She is willing to be out of harmony with the Survey, and with Population Control and even with me. She is frightened by how much she wants this baby. It is a human thing. I do not understand it, but I wish to learn. I wish to understand something that is so precious to Eerin, and to you. It is important, because it will help me understand my atwa."

"Your what?"

"My atwa. An atwa is a piece of the world that we are responsible for. It is our job to keep that piece of the world in harmony with everything else. Every Tendu elder has an atwa. My atwa will be to understand humans. I will be the first Tendu ever to practice this atwa. It will be hard, and I have a lot to learn before I'm ready."

"What about Ukatonen?" Bruce asked. "I thought he was here to learn about humans. Doesn't he have one of these at-thingies?"

"He is an enkar. His atwa is the Tendu. I will be something different." Moki shrugged. "But I don't know what that will be yet. Your daughter will be something new, like me."

"I don't want my daughter to be something new," Bruce told him. "I just want my daughter to be happy."

"I don't understand. What does being happy mean?"

"Don't you know what it means to be happy?"

"I know what it means for me. I know some of what it means for my sitik and for Ukatonen, and even a little for Eerin's family. But I don't know what happiness means for you, and I don't understand how you can know what happiness will mean for your daughter. She isn't even born yet."

Bruce opened his mouth to speak, and then closed it again. "Moki, did anyone ever tell you that you have a knack for asking hard questions?"

"Is that good?" Moki wanted to know.

"It's not a widely appreciated skill," Bruce observed. "I want to be left alone. I don't want to be pushed around. That's what would make me happy."

"I don't understand," Moki said. "How are you being pushed around?"

"I have no say in what happens to my daughter. That lawyer's telling me what I can and cannot do about my own flesh and blood."

"What do you mean by 'flesh and blood,' Bruce?"

Bruce looked impatient. "The baby, Moki. She's my daughter."

"Why are you talking about her as though she were like your arm? She isn't part of your body," Moki pointed out.

"Half of her genetic material came from me. That makes her partly mine."

"How can you own another person?" Moki asked, his confusion growing.

"Moki, I'm her father, I should have a say in how my daughter is raised."

"Why?"

"Because it's right that I should," Bruce snapped.

Moki's head was whirling. He was beginning to understand his sitik's difficulty. This argument was like being sucked into a whirlpool; you went round and round and each circle drew you further down into it. There was simply no way to get Bruce to see another point of view.

"Bruce, can't you see beyond yourself? This child could make a real difference both to your people and to mine. Please, let your daughter belong to herself. Give her the chance to know the Tendu and decide what she wants to do with her own life."

"Moki, stop trying to make me give in. She's my daughter, and I don't want her raised by aliens, not even you."

"I'm not trying to make you give in," Moki said quietly. "I'm trying to find out how to bring us all into harmony. Everyone else involved is in harmony with Eerin's desire to raise this child with the help of Ukatonen and myself. You don't want this because your daughter might grow up to be different from you. Is my understanding incomplete? Is there another explanation?"

Bruce was silent for a long while, scuffing the fallen leaves with his toe. At last he shook his head. "Moki, this is a human thing. You wouldn't understand, and I can't explain it."

Sadness clouded Moki's skin. He couldn't get Bruce to see the path to harmony that stretched out at his feet. All he had to do was to turn his gaze outward, and he would see.

"It pains me to be out of harmony with you, my friend," Moki said, looking up at Bruce. "I have done what I can. The rest is up to you."

Not knowing what else to do, Moki turned and walked away through the drifting rain of angry leaves. Despite his warmsuit, the chill in the air seemed to have settled in his bones.

Juna drove Bruce to the shuttle station. He settled resentfully into the passenger seat of the truck, waving a grudging goodbye to Juna's family and to the aliens. They drove through the orchards and the fields of golden stubble in tense silence.

"I wish we could have come to an agreement, Bruce. It bothers me that we're still so far apart on this," Juna said as they pulled up to the station entrance.

"She's my daughter too, Juna," he said, as he climbed out. He was glad to be leaving. He was tired of this endless wrangling that went nowhere. He stole a longing glance at the door to the station.

"I know, Bruce, and I've done everything I can to include you, but you keep shutting us out. If you want to be part of our daughter's life, you're going to have to accept the fact that Moki and Ukatonen will be part of her family."

Bruce's lips tightened in frustration as he pulled his bag out of the back of the truck. "I guess I'll see you at the hearing, Juna." There was simply no more to be said. Juna was adamant about having the child, and he was equally adamant that the child should not be raised by aliens. There was no foothold for compromise.

"I'm sorry that you got dragged into this, Bruce," Juna told him.

"I know," Bruce said, and picked up his bag and walked away, feeling the weight of dissension slide from his shoulders as he entered the terminal. He glanced back at Juna one last time as the doors swung shut. She was standing by the truck looking after him. He thought of those aliens, with their wet, clingy skin holding a child of his and shuddered. It must not happen.

Juna stood looking after Bruce for a minute, wishing there was something she could say to make things right between them, but it was impossible. Still, she had been among the Tendu so long that the inability to reach harmony was almost a physical ache. She got back into the truck, leaned back, and closed her eyes, wishing somehow to make it all right. Then she took a deep breath, opened her eyes, and started the engine.

Juna sat down at the comm unit and told it to get her mail. She had neglected her mail since she got home, at first because she was on vacation, and then because she had been too busy. Lately she had caught herself avoiding her comm because of the enormous backlog that she knew would be waiting for her.

The accumulation was even bigger than she had imagined. There were over two thousand messages, far too many for a download of her personal mail, especially given the tightness of her filters. Why was there so much mail? She sorted the messages by subject heading, and found that there were about one hundred and fifty personal messages, and thousands of proposals of marriage.

She scanned the proposals, shaking her head in amazement. Some were only a few sentences long, inviting her to visit them and consider their offer of marriage, but many were elaborate proposals, some with graphics of their house, grounds, and families. She replied to the proposals, with a polite notice that she was not accepting marriage offers via E-mail, and set her filters to auto-reply to any other proposals with the same message.

She was being foolish, she knew. In her condition, she should look through these offers, but this was not how she wished to be courted. If they wanted to marry her, let them come in person to make their offers.

"Oh, little one," she said, rubbing her belly. "What am I getting you into?"

Perhaps, she thought, *I could contact a marriage broker when my leave is up. They could filter out the people I wouldn't be interested in.* She sat down on the bed, tears filling her eyes. She didn't want to do that either. She knuckled the tears out of her eyes, and pulled on a shirt. It gapped open over her breasts. She sighed and pulled it off and put on a larger shirt. She needed to get some new clothes. Now that she was pregnant, nothing fit right anymore.

The proposals dealt with, Juna got herself a cup of coffee and settled in to deal with the rest of her mail. She dispensed with several dozen trivial messages, and composed a personal letter that went out to another twenty-odd friends. Another batch was sent to Analin to deal with. There was a note from Mark Manning, to her and Moki.

I went to Snyder Research Hospital, and had my lungs checked out by the doctors there. They said that my lungs were in remarkably healthy condition. You know, I really think the Tendu should consider working with some medical researchers. If you'd like, I'll pull a few strings to get you posted to Snyder. There's several beautiful parks with lots of big trees for Moki and Ukatonen. And you could do so much good for so many people.

Juna smiled, and printed the letter out for the Tendu. They would be glad to hear from Manning. And working at Snyder sounded like a good idea, at least until they had a chance to work out a more permanent assignment. Healing people would improve the Tendu's public image, and she would be near the courthouse where her Pop Con hearing would be held. It was definitely worth thinking about.

There was also mail from the Survey. They wanted to discuss her next assignment with the Tendu. Juna sent back a polite request for a conference with the Survey personnel in charge of the Tendu, and suggested Snyder as a possible short-term assignment.

That done, she turned off the comm unit, and headed out into the bright autumn sunlight to show Manning's letter to the Tendu, and to discuss her plans with them.

"Well?" Toivo asked after Ukatonen finished his examination.

"The bones have set nicely. We're ready to do the final work on your spinal cord. Is that all right with you?"

Toivo nodded, his throat suddenly too tight to speak. He had believed Juna when she said that Ukatonen could work miracles, but now that the Tendu were almost done, he was terrified. He'd held his hope in check before, but now it was soaring out of control. If this didn't work, he was in for one hell of a fall.

"It will take some time for this to work," Ukatonen reminded him. "Your nerves will take a week or two to grow together after we link."

Toivo held out his arms. "I'm ready," he managed to say.

"Teuvo?" Ukatonen asked, turning the light purple shade that Toivo had learned meant polite inquiry. "Are you ready?"

His father nodded. Toivo saw him swallow nervously, and smiled at how alike they were.

Ukatonen glanced at Moki and the little alien flickered a response that must have meant yes.

"All right then, let's begin."

Ukatonen sat beside him and grasped his arm. Moki took the other arm, and reached out to his father, who sat next to Ukatonen. Toivo felt their spurs prick his arms as the link was made and then he was plunged into the now-familiar sensory landscape of linking.

Toivo felt Ukatonen's presence in the link, and through the enkar, the warm, reassuring presence of his father, familiar and human. His presence reminded Toivo of all the times he had fallen asleep as a child with his father sitting on a chair beside the bed, watching over him, keeping bad memories and the demons of the imagination away from him. Toivo relaxed into his father's reassurance and love.

He felt, distantly, the Tendu working on the border between feeling and not-feeling, where his nerves were severed. They flickered in and out of existence like shadows, as they crossed over into the part of his body where his nerves no longer functioned. He felt a warm tingling all along the boundary between feeling and not-feeling. Then the Tendu broke the link.

"Well?" Toivo asked. This link was over so quickly, and he felt almost the same as he had before. There was a barely discernible warmth along the boundary of feeling, but no other change.

"We're done. Your nerves are beginning to grow back and reattach themselves."

"How long will this take?"

A ripple of purple flowed over the Tendu's body. "We don't know. It will be at least a month before your nerves are fully functional again. But you should start to regain some feeling after several days."

Toivo nodded wordlessly. He had irrationally hoped, despite all of the Tendu's warnings, that he would be able to leap out of bed and dance across the room.

"How—how much better will I be?"

Ukatonen rippled purple again. "We don't know. Much of that will depend on you. Once you regain feeling, you will need to relearn to use your body and regain the strength you once had. That will be hard. For now, you should get out of bed and move around as much as you can."

At first there was no change at all. Several days passed before Toivo realized that the boundary between feeling and not-feeling had moved a few inches farther down his body. Then, as he was helping Juna fold some laundry, he felt a sudden pang, and realized that his bladder was full.

"Juna, I need to piss!" he said excitedly.

"Just a minute and I'll help you," Juna said as she finished folding a shirt.

"No, Juna, you don't understand," he said. "I can *feel* that I need to piss. It's working, Juna, I'm really getting better!"

Juna squeezed his shoulder. "Of course you are, Toivo. Ukatonen does good work. Now, let me help you."

"You know, back before the accident, I never dreamed that such a small thing would make me so happy," he confided. "But now . . ." He shook his head. "It's the simplest things that matter the most. I never knew how much I'd miss them. And now you're giving it all back to me."

"Toivo, the Tendu were the ones who healed you," Juna pointed out.

"But they wouldn't be here if it weren't for you."

"Thank you, little brother," Juna said. She bent over and hugged him.

"I'm glad you're my sister," he told her, feeling a rush of love and gratitude.

"I wish I could stay longer," Juna said wistfully. "I want to be here to see you walk again."

"Actually, since you're going to the medical research center over on Snyder Station, I thought I'd go to the rehabilitation wing there for some physical therapy in a couple of weeks. It's a wonderful facility. If anyone can help me get back on my feet, they can."

"Really? Oh, Toivo, that's great! But this is just a temporary posting. The Survey hasn't figured out what they want to do with us yet. I don't know how long we'll be there."

"Juna, once they find out what Ukatonen and Moki are capable of, the trick will be getting the doctors to let go of you."

"Toivo, what about you? Once the doctors find out what the Tendu did to you, they're going to try to turn you into some kind of lab rat."

"Let them. Maybe they'll learn something that will help other people."

"It can be a pretty demoralizing experience," Juna cautioned.

"Then I'll go home. They can't make me stay against my will, Juna. I want to help, if I can. Do you want me there?"

"More than I can say, Toivo. I'm going to feel very alone on Snyder. And it'll be hard on the Tendu, too. They're going to miss all this green."

"The park area has some big trees, and there's a really nice garden designed by Motoyoshi. I bet the Tendu will like that. It'll be all right."

"I suppose, but it'll be good to have you there."

"Thanks, big sister. I wish I knew how to thank you for all you've done."

Juna squeezed his shoulder. "Just get better, little brother. That would be the best present of all."

Ukatonen walked out to the horse pasture with Teuvo. He would miss the old man, and the daily rituals of the horse atwa. The horses were coming along well. They moved as one animal through their paces, and were already hauling light loads. The close synchronization of their movements made them a very strong team.

"I'm going to hate to give these two youngsters up," Teuvo remarked as they led the horses to the pasture after their training session. "I've never seen two horses move so well together. They're wasted as farm horses. These two could win championship prizes."

"The effect will diminish over time, Teuvo," Ukatonen pointed out.

"Yes, I know, but you haven't linked with them for four days, and they're moving almost as well as they did before, in some ways even better."

"But that's your doing, Teuvo. I gave you the seed, but you're the one who has made it grow."

"Ah, they're good kids," Teuvo said as he opened the gate to the pasture. "If they weren't so bright and eager to please, none of our training would have stuck." He fed the horses each another carrot, and then they ambled off to join the other horses.

"It is what we would call *ruwar-a*," Ukatonen said, pushing up the sleeve of his warmsuit so that he could display the word in skin speech for Teuvo.

"What is that?"

"It does not really translate easily," the enkar said. "It means that all the parts of the whole are working well together. Each part of a system makes the other parts stronger, better. It is the kind of harmony we Tendu strive for. In a well-run village, it is common as the rain. Everything flows as easily as water flows downhill, or a wave slides back into the ocean. This seems to be a much rarer quality among humans. Perhaps this is a flaw in my understanding. Your world is so complex, it may be happening all around me and I am unable to see it."

"I think I understand," Teuvo said. "At least I know what it feels like when the horses and I are working well together. You're right, it is a rare thing." He smiled, looking out at the two horses, grazing in unison. "What a world Tiangi must be. I wish I could see it."

"And why not, someday?"

"Because I'm old, Ukatonen, and at my age, 'someday' will never come. In another few years I'll either be too feeble to travel, or dead." Teuvo turned away and looked out over the fields, and Ukatonen realized that the old man was sad.

"I am sorry, Teuvo," the enkar said. "Please forgive me if I have upset you."

Teuvo shrugged. "Old age happens to all humans. It's just hard for us to accept. We're greedy. We want to live forever." He slung the halters over his shoulder, and headed for the barn.

Ukatonen trudged beside him, feeling an emptiness where the comforting feeling of ruwar-a had been. He liked Teuvo, and the old man had taught him much. He was in his debt. It would be so easy to help him live longer.

"Teuvo, let me help," he said as they were hanging up the harnesses in the tack room.

"You are helping," Teuvo said.

"No, I meant let me help you live longer."

Teuvo froze in the midst of hanging up a bridle. He carefully set the bridle on its hanger, and turned to face Ukatonen.

"What do you mean?"

"I mean that you are not ready to die yet, and I can help you live longer."

"How long?"

Ukatonen rippled a shrug. "I don't know. How long would you like?"

Teuvo sat down on the old, blanket-covered couch with a whoosh of pent-up breath.

"That's a difficult question to answer," he replied, "particularly at my age. I've had a good life, with more good fortune than most. It would be greedy to want more, but"— he sighed heavily—"God help me, I do. But living forever?" Teuvo shook his head ruefully. "I don't think so. I'd be leaving too much behind. But it would be nice if my joints didn't hurt and my bowels worked right."

"What if I just fixed the things that are wrong with you? You would live longer and feel better, but you would continue to age."

"How much longer would I live?" Teuvo asked.

"I don't know, Teuvo—perhaps ten or twenty years more than you would as you are now. Enough time to watch your grandchildren grow up and have children of their own, and perhaps to visit Tiangi."

"I'd like that," Teuvo said. "I'd like that very much."

"Then link with me now, and I will do it," Ukatonen said, holding out his arms.

Teuvo did, and Ukatonen linked with him. He could feel the old man's excitement, sharply tinged with the cleanly pungent smell of wonder. Gently, he calmed Teuvo down, then moved through his body, easing and rebuilding swollen joints, cleaning out clogged arteries, removing cells that showed potential for becoming cancerous. Then Ukatonen swept away the accumulated detritus of years out of Teuvo's retinas and cleared the cloudy lenses of his eyes, restoring his sight to youthful sharpness. He strengthened the arterial wall of a bulging aneurysm. He gently awakened Teuvo's brain cells, stimulating them to divide and grow for a few weeks, replacing dead and dying cells, and building new neural pathways, returning his mind to the supple quickness of youth, while keeping the wisdom and experience of his years.

"How do you feel?" Ukatonen asked as Teuvo awoke.

"I'm hungry." He stood, slowly at first, then more quickly as he realized that it didn't hurt, and walked over to the door of the tack room and stood looking out over the vineyard. "I can see better and my joints don't hurt." He took a deep breath and turned back to the enkar. "It's like the whole world just got a little brighter. Thank you, Ukatonen."

"You will improve over the next few weeks. Eat well during that time, your body will be busy rebuilding and repairing itself. You'll want to eat a lot of meat, vegetables, and fruit."

"I'm ready to get a start on that!" Teuvo exclaimed with a smile. "Let's go get some breakfast!"

Juna closed her suitcase and started to lug it downstairs.

"Here, Juna, let me take that," her father said. "You shouldn't be carrying such things."

"*Isi*, it's all right, I can manage."

"I know you can, dear, but humor your poor old dad," he said.

Juna let him carry the bag downstairs. Toivo's recovery seemed to have taken years off her father.

She stepped onto the porch and looked out over the harvested vineyards, bright with red and golden leaves. The arched vault of the station curved overhead, colored in tones of earth and gold and green. She didn't want to leave, but there was so much the Tendu had to do before she was tied down by maternity.

"Breakfast is ready," her aunt called.

"Coming, Netta-*Täti*," she replied, taking a last look out over the vineyards before she went inside.

Breakfast was slow and difficult. Juna pushed her food around her plate, her throat tight with nausea. Anetta fussed over her, concerned by her lack of appetite, while Moki looked on anxiously. Her father meanwhile piled his plate high, and ate like a farmhand in the middle of harvest.

At last the ordeal of breakfast was over. Juna and the Tendu gathered their things together and loaded them into the truck. Then they drove over to the Fortunati house to say goodbye. The whole family was waiting for them as they drove up. Toivo was sitting up straighter today.

"Look!" he said. Slowly, painfully, he raised first one knee and then the other.

"That's wonderful, Toivo!" Juna enthused. "I'm so glad that you'll be coming to Snyder, too. It'll be nice to have some family close by."

Danan came running up. "Juna! I'm coming to the shuttle station to see you off. Can I ride in back with Moki?"

Juna glanced at Selena, who nodded. "Of course, Danan."

"So I hear you're planning on putting me out of business," a voice said.

"Dr. Engle!" Juna cried in delight.

"I couldn't let my favorite patient go away without saying goodbye," he said, giving her a hug.

"I'm glad you could come," Juna told the doctor.

"What you've done for Toivo is just amazing," he told her.

"That was the Tendu. I couldn't even help out much, because of the baby."

"Well, it was miraculous, no matter who did it. I understand you're off to Snyder Research Hospital."

"Yes. They're going to study how the Tendu heal."

"I wish I could be there," the doctor said wistfully. "I envy those researchers, Juna. I only hope they appreciate what they're getting."

"Come visit us," she said. "You hardly ever take time off, and we'd love to see you. You can tell those researchers what to do."

Dr. Engle patted her hand. "Maybe, Juna. But you know I'm needed here."

She smiled. "I know. I wouldn't want to trust my baby to anyone else."

"Thank you, Juna. I'll see you when you come back for the last few months of your term. Just remember to eat well, and don't tire yourself out."

"Moki and Ukatonen won't let me," she said. "They'll take good care of me."

"Good."

Then Toivo was pulling on her sleeve. "Juna, it's time to go."

Juna headed for the truck, hugging people as she went. It had never been this hard before to leave home, but now it felt as though her heart were being pulled out of her chest with every step. What had changed? Not Berry Station or her family. It was still the home she remembered, though the people were older. She was the one that had changed. Living among the Tendu had changed her from a solitary person to someone who needed to be part of a community. How strange that being the only human in a world full of aliens would make her appreciate her family more. She climbed into the truck and waved goodbye to her friends and family.

Moki watched Danan's house recede into the distance. They had been here only a few short weeks, less time than the months spent on the ship, but the time had been so full of people and events that it seemed as though a year had passed since they left the ship. He liked it here, and was sorry to be leaving. He would miss Danan, and the horses, and Netta-*Tāti's* good cooking, and the grapes. He pulled his warmsuit closer around him. It would be warmer where they were going, but there wouldn't be as many trees. It would be more like the space station where the ship had landed. A cloud of regret passed over him at that thought. He could hardly wait to come back here again.

Ukatonen saw the shuttle station draw closer. He had learned a great deal, living here, but it was time to go somewhere else and learn more. He was becoming too close to Eerin's family, and was in danger of losing the detachment expected from an enkar. It would be a good place to come back to, especially when he needed to see green things growing again. The trees here were nice, but he missed the forests of Tiangi, with its dense canopy of vines and leaves. It was strange, seeing trees without their leaves, and he was glad to be leaving them behind, even though the place they were going to didn't have nearly as many trees. But there were healers there, and he was sure that they had much to teach him.

He looked up at the naked trees, and wondered when they would go to a place that was like Tiangi. Juna had said there were places like it on Earth.

Earth. That was where he really wanted to go. He wouldn't fully understand humans until he had seen their world, the place they had come from. He was tired of living in boxes, even in a big, beautiful box like this one. He wanted to be someplace where there was a horizon, and wind, and living things as far as you could see, with the knowledge that there was even more life beyond the horizon. A flicker of impatience passed over him, and he schooled himself to patience. Sooner or later, they would reach Earth, and then everything would make sense.

5

Sohelia and Analin were there to meet them when they arrived at Snyder. They introduced Juna and the Tendu to Ayub Martin, the Snyder Station security chief.

"Welcome to Snyder Station," Chief Martin said. "We're honored to have you here. I've assigned our best security team to look after the three of you. You shouldn't have any worries about your safety here."

They might not have any security worries, Juna thought as she thanked him, but there were plenty of other things to worry about. Her Pop Con hearing was only a few days off. After the hearing there was a long-term-planning meeting with the Survey officials. Hopefully, they could arrange a diplomatic visit to Earth sometime in the next four or five months, before her pregnancy made travel difficult.

Then there was their work at Snyder Research Hospital. The doctors had agreed to a two-week initial assignment in order to study the Tendu's abilities. If things worked out, the assignment would be extended. But there were so many things that could go wrong.

"How is the baby doing?" Sohelia inquired.

"She's fine," Juna said, putting her hand on her belly. "But she doesn't seem to approve of space travel very much. I was a little spacesick."

"How are you feeling now?"

"A little tired, but otherwise fine."

"There's a mob of press outside the terminal," Analin informed her. "Are you up to facing them?"

Juna shook her head. "Not really."

"I can take you through the service tunnels to the hospital," Chief Martin offered.

"That would be wonderful," Juna said.

Martin called for a couple of service carts, then opened a small service panel in the wall and inserted an electronic key. A wide section of wall swung back, exposing a bare grey concrete tunnel lined with conduit and piping for air, water, heating, cooling, electricity, comm lines, and sewage. They waited in the corridor, listening to the pipes gurgle and hiss, until the service carts arrived to take them and their escort to the hospital.

"They're expecting you up at the hospital," Martin said when the carts arrived. "After that, the guards will take you to your quarters."

He handed Juna a card. "Here's my comm code. Let me know if we can be of any help, or if there are any problems with your security detail."

"Thank you Chief Martin," Juna said. "You've been very kind."

He nodded, winked at Moki, and then vanished back into the access tunnels.

The hospital staff were polite, but guarded. Clearly they doubted that the Tendu had anything to offer them. Juna decided that it was not worth getting angry about. She was rather looking forward to their surprise when they discovered what Moki and Ukatonen were capable of.

Their quarters were near the hospital, just down the broad corridor from a park with a grove of large banyan trees. The security team checked out the apartment and then let them inside. The unit was small, but comfortable, with two bedrooms, a bathroom, a small living room, and a tiny kitchen. Juna had stayed in much smaller places. She freshened up, and then joined the others in the living room, where Analin and Sohelia had set out tea, sweet biscuits, and sandwiches. Ukatonen vanished into the bathroom for a shower.

Juna's fragile stomach was not quite ready for sandwiches, but she sipped the tea and nibbled gratefully on the biscuits. The sweetened tea and biscuits settled her queasy stomach.

"Thank you so much for this," Juna told the women. "I needed it."

"Good," Sohelia said. She pulled her comm and a sheaf of paper out of her briefcase. "If you're ready, we should discuss the hearing."

"Go ahead," Juna said. She would have preferred to have a good night's sleep before this discussion, but there wasn't time. The hearing would start tomorrow afternoon.

"You've gotten Judge Matthesen," Sohelia told her. "She's tough, but fair. I'd say our chances were decent."

"Only decent?" Juna asked worriedly.

"It's a difficult case, Juna. In this situation, decent is the best we can hope for. Usually both parents get permanently sterilized or transported to Mars. We'll have to convince the judge that this was an accident, then hope for the best. Judge Matthesen has been kind to other women with extenuating circumstances. Hopefully, she'll be kind to you."

"I see," Juna said. She placed one hand on her stomach, and closed her eyes. She had refused to think about the possibility of losing the baby. But now she could no longer ignore it.

"I was planning on calling Ukatonen as a witness. Do you think he'll have a problem with that?"

Juna took a deep breath and opened her eyes. "You'll have to ask Ukatonen."

"Ask me about what?" Ukatonen said, emerging from the bathroom, still wet, his kilt stained with moisture. He laid a towel over an upholstered chair and sat down on it.

"We would like you to testify on Juna's behalf."

Ukatonen listened intently as Sohelia explained what that involved.

"Yes, I can do that. I will render a formal judgment that what I say will be the truth."

"A-all right, en. Thank you."

"It will be easy to tell the truth here," Ukatonen said. "The facts are plain."

"The difficulty will be in being believed," Sohelia said. She lifted a hand to forestall his protest. "Humans do not know or understand you yet, Ukatonen. And almost all the information that we have about the Tendu comes from Juna. It will necessarily be suspect. I will be calling a few other witnesses to testify to your abilities."

"Excuse me," Analin broke in, "but will the case be open to the press?"

"Usually these hearings are closed. If criminal culpability is determined, then the subsequent trial is open to the press."

"Good." Analin said. "Most of the research reports on the Tendu are still classified. If word of what they can do gets out, then the press will be all over Ukatonen and Moki. I've also encouraged the hospital to keep a tight lid on the Tendu's work."

Sohelia made a note on her comm. "I'll request that the judge enjoin all witnesses to silence on this."

"Thank you," Juna said. "I appreciate that. Sometimes I feel as if I'm living in a goldfish bowl."

"It is hard," her lawyer agreed. "Now, let's go over the details of your testimony."

Juna sat in the courtroom with Sohelia, waiting for the hearing to begin. Security Chief Martin had arranged for them to go through the service tunnels to the courthouse, avoiding the mob of reporters waiting outside. Analin was out there now, issuing a statement. Juna looked at Ukatonen and smiled nervously. Moki reached forward from his seat just behind the defendant's table, and brushed her shoulders with his knuckles. Juna glanced back at him.

"Thanks," she whispered.

He turned a clear, reassuring shade of blue and nodded at her.

At that moment, the clerk came in from the judge's chambers. "All rise," he said as the judge, a severe-looking woman with greying hair and long black robes, came in and sat down. She convened the court, and the prosecutor, a plump, deceptively friendly-looking man named Parker, got up to make his opening remarks.

"Your Honor, the defendant is illegally pregnant. She plans to burden our solar system with another mouth to feed, another set of lungs that will need air. This illegal pregnancy has been on the top screens of all the news nets. If she is allowed to keep this child without punishment, then others will be encouraged to follow her example and flout the laws that humanity has created to save itself from itself. Each new child adds to the burden our solar system must support, during a time when we can ill afford it. I strongly suggest the maximum punishment for this high-profile case."

The prosecutor returned to his seat. Sohelia rose gracefully from her seat.

"Your Honor, if, as my esteemed colleague implies, my client intentionally flouted the population laws, then I agree that she should be sentenced accordingly. Dr. Juna Saari is pregnant without approval from the Population Control Board, but there is compelling evidence that this pregnancy was accidental. Dr. Saari underwent a harrowing physical transformation when she was marooned on the planet Tiangi. The alien responsible for this transformation also undid her contraception, without fully understanding the consequences of his action. When my client was rescued, the Interstellar Survey failed to check her contraceptive status. My client assumed that her contraception was still intact. She had the misfortune to sleep with a man who had never been given a contraceptive shot. Dr. Saari's accidental pregnancy was due to an incredible series of circumstances. The odds of its happening again are astronomical. Punishing my client as an example to others is completely pointless.

"I further state that my client has made great sacrifices, and endured much hardship in order to further humanity's scientific and diplomatic goals. Penalizing her for an accidental pregnancy that occurred as a result of her discoveries would be a shameful thing to do. The remarkable circumstances of Dr. Saari's pregnancy must be taken into account when deciding this case. Thank you, Your Honor."

There were a great many witnesses called to establish the facts of the case. Perhaps the most telling was Dr. Engle. Sohelia quizzed him about how long he had known Juna, and the particulars of her contraceptive shot. Then she asked him about the pregnancy test.

"Dr. Saari complained of symptoms that were very characteristic of pregnancy. So I decided to test her to rule that out."

"Did you consider it a likely possibility, Dr. Engle?"

"Objection!" called the prosecutor. "Counsel is asking for opinion rather than fact."

"Counselor Gheisar?" the judge inquired.

"I have already established that the witness has known the defendant since her childhood. Further questions will reveal a factual basis to this line of inquiry."

"Objection overruled," the judge said. "Please answer Counselor Gheisar's question, Doctor."

"No, I did not."

"While you were giving her the test, did anything happen to support your opinion that this was not an illegal pregnancy?"

"Yes, indeed."

"Please tell us, Dr. Engle, what that was."

"I asked Juna if she was planning on starting a family. She told me that she was considering selling her child-rights, since it looked like she wasn't going to be using them."

"And did she know that you were doing a pregnancy test at the time?"

"No. In cases where there is no pregnancy permit, I do not inform the patient of the nature of the test. Juna didn't know that I was performing a pregnancy test until I told her the results. Actually, I was so surprised, I performed the test a second time."

"And how did Dr. Saari react?"

"She was extremely surprised. She told me several times that it was impossible. She told me that she had been on a Survey ship for the last six months, and before that on another planet. Then she realized what had happened. I saw her face. I believe that her astonishment was completely genuine."

"What did she say then?"

"She told me that the Tendu must have reversed her contraception shot."

"I see. And what did you think of this?"

"I was amazed," Dr. Engle told her.

"Did you believe her?"

"Yes, I did."

"Why?"

"Because she was so completely surprised by it all. She blamed herself for not getting her status checked. I told her that she had done nothing wrong, and that the Survey doctors were the ones who were at fault."

"Objection, Your Honor," said the prosecutor. "The witness is not in a position to determine liability."

"Sustained," the judge said.

"Dr. Engle, did you see anything to convince you that the Tendu could have reversed her contraception?"

"Not then, but later I witnessed something that made me believe that the Tendu could have done it."

"Would you tell the court what happened to convince you?"

"Juna's brother, Toivo Fortunati, was in a spinball accident about a year and a half ago. He was paralyzed from the waist down. There was nothing more the doctors could do for him. The Tendu healed him. I examined him just before I left Berry Station to come here. Feeling had returned to his lower body again, all the way down to his toes. He was able to wiggle his toes, and move his legs." Dr. Engle spread his hands in a gesture of amazement. "It was a miracle, but it happened. If they can do such a thing, then reversing a contraceptive shot would be easy."

"Thank you, Dr. Engle. Your Honor, I have no more questions, but I would like to submit as evidence the following documents on Toivo Fortunati's medical condition following his accident, and Dr. Engle's report on his present medical condition."

"Thank you, Counselor Gheisar," the judge said.

The prosecutor got up and did his best to try to pick holes in Dr. Engle's testimony. But the doctor refused to be rattled despite the unbelievable claims that he was making about the Tendu. Dr. Engle smiled through his beard at Juna as he left the stand. Juna smiled back.

Her smile vanished when the next witness was called. It was Bruce. He gave her a dark, angry glance as he was sworn in, then refused to look at her while he testified.

Sohelia questioned him about his role in the case, most of which had already been established. She quizzed him about his contraceptive status, and he admitted that he had never had the shot.

"My father filed for a religious exemption," he explained. "He was afraid that the shot would permanently affect my fertility. As long as the girls were all getting them, it didn't really matter. Or, at least, I didn't expect it to matter," he added, his skin darkening with embarrassment.

"I see," Counselor Gheisar said. "And has this predicament changed your view of things?"

"Yes," he said. "I got the shot. It was shortly after visiting your client."

"Thank you, Mr. Bowles. No further questions. Your witness, Counselor Parker."

The prosecutor rose, smiling. Juna glanced at her lawyer, who was frowning nervously.

"Mr. Bowles, were you surprised when you heard that you were going to be a father?"

"Very much so, yes," Bruce answered.

"Are you pleased?"

Bruce frowned. "Not really, sir."

"Could you tell the court why you're not pleased at the prospect of being a father?"

Bruce glanced past Juna, at the two Tendu sitting behind her. "I don't agree with how she wants to raise the child."

"Could you please explain?"

"First, I think she's going to be too busy with the aliens to do an adequate job of parenting. Second, she's going to be a single mother. Who is going to be there for the children when she's too tired? And lastly"—Bruce paused, licking his lips nervously—"I want my daughter to be raised by humans, not aliens. Who knows what strange ideas they might teach my daughter?"

"Objection!" Sohelia said. "Witness is stating personal belief, not facts."

The judge looked over at the prosecutor. "Counselor Parker?"

"I believe it's important to hear both sides of this issue, Your Honor. This is Mr. Bowles's daughter we're talking about here."

"This is not a custody hearing, Counselor. In the future please confine yourself to the Population Control regulations in question."

"Yes, Your Honor. No further questions."

The judge adjourned the hearing until the following morning.

Juna watched Bruce gather up his things. Finally she found the courage to approach him. He steadfastly refused to look at her.

"Bruce," Juna said, "I'm sorry you're unhappy about my decision to keep the baby, but you're her father. I hope someday you'll be there for her. She's going to want you in her life too."

He finally looked up at her, his eyes dark with anger. "Juna, the child is more important than those aliens. Let someone else take care of them. You take care of the baby."

"You know I can't do that, Bruce," she said.

"Then I hope you lose. You shouldn't be allowed to have the child." He tucked his pad of notes under his arm and stalked off.

Juna watched the door swing shut behind him. Her lips tightened in sudden anger. "Well, to hell with you, then," she muttered to herself.

Sohelia laid a hand on her arm. "Come on," she said. "You've got more important things to worry about. Let's go get some dinner. Tomorrow I'm putting Ukatonen on the stand. I need you to help get him ready to testify."

The prosecutor objected when Sohelia called Ukatonen to the stand. Juna leaned back in her seat, and watched the two attorneys battle over the enkar.

"Your Honor," the prosecutor said, "calling this witness is highly irregular. We know very little about these aliens. Do they even understand what testifying in court means? How do we know if we can rely on his testimony? What kind of precedents will this be setting?"

"Your Honor," Sohelia responded, "Ukatonen is an unusual witness, but he can provide us with facts and information that no one else can. He knew the accused during her time on Tiangi. He understands what is required of him as a witness. Ukatonen holds a position of great responsibility among his own people. The Tendu hold their officials to an even higher level of responsibility than our own. If he violates his word, he is expected to take his own life."

"That will not be necessary, Mr. Ukatonen," the judge said. "Objection overruled. The witness may take the stand. This court will hold you only to the standards of a human court."

"Thank you, Your Honor," Sohelia said.

"Excuse me, Your Honor," Ukatonen broke in. "Even though you do not hold me to the Tendu standard, I wish you to know that I must hold myself to the standards of my people." He straightened, and speaking formally in both Tendu skin speech and human Standard declared a judgment. "My life is forfeit if I lie."

The judge raised one eyebrow. "If you insist, then so be it. Only I entreat you not to lie in this court. I don't want your death on my conscience."

"Yes, Your Honor," Ukatonen said. The bailiff approached the enkar and instructed him in the human oath, and he raised his right hand and swore it also.

First, Counselor Gheisar asked him to explain to the judge who he was, and what his status was on Tiangi. Then she had him tell the court about the circumstances surrounding Toivo's healing. The judge listened raptly and even the prosecutor left off objecting.

"Ukatonen," Sohelia went on, "would you please tell us the circumstances under which you met the defendant?"

"I met her while I was traveling through the forest. I was on my way to a coastal village to investigate word of strange creatures that had burned part of the forest. She was traveling with Anito, an elder of the village Narmolom. They were also on their way to the coast."

"And when did you first link with Dr. Saari?"

"The night I met her. She was asleep at the time, and didn't know what I was doing."

"And what did you notice?"

"She was very strange. Her metabolism was unlike any living creature I had ever seen on Tiangi."

"Was she fertile?"

Ukatonen said. "I did not notice the presence of the antibodies that would have interfered with pregnancy. In fact, I did not know of their existence until I linked with other humans."

"How difficult would it be for you to undo contraception of this type?"

"It would be extremely easy."

"Would it be easy for most Tendu?"

"Yes. Moki could do it, and he is not yet an elder."

"Would the person know it was happening? Could they tell you were undoing their contraception?"

"Not unless they were told. It is as easy for a Tendu as turning a switch on or off."

"I see."

"Did Dr. Saari ever mention her contraception to you?"

"No."

"Did she ever say anything about wanting children?"

"Not until she knew she was pregnant."

"When you first saw Dr. Saari, did she look like she does now?"

"No. She had been physically transformed."

Counselor Gheisar asked Ukatonen to explain the nature of Juna's physical transformation. He told them about the symbiotic skin that Ilto had grown over her own, and the changes to her immune system that he had made, enabling her to live on Tiangi without being allergic to its foreign proteins.

"Was this transformation a difficult thing for a Tendu to do?"

"Yes, it was. It required an expert healer."

"In your opinion, could the Tendu who performed this transformation have reversed Dr. Saari's contraception?"

"Easily. And he would want to do so."

"I see. Why would that be?"

"He had just captured an extremely strange new animal. He would want it to be able to breed if he found a male of the species."

"Objection! Witness is speculating."

"Sustained," the judge ruled. "Mr. Ukatonen, please speak only to those things that you know to be true from your direct observation."

Juna sat forward, a look of concern on her face. If Ukatonen believed that this was an accusation that he had been lying, then his life would be forfeit.

Ukatonen turned brown with embarrassment. "Please excuse me. I did not mean to speak that which was not true."

"You are not in violation of the truth, Ukatonen," the judge reassured him. "But here we ask only what people know directly."

"I understand," Ukatonen said. "Thank you, Your Honor." His color lightened, going back to a neutral celadon.

Juna sat back with a sigh of relief. She was glad that the judge understood how dangerous Ukatonen's vow could be.

"Ukatonen," Counselor Gheisar asked, "do you know how or when Dr. Saari's contraception was reversed? Do you know who did it?"

"There is no way of knowing," he replied. "I am sorry."

"Thank you, Ukatonen," Sohelia said. "No further questions, Your Honor."

The prosecutor rose. "Mr. Ukatonen. You say that you do not know when Dr. Saari's contraception was reversed."

"I do not," Ukatonen said.

"Is it possible that it could have been reversed before she arrived on the planet?"

"Objection!" Sohelia Gheisar cried. "He is asking the witness to speculate about matters beyond his direct experience."

"Sustained."

"Mr. Ukatonen, how do you feel about Dr. Saari's pregnancy?"

"I'm happy she's having a baby."

"Why?"

"Because she wants this child, and because I look forward to watching her daughter grow up."

"And do you have any long-term goals for this child?"

Sohelia sat up and began taking notes. Juna leaned forward, intent on this new line of questioning. What kind of trap was the prosecutor setting up?

"I hope that she will serve as a bridge between my people and yours."

He looked up at the judge. "The future is not something I have had direct experience with," he told her. "Am I permitted to testify on this matter?"

Juna looked down at the desk, hiding a smile.

"Your Honor," the prosecutor said, "I am trying to establish what the future relationship of these aliens to this unborn child will be."

"Go ahead," said the judge to Ukatonen..

"Dr. Saari will determine that relationship," the enkar said. "She is the baby's parent."

"Yes, but what do you want your relationship to be?"

Ukatonen shrugged, a remarkably human gesture. "I would like to be one of the child's teachers. I would like to teach her about our people, as she will teach me about humans. I value the opportunity to watch a human child grow to be an adult. I am sure that she will teach me a great deal about human nature."

The prosecutor paused, and consulted his notes. "Yes, but did you not say that 'When she is grown, Juna's daughter will help provide a link between our two peoples. There is too much to gain for us to want to hurt her.'?"

"I believe I did," Ukatonen confirmed.

"What did you mean by 'a link between our two peoples,' Mr. Ukatonen?"

The enkar looked down. "I hope that she will occupy the same place between the humans and the Tendu as Juna does."

"What if she doesn't want that?"

"That will be up to her," Ukatonen said. "I hope that she will. We need people who understand both cultures."

"I understand that your people eat their young."

"Yes, that is true, immature tadpoles are part of our diet, but in that same conversation that you mentioned, I also made a formal judgment that no Tendu would harm Dr. Saari's daughter. My life rests on that judgment. Juna's daughter is in no danger of being eaten. Nor is any other human child. Moki and I understand the difference between a tadpole and a human baby."

"Excuse me, Ukatonen, but you are only supposed to answer the question that the prosecutor asks you," the judge said.

"I am sorry," the enkar said, turning brown again.

"Please continue, Counselor,"

"No further questions, Your Honor."

Juna felt a weight lifted from her shoulders. Ukatonen had made it off the stand safely.

There were several more witnesses. Survey personnel testified to Juna's medical condition before and after she left for Tiangi. Her medical records established that her contraceptive vaccine was intact when she left on the Survey mission, and that nothing had happened on the trip to Tiangi to change that. After those witnesses finished their testimony, they adjourned for lunch.

"How are we doing?" Juna asked as they settled into an empty conference room with some limp sandwiches and cold coffee.

"So far, pretty good," Sohelia said. "None of our witnesses' statements have fallen apart under questioning. Ukatonen did a wonderful job up there. But—" she paused for emphasis, "it all depends on what the judge decides, and I haven't the slightest idea what she's thinking."

"Would it help if we linked with her?" Moki asked.

"I suppose it would, bai," Juna said, "but we can't do that."

"I wish it were that easy," Sohelia said fervently. "You know, this is always the hardest part of the hearing for me. I always get nervous at this point in a hearing, no matter how it's going."

"We could link with you and help you relax," Moki offered.

"I'd be honored, Moki," Sohelia said. "But we should wait until after the trial. I'm used to being nervous, it helps me pay attention. Linking might throw me off my stride."

"You really would link with them?" Juna asked, surprised. "Most people are afraid."

"Why should I be afraid? They've done much good and no harm at all."

"May I link with my sitik now?" Moki asked. "I think it would help both of us."

Sohelia glanced at her watch. "We only have a few minutes. Can you do it that quickly?" the lawyer inquired.

Juna linked with the Tendu. They soothed away her fear and nervousness. She emerged from the link feeling relaxed and ready to face the hearing. She took a deep breath and opened her eyes. Sohelia was watching her intently, her face alight with wonder.

"That was fascinating. I could see the worry lines smooth out," she said. "You look much more relaxed."

"I am," Juna said.

"Good." Sohelia checked her watch. "It's time to go."

Juna finished her coffee, grimacing at the taste. "This is almost as bad as Survey coffee," she said. "Let's go."

The judge brought the hearing to order. "Please call in the next witness."

The doors opened and Toivo rolled into the courtroom. He smiled at Juna as he passed by her. A fresh breeze seemed to have blown in with him.

Sohelia had him describe the accident and his subsequent hospitalization. Juna stared at the scarred metal tabletop, unable to watch as Toivo answered her lawyer's questions in a calm, level tone of voice.

Then Sohelia had him describe what occurred while the Tendu were healing him. Toivo's dark face lit up as he described the first signs of life in his formerly paralyzed body.

"And now, Mr. Fortunati, how would you describe the extent of your recovery?" Sohelia asked.

Toivo grasped the arms of his wheelchair, and with a look of fierce concentration and determination, pushed himself onto his feet. He stood on his own two feet, and looked at the judge. "Your Honor, this is how I describe my recovery. I'm weak, but every day I get stronger, every day I have more control over my body. I think I'll be able to walk again soon. It was all because of the Tendu. Without them, I'd still be paralyzed."

He lowered himself carefully back down into his chair.

"I have no further questions, Your Honor," Sohelia said. "Thank you, Mr. Fortunati."

The prosecutor rose. "That was a most remarkable display, Mr. Fortunati. I'm sure that you're very grateful to the Tendu for their work."

Toivo remained silent, waiting for the prosecutor's question. Juna saw Sohelia smile approvingly.

"When did you first realize that your sister wanted children?"

"She's wanted children for a long time. I remember her telling me how much she wanted children back when she first got married."

"How long ago was that?"

"About fifteen years ago."

Startled, Juna did the calculations in her head. It really had been that long since her marriage. That meant that it was almost eight years since her divorce. It was a long time to be alone.

"Why didn't she have children during her marriage?" the prosecutor asked.

"Her marriage fell apart."

"Why?"

"Objection, Your Honor," Sohelia said. "Speculation."

"Sustained."

"Did she tell you why her marriage fell apart?"

"Yes. She said it was because she was away so much on long Survey missions."

"After her marriage fell apart, how did she act?"

"She seemed sad."

"Do you know why she didn't leave the Survey when she got married?"

"She loved her job. She loved being on the edge of known space."

"Even though it meant sacrificing her marriage?"

"Objection!" Sohelia cried.

"Sustained."

"Do you know if she still wanted children when she left on her last Survey mission?"

"I don't know. She didn't talk about it much after her divorce," Toivo explained.

"Did she do anything that might lead you to believe—"

"Objection!" Sohelia protested.

The judge looked down from the bench. "Counselor Parker, if you continue to ask the witness such speculative questions, I'm going to have to ask you to abandon this line of questioning."

"Yes, Your Honor. No further questions."

Sohelia touched Juna's arm. "I'm going to call you next. Are you ready, or do you want me to ask for a recess first?"

Juna swallowed with a throat suddenly gone dry. "Let's get this over with."

Sohelia nodded. She rose. "Your Honor, I would like to call the defendant, Dr. Juna Saari, to the stand."

Juna rose, and was sworn in, and seated herself in the witness chair beside the bench. The safe comfort of her seat at the defendant's table looked a long way away. Moki, sitting in the front row, was dark green with reassurance. Toivo, on his way out of the courtroom, turned and smiled, his teeth white in his dark face. He gave her a thumbs-up as he went out the door. Juna tried to smile, but her face seemed frozen. So much was at stake here. The calmness she'd felt after linking had vanished.

"Dr. Saari, could you tell us your side of the story, please?"

Hesitantly, Juna began telling what happened. At first, Sohelia had to prompt her about details of the story, but eventually she relaxed a bit and the story fell into place.

When she was through, Sohelia asked a few questions underlining details and re-examining certain key events. Juna's nervousness had almost vanished when Sohelia turned her over to the prosecutor.

Juna watched the prosecutor pace in front of her as she sat in the witness box. It was hard to believe that this plump, friendly-looking man was out to get her. He looked like somebody's favorite grandfather.

"Dr. Saari, have you heard of the BirthRight organization?"

"Yes, sir, on the news," Juna replied. He was going to try to link her with the pronatalist movement. Sohelia had warned her that he might try this tactic.

"What about Pro-Child?"

"Also on the news."

"And what about the Parents' Union?"

Juna frowned, searching her memory. "No I have not."

"Do you know Aaron Elijah Miller?"

"Yes, sir, I do. We went to school together. His family stayed behind when the other Amish left," Juna said, wary and puzzled by this seemingly innocuous question.

"Are you aware that he is a member of BirthRight?"

"No, sir."

"Were you aware of his political beliefs?"

"I never really thought much about it," Juna said. "They helped our family prune the vines, and we helped them plow and plant their barley."

"Didn't you ever wonder how he and his wife managed to have five children?"

"I just assumed that he had saved up enough money for the child-rights. They lived very frugally. It was none of our business. We were just glad for the extra hands his family provided."

"And he didn't try to help you get pregnant?"

"No, not in any way."

"Didn't he visit you after word of your pregnancy got out?"

"He came by the house. My father saw him. I was asleep."

"Your father didn't discuss the nature of their conversation with you?"

"No," Juna said.

"Objection, Your Honor," Sohelia broke in. "What is the point of this line of questioning?"

"That's a good question. Counselor Parker?"

The prosecutor frowned down at a sheaf of papers. "It appears my informant was mistaken." He turned back to Juna. "Do you have connections to any pronatalist organizations?"

"Of course not. I do not share their political sympathies."

"Yet you are illegally pregnant."

"Yes, by accident."

"And you wish to keep the baby."

Juna rested her hand on her abdomen. "Very much so. But only with a legally purchased child-right. I didn't plan on being pregnant, but now that I am, I don't want to lose my daughter." She felt tears of longing beginning to form behind her eyelids. Juna looked at the judge, trying to tell her what was in her heart. "I'm not part of any political or religious movement. I just want a child."

"No further questions, Your Honor."

Juna got up slowly, feeling almost giddy with relief at getting off the stand. Sohelia helped her sit down.

"You did great, Juna! That was wonderful!" Sohelia whispered in her ear.

Juna nodded, too nervous to speak. She felt tears sliding down her nose. Her lawyer handed her a handkerchief.

"Are there any further witnesses?" the judge asked. Both attorneys said no. "Well, then, I think we have just enough time for closing statements. Counselor Parker, are you ready?"

"Yes, Your Honor. I am."

"Your Honor, we have a population regulation system that works. Since Population Control was imposed a century ago, our numbers have declined slowly and steadily. There are a billion less people on Earth now than there were when the population regulations were put in place. In space, our numbers are growing at a steady, but sustainable pace. In the next century, Terra Nova will be opened up for colonization, giving us yet another world to expand into. We are making progress, but it is still a precarious balance. Every year, over ten million illegal pregnancies occur on Earth. And over a million illegal babies are born. Each illegal child slows our return to a greener, healthier planet.

"This is a high-profile case. If we let this case go, will we have twenty million illegal pregnancies to contend with next year? And forty million the year after that? We must draw the line here and now. Or once again we will be awash in people, once again we will be the victims of our own fertility. Regardless of our feelings for Dr. Saari, we must take a stand against the tide of fecundity that threatens to overwhelm us. We must not make an exception for even one case. The future of our planet is at stake."

"Thank you, Counselor Parker. Counselor Gheisar?"

Sohelia got up to speak. She approached the judge's bench, turned, and stood looking at Juna for a long, thoughtful moment. Then she turned again and looked up at the judge.

"Your Honor," she said, "our system of population control is inherently coercive. We must never forget this. We render almost every person on Earth infertile when they reach puberty. Each pregnancy must be approved by Population Control. Punishment for evading the law is harsh and absolute.

"And yet, despite this coercion, Population Control is successful. It even has widespread public support. If the Pop Con program did not enjoy this support, it would not work. There would be hundreds of millions of illegal pregnancies, and tens of millions of unauthorized babies.

"Why then, does Pop Con work? Why does it enjoy this wide support? The ecological and social devastation of the Slump convinced most of humanity that a drastic solution was necessary. But more importantly, Pop Con is viewed as harsh, but fair. A family that can afford more children can have them. A poor family can have one child and sell off the remaining fractional child-right to ensure a future for that child. The system is rarely abused, and when such abuse is discovered, punishment is severe and reparations to the injured parties are swift.

"But before the contraceptive vaccine was perfected, Pop Con made exceptions for contraceptive failure. Those regulations are still on the books, even if they have not been used in decades. Dr. Saari's case is truly an accident, improbable as it may seem. If we treat this one accident as a crime, then will people view the Population Control system as fair? I don't think so. How many illegal pregnancies will occur if people begin to rebel against the population regulations?

"But there is another reason for leniency. As you have seen, we have a great deal to gain from good relations with the Tendu. But in order to do that, we need to better understand them. Dr. Saari's child may be an important bridge between the Tendu and humans. Humanity has little to lose and everything to gain from this experiment. A decision to terminate Dr. Saari's pregnancy would also terminate this experiment in Human-Tendu relations.

"Can we afford to throw this chance away?" Sohelia asked. "Your Honor, I urge you to allow this accidental pregnancy, in the name of fairness and decency, and for the sake of the future of Human-Tendu relations. Thank you, Your Honor."

"Court is adjourned until I have a verdict," the judge said. "I hope to be ready sometime tomorrow." She banged her gavel down, gathered her papers, and vanished into her chambers.

"Well, all that's left is the waiting." Sohelia said.

"Let's go home," Juna said. What she really wanted was to open a door and magically be back at her family's house on Berry. She wanted the warmth and solidity and familiarity of home. Instead, she was going back to another one of the anonymous rooms she'd lived in for most of her adult life.

Toivo, Analin, and Dr. Engle were waiting for them outside the courtroom. They swept Juna and the others off to a private room in one of Snyder Station's finest restaurants. The conversation was lively and the food excellent. Toivo praised the wine, flown up from France.

"I traded them three mixed cases of our reserve wines for this dinner," Toivo confided. "I told them that you and the Tendu would autograph the labels after dessert."

"Toivo, you're awful!" Juna laughed.

"Will you do it?" he asked.

"Only if you'll autograph them too," she said. "You had more to do with making the wine than I did. Actually, *Isi* is the person who should sign the labels. You just grow the grapes. He's the artist who crafts the wine."

Toivo sighed. "I know. I wish I had his gift for it."

"Well, he's only been doing it for fifty years. You'll get better over time." Juna sipped at her glass of water. "How is he doing?"

"Since you left, he's been running around like a man half his age. I'd worry, but he looks so good." Toivo glanced over at the Tendu. "I've been wondering if one of those two worked on him," he confided in Amharic, his voice low. "When word of what those two can do gets out—" Toivo shook his head. "Be careful, Juna."

"We will be," she assured him. "We're keeping this stuff under wraps, and we have security escorts."

"Still—" he began.

Just then the manager of the restaurant came over and asked if he could take a picture of Juna and the Tendu, and the subject was dropped.

Juna lay down on the bed, exhausted. Toivo and the others had kept her too busy to think about the verdict, but now, alone in the dark, the buoyant mood of relief that had sustained her all through dinner had evaporated. She rested a sheltering hand on her rounded abdomen. What if the verdict went against her? How could she live without her daughter?

"Oh, little one," she murmured into the darkness. She lay there, feeling tears stream from her eyes into her hair, and then trickle down onto the pillow. Finally she could remain silent no longer. She rolled over, buried her face in the pillow and keened into its muffling softness until there were no tears left in her body, and she fell into an exhausted doze.

She was dreaming that she was holding the baby. Her daughter had reached up a small brown starfish hand to touch her cheek. Juna woke to find Moki gently pushing a strand of hair away from her face.

She smiled sleepily up at her bami for a moment. Then she realized that today the judge would render a decision. She closed her eyes, and turned her face into the pillow.

"Siti, Sohelia just called. She's on her way over with breakfast."

"Mmm," Juna murmured. She wanted to go back to sleep and wake up to find that this day was all a dream.

"Siti, you need to wake up," Moki insisted.

"Mmmph," Juna managed. "All right, bai." She rolled over and opened her eyes.

"You were crying last night, siti. Can I help?"

Juna turned to look at him. "How did you know that, bai? You slept in Ukatonen's room last night."

"I could smell your tears when I came in. Please, siti, let me help." He held his hands out for allu-a.

Juna pushed herself upright. "Okay, bai. Show me the baby. I—We may not have her anymore after today."

For the last few weeks, whenever they linked, Moki would include the baby in the link. Juna could just barely sense the baby's quiet presence, its metabolism ticking away like a fast watch. Recently, she had felt the baby responding to the link. It was nothing more than a vague flutter of sensation, but it happened consistently whenever she or Moki reached inward to sense the child.

Juna grasped Moki's arms, and they linked. She felt him enfold her and reach for the baby. She felt the fluttering sensation of the baby. Juna reached deeper into the link, striving to get as close to the little one as possible.

To her surprise, she felt a faint tickle of awareness in response, a feather-brush against her own presence. Juna sent a gentle surge of warmth and love in reply. The baby responded with another, more focused brush of awareness that touched both Moki and Juna. Juna felt a surge of fierce happiness that carried all three of them soaring sweetly into harmony.

Juna clung to that precarious balance of happiness as long as she could. Then the baby began to tire, and the link was over. Juna opened her eyes, and began to weep.

"Siti, what's the matter? What can I do?"

Juna just shook her head, unable to speak. Moki left, returning with Ukatonen.

"What's the matter?" he asked.

"The baby, I—" and she started crying again.

Just then the doorbell rang. Moki went to answer it, and came back with Sohelia.

"It's the baby, isn't it?" she said squatting beside the bed. "You're afraid you're going to lose the baby."

Juna nodded, and took the handkerchief that Sohelia handed her.

"I won't lie to you, Juna, it could happen. But you have a greater chance for keeping this child than any other client I've ever represented, and I've won a few of those cases as well."

"Really?" Juna asked.

"Of course," Sohelia reassured her. "Don't give up hope until it's ripped out of your hands. Now, put on a robe and come eat breakfast. You need to eat."

Juna nodded and began to pull herself together. Breakfast helped make her feel a little less despairing. Moki had even managed to make her laugh a time or two by the time she'd finished eating. The comm rang as they were clearing the table. Moki answered it and handed it to Sohelia. Everyone stood watching as Sohelia listened.

"All right," she said. "We'll be there in forty-five minutes." She put the comm down. "Judge Matthesen has her verdict."

"Oh," Juna said, her mood suddenly deflated. She returned to her room and got dressed, fighting back her fears and doubts.

Juna sat in the defendant's chair and stared at the scratched plastic table, suppressing the urge to flee. She jumped like a startled cat when the clerk came in and announced the judge. She stood, eyes still anchored to the desk, unable to look up, afraid to hope.

"Please sit," the judge said, arranging her black robes with magisterial grace as she settled into her chair.

"The purpose of this hearing is to decide whether or not criminal culpability was involved in this pregnancy, and to determine the future of the fetus involved. I find that there was no criminal intent in this pregnancy. It was an accidental pregnancy."

Juna looked up from the table in amazement. Sohelia clutched her shoulder.

"However," the judge added, and Juna felt her spirits catch in their soaring. "Due to the unconventional nature of Dr. Saari's alien companions, I feel it is important that there are other human parents to counterbalance the influence of the Tendu. If Juna is not married by the time the child is four months old, she will have to give the child up for adoption. Congratulations, Dr. Saari, you get to have your child. Case dismissed."

Juna looked around, stunned by the decision. It was hard for her to wrap her mind around the good news. Moki and Ukatonen's skins were a riot of celebratory blues and greens.

"Congratulations, Juna," Sohelia said. "You get to keep the baby."

"But—" Juna said. "The marriage."

"Juna, you won!" Sohelia said. "Worry about everything else tomorrow."

"But who will marry me?" Juna said.

"It will work out, you'll see," Sohelia assured her. "There are many families who would love to have you."

"And the Tendu as well?" Juna asked.

Sohelia's dark eyes looked thoughtful for a moment. "The Tendu will make it harder, but you'll find someone, I'm sure of it. But for now, let's celebrate the victory we have rather than worrying about the next battle. At least your daughter will be born. You have over a year to worry about finding her a family."

Juna closed her eyes and took a deep breath. "You're right," she said. "I've just gotten so used to worrying that it's hard to stop."

Analin came in. "Is it good news?"

"Yes," Juna said.

"Hooray!" Analin cheered.

"But there's a catch," Juna added. "I have to be married by the time my daughter's four months old, or give her up for adoption."

"Don't worry," Analin reassured her. "It'll happen. Are you ready to make a statement to the press?"

"Yes, but I don't want to talk about having to get married. It's going to be hard enough without everyone in the world knowing about it."

"I understand," Analin told her. "I'll set up a press conference in an hour, outside the courthouse. Your brother and Dr. Engle are waiting outside the courtroom for you."

Juna headed for the door. "We won!" she announced when she saw Toivo and the doctor. "We won!"

"Juna that's great news!" Dr. Engle said. He hugged her tightly.

Toivo pushed himself up out of his wheelchair to hug her. "I'm so glad, Juna!"

Juna felt tears of joy gather at the corner of her eyes. "So am I!" she said. "So am I!"

The press conference went well. Juna still had the sympathy of the press, and she was able to get away with a simple statement, and five minutes of questions about the baby. She dodged a couple of questions about her pending lawsuit against the Survey.

Then after a couple of light, fluffy questions about the baby's name, and whether it was a boy or a girl, Juna brought the press conference to a close with a huge sense of relief. No one had asked her about their work at the hospital.

"They're going to find out what the Tendu can do someday, Juna," her brother remarked as they headed for a quiet lunch.

"I know," she said, "but I'd rather keep people in the dark as long as possible. My life is going to be complicated enough just trying to find a family to marry."

"You'll find someone, Juna," he told her. "I know you will."

Juna shrugged.

"Seriously, keep me posted. If there's anything I can do, I want to help." Toivo's dark, solemn face was intent. For a moment Juna saw their mother's face reflected in his.

"Thank you, little brother. I'll keep you posted." She grinned. "You can come stand by my door and beat the suitors away with a stick when there are too many of them," she said sardonically. "I'm sure there'll be suitors lined up around the block, just waiting to marry a pregnant woman who lives with two aliens."

"Come on, Juna," Toivo said. "It's not that bad. I'll bet you get some great offers."

"Maybe," Juna said doubtfully.

"Give yourself a few days before you start worrying," Toivo advised. "You're starting at the hospital tomorrow, and that's enough to worry about."

"I know," Juna said. "They didn't seem to be too eager to see us when we stopped in the other day. I don't think that they know what to do with us."

Dr. Engle grinned wolfishly. "That'll change once they understand the Tendu and their capabilities."

"I hope so," she said.

"It will be all right," Ukatonen assured her. "They are healers. It should be easy to achieve harmony."

"Yes, en, but they are also humans. They don't understand you."

"But they will, Eerin," Ukatonen told her. "Moki and I will teach them, as we have taught others."

"I hope so, en. I hope so."

Ukatonen followed Juna and the doctors as they showed him through the hospital. He had expected something like the sickbay on the *Homa Darabi Maru*: a few beds, mostly empty, with one or two injured people on their way to recovery. Instead they were walking past room after room full of sick and injured people.

The heavy sour scent of sick humans constricted his nostrils and caught in the back of his throat. He had to work to keep from breathing through his mouth. He'd never dreamed that there could be this many sick people in the world. It was the most horrific thing he had ever seen.

The humans could build bubbles of life in the emptiness of space. Their sky rafts could sail across the unimaginable distance between their world and his. And yet, they had places like these, full of illness and pain. How could they let this happen?

The farther they walked, the more horrified Ukatonen became. Finally, they stopped at a room full of beeping, blinking machines. In the midst of these machines lay a man. There were tubes and wires going into his nose, on his chest, and out of his arms, connecting the man to the machines. His hair was very white, and his skin was thin and wrinkled in the manner of old humans.

"He is dying," one of the doctors told the Tendu. "Can you help him?"

"We will try," Ukatonen said. The sick man's skin felt dry and thin as paper. He smelled sour, like rising pika dough, and his hand lay limply in Ukatonen's. Ukatonen glanced at Moki, who had moved into position on the other side of the bed. They grasped the man's arms, and linked with him.

The state of the man's body was even more of a shock than the hospital had been. Ukatonen had never felt a creature so out of harmony with itself. The man's body was a mass of out-of-control cells, his heartbeat was thready and thin, and his lungs were filling with fluid. There were deep internal scars where he had been cut open and organs had been removed.

Only the doctors' machines and the medicines were keeping this human alive. The man was frightened and in pain; the sour, bitter tang of it pushed his body even further out of balance. It was appalling. Ukatonen enfolded the sick man's presence, shutting out the pain, and easing the fear. He felt a sweet rush of gratitude and joy; then the man's presence folded in on itself, and went away into death, leaving the shattered husk of his body behind.

Ukatonen gently eased out of the link, taking Moki with him.

"He is gone. You may shut off your machines now."

One of the doctors examined the machines. He lifted the dead man's eyelid and shone a light into his eye.

"His brain function has stopped. He's dead," the doctor reported. He reached over and shut off the machines. "Time of death, nine forty-five A.M.," he reported somberly.

"You killed him!" one of the other doctors protested.

"He is in harmony now. Before—" Ukatonen paused searching for words, "he did not want to live. Only his pain kept him tied here. I stopped the pain and the fear, and he left. Why did you not do this sooner?" he demanded. He could feel flickers of anger crossing his back.

Eerin touched Ukatonen's arm to silence him. "Perhaps," she suggested to the assembled doctors, "the Tendu should work on patients who are not at death's door. There was nothing Ukatonen could do to heal this patient."

She seemed angry, and Ukatonen lifted his ears in surprise.

Eerin began lecturing the doctors, telling them about what the Tendu did, and how they did it. Watching her talk to them, Ukatonen was reminded of her father soothing a skittish horse, and a ripple of amusement coursed down his back.

Moki slipped away from the arguing humans. He walked down the hall, and into a room full of sick children. Some of the children were playing listlessly, others were sitting idly in chairs, too sick to do more than watch the others play. The children stopped what they were doing and stared at him when he walked into the room.

"You're Moki the Tendu!" a fragile little girl exclaimed. "I saw you on the Tri-V!"

She was a small child with pale, almost translucent skin. Her eyes were pale blue and surprisingly large, with dark shadows underneath them.

"Yes, I am," Moki said. "And who are you?"

"My name is Shelley Richter," she said. "Are you sick too?"

"No," Moki answered, "we came here to make people better. Are you sick?"

"We all are," she told him. "That's why we're here."

"What's wrong with you?" he asked.

"There's a hole in my heart, and my lungs don't get enough oxygen," she explained.

"If you hold out your hands, like this," he said, extending his arms for allu-a, "I'll look and see if I can fix it."

"Will it hurt?" she asked.

"It will be like pricking your finger on a thorn, but after that it won't hurt at all."

The little girl considered this information seriously.

"All right," she said, holding out her arms. "Fix me, please."

Moki sat down across from the little girl, and clasped her arms. He linked with her, and found the problem almost immediately. He slowed her heart as much as he could, giving her oxygen through his spurs. Working between beats, he closed the hole by encouraging the growth of overlapping flaps of tissue on either side of the hole, which he then fused together. It was delicate, challenging work. When he was done, Moki paused for a moment, savoring the rich taste of the girl's newly oxygenated blood, then broke the link.

Shelley woke up. Her pale skin now had a faintly pink bloom. "Am I fixed yet?" she asked.

Moki nodded. "How do you feel now?"

She closed her eyes and breathed deeply. "I don't feel tired," she said, "and I'm hungry."

"That's good," Moki told her. "You should eat a big meal as soon as you can. Your body will need that."

A little boy came up to him. "Mr. Moki, can you fix me too? I have leukemia."

"What's that?"

"Don't you know?" he asked. "I thought you were a doctor."

"No," Moki said. "I'm a Tendu. Sit down and let me look inside you, and I'll see if I can fix you."

They linked. This one would be harder, he realized. The cells that ate disease in the boy's blood had proliferated and thrown his entire body out of balance. Moki went deep inside the child's bone marrow, searching for the cells that created the problem, killing those that were out of balance. He gently encouraged the proliferation of healthy cells, and filtered out the unbalanced killer cells.

He was undoing the damage from the medicines the doctors had used, when suddenly he was torn out of the link. He cried out in pain, colors flashing across his body. A human woman was standing over him, shouting. He scrambled away from her, and fled.

Juna walked home with a bag full of groceries, reviewing the day's disastrous events. She still vibrated with anger when she remembered how Moki clung, cringing and terrified, to a small tree in a planter, trying to hide in its inadequate cover. Even with Ukatonen's help, it had taken several hours to get a coherent version of what had happened.

And then there was Ukatonen. Juna rubbed her free hand across her forehead. The doctors should never have asked him to heal someone so seriously ill, especially not as a first attempt. She understood that medical protocols required that any experimental technique be tried on terminally ill patients first, but—

"Dr. Saari?"

Juna looked up, startled out of her reverie.

It was a woman close to her own age. She was thin, worn, and nervous; her clothes were shabby. Juna's security escort moved to cut her off.

"Please, Dr. Saari, I need to talk to you about what Moki did to my daughter."

"It's okay," Juna told the security man. The woman looked too spent and tired to be a threat.

"Dr. Saari, I really don't think—" the guard began.

"It's okay," Juna insisted in a voice that did not invite argument.

"Yes?" she prompted, looking back at the woman.

"I'm Loreena Richter, Shelley's mother."

"What did Moki do, Mrs. Richter?" Juna asked a bit sharply. It had been a long day, and she wasn't really up to dealing with another problem.

"I wanted to thank him. My daughter, he—"

Juna realized the woman was on the edge of tears. "Here," she said, guiding her to a park bench, ignoring the protests of her guard. "Sit down. Tell me what happened." She put her groceries down, fumbled out a clean handkerchief, and handed it to the woman.

"I'm sorry, Dr. Saari. It's just that it's all so sudden and unexpected."

"Yes?" Juna said, and waited.

"My daughter, Shelley has—I mean, she had, a hole in her heart. She was on the waiting list for a transplant, but it's such a long list, and the older she got, the harder it was for her heart to keep up with her. The doctors gave her another six months if we didn't find a heart. I was beginning to give up hope. I mean, the list is so long." She paused, fighting back tears.

"Moki healed her this morning. The doctors haven't seen anything like it. She could leave the hospital today, and live an ordinary life like any child, but the doctors want to study her." The woman took a deep breath and looked up at Juna. "I came straight from the hospital. I wanted to thank Moki for saving my daughter's life."

"Come with me," Juna told Mrs. Richter. "I'll take you to see him." She looked up at the guard, challenging him to make another protest.

"It's your life," he said with a resigned shrug.

When they reached the apartment, Juna asked Mrs. Richter to have a seat while she saw if Moki was awake. The guard stood by the door, watching Mrs. Richter warily.

Juna went into her bedroom. Moki was lying on the bed, his eyes hooded by his nictitating membranes.

"Moki, the mother of the girl you healed is here. She would like to see you."

Moki got up slowly, and pulled on his shorts. "Is she angry at me?" he asked, his skin flaring pale orange with fear.

"It's all right, Moki. She wants to thank you. Come and talk to her."

Mrs. Richter hesitated slightly when Moki came out of the bedroom, but she conquered her uncertainty and stood.

"Moki, this is Mrs. Richter. She's Shelley's mother."

"Pleased to meet you, Mrs. Richter," Moki said. "Is Shelley all right?"

"She's completely healed, Moki. I came to thank you for giving me my daughter back."

Moki nodded.

"My husband died in an accident a couple of years ago," Mrs. Richter continued. "My family is back on Earth, so Shelley is all I've got. I thought I was going to lose her too." She bowed her head, blinking back tears, then looked up. "But now she's going to be all right, thanks to you."

"Does this mean you're not angry at me?" Moki asked.

Mrs. Richter looked startled. "Moki, why would I be angry with you? This is a miracle."

"The other woman was angry," Moki explained. "I was healing a boy with"— he paused, searching for the word—"leukemia. A woman broke the link. She was yelling at me. I don't know why. It isn't good to break a link like that. The boy could have been badly hurt."

Mrs. Richter turned to Juna. "I don't understand."

"Moki got bored while Ukatonen and I were discussing a case with some of the doctors," Juna explained. "He wandered off by himself, into the pediatric ward. That's where he met your daughter. After he healed her, a little boy came up and asked to be healed. While he was in the middle of a link, a nurse came up and saw him with the boy. She ripped Moki's spurs out of the boy's arms, breaking the link." Juna paused, trying to stanch the anger that welled up in her. "Moki is still young. He isn't fully trained yet. Breaking the link like that threw him into shock. He panicked and ran."

"Is he all right?" Mrs. Richter asked.

"He is now. Ukatonen helped bring him out of it. But the hospital isn't very pleased with us, I'm afraid. Moki was healing those children without permission. And—" Juna paused, uncertain about what to tell this woman. "The first patient that Ukatonen was asked to work on was so far gone that he died while Ukatonen was linked with him. I don't think we're going to be here much longer."

"Oh no! That's terrible! They can't send you away! Think of all the good that Moki can do!" Mrs. Richter said. "Please, let me help you. Shelley's been here so long, I know the hospital administration backwards and forwards."

Juna thought it over; she was a stranger here, and didn't know the system. They needed help.

"We'd appreciate any help you could give us, Mrs. Richter," Juna said. "Thank you."

"Dr. Saari, it's you, and Moki, who deserve the thanks. Without you, my daughter might have died."

"We're here to heal people," Moki declared. "Besides, healing Shelley was easy. It was just one simple thing. The boy with leukemia was much harder to heal."

Mrs. Richter shook her head in amazement. "I'll call the hospital administrator first thing tomorrow morning."

Around the middle of the morning, Juna received a comm call from the hospital administrators, asking her to meet with them in an hour.

The hospital's chief administrator, a round, rather jovial-looking African, called the meeting to order.

"Dr. Saari, I wanted to apologize to you about yesterday's misunderstanding. According to Mrs. Richter, your son performed a miracle yesterday. Two miracles, actually. The doctors can find no trace of leukemia in Ian McIntyre. He appears completely cured. Clearly the Tendu are capable of great things. We very much want you to stay here. However, we do need to set up some rules for the Tendu to work under."

"Thank you, Dr. Andraia," Juna said. "The Tendu have a very different view of health and medicine than conventional human doctors. I agree with you. The Tendu and your doctors need to have a better understanding of how to work together. Ukatonen and I have discussed this, and we have two suggestions. First, let the Tendu choose who they can heal. Second, give each of the Tendu a medically qualified escort, someone who can explain the nature of the medical problems they encounter, as well as what human medical ethics are in these situations."

"These seem like good procedures," Dr. Andraia said. "Are there any other suggestions?"

"If the Tendu are going to just wander around the hospital and heal people, how are we going to monitor what is going on?" one doctor protested. "And how are we going to keep this classified?"

"That's a good question, Dr. Shaw," Andraia said. "Juna?"

She turned to the enkar. "Ukatonen, do you have any suggestions?"

"We could include a doctor in the link with us, I suppose."

"I'm afraid that wasn't quite what we had in mind," one of the other doctors said. "We need to hook you up to machines that can monitor your heartbeat, and your brain waves."

"I see," Ukatonen said. "How much time does it take to set up these machines?"

"It takes about fifteen minutes to set everything up. We can use one of the upstairs examining rooms."

"Then Moki and I will heal our patients in that room," Ukatonen said. "I will be interested to see what these machines do."

"But what about those of us who want to investigate how the Tendu heal a specific problem?" another doctor asked.

"We can work on that after we've found the best way to study what the Tendu are doing," Dr. Andraia said. "Ukatonen, Moki, I apologize for the initial misunderstanding and I hope that we can figure out a harmonious working arrangement."

"Thank you, Dr. Andraia," said the enkar. "Moki and I are looking forward to learning from you."

A lavender ripple of relief coursed over Ukatonen's body as he turned on the shower. It had been a very long day. He and Moki had healed five people today, four yesterday, and two the day before. He was drained and weary, and beginning to feel as out of harmony as the people he healed. He needed a green, quiet place in which to restore his balance. Tomorrow, they would rest, he decided. He would get out with Eerin and Moki and they would find a tree, and climb it, and not come down until they felt more in balance.

He emerged from the shower and climbed into his moist, heated bed, and fell asleep.

The next day they explored several of the station's gardens, climbing trees, swinging from branch to branch. They found a small, quiet park with gnarled pine trees and rounded, moss-covered stones. Water trickled from a bamboo pipe into a dark pool where bright orange fish swirled and circled. The garden's tranquillity and balance filled Ukatonen with peace.

"I like this place," he remarked to Eerin. "It has ruwar-a."

"This garden," she told him, "was designed by Motoyoshi XVI. His family have designed gardens for almost a thousand years, first in Japan, then around the world. A branch of the family moved into space two centuries ago. Do you remember the Uenos?" she asked.

Moki nodded. "Your neighbors, the ones with the strange fish."

"Mrs. Ueno is a Motoyoshi; she told me all about her family." Eerin smiled, remembering. "You should see her garden. There's a bonsai that's almost three hundred years old. It was a wedding present from her family."

"I would like to meet the man who created this garden," Ukatonen said. "I think I would like him very much."

"I think you would too," Eerin agreed. "But he died ten years ago. He was Mrs. Ueno's grandfather. She told me about this garden."

A grey cloud of sadness passed over the enkar's skin at this news. "You humans live such short lives," he said. Eerin's people desperately needed the healing he and Moki were providing.

"Actually, Mr. Motoyoshi was nearly one hundred and thirty years old when he died," Eerin said. "He lived a very long life for a human."

"But that would still be young for a Tendu, even with the difference between your years and ours."

Eerin nodded. "We live longer now than we once did. Until the twentieth century, most people were lucky to reach sixty."

"I know, but even a hundred and thirty years seems too short to me. But then, it's hard to believe that most of what I have seen here is no more than a century old. Where are your people's roots?"

"On Earth, where we came from," Eerin said. "But we brought our roots with us." she added, gesturing at the little gnarled tree.

"Earth," Ukatonen said. "When are we going to see it?"

Eerin ran a hand through her hair. "I don't know," she said. "Soon, I hope. In a few more months, I'll be too pregnant to travel."

"Why can't we just get on a shuttle and go?" Moki asked.

"Because people are still afraid of you," Juna replied. "They don't want you on Earth because they think you might spread disease."

Red lightning forks of anger flickered over Ukatonen's skin. "Haven't we been through this already?"

"I agree. It makes no sense," Juna replied. "But this is often true of my people. One of the reasons that we are here, healing people, is to show them how much good you can do."

"I see," Ukatonen said. "This is not just research, then? Healing these people will help your people trust us?"

"I hope so," Eerin said. "I hope so."

* * *

About a week after they had settled things with the hospital, Juna was watching the Tri-V with Moki when the door chime rang.

It was her guard. "Excuse me, Dr. Saari, but this gentleman insists on seeing you. And well—" Glancing beyond the guard Juna saw a handsome, dark-skinned man with sharp-chinned features that looked vaguely Vietnamese. He was dressed in a quietly elegant suit that must have cost a great deal, and he had the presence of someone who expected to be recognized wherever he went.

"My name is Yang Xaviera," the visitor said. "I am here on behalf of the Xaviera family. Please forgive your guard, I really have been most persistent. He has checked my identification, and searched me most thoroughly. I am quite safe."

Juna was too stunned to speak. The Xaviera family was one of the wealthiest and most powerful group families in the solar system. They practically owned the Moon.

"I see," she said, recovering herself. "Please come in."

"Thank you, Dr. Saari. I apologize for not contacting you first, but your comm is very tightly filtered, and we were unable to get through to you. We could have worked through an agent, but this way is both more discreet, and more direct. As I mentioned, I am here on behalf of the Xaviera family. We have come to ask permission to court you."

Juna stared at him, astonished for the second time in a minute.

"It is most gracious of you to see me," he went on. "I apologize for surprising you in this manner." He remained polite and serious, though Juna knew she must present a laughable spectacle.

"Please, sit down," she said at last, motioning him to the couch. "Would you like some tea?"

"Thank you," he replied.

She headed for the kitchen, grateful for a moment to think, but Moki already had the kettle on and was spooning tea into the pot.

"It's all right, siti," he told her. "I'll do it."

Juna returned to the living room. Yang was perched on the sofa like some rare tropical bird. She sat down in the armchair, painfully aware of how untidy the apartment looked. They had been working very hard, and there hadn't been any time to clean.

"Moki will bring the tea," she explained. "He feels that it's his job to look after me."

"Indeed," Yang said. He held out a dossier. "These are our bona fides. We encourage you to have them verified."

Juna took the folder, which was made of rough, expensive paper embossed with the Xaviera's Family seal: "Thank you," she said, putting it down on the table.

"There are many more influential and interesting people for your family to marry. Why are you interested in me?" she asked.

"On the contrary, Dr. Saari—" he began.

"Please, call me Juna."

"Juna, you survived for four and a half years on an unexplored planet, lived among aliens, learned their language, and helped negotiate the beginnings of a most impressive First Contact treaty. Then you bullied some of the most powerful politicians in the system into releasing you and the Tendu from quarantine. By any standards you care to use, you are a most exceptional person, and that has drawn my family's attention to you. We would like to get to know you better, and perhaps"— he gestured at the folder—"arrange a more permanent alliance. I think, under the circumstances, you could use some powerful allies."

Moki brought in the tea things then, carefully arranged on a tray. Their guest's eyes followed his progress from the kitchen to the table.

"Yang Xaviera, this is my adopted son, Moki."

"I'm honored to meet you," Yang said. "I've heard so much about you and your mother on the Tri-V and the net."

"It's good to meet you, too. Do you want to marry my sitik?"

"Moki—" Juna began, but Yang interrupted her.

"Our family would like to get to know her better. If she likes us, and we like her, then yes, the two of you might join our family."

"What about Ukatonen?" Moki asked.

"Ukatonen is welcome as well," Yang said.

"We are a package deal," Juna informed him. She picked up the folder and paged through it. Holograms of spacious mansions and beautiful gardens leaped off the page, pausing at a shot of a well-equipped playground with a dozen happy children at play. It was tempting, and it would indeed be interesting to be courted by a rich and powerful family. She closed the folder.

"You honor me with your interest," she said. "I will give your offer serious consideration. I should warn you that the Tendu and I have a very full schedule at present. I don't know when we can get time off to come and visit you."

"I understand. This invitation has surprised you. Please take all the time you need to consider it. Our offer is open-ended."

She stood, and Yang rose as well.

"Thank you, Juna," he said. "I appreciate your kindness in agreeing to see me." He took one of her hands in his. "It has indeed been a great honor to meet you and Moki. To tell the truth, I did not expect you to be so young and beautiful." He kissed her hand, making the antique gesture seem both appropriate and graceful.

Juna blushed, and lowered her eyes. Her pulse was racing. She felt as giddy as a young girl.

"Thank you for coming, Mr. Xaviera," she said, looking up. "We are honored by your visit."

He inclined his head. "I look forward to seeing you again, Juna. Our family is eager to get to know you better."

Then he was gone. Juna stood staring at the closed door for a moment, then leaned against it and began to laugh. This was like something out of a bad Tri-V series.

Moki touched her arm, ochre with concern. "Are you all right?" he asked.

Juna wiped away the tears of laughter. "I'm fine, Moki. It's just that this is all so strange." She picked up the elegant folder, flipped through it again, and then tossed it onto her pile of mail. "C'mon, let's go find Ukatonen and go out for dinner."

Ukatonen quickly established a routine. For three or four days in a row, he and Moki would go through the wards, healing people. Sometimes it was easy, a matter of adjusting faulty chemistry, or killing off an infection. Other times it was a long, involved process, clearing out plaque-choked arteries, destroying cancer cells, and coaxing damaged tissue to regrow. At the end of each day, Ukatonen went to the Motoyoshi garden, sometimes with Moki, sometimes alone, and sat there in silence beside the trickling water, watching the fish, and drinking in the serenity of the garden.

Occasionally the doctors had them test various medicines to see if they could be changed or improved. Ukatonen liked that work. It was intricate, and tested his skill at allu-a. He was coming to respect human medicine.

Humans had accomplished a great deal, despite the immense handicaps they struggled under. The drugs that they created with their cumbersome chemistry worked surprisingly well. Often, Ukatonen was able to make a drug work more effectively, though communicating what to change proved very difficult. Few of the researchers were willing to link with him, and those that did were faced with the same problem: how to convert the touch/smell/taste of allu-a into the language of chemistry.

And they were discovering ways to help improve a healer's abilities in allu-a. An intravenous feed of glucose and salts enabled them to accomplish much more during a healing session. He recovered faster, as well. They were working on mineral supplements to speed the healing of bones. He looked forward to taking these ideas back to Tiangi.

As rumors about their work spread through the hospital, patients began begging for their help. Moki found this particularly wrenching. Ukatonen tried to explain to Moki that sometimes it was necessary to turn away from need, but it was a lesson that the bami was not yet ready to learn.

As the appeals increased, Ukatonen came to rely more and more on the sense of peace he found in the Japanese garden.

Then one evening, Ukatonen's peaceful refuge was shattered. It had been a particularly trying day. While they were preparing for the last healing, a man barged into the room. He seized Ukatonen's arm and began pleading with him to heal his wife. Security guards rushed in and took him away, but even now, as Ukatonen sat in the garden, he could still feel the hot imprint of the man's pleading hands on his arms and in his spirit. Trying to heal this endless tide of sick humans was like emptying a river with an open-weave basket.

"Mr. Ukatonen?" a voice broke in on his thoughts.

Ukatonen blinked back the nictitating membranes hooding his eyes. A woman was standing a few feet away, microphone in hand. A reporter.

"I understand that you've been performing miracles at the hospital. Would you care to comment?"

"I do not give interviews. You must talk to Ms. Goudrian," he said, and turned away, hooding his eyes again, and letting a broad streak of yellow fork across his torso to indicate that he was not to be disturbed.

But the woman would not leave him alone. Finally Ukatonen got up and walked back to the apartment. The garden was no longer his refuge. If this woman had found it, then others would follow.

Juna was catching up on her correspondence when her comm program signaled her with Analin's familiar chime.

Their press secretary's normally cheerful face looked strained and worried. "There's an exclusive interview on WorldNet with the mother of a child that Moki healed. It's gotten so many hits they've had to put it on twenty different servers. Here," she said, reaching forward to touch a button, "listen to this."

The image on the screen cut to the familiar WorldNet logo, then to the figure of netcaster Natalie Ndabari.

"I'm standing in front of Snyder Research Hospital. Rumors have been emerging recently that Ukatonen and Moki, the two alien Tendu, have been performing miracle cures. I'm here with Loreena Richter." Juna's heart sank when she saw the camera pan to include the woman whose daughter Moki had healed.

"Mrs. Richter, could you please tell us about your daughter?"

"Yes. My daughter, Shelley, had a hole in her heart. She was a candidate for transplant surgery, but there's such a shortage of hearts, I didn't think she was going to live long enough for a transplant. But then Moki, the younger Tendu, healed her."

"How did he do that, Mrs. Richter?"

"From what Shelley tells me, he simply clasped her hands and they went into some kind of trance. But now her heart is as sound as a normal child's. It truly is a miracle."

"Thank you, Mrs. Richter."

The camera zoomed in on the netcaster's face, and she continued. "So far, Snyder Hospital has refused to confirm Mrs. Richter's statement, nor has there been any word from Dr. Saari or the Tendu. I'm Natalie Ndabari, and this has been a WorldNet breaking news report."

The WorldNet logo flickered briefly on the screen, and then Analin reappeared.

"Well, so much for peace and quiet," Juna remarked. "You'd better come on over."

"I'll be there in twenty minutes," Analin promised. "Meanwhile, call station security and have them secure your hallway."

Ukatonen came in just then, slamming the door behind him loudly enough to make her jump. He was so red with anger, he seemed to glow.

"I've got to go," Juna told Analin. "Ukatonen just came in, and he looks upset."

"I'll be over as quickly as I can."

"Thanks," Juna said.

"Hey, that's what you pay me for," Analin said with a smile. "Something like this was inevitable, given the Tendu's talents. I'll do what I can to minimize the impact on you, but you should brace yourself for some heavy weather ahead."

"I think some of it just blew in the door," Juna said, and signed off.

"What's the matter, Ukatonen?"

"There was a reporter in the Japanese garden," he said in skin speech. His words were dark black against the glowing red of his skin. It reminded Juna of cooling lava. "She wanted to know about the work we're doing at the hospital. I told her I wasn't going to talk to her, but she wouldn't leave me alone!"

"Did you say anything?"

Ukatonen shook his head. "No, but she wouldn't leave me alone! Why?"

Juna laid a gentling hand on his arm. Despite the deceptively blazing color of his skin, it was as cool and moist as a spring rain.

"Ukatonen, word of what we've been doing has gotten out." Briefly, she summarized Analin's comm call. "It looks like the press are going to be all over us again," she said with a sigh.

"Why wouldn't she leave me alone?" Ukatonen repeated. "I told her I wasn't going to talk to her. Didn't she believe me?"

He was an enkar, and on Tiangi no one would dream of being so rude to someone of his status.

Juna sighed and rubbed her forehead. She was tired, her breasts and back were sore. All she wanted to do was lie down and sleep until the baby came.

"You did exactly the right thing, Ukatonen," she told him. "But reporters are paid to be persistent. They don't care that you're an enkar. To them you're only a story. That's why we have Analin to deal with them."

Ukatonen's color had cooled somewhat, but he was still clearly agitated. "She was so rude," he said aloud and then again in skin speech. The words flared black against his red skin. They faded and flared over and over again, gradually growing fainter, like a dying echo of his spoken words.

Analin's warning proved all too true. Despite everything Analin did to minimize the impact, they were mobbed, first by the press, and then by people begging to be healed. The hospital called Juna and told her to stay home. They were afraid there would be a riot if the Tendu showed up.

So they remained caged at home. Ukatonen and Moki helped her clean house, after which the two Tendu sought comfort in a long, intense link. Juna looked around at the clean apartment, trying to find something else that needed tidying. Finally, desperate for something to do, she attacked the enormous pile of mail on her desk. As she was sorting through it, she came across the folder from the Xaviera family. She picked it up and began paging through it. Juna was pleasantly surprised to see that the Xaviera family residences, though gracious and beautiful, were not nearly as grand as she would have imagined. There were plenty of amenities, but very little overt display of wealth.

The gardens, however, were another story. They were filled with rare and beautiful plants and animals, many extinct in their native habitat. Every effort had been made to create and preserve full ecosystems. She turned to a double page hologram of their fifty-hectare rain forest preserve on the Moon, and smiled wistfully. Ukatonen and Moki would love that.

She looked up at the closed door of their room. Yang had said that their invitation to visit was open-ended. The hospital couldn't use them, and there was nothing else for her to do here except answer mail. If they were out of the public eye for a week or so, perhaps the furor would die down and they could slip quietly back to Snyder and continue their work.

She put a call through to the Xaviera family and left a message for Yang. He returned her call after only two hours.

"Juna! I'm glad you called! Are you coming to visit?"

"I'd like to, but—" She paused. "Have you seen the news? I'm afraid that we're all over the net. The hospital is mobbed, and they're afraid of a riot if we show up. It looks like we finally have time to visit, but I'm afraid that we'd be bringing trouble with us."

"Nonsense, Juna. Discretion is one of our family specialties. The Tendu will be coming with you of course?" he inquired politely.

"I couldn't leave them behind."

"Of course, and they will be welcome. You've seen our rain forest?"

"Oh, yes. The Tendu will love it."

Yang smiled. "We hope so. Now, let me make some arrangements, and then I'll call you right back."

Discretion was, indeed, a family specialty. Somehow, Juna and the Tendu were whisked off the station in the middle of the night, escaping through the service tunnels, and onto a private shuttle. Only Analin and Toivo knew where they were going.

"It's the Tendu," Analin had said, when Juna told her about the proposal. "They want access to the Tendu."

"I know," Juna replied. "But I'm tired of doing all this by myself. I need someone powerful in my corner."

"Be careful, Juna," Analin warned.

"I will be," she said.

Now, staring out through the filtered window at the sunlit surface of the Moon, she wondered how wise she was being. The Xavieras were immensely powerful. They could ruin her, or kill Toivo and Analin, and kidnap her and the Tendu. She took a deep breath, fighting off the crawling paranoia that had risen from the depths of her psyche. There was no turning back now. The shuttle was landing.

Yang met them at the gate. "Welcome to Jóia da Lua, Juna. I am honored to meet you, Ukatonen, and it is good to see you again, Moki. I hope you enjoy your stay with us." He escorted them to a ground car with fat rubber moon wheels.

"What about our bags?" Moki asked.

"Don't worry, they're being taken directly to your rooms," Yang told him. Yang opened the door to the ground car, a big, luxurious model that could seat at least six people in the back, and waved them graciously inside before climbing in himself. "We're so glad you were able to come. The rest of the family can't wait to meet you."

"I'm looking forward to meeting them as well," Juna said. "Getting us here must have been a great deal of work. I'm sorry if we caused you any additional trouble."

Yang shrugged elegantly. "My family has often had to travel discreetly. We have systems in place to do so. The hardest part was getting you out of your apartment and into the service tunnels without being seen. Every-thing else was easy."

The car entered a tunnel. Juna felt her throat close in sudden terror. Perhaps all this was a ruse, a cover for kidnapping them. They stopped at a huge airlock door. There was a rumbling and a heavy thud behind them as the back door of the massive cargo airlock closed. Then the front door opened, and green forest light flooded in.

They drove out into the midst of a jungle. The trees, in the Moon's re-duced gravity were hugely tall. Ukatonen and Moki chittered excitedly, staring out the windows at the passing forest, their skins bright pink with excitement.

Yang smiled. "They like the forest?" he asked.

"It's like water on parched soil for them. They haven't seen a proper rain forest in—" She thought for a minute. "It's been almost a year. They spent some time in our satellite's Diversity Plot, but that was a temperate-zone forest, nothing like this."

"It was my great-grandfather's project. He wanted to create a rain for-est like the ones in Brazil. It took ten years just to create the proper soil, then another twenty to establish a canopy so that the understory plants could go in. It's still maturing after nearly fifty years, and we keep expand-ing it. Last year, we roofed another five-hectare section, and we've started processing the soil. Our ecologists are looking forward to showing you the forest."

Ukatonen tore himself away from the window. "Ecologists?" he asked. "Are these the people whose atwa is this forest?"

"Yes," Juna told him.

"Then I would be most interested in speaking with them," the enkar said. "But first, Moki and I will need to inspect the forest."

Juna turned toward the window to hide a smile. It was the closest to a direct request that Ukatonen's dignity would allow.

"There will be plenty of time for you and Moki to explore. You'll be here for eight days," Yang assured them.

Glancing back, Juna could see Moki's ears droop, and Ukatonen's color fade slightly. For them, a month would be barely enough time to get to know the forest.

The forest opened up and they drove through a gate and into the com-pound. The car came to a stop in front of a long, low-slung wooden house with a gracious and welcoming front porch. Several young servants in livery stepped forward to open the doors of the ground car.

A fine-boned middle-aged Asian man stepped down from the porch to greet them. He said something in Vietnamese and Yang nodded. There was an air of command about the older man, as though he was used to having his orders followed.

"Dr. Saari, Ukatonen, Moki, I am honored to introduce you to my bio-father, Quang Nguyen Xaviera, current head of the Xaviera family."

Juna's eyes widened fractionally in surprise. They must really want the Tendu, if they were sending the son of the head of the family to court her.

"I am honored to meet you, Mr. Xaviera," Juna said.

Mr. Xaviera bowed to her. "Thank you Dr. Saari, I am honored to meet you as well."

Mr. Xaviera greeted the two Tendu as formally and as ceremoniously as he had greeted Juna. Ukatonen and Moki returned his bow and greeted him in equally formal Standard and Tendu skin speech. Then Quang Nguyen Xaviera escorted them into the house and introduced them to his wife, Abeo, a tall, commanding African woman who ran one of the largest shipping concerns in space. She was dressed magnificently in brightly printed African robes, and wore heavy gold jewelry.

"Welcome, Juna. Welcome, Ukatonen. Welcome, Moki," she said. "Welcome to our house." She clapped her hands and a dark-skinned girl came forward bearing a tray with a fragrant bowl of rose water and crisp linen hand towels.

"This is my daughter Oseye." Oseye bowed her head, peering sideways at the Tendu.

"Please accept our humble hospitality," she said, proffering the tray. They washed their hands and Oseye carried off the tray.

"Your journey must have been very long," Mrs. Xaviera said. "My other daughter, Ngoc, will show you to your rooms. I am sorry that my other son, Raoul, is not here to meet you, but he is studying on Earth."

Ngoc, a somewhat older version of Oseye, escorted the guests down a long hallway to an elegant suite, then bowed and left them.

"When can we go see the forest?" Moki asked.

"I don't know, Moki," Juna answered. "I'll try to arrange something as soon as possible. Right now, let's unpack and get settled."

They showered and changed. Half an hour later, a young boy knocked on their door. He was bearing a tray with tea things artfully arranged on it. He introduced himself as Joao, a member of a collateral branch of the Xavieras, one of Yang's cousins.

Moki watched Joao intently as he deftly poured the tea and served each of them.

"Our father, Quang Nguyen, respectfully invites you to visit him in the aviary when you have finished your tea. I will be honored to escort you there."

The young man was well trained. He didn't stare at the Tendu, though Juna noticed a few covert glances in their direction when he thought they weren't looking. Once he had served them, he glided quietly to the door and stood beside it like a statue.

Moki's ears lifted and he flushed purple with curiosity. "Isn't he going to eat with us?" he said in skin speech.

Juna shook her head. "No, Moki, he's supposed to be invisible, like a tinka, only he's a person."

"You treat people like tinka?" Ukatonen asked. His skin turned beige. He was clearly appalled at the thought of such rudeness.

Juna shrugged. "I don't entirely understand this, Ukatonen, but even though he's a member of the family, he is functioning in the role of servant. As a servant he's supposed to be invisible. But he's considered to be a person, and has the legal rights of a person, unlike a tinka. So he's more like a bami. Perhaps later, when he is off duty, you can ask him about it. But," she added, taking one of the exquisite tea biscuits from the silver tray, "it is not polite to discuss such things in front of Joao now, not when he is unable to participate in this discussion."

They finished their tea, with Moki sneaking occasional wide-eyed glances at their young servitor. Joao watched him back. Ukatonen watched all the watching, slow blue and green ripples of amusement sliding across his body.

Joao escorted them through the compound and down a long breezeway that ran along a courtyard dominated by a large steel sculpture. Several children were sliding down it, and they left off what they were doing and followed the visitors, staring curiously at the Tendu and giggling. They were bright and happy children, brown and beautiful. It was easy for Juna to imagine her own daughter playing among them. This would be a wonderful place to bring up a child.

Then they rounded the corner of a large building, and found Quang Nguyen Xaviera standing inside a huge aviary, watching a cloud of hummingbirds zooming around a feeder. The tiny birds were almost too fast to see as they dove and hovered in front of the bright red feeder. Quang Nguyen looked up as they came in.

"Welcome," he said. "I wanted to show you around our compound. I thought that the aviary would be an interesting place to start."

"What is this?" Moki asked.

"It's a place where we keep birds, Moki. Most of these are hummingbirds from Brazil, one of the places on Earth where my family comes from."

"Why are you keeping hummingbirds?" Moki asked.

Mr. Xaviera smiled. "We keep them because they are beautiful, and rare. The rain forests where they once lived were destroyed. Until they can be replaced, we keep them safe here."

Ukatonen's hand darted out and he plucked one of the brilliant birds from the air and stuck his spur into it. Mr. Xaviera's eyes widened in surprise and alarm.

"Ukatonen!" Juna cried, terrified that the enkar had offended this rich and powerful man.

Ukatonen released the bird. It zipped off unharmed, to Quang Nguyen's evident relief.

"Fascinating. They are much like the watani at home. They eat nectar?"

Mr. Xaviera nodded hesitantly. "Yes, yes they do. That feeder is full of it. The red attracts them."

Ukatonen held up his arm, and let the skin around his spurs turn bright red. As they watched, one of the hummingbirds came up and sipped drops of nectar from his spurs.

"When I was a bami, I used to do this all the time," Ukatonen said. "It was harder with the watani, but these birds are extremely tame. There was one who I trained to come to my hand. It used to follow me around, pestering me for nectar."

"Did it have a name?" Joao asked.

Ukatonen shook his head. "My people do not name animals. They simply are. Sometimes we tame them, but they are not really pets, not as you humans know them. We tame them to understand their nature better."

It was an awkward moment, until Moki broke the tension. "Mr. Xaviera, when can we see the forest?"

He smiled down at Moki. "How about right now?"

They followed him out of the aviary, and down a path into the jungle. Soon they were surrounded by tall trees.

"This is the oldest part of the forest," Mr. Xaviera explained. "These trees were planted by my grandfather. I look at them, and feel young."

Moki and Ukatonen were both looking up at the trees, their skin blue-grey with longing.

"Mr. Xaviera, can we climb these trees?" Moki asked.

"Are you sure you can climb them safely?"

Moki nodded.

"And you will not hurt any of the plants or animals?"

"Yes, Mr. Xaviera, we will be careful," Moki said reassuringly.

"Is it all right with you, Juna?"

"Of course, Mr. Xaviera. They're both expert climbers, and I can assure you that the creatures and plants will not be harmed."

"Then please," he said spreading his hands palms upward, "be my guests."

Moki scrambled up the trunk of the nearest tree. Ukatonen followed him, moving as swiftly as his dignity would allow. They were up the tree and out of sight in less than a minute.

"Wow! Just like a monkey!" Joao said, staring upward, his mouth agape in amazement. Then he remembered himself, and looked embarrassed.

"Joao!" Quang Nguyen snapped. "That's no way to talk about our guests."

Juna laughed. "It's all right, Quang Nguyen. Sometimes they remind me of monkeys, too, but they're much more civilized. Look at them now," she said, pointing at the two Tendu flickering blue and green as they leaped through the trees, the lighter gravity making it look as though they were flying. "Aren't they beautiful?"

It took the Xavieras a while to pick them out, but finally she saw Joao's face open in delighted recognition, and then Quang Nguyen saw them too. Juna watched them wistfully, longing to climb with them, but held down by her human responsibilities.

"I'm afraid that they'll be up there for a while," she said apologetically. "It's been a long time since they've been in an environment that was anything like their own."

Quang Nguyen smiled. "I understand. I feel much the same way when

I'm back in Vietnam. I'm glad we are able to make them happy. May I show you the rest of the compound?"

He gave her the grand tour, introducing her to various members of the family as they encountered them, making a particular effort to bring eligible bachelors to her attention.

"This is one of our retreats," he told Juna. "Most of the people here are on family leave or sabbatical. We encourage the members of our family to take long family leaves, and allow a two-year sabbatical once every seven years. After all, what is the point of having wealth if one does not have the time to enjoy it?"

Juna smiled but didn't comment, not really knowing what to say to this. She had never thought about what it would be like to be wealthy. The idea felt strange to her.

The clamor of children's voices came to her. They rounded a corner and were facing a schoolhouse with a large, well-equipped playground filled with children.

"This is our school," Quang Nguyen said. "It has just let out for the day."

"Surely these are not all your children!" Juna exclaimed.

He shook his head, his dark eyes alight with amusement. "No, most of them are from Copernicus City. We take as many of their best and brightest as we can, and we run a lottery, giving chances to the poorest thirty percent of the families. It gives us an interesting mix of students. Only about five percent of the students are actually family members."

"Sir, my shift is over," Joao said. "May I please be excused?"

"I'm sorry, Joao. Please run along."

"It's been a pleasure serving you, Dr. Saari. I liked meeting the Tendu."

"Thank you, Joao. Please feel free to come and visit us later, if you wish. I know Moki would like to get to know you better."

"Thank you, Dr. Saari!" Joao bowed and ran off.

"Mr. Xaviera, may I ask you a personal question?"

"Please, go ahead."

"I notice that your children work as servants. Why is this?"

"That is a very good question, my dear," he said, sitting down on a bench. "Employing our children as servants has been Xaviera family policy for several generations. We even emigrated from the Earth to the Moon in order to continue doing so.

"Many of our children will go on to run large organizations. We feel that it's important for them to learn to serve before they learn to rule. That way they do not take their privilege for granted. We are very strict with them during the years they are in service to the family. They must each work three days a week, and make up for the schooling that they miss. We have tutors to help them. They are paid what we would pay a regular servant. Half of this money goes into a fund that they receive when they reach majority. The other half is theirs to spend, save, or invest."

He smiled. "I invested most of my spending money in an older cousin's start-up company. We lost our shirts, but we learned a great deal from the experience. What we ask our children to do is both difficult and controversial, but I was raised that way, and I feel that it was a valuable experience. As a servant, I learned things that I never would have in school, things that served me well, and are still serving me well."

"You know," Juna said thoughtfully, "this is very similar to how the Tendu treat their bami. I assume that Moki would also be expected to serve?"

Quang Nguyen looked surprised. "We had not really thought about that."

"He is my adopted child," Juna pointed out.

"I apologize. How old is Moki?"

"There's no way to know for sure, but Ukatonen thinks he's about thirty-six Tendu-years-old, which would make him approximately thirty-three or thirty-four Earth-years-old."

Quang Nguyen raised his eyebrows in surprise.

"The Tendu mature very differently than we do," Juna explained. "In many ways, Moki is more independent than a human child. He would make a good servant. He is extremely obedient, and he already has many of the necessary skills. But," she continued, "he has a deeply stubborn streak. It does not show itself often, but when it does, he would rather die than give up.

"He nearly died twice," Juna recalled. "Once when he was trying to get me to become his sitik, and again when he tried to sneak on board our starship, so that he could go with me. Both times it was because he refused to give up."

"I see," Quang Nguyen remarked. There was a long silence.

"It's the Tendu, isn't it? That's why your family is interested in me."

"It would be counterproductive to lie," he said. "Humanity stands to gain a great deal from the Tendu. They stand to gain a great deal from us. An alliance would be very advantageous to our family, but I think you underrate yourself, my dear. You are young, intelligent, and beautiful. More importantly, you are strong and determined. You survived four difficult years among the Tendu. You brokered a most impressive treaty; and you have withstood and triumphed over some extremely powerful political pressure."

"I had help," Juna said. "Without the Tendu, I would have died on Tiangi. Some of the finest minds of both our people helped to forge that treaty. And Mr. Manning, and Analin Goudrian helped get us out of quarantine."

"But you stood at the center of all of those things, Juna. You helped make them happen," Quang Nguyen replied. "You have met my wife, Abeo. She possesses strength like yours. She is both the rock, and the river raging around it. That is why I cherish her as I do. That is why I proposed that we court you. A woman of your strength and vision would be an asset to our family, even without your ties to the Tendu."

"Still, this is a marriage for gain," Juna said with a shrug. "I'm not entirely comfortable with that."

Quang laid a gentle hand on her arm. "Juna, every marriage is for gain, else, why would we do it?"

"But I want to gain a family," Juna explained.

"And you will be," he said. "Tonight we will have a reception in your honor. Most of the rest of this branch of the family will be there, including all our unpaired men. Hopefully one of them will strike a spark in your heart. Please, give our family a chance, Juna. We would be honored to have you join us."

"All right," Juna said. Perhaps she would be drawn to someone at the reception. Belonging to a family like this certainly would have advantages—for the Tendu, for the child beneath her heart, and for herself. It would not be wise to turn away just yet.

He glanced at his watch. "I'm afraid that I must leave you to attend to some other duties. Please, feel free to wander wherever you like."

"Thank you, Quang Nguyen."

"You're welcome. I'll see you tonight." He turned and walked off across the compound.

Juna headed for the forest. She wandered through the woods on the neatly groomed, cleared path. It was good to be in the forest, alone. Up overhead, a bird called, a loud, sonorous call. Farther away, another bird replied. There were faint rustlings here and there in the foliage, as unseen animals fed or fought, or courted. She looked longingly up at the treetops, aching to be up in the hidden world of the canopy. Finally, she could stand it no longer. She stripped down to her bra and underwear, wrapping her clothes in a couple of broad green heliconia leaves, pinned together with twigs. She tied the package around her waist with several strands of vine and started climbing.

Juna climbed steadily until she reached the treetops. She found a sturdy branch and sat for a few minutes, admiring the glorious view. The trees stretched away to the edges of the dome, and beyond that was the sterile grey surface of the Moon. Beyond the dome overhead the crescent Earth hovered in the sky, against a background of brilliant, untwinkling stars. This would, indeed be a wonderful place for her and the Tendu to live.

On Tiangi, she would never have been able to sit in such a vulnerable spot. The sky belonged to the enormous raptors that patrolled the canopy, looking for any animal unwary enough to stick its head above the treetops. She had been attacked and nearly killed by one of the huge, soaring creatures as she sat in an exposed treetop.

After spending a long pleasant interval admiring the view, Juna climbed back down into the canopy, and called to the Tendu. She heard a pair of answering calls, and headed toward them.

Moki came swinging up to her, his skin rippling blue and pink with excitement. "It's wonderful! It's like home, only different. Everything is from Earth, like you!" he exclaimed.

"Yes, Moki, everything is from Earth, like me," Juna said, amused by his excitement.

Ukatonen leaped onto the branch, his skin azure with joy.

"It's good to be here," he said. "Moki's right, it is a great deal like home. Thank you for bringing us here."

"You're welcome," Juna said. "Have you looked above the trees yet?"

They shook their heads.

"There are no koirah here," she said. "It's safe. And the view is incredible."

She led them up into the clear, bright sunlight. "Look," she said. "Isn't it amazing?"

Slowly, tentatively, the Tendu looked around at the dark sky, the crescent Earth, the myriad pinpoint stars, the harsh sunlight.

"It's very strange," Ukatonen said. "It looks like night, but the sun—" He shook his head.

Moki's ears were spread wide as he looked around. "Is that Earth?" he said, pointing.

Juna nodded.

"Where's the rest of it?"

Juna was explaining about how part of the Earth was in shadow so that you couldn't see it, when a shuttle passed overhead. The two Tendu vanished into the canopy. Juna sighed sadly. Even here, in this safe place, their instinct to avoid high, exposed places was too strong.

Juna climbed down after them.

"It's all right," she said, when she found them several layers down, looking anxiously upward. "It's just a shuttle. Nothing to worry about."

"I understand," Ukatonen said, "but this is how the Tendu have managed to survive for so long. I have been avoiding the treetops for a thousand years or more. I cannot stop doing it now."

"I'm sorry," Juna said. "I shouldn't have asked this of you."

"It is a wonderful view, siti," Moki offered. "I'm sorry that we can't enjoy it as you do."

"It's all right, bai, you were very brave to go up there at all. So, why don't you show me the forest?" she suggested.

And so they spent the next several hours exploring the jungle. Juna was amazed at how quickly they adapted to this jungle, even though everything in it, including the gravity, was alien to them. Juna's watch chimed, reminding her that it was time to get ready for the evening's reception.

Ukatonen led her to a pool with a waterfall. She stripped naked and plunged in, washing away the dirt from her climb. Moki brought her clothes, and she sat on a warm rock, letting the sun dry her off while the other two splashed in the pool.

They're so happy here, Juna thought. *It's going to be hard for them to return to Snyder Station after this.* She sighed and got up and began putting on her clothes.

"Come on," she said. "There's a party we have to go to."

The Tendu followed her back to their rooms reluctantly. They watched as she hurriedly washed and dried her hair, combing it out into a tight Afro that clung to her head, emphasizing the planes of her face. She slipped into the purple-and-red evening dress that she'd bought for the trip and regarded herself in the mirror. The dress was all right, she decided. It harmonized with her rich brown skin, and maximized her bustline, which had filled out remarkably with her pregnancy. The gown's full skirt hid the slight potbelly of her pregnancy. It made her look smooth, elegant, and surprisingly young. She painted a little kohl around her eyes, dabbed on a little blusher and lipstick, and decided that she was ready.

There was a knock on the door. It was Yang. He gave her a beautiful spray of white tuberoses, which she pinned into her hair.

"You look lovely, Juna," he told her. "I'm honored to be seen with you. All the other men will be jealous."

Juna blushed. "Thank you, Yang," she said. "You're very kind."

He held out his arm, and she slipped her hand through it. They walked out together, the Tendu following behind them. The dome filters had been polarized, and the compound was dark. Night-blooming flowers poured their fragrance into the warm air. Cicadas chirred away, filling the air with a curtain of shimmering sound.

"It's a beautiful night," Juna said.

"Thank you," Yang responded. "We've done our best to make it so."

Juna gave him a sidelong glance. He seemed to see nothing unusual in his remark, but it reminded her of the enormous power that this family took for granted.

"Yes, I suppose you have," she said, her face carefully neutral.

"Here we are," he said, opening a door and ushering her and the Tendu into a large, elegant room filled with people. Quang Nguyen and his wife greeted Juna, guiding her to a comfortable sofa. Children dressed in house livery brought her appetizers, which she accepted gratefully. All that exploring had made her hungry. Another child-servant slipped up to her and took her drink order.

"Dinner will be served in about forty-five minutes," Quang Nguyen told her.

"Thank you," she said. "The Tendu and I were so busy exploring your lovely rain forest that we forgot to eat."

"Would you like to meet our head ecologist?" he asked.

"Yes, I would," Juna replied.

"I'll go get him," he said.

While he was gone, Juna sat back and watched the glittering crowd dressed in beautifully tailored silks, and adorned with gold and precious gems from the family's mines here on the Moon. The name of this place, Jóia da Lua, memorialized the gemstones that were this family's initial source of wealth. She felt plain and out of place amongst all this opulence.

Quang's wife, Abeo, came up with a handsome Asian man on her arm. "Juna, this is Hideo Tanaka Xaviera, one of my fleet captains. He's asked to meet you."

"I am honored to make your acquaintance, Tanaka-san."

"I am honored to meet you, as well, Dr. Saari. Please, tell me about Tiangi. What was it like?"

Juna smiled reminiscently. "Like Earth, but greener. It was beautiful in a way that Earth has not been for many centuries. But dangerous too. I spent a great deal of my time trying not to get eaten or fall out of a tree."

Just then Quang Nguyen brought over the ecologist, and then several other men were introduced to Juna. She was soon caught up in a whirl of introductions and flirting. Everyone, it seemed, had a man to introduce to Juna. At one point, she was formally introduced to a man by a four-year-old girl, who turned out to be his niece. She barely had a chance to talk to the two Tendu, who were surrounded by their own coterie of admirers.

The party went on until well past three o'clock. Juna tiptoed into her room careful not to wake the sleeping Tendu, slid out of her dress, and climbed into bed, tired, but still too excited to sleep. She had never been the center of so much masculine attention before. It was a heady experience. She lay in the darkness, looking up at the ceiling, and thinking over the evening.

While the attention paid her was flattering, she was not really drawn to any particular man. Yang was familiar, but his smooth, withdrawn nature didn't attract her. She had the most in common with the ecologist, Jacques Quanh Xaviera, and had agreed to tour the forest with him and the Tendu the next day. Jacques had been in the Survey, but had retired to take over the management of the Xavieras' various preserves.

"We've preserved so many rare and endangered species. Some day, we'll be able to reintroduce them back into the wild," he'd told her. "And I was ready to settle down. I knew I could make a difference here."

Juna rolled over onto her side and pulled the pillow down a bit. Jacques seemed nice enough, but there was no spark there either. She had met a lot of men tonight. Perhaps in a few days, when she got to know some of them better, she would feel attracted by one of the Xavieras.

And if not, what then? She rolled over onto her back and stared up at the shadowy ceiling again. The Tendu did love it here, and it would be a wonderful place for her child. . . .

"Siti?" Moki said. "Why are you alone? I thought you would have found someone to mate with."

Juna sat up. Moki was standing on the doorway. "This isn't like Tiangi, Moki. I'm not just looking for someone to fertilize my eggs." She patted her stomach. "It's a little late for that. I'm looking for someone I can fall in love with."

"Why?"

"For as long as there have been human poets, philosophers, and lovers, they have been trying to answer that very question. I guess the best answer is that I would be happier in a marriage where there were bonds of love. It's a tie that binds people together. It's like allu-a in that way."

"And what if you don't fall in love with any of the Xavieras?"

Juna looked down at the rumpled sheets. "That was just what I was trying to decide, Moki. If it were as simple as finding a place where you and Ukatonen could both be happy, then I would marry the Xavieras. But the Xavieras are a rich and powerful family. They want access to the Tendu. There are good things and bad things about that. We would gain powerful protectors, but"— she held up her hands in a gesture of helplessness— "they would expect favors in return. Those may not be things that would be good for the Tendu."

"Then we should not tie ourselves to them," Ukatonen said from the doorway. He spoke in skin speech, his words glowing in the shadowy room.

"Even when they can provide you with a rain forest to live in?" Juna asked.

"I did not come here to live in a rain forest, Eerin," he told her. "I can do that on Tiangi. I came here to learn about your people, and I have learned a great deal. For instance," he said, still in skin speech, "they have listening devices in these rooms. They can hear everything you say aloud."

Juna covered her mouth, horrified. Had she said anything she would regret them overhearing?

"I overheard Abeo and another woman discussing it," the enkar explained.

Juna turned on a light, and found a pad of paper. "Did they see you?" she asked, sketching the skin speech symbols on the paper. The glyphs would be completely incomprehensible to the Xavieras, even if they had video cameras installed.

"I don't think so. I was standing outside, near an open window," Ukatonen said in skin speech.

"What else did they say?" Juna wrote.

"Abeo asked if the microphone in our rooms was working. The other woman said that it was, and that they could hear us perfectly, but that so far you'd said nothing of interest. Then they started speculating about which of the men you would choose. Quang Nguyen wants you to settle on Yang, but Abeo wants him to marry someone else. The other woman thought you would go for the ecologist."

"Thank you for telling me this," Juna wrote. "I will not be marrying these people. We can discuss it tomorrow, out in the jungle."

She yawned, and said aloud, "God, it's late! I should get some sleep."

"Good night Eerin," Ukatonen said. "Come, Moki, let's go to bed. Sleep well."

Now that her decision was made, the rest of Juna's time among the Xavieras felt almost like a vacation. She flirted with the men, explored the rain forest with the Tendu and Jacques, got to know the women, and played with the children. Despite their eavesdropping, Juna liked the Xavieras. They were witty, personable, and very intelligent. At times, she even regretted the fact that she had to refuse their proposal, but nothing happened to change her mind.

She and the Tendu spoke only of inconsequential things in their suite, reserving any serious discussion for the time they spent up in the canopy, where Juna was reasonably certain they could neither be seen nor heard.

On the evening of the last day of their visit, Quang Nguyen, Abeo, and their son Yang invited her and the Tendu for a quiet farewell dinner. Just before dinner, Yang handed her a small, exquisitely crafted wooden box.

"For you," he explained, "a courting present. The wood is from our forest."

"Thank you," Juna said, her voice hushed in admiration. "It's beautiful."

"Here, let me show you how it opens." He slid aside an invisible panel, releasing the lid. "There," he said, handing it to her.

She opened it. Inside, cradled on deep green velvet, was a beautifully worked golden brooch, made in the shape of a Tendu, the red stripes along its back picked out in tiny rubies, its eyes made of emeralds. The workmanship was exquisite. The Tendu seemed almost alive. Juna glanced up and saw a flicker of amusement flash across Moki's body, and she fought back a flush of embarrassment. It was exactly the color of a Tendu in heat.

"I can't accept this," Juna said. "It's too much!"

Quang Nguyen folded her hands around their gift.

"Please," he said. "You are a remarkable woman. This is a barely adequate tribute to all you have done. We wished to thank you for the honor you have done us in considering our proposal of marriage."

If he were Yang's age, and unpaired, Juna realized, it would have been much harder to refuse the Xavieras' proposal. She looked up and saw Abeo's eyes on her, and realized that Abeo knew this too. The knowledge chilled her.

"Thank you, Quang Nguyen," Juna said. "You honor me with this gift."

Just then a little girl in a white uniform came out and rang a dinner gong, rescuing Juna from this awkward conversation.

"Dinner is served," she announced, and the thick tension of the moment evaporated.

Conversation over dinner was light and inconsequential.

"So," Quang Nguyen said, as the children served dessert and poured tea into translucent porcelain cups. "Have you decided whether you will you do our family the honor of marrying us?"

"Yes, Quang Nguyen, I have," Juna replied. Her hands were sweaty with nervousness. "Though I am deeply honored by your proposal, I am sorry to say that I must refuse your offer."

A light seemed to go out of Quang Nguyen's eyes. His visible disappointment surprised Juna. "I am very sorry to hear that, Juna. May I ask why?"

"Someone placed a listening device in my room," she said.

Quang Nguyen's eyes flicked to Abeo and back again, so swiftly that if Juna hadn't been looking for it, she might have missed it.

"On behalf of the entire family, I apologize for this insult." His eyes were hard and bright with anger, and Juna realized that he could be a formidable adversary.

"It wasn't just the microphone," Juna told him. "There are other reasons as well. The Tendu and I must remain as neutral as possible. Tying myself to your family would interfere with that neutrality. And I prefer a marriage of affection to one of convenience. It is possible that I might have found someone to pair with, but—" She shrugged. "Were the circumstances different, I would have accepted your offer, but if the circumstances were different, I think the offer would never have been made."

"Dr. Saari," Abeo said, "I appreciate your tact in not mentioning my role in this, but it is not necessary. I like you, Juna Saari, and I'm truly sorry that this has come between us. But the Xavieras are a wealthy and powerful family, and we have enemies. I wished to keep my family safe. If you would like, we will destroy the recordings before your eyes. There is nothing particularly revealing on them."

"That will not be necessary," Juna told her. She admired Abeo, despite the invasion of their privacy. She, too, was sorry that this had come between them.

"I am most sorry that you cannot accept our offer," Quang Nguyen said. "Despite this unfortunate incident, I hope you will consider our family as your friends. If there is ever anything that we can do for you, please ask, and if it will not harm our interests, we will do it."

"Thank you, Quang Nguyen," Juna replied. "Your friendship does us honor."

He laid a hand on her arm. "Juna," he said, "I want you to understand something. We are not attempting to set up a quid pro quo arrangement here. We are asking for something much deeper. The Tendu have much to give humanity, but there are powerful forces allied against you. They are afraid of the challenge and the changes that the Tendu bring with them. The Xaviera family does not want these people to succeed, and we are willing to commit our resources to stopping them. Do you understand?"

She looked into his dark, almond-shaped eyes. She could see only truth there. "Yes, Quang Nguyen, I do."

"The Tendu will remember that you have offered your help," Ukatonen declared.

"Thank you, Ukatonen," Quang Nguyen said. "We are grateful."

Ukatonen inclined his head graciously. It was a gesture he had learned from Quang Nguyen, but it fit him well.

"We have been trying to visit Earth," Ukatonen said, "but we cannot get permission. Is this something that the Xavieras can help us with?"

"I will see to this," Abeo volunteered. "I'll will put Raoul on it. He enjoys this kind of thing," she told her husband.

"Thank you, Abeo," Juna said. "We appreciate it."

"I will tell Raoul to hurry," Abeo went on. "In a few months, your pregnancy will interfere with your ability to travel. And you should have time to spend with your child when it's born."

Her dark face lit up with a fond smile. "Having a baby is such a pleasure, especially the first time. Don't let anyone or anything come between you and that baby for the first six months, longer if you can possibly manage it."

Juna nodded. "Don't worry, I'm taking my full child-leave. The rest of the world can go hang."

Ukatonen walked with Eerin and their security detail down the hall to their meeting with the hospital staff. He thought of the Xavieras' compound and a faint mist of regret clouded his skin. It was too bad that they could not stay there, but Eerin was right. Despite the powerful inducements that the Xavieras had to offer, they could not tie themselves to so powerful a family. Still, he was tired of this cold, dry station, and the continual presence of security escorts. They kept him from meeting people, and learning what they thought, which was an important part of an enkar's work. He hoped that Eerin could figure out a way to rid themselves of their escort.

Dr. Andraia met them at the door to the conference room.

"Welcome back," he said, as he opened the door for them. "We missed you."

"Thank you," Ukatonen said.

He waited while the humans settled down and the meeting got underway.

"Because of the security problems we've been having," Dr. Andraia began, "we need to make some changes. We've made arrangements for you to be quartered here at the hospital. We're doubling your security escort, for additional protection."

Ukatonen let a private flicker of irritation fork down one leg, where it could not be seen.

"Why do we need so much security?" he asked.

"We're afraid that you might get hurt. Someone might try to kidnap you, or hold you hostage," Dr. Andraia replied.

Ukatonen looked at Eerin, ears spread wide.

"He means that someone might catch you and try to keep you against your will," she explained.

"Like taming an animal?" Moki asked.

Eerin shook her head. "No, they want to keep you because you're valuable, because they think they can get things from the government by threatening to harm you."

"Or someone might simply want to kill you," Dr. Andraia put in. "The hospital has already received a number of death threats against you."

Ukatonen was puzzled. "Why would they try to do such a thing? Have I harmed anyone without realizing it?"

"By coming here and healing the sick and injured, you have given people who had no hope a chance at a miracle. But it is a very scarce miracle. You can only heal a fraction of the people who need it. That is what makes you so valuable as a hostage," Dr. Andraia explained. "Dying people are desperate people, and some of them will resort to violence in order to get your help."

"I don't understand," Ukatonen said.

"You're doing things that are completely beyond our medical capabilities. That is what makes you so valuable, and why we need the security guards to protect you."

"I see," Ukatonen said. "So, Eerin, Moki, and I need security escorts because we are changing your world by healing people, yes?"

"I'm afraid so, Ukatonen," Dr. Andraia agreed.

"I see," Ukatonen said once again. "Then we have violated Contact Protocols by healing people. I must think about the implications of this." He rose and walked out of the meeting, ignoring the doctors' attempts to call him back. Eerin and Moki scrambled to follow him.

He said nothing as they were shown to their new quarters. He remembered the man who had grabbed his arm and begged him to heal his wife. He should have wondered why this human was acting so desperate, but he had been so eager to get to Earth, to set foot on a real world, that he had forgotten all about the Contact Protocols. He had violated his own judgment, dishonoring himself and casting doubt on all of the other enkar. There was only one honorable way out.

"En, tell me what you're thinking," Eerin asked when they had reached the privacy of their quarters.

"I had hoped that healing those people and working with the doctors would help us get to Earth. I let my desire to go to Earth cloud my sight." He paused, the deep brown of his shame clouded by grey regret. "I have failed in my judgment as an enkar. The only honorable thing for me to do is to die."

"You can't die, en," Eerin told him. "We need you, Moki needs you."

"It is a question of honor," he said with a shrug.

"How are we going to explain your death to the Tendu?"

"The enkar will understand," Ukatonen told her.

"And my people," she said. "What about them? What do you think they'll do when you commit suicide? They'll slap a Non-Contact order on Tiangi. It'll be impossible for Moki. Either he'll be sent home without me and die, or have to stay here with me and never see another Tendu for as long as he lives. Yes, you tampered with the protocols, but that's my fault as much as yours. I was the one who should have taken the protocols into account, not you."

"Why didn't you?" Ukatonen demanded.

Eerin looked down, her dark skin reddening slightly with embarrassment. She lifted her hands in a gesture of helplessness. "I wanted to do something that would show my people what you were capable of. I wanted them to understand how much they had to gain from the Tendu." She shook her head ruefully. "I succeeded too well, I'm afraid. But," she said, looking up at Ukatonen, "the point is that this is not your mistake. It is mine."

"But I am an enkar. I should have seen this."

"Ukatonen," Eerin said, "you became an enkar because you knew your people and your world inside and out. You spent years in training, acquiring knowledge that the Tendu had gathered over many millenia. Humans are something completely new and strange to your people. We don't work by your rules. There's no reason for your judgment to be perfect. We humans survive and learn from our mistakes. So should you, Ukatonen."

Ukatonen felt the first stirrings of doubt. He looked away, not wanting to hear any more. He was afraid she was right, and that made him feel like he'd been covered in dung. He was caught between his honor and his duty.

Moki touched his shoulder. "I need you to show me what it means to be a Tendu, every bit as much as I need my sitik to show me what it means to be human. What good will I be to our people if I am too much a stranger to them? Eerin is right, en. We must take what we learn back to our people. What you have learned is more important than your honor. Dying before you pass along what you have learned to the other Tendu would be selfish."

The disadvantage to sound speech, Ukatonen realized, was that you had to listen to it. With skin speech, you could look away and not see it. A flicker of regret passed over his body, and he reached out and touched Moki affectionately on the shoulder.

"It is not often that a bami has something to teach an enkar," Ukatonen said in skin speech, taking care to keep the colors of his words soft and gentle.

"Forgive me, en."

The black bars of negation flickered over his skin. "Being right does not require forgiveness, Moki."

"Then you are not going to kill yourself?" Eerin asked.

Ukatonen shook his head. "Not now." He found himself turning the idea of living over in his mind, and discovered that he was relieved at the prospect.

Eerin let out an explosive sigh and relaxed. "Thank god," she said. "You really scared me."

"I know," Ukatonen said.

"What now?" Eerin asked.

"I haven't thought that far yet," Ukatonen confessed, brown with embarrassment. "I was too busy dying."

"I think—" Eerin began.

Ukatonen looked up at her questioningly.

"I think we should stop healing people," she finished. "We've shown what the Tendu are capable of, and that's enough for now. The problem is how to break the news. We'll need to speak to Analin about that."

Ukatonen stood looking out a hospital window at the garden below, letting the small patch of green refresh his eyes and his spirit. This was their last day at Snyder Hospital. They were meeting with the doctors on their team to discuss the best therapies for the people he and Moki had been healing.

He had learned a great deal in this place, but little of it was what he'd expected. A grey cloud of sadness passed over his skin as he turned away from the window. He could do so much good here, but now was not the time to do it. Later, perhaps, when humans and Tendu were more in harmony.

"Our security escort is waiting," Eerin said. "Are you ready to go?"

Ukatonen nodded and turned to follow her down the long hallway.

Suddenly a man darted out of one of the rooms and pulled Eerin inside. He pressed a scalpel against her throat.

"That's my daughter in the bed there," he said, "and you're going to heal her, or"— he pulled Eerin's head a little further back—"I'll slit her throat."

"I don't understand," Ukatonen said, puzzled and frightened. "Why are you doing this?"

"My daughter's dying."

"I see," he said. "You want me to heal her. And if I do not?"

"Then I kill the woman."

Ukatonen glanced over at Moki, whose skin was a roiling turmoil of red and orange. He reached out and touched the bami. "It's going to be all right, Moki," he said aloud. Meanwhile, in skin speech he was saying, "I'm going to try to get you close to the man. If you get a chance, grab his knife hand and pull it away, and sting him unconscious." Ukatonen saw Eerin's eyes widen fractionally as he said this, and knew that she would be ready when the chance came.

"Moki's very scared," he told the man. "I'm afraid of what he might do. It would be best if you let him stand near Dr. Saari. She's his adopted mother, and he will be calmer when he's near her."

"Please, sir, don't hurt my mother," Moki said, in a frightened child's voice. Ukatonen flickered approval; clearly Moki knew what he was doing.

"He's only a child," Ukatonen said. "It will make it easier for me to heal your daughter if he's kept out of the way."

"Ukatonen, what's happening? Why is that man scaring my mommy?" Moki asked, an almost human quaver in his voice.

The man's eyes traveled from Ukatonen to Moki to the security escorts clustered around the door, weapons bristling, and then back to Moki again.

"All right," he said, after a long, dangerous silence. "He can come and stand between me and the door. That way if the security people try shooting me, the bullet will have to go through him and his mother first."

"Perhaps we would all feel calmer if the guards backed away from the door," Ukatonen suggested.

The man nodded. "Do what he says. Get away from the door."

The security guards backed away, and Ukatonen was relieved when the man instantly became calmer. This was like taming an animal. The more cornered the animal felt, the harder it was to get him to calm down.

"What's wrong with your daughter?"

"Leukemia. Like that little boy you healed. Carlo."

It had been Moki who healed the little boy, Ukatonen recalled, but that was all right. It meant that the man was underestimating Moki.

"I remember that," Ukatonen said. "I'll need to touch your daughter in order to heal her."

The man hesitated for a moment. "All right, but if anything happens to her, the woman dies."

"I will not hurt your daughter," the enkar promised.

He stepped over to the bed. The little girl lying there was pale, and there were dark shadows under her eyes. Her eyes darted between her father and the door, quick nervous glances that were the only sign of her fear. "Hello, my name is Ukatonen. What's yours?"

She looked over at her father for a second. He nodded.

"I'm Sarah. Are they going to hurt my father?"

"I don't know, Sarah," Ukatonen said. "He must love you very much to do this. Are you scared?"

She hesitated a moment, then nodded.

"So am I, a little bit, but right now I'm going to try to make you better. Do you want to get better, Sarah?"

Sarah's eyes went to her father and then back to Ukatonen. "Yes, please," she replied in a voice barely above a whisper.

"All right, then," he said. "I'm going to hold your arm like this," he said, taking her arm. "It will sting a little, like a shot, and then you'll go to sleep. I'll be inside you then, and I'll find out where you're sick and make it better. All right?"

Sarah nodded. "What about my dad?"

Ukatonen glanced over at the child's father. He was watching them intently, Moki was apparently forgotten.

"We'll worry about that later."

Ukatonen linked with the child. He could feel the wrongness inside her as soon as he linked. The cancer was very bad. He cleared out what he could of the immediate damage, and left killer cells behind to eliminate the rest of the cancer. He paused, looking over his work. It was good. The girl would seem to go into a gradual spontaneous remission.

Finished, Ukatonen pulled out of the link, leaving his eyes hooded and his body relaxed, as though he were still linked. He glanced sidelong at the child's father. He was completely ignoring Moki, and his arm had relaxed a little. The sharp blade had fallen slightly away from Eerin's throat.

"Now, Moki!" Ukatonen signed in skin speech.

Moki moved with reflexes honed by a lifetime of being both predator and prey. He pulled the knife away from Eerin's neck, and stung him asleep almost before the man knew what had happened.

Security came rushing in, taking the man into custody.

"Wait!" Ukatonen commanded as they started to haul the sleeping man away.

To his surprise, the security people halted.

"Let me wake him up so he can say goodbye to his daughter."

They looked at Eerin, who nodded, and they let Ukatonen sting him awake.

He looked blearily up at Ukatonen. "How is she?" he asked.

"Your daughter was very sick," Ukatonen told him. "I've done what I could, but"— he paused. "I don't know if it was enough. I can wake her so that you can say goodbye, if you'd like."

"No," the man said, shaking his head. "I don't want her to see me like this. Tell her I love her, and that I'm proud of her." He looked at Eerin, "I-I'm sorry to have scared you, but"— he glanced at his daughter sleeping in the bed—"she's all we have. I couldn't let her die."

"I understand," Eerin said. "But if Moki or Ukatonen had gotten hurt—" She turned away, anger on her face.

The man looked down, "I'm sorry," he said. He looked up at the security guards and nodded. They led him away.

"What will happen to him?" Moki asked.

"He'll be put in jail, like I was," Eerin told him. "But he'll have to stay there for a long, long time. His daughter Sarah will be an adult before they let him out." She looked away for a moment. "He gave up the chance to watch her grow up, in order to know that she would."

"Why doesn't he kill himself?" Ukatonen asked.

"That's a difficult question to answer, Ukatonen," Eerin replied. "In some cultures he might. In others, he would be tried and killed. Here, he will be expected to serve a long prison sentence at a penal colony far from his family. Eventually, he will be released and be free again. We think of that as punishment enough."

"Doesn't he have any honor?" Ukatonen asked, thinking of his own painful decision to keep living. He wished he could link with the man, and understand why he had done this. Perhaps he would never understand humans; perhaps harmony with them was impossible. He turned away from the thought. His spirit was already weighed down by despair. He couldn't deal with any more of it.

"It is not so simple as that, Ukatonen. Even if he wanted to commit suicide, he would be stopped by the prison guards. Many of our religions prohibit suicide."

"Every time I think I understand you humans, you surprise me," Ukatonen said, purple with puzzlement.

Eerin grinned at him. "That's okay. We surprise ourselves all the time, too. Come on, let's get out of here."

* * *

Juna stood at the window of her bedroom, looking out over the rows of vines, their gnarled trunks obscured by tangles of last season's canes. Midwinter was a quiet time on the farm. Most of the work went on in the vast vaulted cellars, racking and aging the wine in huge oak barrels, bottling the mature vintages. Juna felt like one of those barrels, waiting here with the baby maturing inside her. It was good to come home again and rest after their demanding work at the hospital.

Just then the baby stirred inside her. She smiled and put her hand on her abdomen. She had first felt the baby move the day before, when they were descending in the elevator from the shuttle dock to the terminal. At first she thought it was some internal shifting caused by the increasing gravity. But the little flutters and sudden shifts had continued at odd times ever since. The movement of the baby thrilled her, but it also reminded her of how little time she had before the baby arrived. She was starting to show. In another month, it would be time for maternity clothes. And she had done nothing about getting married since her visit to the Xavieras. She dreaded the task of looking for a family to marry into, but she was going to have to face it soon.

There was a knock on the door.

It was Toivo. "*Hei*, Juna, look! I walked all the way over here!"

"Oh, Toivo, that's great! I'm so pleased!"

He flopped into a chair with a tired sigh. "Dr. Engle says that if I keep improving at this pace, I'll be able to help with spring planting."

"That's good," she said. "I'll be so pregnant by then that I won't be any use at all."

"You can be our fertility goddess," he said, teasing her.

Juna looked down at a pale square of wintry sunlight on the floor. "Oh, Toivo, what am I going to do?"

"I thought you were planning to go to Earth with the Tendu."

"Yes," Juna said, not taking her eyes off the carpet, "we are. But that's not what I'm worried about. If I don't get married, they'll take the baby away. I should be looking, but frankly, I haven't a clue about how or where to start."

The patch of sunlight blurred as tears clouded her vision.

"That's what I came over here to talk to you about," Toivo said, resting a comforting hand on her shoulder. "I've talked it over with the rest of the Fortunatis, and we were hoping that you would marry us. I know it's not a romantic match, but we all love and care about you, and we're fond of the Tendu, too."

Juna stared at him for a long moment, blinking in surprise. Then she burst out laughing.

"It's not a joke, Juna," Toivo said. "We're serious."

She got control of herself. "I know you are," she said, wiping tears of hysterical laughter out of her eyes. "It's just— Well, it isn't every day that I get proposed to by my own brother."

"Come on, Juna, it isn't like that."

"I know, Toivo, but it *is* funny."

"I guess so, but it's not that unusual. There are lots of group marriages with sibs in them."

"What about *Isi* and Netta *Täti*? Have you talked to them about this?"

"*Isi* thinks it's a good idea. He said that if you would marry into the Fortunati group, he will too. That way the vineyard would stay in the family."

"And Netta?"

"Well, she isn't as keen on it as *Isi*, but she understands. Anetta wants you to be happy, Juna. If this solution brings you happiness, then she approves."

"I need to talk this over with the Tendu."

Toivo nodded.

"How does the family feel about them?"

"The kids are all excited about having Moki around, and Selena practically worships the ground that Ukatonen walks on. The rest are fond of Moki and impressed by Ukatonen. The important thing is that they all want you, Juna. They trust you, and they're willing to trust the Tendu."

"Can you give us a day or two to think about it?"

"Take all the time you need, Juna. There's no rush. As far as the Fortunati are concerned, the wedding is just a formality. You're already part of the family."

"It seems like a good solution for everyone," Ukatonen said, after Juna told him about the proposal. "You would be marrying into a family that cares about you. The family likes Moki, and you've said that they trust me. What other problems are there?"

"I'm marrying into my brother's family, for one."

"I thought you said that sibs often married into the same group marriage."

"Yes, but it's usually a pair of brothers, or a pair of sisters. It's much less common for a brother and a sister to enter into the same group marriage." She shook her head. "If we weren't well known, then it wouldn't matter much. A few of the neighbors might gossip, but that would be it. Because we're famous, it'll make the top screen on Net News."

"I don't understand," Moki said. "What's wrong with brothers and sisters marrying?"

"A taboo against close relatives marrying is how we have traditionally prevented inbreeding."

"I wondered how humans prevented this. Our offspring are so widely scattered that inbreeding is highly unlikely."

"Let others talk. This is what is good for you and your daughter, and you should do it," Ukatonen advised. "As an enkar, I cannot be formally joined to your brother's family, but I am honored that they trust me enough to let me live with you."

"Moki?" Juna asked. "How do you feel about it?"

"It will be great to live with Danan and Toivo, and everyone else!" he said enthusiastically. "But won't Anetta and Teuvo be lonely?"

"We'll see them all the time," Juna assured him. "They'll be all right. Isi is going to marry into the Fortunati family also. And Aunt Anetta understands."

"If it's all right with them, then I want to do it," Moki said.

"Then it's settled. Let's go over to the Fortunati's and tell them that we'll marry them," Juna said. She felt an immense sense of relief wash over her with these words. She was going to be able to keep her daughter.

"I don't know, the lavender is too washed out, and the red is just a little too bright for a wedding gown," Juna remarked to Selena as they looked through a slate full of wedding catalogs. They had been looking through the catalogs for over a week, and still hadn't settled on a dress.

Just then the comm chimed. Juna recognized the ring. It was for her. She set the reading slate down and got up to answer it.

It was Abeo Xaviera. "It's good to see you again, Juna," she said. "I have good news. Raoul tells me that the Survey has arranged for you and the Tendu to go to Earth."

Juna's throat tightened in sudden excitement. Somehow the Xavieras had done it! They were going to Earth!

"That's wonderful news! When?"

"In about six weeks."

"Um," Juna said, glancing over at Selena on the couch. She had hoped for a longer honeymoon. "I'm getting married in about a month."

"So I hear," Abeo said. "I wanted to congratulate you and wish you every happiness."

Juna blushed. She kept forgetting that her life was headline news. "Thank you," she said.

Abeo shrugged. "It was not only my doing. Ukatonen and Moki's work at Snyder Hospital made the diplomats realize what they had. It didn't take much leverage to get the door open after that. It was merely a matter of speeding up what was already in the works."

"Well, thank you for whatever you did, and please thank Raoul for me as well. I wish the Tendu were here so that they could thank you too."

"You are most welcome, Juna. I was glad to have so easily paid the debt my family owed you."

"Easy for you, not for us," Juna said.

"Ah, yes. That is the seed from which commerce grows, is it not?"

Juna nodded.

"I was glad to have been of service. Please pass our family's greetings on to the Tendu."

"I will, and please pass ours along to your family. We would be honored if you came to our wedding."

Abeo inclined her head graciously. "Thank you, Juna. I shall see if Quang and I can make it. Your new family is fortunate indeed to be acquiring such a gifted new wife," she said. "I will leave you to your wedding plans. You have a great deal to do in a very short time."

"Goodbye, Abeo, and thank you," Juna said. She was coming to like Abeo, she realized, though she was grateful that she was not one of her co-wives.

The screen went blank, and Juna looked up. Selena was staring at her openly.

"Was that—?" she asked.

"Abeo Xaviera," Juna finished for her. "Yes, it was. She owed me a favor."

"She owed you a favor. Abeo Xaviera owed you a favor." Selena sounded stunned.

"The Xavieras courted me, very briefly," Juna explained. "It didn't work out. They felt that they owed me a favor because of it."

"You were courted by the Xavieras," Selena repeated incredulously.

"Didn't Toivo tell you? That's where we went after the news of the Tendu's healings broke."

"You turned them down?" Selena said, still amazed.

"Selena, the Xavieras wanted access to the Tendu. So I turned them down. It wouldn't have been good for either the Tendu or me. I know I'll be happier here with you. You've always been family, and that's what I want."

Selena lifted her chin toward the comm unit. "She sounded disappointed that you didn't marry them, and I don't blame her. I don't think I've told you how glad I am that you're joining our family. I've always admired you, Juna. You're so strong-willed and determined."

Juna let out a short, derisive laugh. "That's what ended my first marriage. I didn't want to stay home and mind the children."

"They were fools," Selena said. "They didn't know what they had. You would have come home when it was time and you were ready. Meanwhile, you were learning things that were worth passing on. You'd have come home with wonderful things to teach the children. Well, their loss is our gain. I'm looking forward to having you as a co-wife."

"And the Tendu?" Juna asked.

"Them too," she said. "Moki's taught Danan a lot, and Ukatonen—" She paused and smiled. "He's got a lot to teach all of us. I like him."

"I used to be jealous of the Fortunati," Juna said, "especially after my first marriage didn't work out. I wanted to belong to a marriage as happy as yours. Now—" She shrugged. "Suddenly I've gotten what I wished for, and I'm scared, a little bit. I'm afraid it won't work out, or I'll bring trouble to your house." She blinked away the unshed tears pricking at the back of her eyelids. "I love you all so much, Selena. I don't want that to happen."

Selena hugged her, "Oh, Juna, trouble comes to everyone—we know that. We're willing to share in your troubles every bit as much as we will share in your joys. That's what family is all about. Besides," she continued as Juna started to interrupt, "it's not like we don't know you. This marriage formalizes a relationship that's been there for years. You've been family since Toivo married us. We know what we're getting into, Juna."

"You're sure?" Juna asked.

Selena laughed. "We're sure." She picked up the reading slate and pressed the wake-up switch. "Now we've settled that, let's get back to picking out a dress for the wedding."

Moki waited with Danan and the other Fortunati children for the ceremony to begin. They were supposed to walk down the aisles, strewing fragrant flowers and herbs for their elders to walk on, in order to make their elders' passage through life sweet. Today they were joining the Fortunati family. It was like becoming part of a village. The whole thing puzzled Moki. One did not become part of a village; one simply was part of a village. The village, through its elders, chose the bami. Tinka, when they came to a village, were merely looking for a place where they could be safe. One either fought for and won a place among the village tinka, or one stayed in the forest and was eaten. There was no choice there.

Humans had so many choices to make. What kind of marriage to have, who to marry, where to live, what kind of work to do, whether to have children, and how to marry. The list went on and on. He wondered how they managed with all those choices. On Tiangi, obligation and tradition replaced choice. It made life much simpler.

The music started, and Moki followed Danan down the aisle, strewing herbs. Quang, Abeo, and Yang Xaviera nodded at him as he passed their chairs. He nodded back, and they smiled at him as he passed. Dr. Engle caught his eye and winked at him.

Then they reached the center of the circle of chairs. Moki followed the other children as they strewed herbs in the circle. The smell of the pungent herbs crushed underfoot made his eyes water, but it didn't bother the humans at all. At last the music stopped and he sat down, quickly flicking his nictitating membranes across his eyes to clear them.

Then a new tune, slower, and more solemn began, and everyone stood as Niccolo Fortunati, the family Eldest, came out on the arm of the priest. They walked slowly to a small raised dais in the center of the circle and waited as the rest of the family strode down the four aisles leading to the center and stood in a semicircle behind Niccolo and the priest.

The music changed again, becoming louder and more triumphant.

Toivo and Eerin walked down the aisle, followed by Selena and Teuvo, with Anetta bringing up the rear. Eerin looked beautiful in her dark green gown. She glanced at Moki nervously as she entered the central ring with Toivo, and Moki turned dark blue in reassurance. She smiled at him, and her nervousness seemed to vanish.

They stood before the Eldest and the priest. The music stopped and there was a moment of stillness.

"Welcome, friends and family, to this celebration of joining," the priest said. "Today, we witness not just the joining of one person to a new family, but the merging of two families. Today we come to join the Saari family and the Fortunati family. You, their friends and their neighbors, are here to witness this joining. You have watched these two families strive and struggle to build new lives here on Berry Station. You've watched their triumphs and their tragedies as they have done so. You've welcomed their children into the world, and comforted them when a beloved one has died. Now you are here to see them begin a new stage in their lives together. Thank you for coming to support their joining.

"Juna Saari, do you come to this joining of your own free will, without coercion?" the priest asked

"Yes, I do," Eerin replied.

"Toivo Saari Fortunati and Selena Anderson Fortunati, do you represent your family in this joining?"

"Yes, we do," Selena and Toivo said.

"And you and your family come to this joining of your own free will?"

"We do."

"Juna Saari, do you join yourself to this family to give aid and comfort in times of trouble, to share your joys, and to strive for peace and harmony within your family and in the world at large?"

"I do," Eerin replied.

"And will you raise your children in common with theirs?"

Eerin glanced over at Moki, eyebrows raised in a silent question. They had discussed this before the wedding. The other adults in the Fortunati family would be able to tell him what to do. It was like any Tendu village, and was what he had expected. He nodded.

Eerin looked back at the priest. "I do," she said.

*   *   *

Juna watched as her father repeated the wedding vows, relieved that her part was over. She looked over at Moki and Ukatonen. Happiness and approval danced across their skins. The baby shifted gently within her, as though it approved too.

Her father said the last of the vows. The priest touched Teuvo's forehead with scented oil, and then she took both their hands and placed them in the hands of the Eldest.

"I now pronounce you joined," the priest said.

Niccolo Fortunati kissed Teuvo formally on each cheek, and then kissed Juna on the forehead.

"Welcome to the family," he said, beaming happily at them.

There was a ripple of applause from the wedding guests.

The priest held her hands up for silence. "This ceremony is more than the joining of two families. As you know, Dr. Saari Fortunati is the adviser to the two Tendu envoys, Ukatonen and Moki. Moki is her adopted son, and as such, will become a part of the Fortunati family. Would Moki and Ukatonen please come forward now?"

The Tendu got up and came to the dais. Juna took Moki's hand, enfolding it in both of hers.

"Moki, do you agree to accept the Fortunati as your family, to love and obey them as you do Juna?" the priest asked.

"Yes," Moki said, aloud and in formal skin speech.

The priest turned to Toivo. "Does your family agree to accept Moki as their child?"

Toivo smiled at Moki, and took his other hand. "We do."

The priest turned to Ukatonen. "Your position as enkar forbids you from entering into any ties that we would recognize as the ties of marriage, but you are one of Moki's guardians. Do you accept Moki's adoption into the Fortunati family?"

"I do."

"Do you agree to work with them to raise Moki to understand both human and Tendu cultures, and to attempt to achieve harmony with them should any conflict between the needs of these two cultures arise?"

"I will," Ukatonen said aloud and in formal skin speech. The elaborate black border around his words indicated that his words had the weight of a formal judgment. Juna raised her eyebrows in surprise.

The priest repeated these vows to the Fortunati family and they agreed to abide by them.

Then Danan and the other children rose. The priest smiled.

"Anetta Rovainen, the Fortunati children have asked to adopt you as an honorary grandmother. Do you accept this?"

Anetta looked at the children, her eyes glittering with tears. "Yes, I do."

The priest pronounced a final blessing and the music began. The children bent and picked up the thick garland of ti leaves and flowers that encircled the central dias, and held it up. Each member of the Fortunati family took hold of it, in order, from Eldest to youngest. The music started, and Eldest led the rest in a complex, stately wedding dance. Juna glanced up to see Ukatonen watching them, ears spread wide. She smiled at him, then turned back to the dance, lowering the garland to let Eldest's end of the braid pass over hers. Soon she was lost in the careful, complex weaving of the wedding garland. At the end, the braid was so tight that the dancers had to squeeze past each other, amid much laughter and joking. Then the music ended and the dance was done. The garland was woven around each member of the family, tying them together in a single, unifying knot.

"Go now, as a united whole," the priest said.

Carefully, gently, the family set the garland down and stepped out of the complex knot they had woven. Some of the leaves were crushed and broken, but it formed a tangible picture of a family's unity.

The honeymoon was all too brief. After only a week spent settling in with her family, Juna and the Tendu boarded the shuttle bound for Copernicus City on Luna, where they would meet the diplomatic corps and begin a week-long series of briefings to prepare them for their visit to Earth. Juna laid her head against the seat back and closed her eyes. If only there had been more time. Leaving this soon after the marriage worried her. It reminded her too much of her first marriage. She didn't want to destroy this marriage by spending too much time away.

She cradled her burgeoning belly with one hand. She was five months along. It was now or never. If she waited, it would be too late. Two months, and then she would be home again. Then nothing was going to pry her loose from home until the baby was weaned.

Moki touched her arm. "Look, siti, you can see the station through the viewport."

Juna looked out the window. Berry Station gleamed against the empty black night, its red and green warning lights blinking against the rough stone exterior. Berry looked like one of last year's potatoes from the outside, but it was home. She looked back at Moki and smiled.

"I miss it already," she said.

"We'll be back soon," he told her.

Juna held out her arms, and the three of them linked. Ukatonen's presence thrummed with excitement, belying his apparently calm exterior. Moki, too, was excited, but Juna felt a concern for her threading through his excitement. Juna soothed his concern and let the Tendu's excitement buoy her up into exhilaration. Then she turned and reached for the tightly coiled presence of the baby, a flicker of sensation inside her, aware only of warmth and movement. She felt the familiar salty spark of neurons firing in the baby's brain. The baby responded to her presence with a warm surge of curiosity. It moved its arm, and she felt the movement inside her womb. It was a strange and wondrous thing to feel the baby and its movement simultaneously. Gently she enfolded the baby in her presence for a few moments, then let Ukatonen, and then Moki enfold the baby within her.

Then they slid out of the link. Juna rested her hand on her belly, smiled, and slid into sleep.

Ukatonen left the briefing session, his brain heavy with a thick sludge of facts. There was so much to remember, so many countries, and each country was different! In some ways it was even harder than his enkar training had been. His self-confidence had been badly shaken by his inability to see the consequences of their work at the hospital. Was he really up to this task? He felt overwhelmed and alone. This was more than he could do by himself. If only there were another enkar here to share this burden.

A yellow flicker of irritation forked down one leg. Enough of these doubts. He was here, and he would do what needed to be done. And soon he would get to see an actual Earth rain forest. The Xavieras' jungle had been small and incomplete, but it was enough to show him that the rain forests of Earth, for all the alienness of their life forms, had much the same ecology as those on Tiangi. He had viewed some of the humans' tapes and laboriously plowed through several books on the subject. He had learned much more from Eerin and from Jacques Quanh Xaviera, the ecologist in charge of the Xavieras' rain forest, than he had from the tapes and books. He could not ask questions of the books and tapes.

"That was a tough briefing," Eerin remarked. "I'm looking forward to lunch. It'll be nice to spend an hour stuffing my body instead of stuffing my brain."

"You found it hard too?" Ukatonen asked, spreading his ears in surprise.

"Of course I did. They shoved an awful lot of stuff at us today."

"But you know what a President is already. You understand human governments."

Eerin smiled and shook her head. "I may know what a President is, but I can't claim to understand government."

She was making a joke, Ukatonen realized.

"There's just so much to remember," Ukatonen said, fighting to keep his words slow and calm. "I don't want to make any mistakes."

"Ukatonen," Eerin said, "no one expects you to remember it all perfectly, and even if you did, someone else might forget. This is just to help prevent misunderstandings. The presidents and royalty you'll be meeting are as worried about making mistakes as you are, and they know much less about your people than you know about us. Don't worry, there will be people there to help remind us of what to do."

"But I'm an enkar," he insisted. "I should know what to do."

"Ukatonen, this isn't Tiangi. Everything here is new for you. In a situation like this even an enkar can make a mistake or two. Personally, I think you'll do better than I will."

"Really?" he said, surprised.

"En, I've never done anything like this before," she told him. "You've spent hundreds of years visiting the chiefs of different villages. This isn't really all that much different. There are different titles and ceremonies, but it's the same basic situation. We're just trying to make sure that you don't do anything that will cause you or the leaders to lose face. That's why they're teaching us all this protocol. But we're not visiting every single government on Earth. We've had to choose the ones that are the most important. So just by visiting them, you'll be giving them status."

"I see," Ukatonen said. "Then why are we learning all of this?"

"Because these are the things that human diplomats must know. If the people you're going to meet have a familiar framework in which to place you, they'll feel more at ease."

"But I'm not a human diplomat," he pointed out.

Eerin nodded. "That's why you don't have to do everything perfectly."

Ukatonen shook his head, more confused than ever. "I don't understand."

"Look, en," Eerin said, "you're an alien. They expect you to be different. They expect there to be misunderstandings and mistakes. There are misunderstandings and mistakes enough between humans from different cultures. That's why we have all of this protocol in the first place. To prevent misunderstandings. Just do the best you can, and rely on me and the other members of the team to help out if you get confused. Trust us, okay?"

"All right," he said. *But I'm an enkar*, he thought, *and I'm not supposed to make mistakes.* All of the truths that made up his world seemed to be crumbling away to nothing while he put on a brave front.

Moki sat through another long meeting with some famous human, trying not to look bored. They had been on Earth for over a week and all they had done was have meetings with important people. He had tried telling himself that it was just like being a bami for the chief elder of a village, but it wasn't. A chief elder would have kept him busy waiting on the needs of his visitors. Here he had to sit still and watch, and pretend to listen. He wasn't really learning anything, not after the first week of this. They spent all their time in buildings and trains and cars. There had been a few nice gardens, but they were all clipped and tame. When were they going to see the real Earth, the jungles and the forests? He hadn't climbed a tree since they left Berry Station.

Moki glanced over at Ukatonen, who sat leaning forward, ears spread wide, apparently listening intently to everything this current leader, President of a country called the Re-United States, had to say. It wasn't anything that they hadn't heard a dozen times before. His country welcomed the Tendu, and wished for better relations with them. They were eager to trade with the Tendu when the opportunity arose. Glapetty, glap, glap, glah . . . It went on and on, and was apparently meaningless.

Finally the meeting broke up, and they went for a walk in a garden behind the big white house that the President lived in. It was full of huge old rosebushes, their blossoms filling the air with scent. He liked roses. Waiting until the others were farther ahead, he tore off a handful of pale pink rose petals, and popped them into his mouth, savoring their subtle, flowery taste. He glanced up and saw one of the silent security men in dark suits smiling at him behind his sunglasses.

Moki turned a deep, embarrassed brown, and hurried to catch up to the rest of the group. Ukatonen gave him a brownish yellow flicker of reproof for lagging behind.

That evening, when they returned to their hotel room, there was a large bouquet of roses from the head gardener of the rose garden waiting for Moki, and a small tin of candied rose petals from the security people. Eerin and Analin laughed out loud when he told them the story. Ukatonen, however, turned a disapproving shade of yellowish brown.

"This embarrasses us all, Moki. I thought you knew how to behave well."

"Oh, come on, Ukatonen," Eerin said. "So he sneaks a few rose petals. It doesn't matter. They think he's just a kid."

"If anything," Analin added, "it will make people like him even more."

"It does matter, Eerin. He is a bami, and he represents our people here. I will not have him behaving in a way that makes us lose face."

"But I cannot be a bami here," Moki complained. "At home, I would be helping to serve my sitik through these meetings. Here I can only sit and watch and try to listen. And all the meetings are the same."

"Yes, they are, Moki, but they are all equally important as well," Ukatonen lectured. "These people we are meeting are the chiefs of their countries. If we are to achieve harmony with humans, we must know and understand their leaders. You serve your sitik here by watching and listening. You must watch these humans closely, study them, find out what is in their hearts. If you understand the leaders, you will begin to understand their people."

Eerin touched the enkar's shoulder. "You are right, Ukatonen, but I think, for now, it would be wise if the humans underestimated Moki. They will speak less guardedly around him because they believe he is a child and doesn't understand them. He will learn more, and through him we will learn more."

Ukatonen looked thoughtful for a moment. "You're right. I will teach Moki the art of ang ar-gora, invisible listening. Normally we teach this skill only to enkar-in-training, but this is not a normal situation, and you are not a normal bami, Moki."

Moki's ears spread wide, and his skin turned blue with delight. "I am honored, en."

Ukatonen's skin took on a faint ochre tinge of concern. "It is a hard discipline, Moki. I hope that I am not wrong to teach you this. Ang ar-gora must be used wisely and responsibly. Please do not demonstrate that I was wrong in my judgment of you."

Moki's ears drooped. "Yes, en," he promised. "I will try not to disappoint you."

Ukatonen looked suddenly tired. "I don't think you will, Moki, but I want you to understand what I am trusting you with." He stood. "It is time for me to sleep," he said. "Good night."

Concern was written across his sitik's face as she watched Ukatonen leave. She opened her mouth to say something, but the door swung closed behind the enkar and it was too late.

"He looks tired," she said to Moki. "I hope it's not the greensickness returning."

"I think he is as tired of these meetings as I am, siti," Moki admitted. "But he is an enkar and may not say so."

Juna woke up, went to the bathroom, and then came back to bed. It was early yet. She should get more sleep, but her body's clock was still somewhere out over the Atlantic. She adjusted the pillow that supported her growing belly. Ukatonen had been unusually short-tempered with Moki last night. The heavy schedule and Earth's higher gravity combined to wear them down into exhaustion. She barely got through the day, and she was worried about what their demanding schedule was doing to the baby.

She rolled over onto her back and then shifted back onto her side again with a sigh. It was getting harder to find a comfortable position. She felt a sudden longing for home. She wanted to be surrounded by women who understood being pregnant and who could help her through this increasingly awkward and uncomfortable time. Instead, she was far from home, surrounded by people who expected her to function at peak efficiency, despite the demands of her pregnancy. She felt sudden tears of self-pity leaking from the corners of her eyes, and decided that it was time to get up before she dissolved into a soggy victim of pregnancy hormones.

Juna and Analin prevailed firmly upon the protocol minister to rework their schedule to allow for a free day in Costa Rica, where they would tour the cloud forests of Monteverde. There were still state visits to the leaders of Canada, Texas, and Mexico, but it gave them something to look forward to.

When they got off the plane in San José, Ukatonen was almost vibrating with excitement. Moki, who had begun to shrink quietly into the background, in order to practice the art of invisible listening, was a blue and yellow blaze of anticipation. Juna smiled. She, too, longed for a day off in the shady depths of the jungle.

At last they were loaded into a military helicopter with the Minister of the Environment, who pointed out the various environmental reclamation projects the government had undertaken. After an hour of flying over scattered farms and plantations, they swung out over the bay and then up toward the forested peaks of the Monteverde cloud forest.

Below them, a broad green ribbon of jungle stretched from the mountains to the sea, most of which was part of the Monteverde restoration project. Moki and Ukatonen's ears fanned wide, despite the roar of the helicopter engines. They had never seen a jungle from above before.

The helicopter landed at the edge of the airstrip and their party was escorted to a string of jeeps that took them past patches of lush pasture where cows and horses grazed placidly, then along slopes covered with coffee trees, and then into fruit trees which faded almost imperceptibly into jungle, though Juna could still detect rows of trees. A cacao plantation, Ministro Gomez explained. Then they rattled over another cattle guard and the landscape changed to true jungle. The road ended in a gravel parking lot. Their entourage rumbled to a stop, and the noisy silence of the jungle settled around them.

Juna closed her eyes and inhaled. Almost, she thought, almost she could believe she was back on Tiangi, but there were subtle differences in the scent of the forest, sweet fruitiness where there should have been musk, and the underlying scent of vegetable decay was less pungent. But these were tiny differences. She heard a buzzing noise whiz past her head, and then back again, and opened her eyes to see a shimmering green and pur-

ple hummingbird hovering in front of her, clearly puzzled by the red flowers on her shirt. She laughed and the hummingbird zoomed off into the
forest. Moki and Ukatonen laughed with her, their skins a riot of blue and
green. It was good to be back in a jungle, any jungle.

The director of the park guided them through the visitors' center. The
Tendu followed dutifully, though it was clear that their minds were else-
where. After a torturous half-hour of being guided, centimeter by centimeter through the exhibits at the visitors' center, Juna finally laid a hand on
the director's arm.

"Señor O'Brian, your visitors' center is amazing, but perhaps we would
learn more from it after we have seen the forest," Juna suggested tactfully.

"Oh, of course, Profesora," he said, and showed them out of the over
air-conditioned visitors' center, and down a path into the forest. Moki and
Ukatonen's ears were fanned wide and quivering, their nostrils dilated. The
park director began droning statistics at them again. They heard none of it.
There was a rustling in the treetops and a patter of falling leaves. It was the
last straw. Moki was up the tree in a twinkling, vanishing into the canopy.
A minute later, something whirled down out of the branches onto the path.
It was Moki's shorts. Juna fought back a peal of laughter. She picked up the
shorts, and looked at Ukatonen, who was quivering in his eagerness to follow Moki, held back only by the iron discipline of the enkar.

"I suppose," she said dryly, "that you should go after him, en. I'm a bit
too pregnant for clambering about in the trees."

Ukatonen nodded, and vanished up into the trees like a green shadow.
Juna smiled wistfully up at him, wishing that she could follow the Tendu.
But her body was growing ungainly, and someone needed to keep the officials off their backs for as long as it took for the Tendu to come back. She
turned to the director, who was staring up into the trees, a horrified expression on his face. She fought back a sudden surge of laughter.

"Shall we continue with the tour, Señor O'Brian?" she said.

"But the aliens—" he began.

"The Tendu will be fine, Señor O'Brian. They live in a rain forest. This
one is different, yes, but they will be careful."

"What if they get lost?" one of his aides said.

Juna shook her head. "It would be like getting lost inside your own
house. We will see them when they are ready to return."

"But—" the director began.

"It will be all right," Juna assured him. "The Tendu won't hurt anything, and I very much doubt that anything in this forest could hurt the Tendu."

Ukatonen swung through the trees, feeling the branches swing and sway under his weight. They were heavier here than on Tiangi, and the canopy was lower to the ground. He was as blue with joy as a clear morning sky, and so was Moki. At last, panting, he swung to a halt. On Tiangi, he could have moved at this pace from dawn to dark, but here on Earth the heavier gravity and months of inactivity made him tire more quickly. But it was enough to be here, in a forest on another world. It was worth all the months of deprivation and waiting to be here.

Moki swung up beside him on the branch, pink flickers of excitement forking across his body and down his arms and legs.

"What shall we do first?" Moki asked.

"Sit for a while and listen. You may practice your ang-ar-gora here, where it was meant to be practiced."

So they sat, still as the branches they sat on, as the afternoon progressed around them, bringing them a parade of animals, small and large. Lizards crawled over them, tongues flickering at their strange scent, birds flew past, and a slow-moving, furry animal munched on leaves only a few feet away, oblivious of their presence. They seemed like friends, strangely transformed, yet familiar in their roles in the forest.

As the afternoon light became golden and slanting, hunger drove them to move. Moki found a tree ripe with fruit, and they ate till their stomachs bulged. Then they found a suitable tree and built a nest.

Neither of them spoke of going back. Ukatonen knew Eerin would understand. They had waited so long for this, and the humans were only allowing them a few scant hours. It wasn't enough, and Eerin knew it as well as they did. Moki would begin hungering for his sitik in a day or two. They would go back then. It would throw the humans' precious schedule off, but this was more important. How could he know a world without living in its wild places?

A deep burgundy ripple of irony coursed over Ukatonen's skin. Before he'd come here he would never have thought of such a thing as wild places. On Tiangi, everything was wild. Here, there seemed to be almost no wilderness. How could the humans stand to be so cut off from the wild places of their world? He closed his eyes, taking a deep breath of the richly scented air, so different, yet so soothing. He felt more at home here than he had since he left Tiangi. The weight of these months of isolation fell away, and he slid into a deep, relaxed sleep.

He woke an hour or two after dawn, feeling as frisky as a courting tillara. Moki had already gone out and gotten breakfast. There was fresh fruit, some young fern shoots, and one of the slow-moving mammals they had seen the day before, neatly butchered and lying on the inside of its coarse, greenish-furred skin.

"I didn't know what was protected here," Moki said, "so I tried to take a little of several different things that seemed plentiful."

Ukatonen flickered acknowledgement. "We will only be here a few days. I don't think that we can alter the balance very much in that time. Still," he added, "we should try to eat as little meat as possible." He helped himself to a piece of fruit, swallowing it with evident delight.

Juna, meanwhile, was busy trying to calm diplomats horrified by the crumbling of their carefully planned schedules, and appease government ministers certain that the aliens were dying from snakebites or were slaughtering endangered species by the score.

Juna patiently stood her ground. She explained to the diplomats that the nature of her bond with Moki meant that the roaming Tendu would return in a day or two, and reassured the government ministers that the Tendu knew how to survive in the forest, and that they would avoid poisonous snakes, and would not wantonly destroy the forest. On the third day, she went out with the search party. They spent all day exploring the forest, using dogs to try to track the Tendu, with no luck at all. When they returned to camp at sunset, Moki and Ukatonen were waiting for her in her tent. They had slipped into camp several hours before, in a test of Moki's skill at ang-ar-gora.

Juna briefed them about what had been happening at camp. Then they slipped like shadows through the dusk, back into the jungle. Juna finished freshening up and went to meet with Señor O'Brian, to discuss what to do next. As she sat down, there was a loud crashing in the trees overhead. Moki and Ukatonen scrabbled down the trunk of a tree. Juna smiled inwardly at the racket they were making.

"Siti?" Moki called loudly, a very convincing note of fear in his voice, "Siti, are you there?"

"Moki!" Juna called. "I'm right here!" She ran to embrace him, and he clung to her as though he had not seen her for months. Ukatonen came up behind him. Juna reached out to embrace the enkar. Altogether it was a most touching and convincing homecoming.

"Is there any food left?" Moki asked. "I'm hungry. We've had nothing but fruit and greens for the last three days."

Juna saw Señor O'Brian and Ministro Gomez visibly relax at Moki's words. It was another cleverly planned deception. It was easier than proving to the ministers that the Tendu would kill sparingly and only at need.

"Perhaps we should continue this discussion in the mess tent," Juna suggested. "That way Moki and Ukatonen can get something to eat while we discuss rearranging our schedules."

Señor O'Brian agreed.

After Moki and Ukatonen had filled their plates full of meat and beans and rice, and before they began to eat, Ukatonen made Moki apologize to their delegation and to the governmental ministers. It was another face-saving gesture that Juna and the two Tendu had cooked up. Moki, as a "child" and an alien one at that, could not be expected to understand the importance of their schedule. Ukatonen claimed to have been looking for him until late the day before, and that it had taken them all day to find their way back.

Moki looked up forlornly at the officials and ministers. "It's just been such a long time since I've been in a real rain forest. I was just so homesick," he said, his ears drooping so miserably that Juna had to fight to keep from laughing.

Moki was a very good actor. Juna heard a murmur of sympathy from members of their entourage. Good. Perhaps the diplomats would not push them so hard after this.

"Moki, it was very bad of you to run away like that," she said. "You realize that I'm going to have to punish you. You're not allowed to eat any sweets for a solid month. I expect you to help wash all the dishes here until we leave. And you're to pour tea and serve the ministers at all our next meetings. Is that clear?"

"Yes, siti," Moki said, looking mournfully down at the ground.

"Don't you think you're being a bit hard on the boy?" Señor O'Brian said.

Juna fought back a smile. Dishwashing was the only real punishment, and it was a mild one. Moki only craved sweets when he was healing people, and he would be glad to be able to actually do something useful during those long, boring meetings.

After dinner, Juna met with the diplomats to repair their battered schedule. Actually, they had only missed a couple of meetings with the heads of state of Guyana and Suriname, and a "day off" that included a military review, which she was frankly relieved to have avoided. She didn't know how to explain war to the Tendu. The concept wasn't part of their universe.

"Look," she said, after the diplomats had debated the issue for several minutes. "These meetings and briefings are very hard on the Tendu. The whole situation is completely foreign to them, and very stressful. They need time off in wild places like this park. Otherwise we're going to have more embarrassments like this last one. You've been expecting the Tendu to accommodate to human ways, and it's strained them to their limits. It's time we humans accommodated ourselves to the Tendu. After all, they've come a long way to see us."

"Dr. Saari, we don't have a lot of control over what the various governments choose to show to the Tendu," one of the diplomats replied.

"But the Tendu can refuse to see the things that don't interest them, can't they?"

"To a certain extent, yes," the diplomat replied. "But some things are unavoidable."

"I see. But perhaps we can negotiate a few more visits to national parks and reclamation sites, and a few less displays of military might. And a couple more days off that really are days off. It isn't just the Tendu I'm concerned about. There's the baby as well. I'm exhausted, and I'm afraid that it might harm the baby if I continue to overwork myself like this."

"We'll do what we can, Dr. Saari."

And to Juna's surprise, they accomplished quite a lot. Part of their success was due to Moki's running away, which had gotten into the papers. Analin's spin on the incident underlined the extent of Moki's (and by implication, Ukatonen's) homesickness.

Suddenly their meetings took place outside, in gardens. Instead of parades and teeming crowds of people, Moki and Ukatonen were led through vast reclamation projects, forests of replanted saplings growing over the scars of old strip mines and industrial sites. In Brazil they were taken through the restoration of the great coastal forests. The members of the Central African Federation of Countries showed them the Green Sahel project, where they were slowly, painfully, pushing back the desert. The Chinese took them through the Huang He project, where they saw the vast factories devoted to rebuilding the long-vanished topsoil, and acres where that topsoil had been painstakingly laid down and held in place by plantations of clover and grasses, from which forests of bamboo, poplar, pine, and ginkgo were rising. Ukatonen and Moki conferred with the environmental engineers, and often were able to make useful suggestions. More importantly, the Tendu's interest in these projects focused human interest on them as well. The last three weeks of their trip were much more fun. Ukatonen seemed reinvigorated; he listened to the people he met with a new intensity and focus.

Ukatonen sat in the hot, dusty bus, looking out the window at the ravaged land around him. This was their tenth tour of an environmental reclamation site in the last eight days. Every country seemed to have several. Some countries seemed to be nothing but reclamation zones.

The tours were always the same. First they would be shown the ravaged land, barren, eroded, sick with chemicals. Then they would be shown the repair efforts under way—decontamination, replacement of topsoil, and replanting. Then finally they would be shown the most advanced stage of regrowth—forest, prairie, desert, whatever. It always felt empty and incomplete. There weren't enough birds or small animals rustling in the undergrowth. The plants weren't quite right, too far apart, or growing in neat rows. It all felt subtly wrong, and there was never enough time to figure out what was the matter. And he never got to compare the reclamation site with a real forest or prairie or whatever. It left him feeling as incomplete and unharmonious as the sites he visited.

What made humans do this to their world? How could they foul their nest this way?

He began listening to the leaders more closely, asking probing, difficult questions that made the diplomats and even Eerin squirm uncomfortably. He knew he was being difficult, but he was an enkar, and understanding this conundrum was what he needed to do. With Eerin's encouragement and help, he began watching videos and laboriously reading through history texts. It was hard work, as dry and dusty and dead as the reclaimed lands he had visited.

Gradually, a picture began to emerge. It was an ugly picture of greed and devastation on a scale so vast that he still had trouble believing it had really happened.

Within the space of two centuries these otherwise intelligent, thoughtful people had cut down their forests, mined their hills and poisoned their land, water, and air. Ukatonen found it painful to try to come to grips with this fact. Eerin had tried to explain the complicated tangle of greed, prejudice, narrow-mindedness, and shortsightedness that led to this, but he found it hard to wrap his mind around the necessary concepts.

The humans had paid a heavy price before they realized their mistake. Billions of humans had lived short, harsh, and painful lives, dying of the diseases inherent in starvation and overcrowding. Now, millions still lived hard lives, but at least they were getting enough to eat. The population on Earth had been shrinking for the last century. It was falling more slowly than Ukatonen would have liked, but it was declining. They would reach a sustainable level in another century or two. But it would take even longer before every human's life would be a comfortable one.

Eventually Ukatonen gave up trying to understand why or how humans had done this to their world. It was easier for him to help humanity restore their battered planet's ecosystem than it was for him to understand why they had destroyed it. At least restoring the ecology felt familiar. It would take him out into the forest, where he was at home. And he would see to it that there were as few schedules and meetings and little boxy rooms full of people as possible. He woke up the computer and began doing a little research, while the bus ground its way slowly uphill.

Juna shook hands with the team of diplomats who had helped them, thanking them and bidding them goodbye. Oddly enough, she was going to miss working with them, though she wasn't going to miss the demanding schedules and the punctilious attention to protocol that went with this work. She was glad the diplomatic portion of their trip was over.

She watched Moki making his final farewells. As usual, he had made a lot of friends. She saw M. Pichot slip Moki a small round tin of the candied rose petals that he had become so fond of. Ukatonen, moving at a slower, more dignified pace, brought up the rear. People's faces changed as they turned from Moki to Ukatonen, becoming serious and respectful. He might not generate the bubbly popularity that Moki did, but the diplomats and their staff clearly honored and admired the alien elder. Despite all the difficulties, the two Tendu had managed to accomplish an incredible amount of valuable face-to-face diplomacy on this trip.

Moki and Ukatonen finished their goodbyes, and the three of them boarded the zeppelin.

Juna watched as Analin stowed her gear and strapped herself into one of the seats by the window of the cabin they would be sharing for the three-day flight to Darwin, Australia. Analin had performed one miracle of public relations after another for them. Her deft handling of the Tendu's disappearance into the forest had turned the whole trip around. She was the one who made the world aware of how homesick the Tendu were for the forest, gently shaming the leaders of the world into accommodating the Tendu's interests and needs.

"I wanted to thank you again for all your hard work. I'm afraid we made things pretty hard for you sometimes," Juna told her press secretary when they were settled. "But you made us look good despite all our mistakes."

Analin shook her head. "It wasn't that bad. The three of you are fun to work with. And you tried to make my job easy whenever you could."

"I guess we make a great team, then," Juna said with a smile. "You made our work easier too. We'll miss you. Are you looking forward to seeing your relatives in Indonesia?"

"I've never met them. They're my grandmother's family. Second cousins several times removed. My grandmother kept in touch with them, and my mother sent them cards at New Year's and visited a few times." She shrugged. "We may not have all that much in common."

The zeppelin lifted off then. They watched the ground move away from them with a barely perceptible shudder of the engines. Juna had never traveled on a zeppelin before. She had never had the time or the money for such a slow, luxurious method of travel. But there had been enough money left over in their travel budget, and they were ready for a little pampering after all their hard work.

"You know," Juna offered as a bank of clouds obscured their view of the ground. "We'd love it if you could visit us at the reserve. It would be nice to spend some time with you when we weren't in the middle of a crisis."

"I'd like that too," Analin said with a smile. "I'll try to come up and spend a few days with you and the Tendu. I've never really seen them in the jungle," she said wistfully. "I was too busy in Costa Rica, and I think they didn't really want to be seen."

Juna nodded. "I wish I could climb with them, but this belly throws my balance off. And if I fell it wouldn't just be me falling." She sighed and then added, "but I'll miss the treetops. It's like another world up in the canopy. It's wonderful." Juna yawned. "I think this trip is catching up with me," she said. "I'm going to take a nap."

Juna napped her way across most of Australia, getting up only to eat and to pee, and to look down at the scenery or up past the bellying bag of the zeppelin at the incredible array of Southern stars. The distant drone of the zeppelin motors wove in and out of her dreams, becoming a small plane soaring by overhead in a bright summer sky, or the distant drone of a tractor on a long, hot summer's day.

Shortly after they landed at Alice Springs, Ukatonen heard Eerin being paged over the zeppelin's comm system. A few minutes later she tapped on his door. There were some Australian Aboriginal elders who wished to meet with him and Moki. Clearly Eerin seemed to think this was something special, so he agreed to meet with them.

They were shown to a small private lounge. As soon as they were settled, the doors opened to admit a pair of ancient elders escorted by respectful grandchildren. They wore nothing but their loincloths and their dignity, but they carried themselves with more majesty than most of the rulers the Tendu had met. The Aboriginals were the first people he had met on Earth who reminded him of Tendu. He longed to link with them.

Ukatonen struggled to follow their heavily accented Standard as they told him about their history, how their land had been taken and their people killed like animals, the imported illnesses that swept through their people, how their children were taken away from them and raised to be white. It was a fearful and frightening story.

"So far you've only talked to the people who won their struggles," the male elder, Stan Akuka told him. "You've been talking to the wrong people, mate. Talk to the losers. They'll tell you a thing or two. Be careful the whites don't come to your place and steal your land."

"It is very far away," Ukatonen said.

"So was Australia," the female elder said. "Once."

"Tell us about your place," Stan said. He sounded hungry, eager to hear about Tiangi.

Ukatonen stood. "There are no words for my world. I will perform a quarbirri for you, instead." He pulled a small flute from his gathering bag, and began to play the melody for the quarbirri he had been working on. His skin flared and died as the music rose and fell. Then his skin and the music shifted into the main portion of the quarbirri. The main section of the quarbirri began by depicting the dawn as the sun rose from the sea over the Outer Islands on Tiangi. His skin speech gradually brightened as the sun rose, flaring big and brilliant as the first rays lit up the treetops of the island. Then he told them of swimming with the lyali-Tendu, the people of the sea, his words shimmering like schools of brightly colored fish against the blue depths of his skin. He depicted the coastal forests, singing and dancing their green mystery. He told them of rivers, wide and slow, and fast and treacherous; and of the ancient inland forests, sloping up into the bunched foothills. He sang the rugged rocky outline of the mountains, with their cool, misty slopes.

Then he showed them sunset on the shoulders of the mountain passes overlooking the dry savannas and deserts where vast herds of animals roamed. The savannas were lands of mystery and legend to the Tendu. They were visited only rarely by adventurous hermits and enkar. In the distance, further mountains loomed black against the red sunset. No Tendu had ever been there. As night fell, Ukatonen sang of the soft glow inside a village tree, and the sounds and sights of the villagers as they settled in for the evening. He ended with darkness and the distant sounds of the night forest.

The Aboriginal elders watched intently as he performed for them, their faces calm, like a wide river where the water runs smooth and deep. They had the patience and deliberation of boulders, as though they had existed for centuries, despite their short-lived humanity.

Ukatonen stood silent and still for a moment after the quarbirri ended. Then he held out his arms, offering to link with them. The two elders reached out and grasped his arms as he instructed them. Moki joined them, holding out one hand to Eerin, who joined the link.

Ukatonen felt a moment of panic from the man. He reached out and enfolded the elder in calmness, steadying him until he could get his balance in the rush of sensation. There was an internal complexity to the woman that belied her stolid outward appearance. Her presence reminded him of a stretch of bright, rippling water. The man felt dark and solid all the way through, a good, well-worn darkness like the wooden handle of a tool, polished and stained from years of use. The human's sense of patient craftsmanship reminded Ukatonen of Domatonen, the enkar who had trained him in healing and allu-a.

The memory of Domatonen triggered a sudden, explosive upwelling of longing and loneliness. As he struggled to control himself, he felt the sudden sharpness of surprise from Moki, Eerin, and the two elders. Moki and Eerin moved first, enfolding Ukatonen in reassurance. Slowly and uncertainly, the Aboriginal elders opened themselves to him, exposing the depths that lay under the bright rippling thoughts and the core of dark wood to comfort him.

Ukatonen struggled against their help, but the pressure of loneliness was too much. He gave up and opened himself to them. He had not realized how much loneliness and homesickness had poisoned his spirit. He let go of his loneliness and pain, allowing the others to wash it away, until the link dissolved. He felt light, almost hollow, like the shed skin of a snake, empty of all the pain that had filled him.

"You have been too long in the cities of the ghosts," the man told him. "You need to go walkabout in the bush for a while."

Ukatonen nodded. They were right. He needed to lose himself in the familiarity of the forest.

Stan Akuka stood. "Thank you," he said. "Come visit us. There's a lot of good jungle up around the north end of Queensland. We'll share songs, and dance and eat and talk, and do this new thing you have shown us." He took a battered card out of his waist pouch. "Here's my comm number. Let me know when you're coming, and I'll get everybody together. We'll have a right big party."

"You and the little one should come too," the woman told Eerin.

Eerin nodded, and then the Aboriginals filed out of the room, leaving the ship as unceremoniously and quietly as they had come.

Ukatonen looked out the window of the lounge and saw them heading, not for the airdrome, but across the hot tarmac and into the grey-green bush.

Juna touched his shoulder. "I'm sorry, en," she said. "I should have gotten you down here sooner. I didn't know how bad it was."

"You did the best you could, Eerin," Ukatonen reassured her. "We are here now, and we will be in the forest in two days' time."

"I can hardly wait," she said, yawning sleepily.

Ukatonen nodded absently. He was thinking about the Aboriginals, and their warnings. He would have to go to Darwin and talk to them someday soon.

A day and a half later, the zeppelin touched down at Darwin. When they reached the arrival lounge, Juna looked around. Serena had arranged for one of the family's older sons, Marcus Fortunati, to meet her here. He would look after her and the Tendu until she went back up to the station.

A tall, dark-haired man came up to them. "Dr. Saari?"

"Marcus?" Juna inquired. Juna had remembered him as a solemn-eyed toddler when she was a teenager. He had become a handsome adolescent while she was in the Survey Academy. She hadn't seen him for years, and the image of him as a handsome teen had remained in her mind's eye. He must be in his early thirties by now.

"Marcus? Is that you?"

"Hello, Aunt Juna."

"For some reason, I thought you were younger."

He blushed, looking suddenly a lot more like the teenager Juna remembered. "It's been a long time, Aunt Juna."

It was Juna's turn to be embarrassed. "I know," she said. "I was expecting a twenty-year-old. Serena told me you were in college."

"I'm in graduate school now," he told her. "I wanted to go to the Survey Academy, but they've cut back on admissions."

Juna touched his arm sympathetically. "I'm sorry, Marcus."

He shrugged. "It's all right, Aunt Juna."

"Please, Marcus, don't make me feel any more of an old lady than I already do. Just call me Juna."

"All right," he said with a grin. "You look too young to be my auntie, anyway."

Juna blushed at the compliment. Then she introduced him to Analin, the Tendu, and their squad of security escorts.

"If we had an elephant and a tent, we could call ourselves a circus," she quipped.

Moki got their luggage while Marcus arranged for a shuttle to take them to the airport for their flight to Jakarta.

"What are you studying?" she asked him, when they were settled in the shuttle.

"I'm getting my Ph.D. in Anthropology," he said. "I thought about doing Alien Contact studies, but since I couldn't get into the Academy, anthropology seemed like a more practical goal.

"It's just as well," Juna said. "The A-C people are all theory and no practice. You'll learn more in Anthropology. Where are you doing your fieldwork?"

He shook his head. "I haven't decided yet. I was hoping I'd find something interesting in Indonesia."

"I'm sure you will," Juna told him. "It's an interesting part of the world."

Ukatonen and the others said goodbye to Analin in Palang, then flew on to Medan. They got to their hotel, ate a quick meal and collapsed into bed. The next day, a ranger from Gunung Leuser Park collected them in a van, glancing sidelong at the Tendu. Her name was Nesa, and she let Moki help load the bags, which endeared her to him immediately.

An hour out of the city, trees closed over their heads, and they were in the forest. Ukatonen had to fight the urge to leap out of the truck and head for the treetops. They stopped at a village market to pick up supplies. He and Moki were immediately surrounded by eager, staring children, chattering at them in their native language and broken Standard. Their security guards shifted nervously, but Eerin shook her head.

"Let them go," she said.

Ukatonen bought two beautifully made mesh bags that looked rather like Tendu gathering bags except for their longer straps and their weaving pattern. He and Moki filled the bags with ripe fruit. They found a quiet corner of the market and spread the fruit out to eat, sharing it with the curious crowd of children, who darted in to take pieces from the aliens' hands then darted back again, exclaiming at their own bravery. By that time, a crowd of adults had gathered and stood watching. When the fruit was all eaten, Ukatonen stepped onto a packing crate, and, drawing himself up, performed the bird chant.

The villagers clapped excitedly, and then one old man, clad in a faded sarong, his face a mass of wrinkles, brought out a gong and started to play. Other people came running with their musical instruments. Soon the air rang with complex rhythms and plaintive chants. People started dancing, drawing the Tendu and Juna and the park ranger into the performance. Ukatonen wove snatches of quarbirri into the dance. Moki simply improvised.

The villagers were absolutely delighted, and it was several hours before they got out of the village and back on the road, laden with gifts of fruit, cloth, and a couple of small flutes. Ukatonen felt more lighthearted than he had in months, and Moki was so excited that he could hardly sit still.

Nesa, the park ranger, was grinning from ear to ear as they pulled out of the village.

"We'll have to arrange a show for you some evening," she said. "The rangers and some of the villagers have put together an orchestra, and we can have some dancing and puppets."

"I'd like that," Ukatonen said. "I would be happy to perform a quarbirri for them, if you think they would be interested."

"What you did in the village was incredible," Nesa told him. "I'm sure they'd be eager to see you perform again."

They reached the research station just before dark. Juna and the Tendu piled out of the van, and followed Nesa to their rooms in a traditional high-roofed *adat* house with its beautifully carved and painted roof gables. Ukatonen threw his suitcase in the corner, picked up one of the gathering bags, swung down off their balcony, and walked into the forest. Juna didn't try to stop him. She knew how much he needed the peace and familiarity of the jungle. Moki put Juna's suitcase on the bed and looked at her pleadingly.

"Go ahead, Moki. Come back when you need me."

He followed Ukatonen into the forest, just as Marcus stepped onto the balcony of Juna's room.

"Are they going to be all right?"

Juna smiled. "They're going to be happier than they've been since they left Tiangi. It's as close to home as they can come on Earth. They'll be back in a couple of days, full of questions."

"But aren't you worried about Moki?"

"Moki can survive anything this rain forest can throw at him, Marcus."

"I—" Marcus began. He looked terribly crestfallen, like some wet baby bird.

"You wanted to spend some time with them, is that it?" Juna said. "Don't worry, you will, but they've been through so much in the last few weeks. It's time to let them be who they are without humans around."

Her stomach growled loudly. "The baby says it's time to eat," she said, patting her swelling belly. "Come on, let's go find out what's for dinner. We'll see the Tendu when they're ready for our company and not before."

Ukatonen sat on a high branch, feeling a welcome warm rain running down his skin. He had a rain forest around him, this time for more than a few days. He could actually get to know this forest, and compare it to those on Tiangi. He took a deep breath, breathing in the warm, sweet scent of this forest. It was different from the forest in Monteverde; the underlying scents were spicier and more pungent here.

Somewhere nearby, a bird honked loudly. Ukatonen sat still, waiting, and soon an ungainly black bird with an enormous bill fluttered onto a nearby branch. He watched as it gazed suspiciously around for a few moments, then settled into the serious business of stripping fruit off the branch it was perched on.

Watching the bird, so reminiscent of the poo-eet bird of Tiangi, yet so different, Ukatonen felt a weight lift from his heart. He was home and not-home simultaneously. He was surrounded by the familiarity of a rain forest that was different from anything on Tiangi. Here was what he had traveled so long and so far to see.

Moki swung up beside him, startling the bird, which flew off, honking sonorously.

"I wish we could stay longer," Moki said in skin speech, "It's nice being back."

Ukatonen flickered agreement, but looked away. Sadness clouded his skin at the thought of going back to Berry Station. Interesting as it was, it didn't feel like home.

"I'm sorry, en." Moki said. "I didn't mean to make you sad."

"Let's just enjoy the time we have here," Ukatonen told him. "We can think about going home when the time comes." But as he said this, he knew he couldn't go back with Eerin and Moki. It would be hard on Moki, but he was clever and adaptable. He would be all right. Perhaps Moki would learn more about humans without another Tendu around to distract him.

For Juna, the green and golden days passed swiftly. Moki and Ukatonen emerged from the forest a couple of days later, their bags bulging with freshly gathered fruit. Ukatonen spent several days conferring with the researchers, while Moki spent time lounging on the riverbank with her. Then the Tendu vanished into the forest again. Each time they emerged from the green gloom they seemed happier and more relaxed, but also more alien. Moki and Ukatonen spoke more in skin speech and less in Standard. It was as though they were shedding the part of themselves that had learned to live in the human world.

Marcus hung around Ukatonen whenever the enkar was in camp. Ukatonen seemed to enjoy his company. He took Marcus along on walks through the forest, and started teaching him how to climb trees.

When he was not exploring with Marcus, Ukatonen spent most of his time talking with the researchers, listening to their plans for restoring the original ecology. Moki and Juna spent most of their time swimming in the river or resting on the shore, watching flocks of brilliant butterflies alight on the sandy bank to drink and sun themselves. Sometimes Juna closed her eyes and let herself imagine that they were all still on Tiangi.

A few days before they were due to leave, Ukatonen came down and sat beside Juna, on the bank of the river. There was a serious, thoughtful cast to his skin.

"What is it, en?"

"Dr. Sivagnam has invited me to work with the restoration team. I want to stay here."

Juna felt a welling of sadness within her, like blood from a wound, but she wasn't surprised by the enkar's decision. She propped herself up on her arms to see him better. "What about Moki?" she asked.

"He'll be all right. He's happy to be wherever you are, you know that. But I—" He hesitated. "I *need* this, Eerin. I can't go back to Berry, not yet.

I'll be there to help you have the baby, but then I'll come back here. I need to be here."

"Who'll look after you?"

"Marcus has offered. He wants to study me, and how I interact with humans." He shrugged, looking away. "I'll get a comm account, so that we can talk."

"We'll miss you," she said, squinting up at him.

Ukatonen brushed her shoulder affectionately with his knuckles. "I'll miss you too."

They sat there for a long time, watching the sun dance on the river and the butterflies and birds come and go. Then Ukatonen got up, ducked into the river, and came out again, gleaming in the sun. He touched her shoulder again and walked into the forest.

The last few days were very subdued. The three of them spent a lot of time together. They linked as often as they could, bringing themselves into a strange, almost prescient state where each knew what the other was going to do almost as soon as the other thought of it. They spoke very little, there was no need.

At last it was time to go. Ukatonen went with them to the airport in Medan. They clasped hands in a last brief link and then Moki and Juna turned and got on the plane.

Ukatonen spent most of the next month alone in the forest. It felt good to have cast off his connections again, to be free of obligations, free to study this strange and tattered ecosystem. He had seen enough restoration projects to appreciate how much the humans had done to repair this badly damaged ecosystem. Still there were holes, places where species were missing. He brooded over his observations, trying to create a pattern out of the remnants of the whole.

Finally he returned to the research station.

"The forest is too broken," he said, defeated. "I cannot repair it without samples from the creatures that are dead now," he told them. "Without samples, I cannot re-create the species that the forest needs in order to be whole again."

"How big a sample do you need?" Dr. Fardhi, the head biologist, asked hesitantly.

"Just a few cells." He looked up in surprise. "You mean you've got some? Why didn't you tell me?"

"Here," he said, and led him to a computer.

"We have a database containing all preserved samples of extinct species. If a sample exists, we can find it for you."

Ukatonen watched columns of names and code numbers scroll by. "I don't know the names of the animals we're looking for. I know what they do, though."

"We'll help you," Dr. Fardhi said eagerly.

Several hours later, they had come up with several possibilities.

"How about this one?" Dr. Karim suggested, pointing at the listing for a bird. "We have a lot of samples of that one."

Ukatonen shook his head. "It would be better to start with something small and simple. An insect, perhaps."

"Let's use this butterfly, then," said Dr. Nugroho, the entomologist. "We have samples on site."

"Yes," Ukatonen replied. "It would pollinate several important species. I'll need some supplies, though," he said, picking up a pencil and some paper to make a list.

Three weeks later, Ukatonen peered into the cracked aquarium that held the pupating butterflies.

"They're hatching," he said.

Dr. Nugroho leaned forward, his breath fogging the glass, as a wet-winged butterfly emerged from its smooth brown pupa, and slowly flapped its wings to dry them.

"Look at it! Look at it!" he whispered, as excited as a child. "I can't believe it's real!" He remembered himself long enough to stick his head out of the door to the lab and shout that the butterflies were hatching, before he returned to watching them emerge. The room filled with people. Ukatonen waited until the initial excitement had died down, then picked up the aquarium.

"What are you doing!" Dr. Nugroho cried.

"I was going to set them free," Ukatonen said.

"But—"

"There are three more tanks full of butterflies, if you want to study them," Ukatonen said, a flicker of amusement running down his back.

Dr. Nugroho nodded grudgingly. "All right," he said. "We'll let these go."

They trooped out into the forest. Ukatonen set the tank of butterflies down in the middle of a sunbreak near the trees they pollinated. He put his arms into the cage, drops of nectar beading up from his spurs. Soon his forearms were covered with butterflies, eagerly drinking nectar from his spurs. He lifted his arms up into a shaft of sunlight, waited a few moments while the sun warmed the insects, then gently shook his arms. The startled butterflies fluttered up into the air like colored pieces of paper caught in an updraft. The humans watched quietly, their faces alight with awe. One or two of them had tears running down their cheeks.

Ukatonen felt suddenly light inside, as though he could soar like one of the butterflies he had just released. It had been a very long time since he had felt such pure joy. He had found the right work to do.

The call woke Juna in the middle of the night. She struggled to sit up, aware that her bladder was full again.

"Comm on!" she called. "Hello, who is it?"

"Juna, it's Analin. Ukatonen's done it again! He's revived an extinct species!"

"Oh," Juna said, struggling to wrap her tired brain around the news. "It's the middle of the night here. Can you call me back in about four hours, when I'm awake?"

"I'm sorry, Juna, but the press has gone crazy. I need a statement now."

Juna sighed. "Give me a couple of minutes, okay? I'll call you back."

When the comm winked off, Juna rolled out of bed and waddled down the hall to the bathroom. There was a month to go now, and the increasingly tyrannical demands the baby was putting on her body were getting tedious. She was tired of getting up several times a night to pee.

She stood up and rearranged her voluminous nightgown over the bulk of her belly, then waddled back to her room.

She turned on the light and sat down in front of the comm unit, trying to think through a fog of sleepiness. Ukatonen had brought back an extinct species. She smiled. It sounded like something he would do. She hoped that he wouldn't get so involved in this project that he would forget to come up and help her have the baby. She and Moki both missed him a great deal, and she wanted his reassuring presence in the link when she went into labor.

She reached out to activate the comm. *The sooner I deal with this problem, the sooner I can get back to bed*, she thought, and punched the activation button.

"Comm on. Return last call."

I've wet the bed, Juna thought as she awoke. Then realization dawned on her. *Thank god Ukatonen got here on Tuesday*, she thought with a sudden sense of relief.

"Moki, wake up," she called. "My water's broken. It's time. Get Ukatonen and Selena, call Dr. Engle." As she was getting out of bed, she had a contraction. She propped herself up and tried to breathe through it, then got up, grabbed a clean, dry nightgown, and headed for the bathroom.

Ukatonen met her as she was emerging from the bathroom. "Moki said the baby is coming."

"Yes, my water has broken."

"Shouldn't you be lying down?"

"It's all right, Ukatonen," Selena told him as she came down the hallway with Moki. "The baby won't be coming for a while yet."

"Here," Juna said, holding out her arms. "Let's go into my room and link. That'll help you understand what's happening."

They sat in a circle on the floor.

Selena touched her shoulder as they were reaching out to link. "Juna?"

"Yes?" Juna said, concerned that Selena was going to try to stop the link.

"Can I join this link? If I'm to be your midwife, it might help me see how things are going."

"A-are you sure?" Juna asked, surprised.

Selena gave her a long, serious look. "I think it will help."

"Thank you," Juna said.

While Moki and Ukatonen were showing Selena how to link, another contraction rippled through Juna's abdomen. They waited until it passed, and then the four of them linked.

Juna could feel her daughter's cloudy, unfocused fear and confusion. She enfolded the baby with love and reassurance. Cradled in her mother's familiar presence, the baby relaxed. Moki and the others surrounded the child with their love and comfort. Juna felt Selena's quiet, joyful presence watching over her and the baby, and her own worry was eased.

Another contraction went through her like some internal earthquake. The baby's fear surged and Moki and Ukatonen soothed the frightened child. There was a stretching pain as Juna's womb squeezed the baby downward, and she remembered to pant hard. Ukatonen blocked her pain, and helped her relax and breathe. When the contraction was over, they gently eased out of the link.

Dr. Engle was watching with Toivo, Astrid, and several other women in the family.

"It's all right. They were just checking the baby," Juna reassured them.

"And how is she?" Dr. Engle asked.

Juna smiled. "Scared but strong."

"And Mom?" he asked.

Selena nodded. "She just had a nice strong contraction. Her cervix is dilating. She's not in a lot of pain, and she's relaxed. The baby's head is exactly where it needs to be. It should be an easy labor."

"Good. Next time, let me in the link. I want to see what's going on."

After that, it was just a matter of time, walking up and down the long hallway to the common room, pausing to breathe through the contractions. They linked every few contractions, reassuring the baby, and helping Juna relax, easing her cervix open.

Juna and the baby rode out the labor and delivery cushioned on the love and support of the women of the Fortunati family, assisted by Dr. Engle and the Tendu. The older children tiptoed in and out of the delivery room, fetching and carrying, or just watching quietly in a corner. The youngest watched with their mothers. When the baby crowned, every child old enough to understand was there to watch the delivery.

In a corner of her mind, in between the waves of contractions, Juna smiled. The public nature of this delivery reminded her of the village of Narmolom, on Tiangi, where the idea of a closed door was an unknown concept. She could feel Dr. Engle's hidden irritation at this small audience when they linked.

"It's all right, Doctor, they aren't distracting me. I like having them here," she murmured.

Then there was one last push, and the baby was out. The link between them remained, a little fainter now, but still there as Dr. Engle cleaned out the baby's mouth and turned her upside down to drain any remaining fluid from her lungs. The infant, confused by the sudden transition from the womb to the outside world, cried out, a lusty, healthy squall that brought tears of happiness to Juna's eyes. Selena took the baby and laid her on Juna's chest. Moki moved closer so that she could bring her linked arm up to hold the child.

Juna looked down at her daughter, enfolding her in love and happiness through the fading link. It was strange, seeing this baby she knew so well for the very first time. The infant grew still, her unfocused eyes wide with surprise and wonder.

"Hello, little one. Welcome. Welcome and love. Your name is Mariam. That was your grandmother's name." Juna remembered her mother holding Toivo out for her to see, how his small brown fingers had held her finger. If only her mother had lived to see her namesake. Tears of mingled joy and sorrow came at the thought.

Ukatonen gently eased them out of the link. Dr. Engle stripped the blood out of the umbilical cord and cut it. Confused, Mariam began to cry again. Juna held her until the crying stopped. Then she handed the baby to Selena, who washed her off and swaddled her warmly, while Moki watched.

"Here's your sister, Moki," Selena said, handing him the baby. "Why don't you take her out into the common room and show her to the rest of the family?"

Moki took the infant, cradling her carefully. This was his sister, something no Tendu had ever had before. He proudly carried Mariam out to show to the rest of the family, handing her first to the family's Eldest, Niccolo. Mariam stared muzzily up at his beaming, wrinkled face and white beard. Niccolo's eyes shone with happiness as he held his new great-grandchild, gently bouncing her up and down for a few moments.

Niccolo passed the baby to Teuvo. "Congratulations, on your new granddaughter," he said. Their eyes met over the newborn baby. Niccolo patted him on the shoulder. "It never gets old, does it?"

Teuvo shook his head as he smiled down at his new granddaughter, a look of wonder and awe on his face. Then he gently passed her along to Anetta.

"Welcome, Mariam," Anetta said. "It's good to finally meet you!"

Mariam began to fuss and Moki took her back. He slipped a spur into her skin to find out what was bothering her. She was hungry and frightened by the noise and the bright lights. He calmed her down and fed her a little through his spurs, then took her back to Selena.

"My sister, Mariam, wants to be some place quiet and dark," he told her. "She's hungry too."

"Poor thing," Selena said. "It'll be a few hours before Juna's milk comes in. I'll give her a little water, but it's better if she's really hungry when she starts to nurse. We'll put her down for a bit, and let her get used to being born."

Selena laid her in the crib. "Isn't she wonderful, Moki?"

"She's so helpless," Moki said. "She'd die without us to protect her." He felt a sudden fierce protectiveness for this tiny mite. It surprised him to feel like this. It was not a particularly Tendu sort of feeling.

"But we are here," Selena said, "and we'll do our best to keep her safe and happy, won't we?"

Moki nodded, and stuck his finger into the baby's waving hand. Her fingers closed around his fist with surprising strength. She was not as helpless as he had first thought. Blue and green laughter rippled over his skin. "She's strong," he said. He looked up at Selena. "I'm glad she's my sister."

Selena touched Mariam's soft tan cheek. "It's going to be wonderful watching her grow up."

Moki's skin flared a clear, strong blue. "Yes," he replied. "Yes, it will be."

Ukatonen excused himself and went to the kitchen, where he downed two apples, three slices of bread, and a cup of the humans' honey, so much like that on Tiangi. Then he arranged a platter of food for Moki and the others. After helping Eerin through her daughter's birth, he was profoundly glad that the Tendu laid eggs, and small ones, at that.

He pushed open the door to the delivery room with his foot, and set his tray on a counter. While Moki, Selena, and Dr. Engle were eating, he sat beside Eerin.

"How are you feeling?"

She smiled down at the baby, and then back up at him. "Happy, but sore."

"Shall I—" Ukatonen began.

Eerin shook her head. "No. With all you and Moki did to ease my

before. But could they keep on doing it? How long before they made a fatal misstep?

He shook his head. It wasn't just the promise he had made to abide by the Contact Protocols that held him back. The truth was that he liked humans the way they were. They were suspicious and quarrelsome, true, but they had a vitality and a curiosity about the universe that the Tendu lacked. But their curiosity and aggressiveness were woven together as tightly as a weedah's nest. Pulling out even one strand would make the whole thing fall apart.

He settled back in his seat, closed his eyes, and repeated the verbal portion of the Hitchee quarbirri to himself. The Hitchee quarbirri told the story of a foolish hermit who tried to empty the forests of everything that could possibly harm him. On Tiangi, the quarbirri was regarded as hugely funny, but here among the humans, faced with the kinds of decisions that he was expected to make, the story became deadly serious.

After the foolish hermit had finished making the forest safe, everything was in chaos. Would the same thing happen here? It was clearly not yet time to decide. He needed to know more. That would take time, and study. He took out his computer and told it to wake up.

CHAPTER 8

Moki came in from the forest with a live bird in his hand to show Eerin. He bounded up the stairs to the nursery, then paused at the door and peered inside. Eerin was nursing the baby. He turned away, fighting back his loneliness and anger. He went outside and stung the bird awake. It flew from his open hands with a harsh cry of alarm. The bright orange patch on its head made it easy to track the bird as it flew into the forest.

He had wanted to show Eerin how he had gotten the bird to grow orange feathers, but she was preoccupied with the baby. Mariam took so much of her attention these days. Disconsolate, he found a quiet, cool spot by the horse trough, and settled down to wait until his siti had time for him.

"*Hei, pikkuinen.* What are you doing?"

Moki looked up, startled. It was Eerin's father. He had been so lost in thought that he hadn't heard the old man coming.

"Just sitting," Moki told him.

"Well, why don't you come help me with the horses? We need to take lunch out to the workers in the fields."

Moki shrugged and got up. He didn't particularly want to help out now, but he didn't have anything better to do.

"*Isoisi,* how long does it take for babies to grow up?" he asked as they drove the cart out to the long tables where the laborers would eat.

"That depends, Moki," Teuvo replied, "on what you mean when you say 'grown up'. Most of us leave home between the ages of seventeen and twenty. But we're able to get by without parents several years earlier than that, though it's usually better if the children stay with their parents longer."

"That's a long time," Moki said, horrified by the prospect of sharing Eerin for so long.

His grandfather smiled. "That depends on which way you're looking at it. It seems long when you're the one doing the growing up. It seems much shorter when you're watching your own children and grandchildren grow up."

They rode in silence, while Moki tried to accept the idea that Eerin would be preoccupied with Mariam for a very long time.

"Moki, how long does it take before a bami is all grown up?"

"You are grown up when your sitik says you are ready to become an elder. Sometimes it takes"— Moki paused to calculate the time in Earth years—"only fifteen or twenty years, sometimes it can take sixty or even seventy years. It all depends on your sitik and on the harmony of the village. If the village needs new elders, the time can be shorter. If the village is stable and happy, the time is longer. No one is really in any hurry. After all, your sitik must die or be exiled from the village when you become an elder."

It was Teuvo's turn to be silent for a while.

"What will happen to Juna when it is time for you to become an elder?" he asked.

Moki shrugged. "I don't know, *Isoisi*," he said. "I suppose that will be decided by the enkar when the time comes. It will be a long time before I am ready to be an elder. I have so much to learn."

"And what if they say that Juna must die?"

"All elders are offered a choice—death or exile," Moki told him. "Most Tendu elders choose death, because they cannot imagine a life outside of their village. It may be that Eerin will have to leave me on Tiangi. It may be that we simply will not be permitted to see each other ever again. But no one will expect her to die if she does not want to."

"I hope you're right, Moki, because I would kill anyone who tried to hurt my daughter."

Moki felt a trickle of orange fear ooze down his back at this sudden flash of violence.

"I love her very much, Moki," Teuvo continued. "She and Toivo are more important to me than anything else. I created all of this"—he gestured at the vineyards—"so that I would have something to pass on to my children."

Moki touched his arm. "*Isoisi*, do not worry. I promise that I will not let Eerin die when I become an elder. I'm not an enkar, but if I was, I would make this a formal judgment, with my life as forfeit."

"Then I am glad you are not an enkar, Moki," Teuvo said. "I don't want to trade your life for Juna's. I love you both."

Moki felt a strange welter of emotions. This was so strange, so un-Tendu, yet it moved him deeply.

"Thank you, *Isoisi*," he said. "I love you too."

Ukatonen watched as the gangly chick broke free of its shell and wobbled toward the warmth of the brood lamp. It tried to settle itself under the brooder and fell backwards on its rump. It sat there for a second, blinking in confusion at the world, and then set about preening its dirty grey feathers.

"Congratulations, Ukatonen," Dr. Lindberl said. "You've brought back another species." He was a short, squat man, with a wide mouth and a couple of moles on his chin.

Ukatonen shrugged. "The DNA was old, but there was a lot of it," he said. "Once I'd gotten a big enough sample, the rest was easy. What I don't understand is why you wanted to resurrect this particular creature."

Dr. Lindberl's wide-mouthed grin stretched across his face. "They sure are ugly, ain't they?" he drawled.

Ukatonen nodded.

"And clumsy and stupid on top of that. But they're a symbol, Ukatonen, a very powerful symbol. We can use these birds to raise money to help restore thousands of acres of habitat. Hell, we might even manage to wipe out all of the exotics on Reunion, and put them back where they belong. The rats'll be the hardest to get rid of." Dr. Lindberl shook his head. "Rats've killed almost as many species as we have. But we helped them get where they could do the damage. Frankly, I wouldn't miss ol' *Rattus norvegicus* one bit if it was wiped off the face of the Earth tomorrow."

"Surely they must have an ecological niche," Ukatonen said.

"Course they do. They're vermin. They killed half of the people in Europe during the Black Plague, and a goodly number more during the Slump. Actually, it was the disease that did them in, but the plague was carried in the fleas on the rats." He paused. "Technically you're right. They're a major food source for a lot of predators. Even so, I wouldn't miss rats much at all. Not many people would."

"There are animals my people would not miss either, but we keep them in the world."

"I suppose you're right," Dr. Lindberl conceded. "After all, the rattlesnake is the symbol of the Republic of Texas, sort of the state bird, but there ain't no one in Texas that would want one living under his house, even if they do eat rats. That's about the only useful thing a rattlesnake does."

"Why is a snake the state bird?" Ukatonen asked. "Does it have feathers?"

Dr. Lindberl grinned broadly. "That was by way of bein' a joke, son."

"Ah."

They stood silent for a while, watching the chick preening its feathers under the brooder.

"So what're you gonna do next?" Lindberl asked. "This's a pretty difficult thing to follow up on, you know."

"I'm going to travel for the next few months. I want to see some more of the world, at least as much of it as my security escort will let me."

"Where're you goin'?"

"I'm not sure yet. I want to see some more of the ecological restoration projects, actually spend time there, and see what people are doing. I've tried doing book research, but it's better for me to go and see places. The books are too static to hold my attention. I'm used to words that move."

"What are you tryin' to find out?"

"I'm not exactly sure," Ukatonen confessed. "I'm trying to learn more about how humans think. I want to see the world through your eyes."

"That's a mighty big project," Dr. Lindberl said.

"I know," Ukatonen agreed.

"Well, in order to further your research, I propose that we go on out and get sloppy drunk."

"Why is it that your people drink so much alcohol?" Ukatonen inquired. "Surely you must have better euphorics."

"Tradition, I suppose. What do the Tendu do to get high?"

"There are a number of substances we use. Most would not be compatible with your physiology."

"You miss them much?"

"Sometimes. But if I want to, I can synthesize their effects through my allu."

Lindberl's sandy eyebrows shot up. "You can do that? Man, you all are pretty cheap drunks. Why take drugs at all, then?"

"It's less work," Ukatonen explained. "You cannot get as high, because it takes a certain focus to synthesize the drug."

"Well then, why don't we go celebrate? I can get drunk and you can get—What do you call it?"

"Gun-a."

"Well, then, let's go out and get good and gun-a. It isn't every day we resurrect the dodo."

Ukatonen leaned back in his chair and admired the rainbow halos surrounding the lights. The halos pulsed in time to the music, which was too loud, but complex enough to be good anyway. Ignoring his security escort's obvious dismay, Ukatonen got up and started dancing to it, skin speech and pictures cascading over his skin in time to the music. The humans drew back to watch him.

One of the musicians spotted him on the dance floor, and his eyes widened. He motioned to the other humans in the band, and they all turned to watch the enkar dance, shifting the music in response to his pictures. Then one of the musicians set aside his instrument, came down, and invited Ukatonen onto the stage. Half-blinded by the lights, Ukatonen performed the bird chant in time to the music. The song ended, and the audience went wild.

The lead musician picked up a golden, curved instrument with a complex mechanism on the front.

"Let's jam," he said, and started to play something sweet and slow and haunting on his mellow, rich instrument. Puzzled, Ukatonen stood watching. Under the red lights the man's dark sweat-sheened skin shone like the surface of a vat of deep purple grape juice.

"He wants you to do the picture thing along with the music, man," one of the other musicians whispered to him.

Ukatonen nodded, drew himself up as for a quarbirri, closed his eyes, and listened. Slowly, he let his skin change to a dark and bruised purple, like the night sky over a large city. Red and blue patches of color flared on his skin, sliding over his body like the blaring notes sliding out of the gleaming musical instrument.

Point by point, brilliant lights appeared on his skin, moving in time to the hot, slow music. Sometimes his skin became the night sky seen through leaves. Then it shifted through the glowing phosphorescence of the warm seas of Tiangi, and then the harsh, static brilliance of stars in space, writ large on his skin.

The music drew to a close, and Ukatonen's skin flared and died with the sound of the final note.

There was silence for a moment; then the audience cut loose with cheers and whistles, and shouts of "More! More!"

The musicians waited until the applause died down. Then the horn player stepped up to the microphone.

"Do you want us to do one more?" he asked.

The audience's response was so loud that for a moment Ukatonen thought the roof was falling in.

"You ready?" the musician asked.

Ukatonen nodded.

"It's your turn, then. You lead, we'll follow."

"I'll do a piece from one of our quarbirri, then. It tells the story of a bami who was separated from her sitik on a trading voyage, and how she found him again," he told the waiting audience.

He turned away from the mike, "Watch my back," he told the musicians, "I'll mirror what I'm doing on the front of my body." It was an old quarbirri technique, but it should work just as well with these human musicians and their alien instruments.

Ukatonen walked to the front of the stage, feeling the heat of the lights on his skin. The synthesized drugs had worn off, the lights had lost their halos. Through the glare, he could dimly make out the audience sitting at their tables with their drinks, waiting for him to begin. Looking out at the crowd, he felt suddenly afraid.

Pushing the feeling aside, he drew himself up and began. He started slowly, testing the musician's ability to follow. He speeded up as the players found the trail of the music. They built a musical structure on his skin speech that was different and more complex than anything a Tendu would do. It was disquietingly beautiful, and he loved it. The complex interplay between the musicians made him feel strangely at home. The music was alien, but the togetherness of it, the ruwar-a, was very Tendu. It was too bad that Moki and Eerin were not here. He would have liked to share this experience with them.

The quarbirri and the music ended with a bright crescendo of joy as the bami and her sitik were reunited. The audience went wild again.

"Man, you're really solar," one of the musicians said.

"Thank you," Ukatonen said. "Can we do one more?"

The musician laughed. "I don't think they're going to let you go without an encore," he said, gesturing at the audience with his chin. "What do you want to do?"

"I was thinking something slow, something quiet," Ukatonen said. "Something to calm the audience down."

"Good idea," the musician agreed.

"Could we lower the lights?"

When they were ready, Ukatonen stepped forward, wishing he had brought his flute. It would have been nice to play along with the other musicians, but the quarbirri would have to do for tonight.

He drew himself up a third time, and in the hushed darkness began to tell about everything he missed on his home world: the smell of the forest after rain; swimming with the Lyali-Tendu; the familiarity and comfort of village life, and the reassurance of allu-a. As fond as he was of Moki, he ached to link with a different Tendu.

He started in silence, the musicians watching his words; then slowly a single horn began to play. Then came a silvery rush of sound, like the wind in the trees, and a quiet thunder and hush from the drummer. From that the structure built to muffled horns and then the sweetness of voices in harmony, no words, just sound. Bit by bit, it died away, leaving him alone with his silent skin speech and the slow full notes of the horn. When that died away, he let the last words appear and reappear, fading slowly. He held out his hands, spurs upward, and bowed his head as the last words faded. No one here understood a word he had said, and yet the music had followed his meaning, sweet and sad. He saw a woman sitting close to the front of the stage wipe away a tear. Across all the distance between his world and theirs, he had managed a sharing.

After the applause ended, he found Dr. Lindberl waiting for him at the edge of the stage. Manuel, Ukatonen's security escort, was standing behind him.

"Your security guy's about to have kittens," he drawled, "but everyone else loved it. What other talents have you got hidden up your sleeve?"

Ukatonen shrugged. "I'm an enkar. We are expected to have a wide range of skills."

"Hey, you guys want to come with us and jam?" the horn player asked. "I know a quiet spot where we won't get bothered."

"I would like that, but—" Ukatonen gestured toward Dr. Lindberl and Manuel. "What about my companions?"

"They can come too," the musician said. "Either of you two play anything?"

"I've been known to blow blues on a harmonica," Dr. Lindberl said.

"I play the guitar," Manuel said, "but unfortunately, I am on duty." He turned to Ukatonen. "Excuse me, en, but you must be more careful. I cannot protect you when you're on stage. If someone had wanted to kill you while you were up there, you would be dead now."

"I'll try to be more careful in the future, Manuel," Ukatonen reassured him blandly.

"It would reflect badly on me if I allowed you to get hurt," Manuel pointed out.

"I understand," the enkar said. "But I need to take chances sometimes."

It was an old disagreement between them. Each tried to respect the other's needs, but inevitably, they were in conflict with each other. It bothered Ukatonen that he could not achieve harmony with Manuel, but that was not going to stop him from doing his duty as an enkar, even if it meant risking his life. He risked his life every time he made a formal judgment. Performing on a stage seemed safe by comparison.

So, despite Manuel's disapproval, he agreed to go, and the three of them set off in the company of the musicians.

Juna sighed as she read Manuel's latest e-mail. It was yet another attempt to get her to convince Ukatonen to be more careful. If it continued, Manuel wrote, he would be forced to resign. Juna sighed heavily. She wasn't any more likely to change Ukatonen's mind than Manuel was.

She smiled as she read of Ukatonen's latest adventures. He was hanging out with jazz and improv junk musicians. He had actually gotten up and performed in public several times, exposing himself to the possibility of an assassination attempt. Juna scrolled through the letter, hoping that

Manuel would provide a few details about Ukatonen's performances, but the security man only complained about how difficult it was to guard the enkar.

Mariam began to fuss, and Juna got up and lifted her out of the crib. She was crawling now, and didn't like to be cooped up in her crib. Mariam was growing up fast. At five and a half months, she was already ahead of most babies her age in terms of physical coordination. She and Moki linked with Mariam, helping her learn to reach and grab and crawl.

Part of Juna worried that her little amber-skinned girl was growing up too fast, but the linking sessions brought her so close to Mariam. It was good, but it was a little scary, too. She remembered Bruce's fear that Mariam would grow up to be alien. Was he right?

Mariam began pulling the buttons on Juna's shirt, trying to unbutton it. She hadn't quite figured out how to open it, but her plump golden fingers handled the small buttons with the deftness of an older child.

"Are you hungry, pumpkin?" Juna asked, unbuttoning the nursing flaps of her shirt. Although Mariam was starting to show an interest in solid food, she still clamped onto the nipple and nursed strongly and eagerly. Juna smiled down at her daughter. The chief joy and the chief sorrow in raising children was watching them grow and change. Linking with Mariam only helped her enjoy her baby's all-too-brief infancy more intensely.

Moki squatted by the back corner of the barn, watching the chickens peck and scratch at their grain. He was bored, and he itched to work on something. On Tiangi, he had watched other bami catch small animals and transform them through allu-a, then change them back again, learning how to use their spurs to transform and heal. Helping Eerin and Ukatonen at the hospital had been fun, but now there was nothing to use his spurs on.

He went to the feed bin and grabbed a handful of grain. It was easy to lure the tame, hungry chickens close to him. With a quick grab, one of the peeping chicks was his.

A prick from his spurs silenced the small yellow ball of fluff's piercing cheeps of alarm. Moki squatted there, and pondered what to do next. He could try growing an extra leg, but that was too easy. Perhaps a second heart, or another liver—they were complex organs requiring a great deal of precision to duplicate. Or he could change the chick's sex. That required delicate systemic changes, and wasn't particularly noticeable. It seemed like a good and challenging choice. And it wouldn't upset Eerin's family.

He went into the hayloft, where he wouldn't be disturbed, and began to work. He decided to begin on the easiest level, transforming the sex organs from female to male. On such a small, immature animal, the process was very easy. Later, he would work on a deeper level, changing the brain chemistry and the endocrine system to be fully in harmony with the changed organs. Then, eventually, he would work on the cellular level, changing each cell so that its genetic complement matched its sex. He emerged, blinking, from the hayloft an hour later, slipping the chick in amongst its siblings, marked now with a distinctive brown patch on its chest and one darkened toenail. He felt better than he had in weeks.

Selena tiptoed out of the toddlers' room. The childern were finally asleep, and she didn't want to wake them. At last she could put her feet up for a few minutes, before beginning to think about getting dinner ready. A cup of coffee sounded good about now. She spooned the fragrant coffee into the filter. They ate well here on Berry, where they could barter apples and wine for coffee, tea, chocolate, and bananas from the plantations in the tropical sectors.

She leaned against the counter, listening to the breathy gurgle and splash of the coffeemaker. Looking out the window, she saw Moki, head down, cut across the barnyard, and back out to the fields. There was a furtive air about him, as though he had been doing something he knew was wrong. He was spending a lot of time lurking in corners alone, or watching Juna and the baby. If he had been a human child, Selena would have suspected him of being jealous of the new baby. But he seemed so self-sufficient, and besides, Juna had told her that Moki was nearly as old as she was.

She could hear, faintly, Juna talking on her comm unit. Juna's daughter was getting stranger every day. The other morning she had come in and found the baby sitting in the front hall, methodically tying and untying the laces on Toivo's work boots! Mariam couldn't even walk yet, but she could do things that much older toddlers had trouble with. And the way that child looked at you! It was like she was seeing your thoughts projected on the back of your skull!

A couple of days ago Selena had found Juna and Moki linking with the baby. She understood using the alien's strange linking for urgent situations like labor, but this casual linking with the baby bothered her.

With a final wheeze and a soggy chuckle, the coffeemaker finished its work. Selena poured herself a cup, and then, with a sudden resolve, poured another cup, and set it on a tray with some cookies. It was time to talk to Juna about her concerns.

Toivo was putting some tools back in the barn when he saw the chicken with three legs and four eyes. He watched it limping awkwardly along for a moment, then picked it up and wrung its neck with one swift movement. He reached to pick up the shovel he had just set down, when he saw Moki.

"I was going to fix it after lunch," the little alien said. Toivo was startled by Moki's sullen and resentful tone.

With an effort, Toivo swallowed his anger. "Come with me," he said, gripping Moki's shoulder. "We need to talk to your mother."

He strode into the house, not even bothering to remove his shoes. Juna was talking to Selena in the family room, the baby asleep beside her. He tossed the dead chicken into Juna's lap.

"Moki did this."

Juna looked from the malformed bird to Moki and back again. She closed her eyes in pain. "I'm sorry, brother," she said in Amharic.

"I was going to fix it." Moki explained. "I just needed to eat first."

"But Moki—" She paused, looking from Selena to Toivo to Moki and back again.

"Moki, these animals are under our protection. We don't do things like this to them."

"But how will I learn?" he asked.

"I don't know, Moki, but these are not your birds, and you shouldn't play with them without permission. Do you understand?"

Moki shook his head. "What can I work on, then? I need something to do."

"I don't know," Juna said again. "I need to talk to Ukatonen about this. All of this," she added with a significant look at Selena.

Selena reached out and touched Moki on the arm. "Do you miss Juna?"

Moki's skin turned deep walnut brown. "Yes," he said. "I need her too much."

"No, Moki," Selena told him gently, "you need her as much as you need her. It isn't always easy being a brother. Human children get jealous of their siblings all the time."

"Really?" Moki said, the deep tone of shame on his skin lightening.

"Really," Selena said. She turned to Juna. "You need to spend more time with Moki."

"But Mariam—" Juna began.

"Mariam has other parents who love her. Let them look after her a little more. Right now, Moki needs you."

Juna looked at her bami, tears forming in her eyes. "I'm sorry bai," she said. "Let's go for a walk and talk things over."

Moki nodded. Juna put a hand on Selena's arm. "Can you watch Mariam for a while?"

"Of course, Juna. It's my turn in the nursery today. You two go on, and don't worry about a thing."

"Thank you." Juna scooped up the deformed chicken. "We'll bury it, and I'll try to explain the problem a bit better to him."

Toivo nodded. He glanced at Selena, who was watching Juna and Moki leave, a worried frown on her face.

"What is it?" he asked.

"I was going to talk to her about Mariam, when you came in," she said. "That chicken isn't the only thing Moki's been playing with."

"What do you mean?"

"Mariam was sitting in the front hall, tying and untying the shoelaces on your boots the other day. She's still crawling, but already she can do things like that."

Toivo looked down. "Juna told me that she and Moki had been working with Mariam. Juna wouldn't let the baby come to harm." Despite his reassuring words, the situation made him uneasy.

"I don't know, Toivo," Selena said. "But I think Mariam should have a chance to prove what she can do on her own. She's only a baby, after all."

Toivo sat beside his wife. "You're right. We should talk to her about it. But let's wait a while. I don't want to say anything to Juna until we understand what's happening."

"We should give this thing with Moki a chance to settle," Selena agreed. She smiled at him. "It isn't all bad, Toivo. It's just—different."

"And being different can be hard," Toivo observed.

*   *   *

Juna and Moki walked hand in hand along the edge of the vineyard. The dark, gnarled grapevines were sporting bright green new shoots. Juna was silent, trying to find the words to express how sorry she was. They came to the grove of three large chestnut trees, overlooking the weathered tables where the laborers ate their meals. Juna sat at one of them.

"I'm sorry, bai. I—" Juna stopped and held out her arms for a link. Moki sat down across from her. He reached out to her and they linked. Juna felt her bami's wall of silent frustration and loneliness dissolve as she enfolded him in love and affection. His need was intense, and their link was long. The light was dimming toward dusk when they emerged, and it was growing cold.

"Bai, when you need me, please tell me. I may not always be available right away, but I will make time as soon as I can. I promise," Juna told him.

"Yes, siti," Moki said. "Thank you."

"Now," she said. "What are we going to do about the chickens?"

"I don't know, siti," Moki told her. "I'm bored. There's nothing to do."

"Well, we can't have you messing with the chickens. It upsets people."

"But I need to *do* something."

"Let's go see Isi and Netta. Maybe they can help us. Besides, it's getting too cold for you to be out. Isi can run us home in the truck."

Moki brightened. "I'd like that," he said.

They wound up staying for dinner. When the meal was over, Teuvo stumped down into the cellar, coming back with a bottle of gleaming golden wine. Juna's eyes widened when she saw the label.

"*Isi*, that's from Earth!"

He nodded, his work-roughened hands peeling away the foil over the cork. "Bernkastler Doktor '36, beerenauslese, one of the classic vintages, heavily botrytized." He smiled, "It's like drinking flowers! Even this little one may like it," he said, nodding at Moki.

"But why now?" Juna asked. "Is there some reason for celebrating?"

Her father shrugged. "Life is a celebration, if you look at it the right way. But, no, I got it out for my grandson here. I want him to try it."

"Why?" Moki asked. "You know I don't like wine."

"Try some," Teuvo urged him. "It involves a project I want you to do for me. Something to keep your spurs busy without bothering the chickens."

"All right," Moki said.

Anetta got down some small wineglasses, and Teuvo solemnly filled everyone's glass. A reverent silence fell as they swirled, sniffed, and then tasted it. Moki took his first sip warily. Then he turned blue, and spread his ears wide.

"You like it?" Teuvo asked him.

"It's better than most wine. Sweeter, and like—like flowers, roses perhaps, and a little bit like honey. But there's still that alcohol in it."

"Can you isolate that flowery taste pikkuinen?" Teuvo asked. "Memorize it in your spurs?"

Moki stuck a spur into his glass. He closed his eyes in concentration for a long moment, then nodded.

"Could you re-create it, if you had to?"

"I think so, *Isoisi.* Why? What do you want me to do?"

"That wine is rare and precious because of a certain mold, botrytis, that grows only under very special conditions. Autumns have to be long and dry, and warm, and the botrytis mold must be present. If it is, then you get that amazing flavor, but up here, there is no botrytis, because it gets on other fruits and makes them rot. So, we can reproduce the weather, but without the mold"— he lifted his hands and spread his fingers—"all you have is sweet wine."

Teuvo leaned forward. "Could you build me a grapevine that would make wine that tastes like that, without the mold?"

"I'm not sure, *Isi*," Moki said. "But I could try."

"Then instead of bothering the chickens, let's see what you can do with a grapevine."

The comm chimed.

"Comm on, speaker on," Ukatonen told it. He was used to ordering the human's machines around by now.

Eerin looked tired and tense.

"What is it?" he asked. "What's wrong?"

"It's Moki," she said.

He sat back and listened while she told him what Moki had been doing.

"I'm going to try to spend at least a full morning or a full afternoon with him every day, but I think he also needs you around. It's been months since we last saw you, en."

Ukatonen looked away, browning with shame. Spending time with the musicians had been fun, but he needed to remember his duties as an enkar.

"I'll try to come up at the end of the month," he said. "I'm working on a project in Brazil until then."

"Why don't we come down and visit you?" Eerin suggested. "Mariam's getting close to being weaned. Moki and I could come down when you're done there. We're both dying to see the projects you're working on, and I want to see you perform. Manuel hasn't said anything about what you're like on stage."

"I'd like that," Ukatonen told her.

They talked of inconsequentials for a while, and then Eerin signed off.

Ukatonen stood up and stretched. It would be good to see Eerin and Moki again. It was time to focus on his duty, he thought, regret misting his skin with grey. Humans came closest to understanding harmony in their art. He had felt it in the Motoyoshi garden, and sometimes, fleetingly, looking at a painting or a sculpture in one of their museums. Music had been the easiest for him to grasp, and it came the closest to his own concept of harmony. Indeed, the Standard word for harmony had a second, musical meaning, and this carried over to many of humanity's other languages as well. It seemed ironically appropriate.

Music was certainly one way to achieve harmony with the humans, but it was a fragile, tenuous link at best. He needed to find a more compelling connection. Certainly there was the promise of better medical care, but how many Tendu would be willing to leave their cozy jungle to spend time in the aseptic environment of a hospital? No village elders, and very few enkar, he supposed. Perhaps a few of the stranger hermits, but they needed hundreds of experienced healers. But providing better medical care would only help more humans live longer at a time when they desperately needed to slow their population growth.

Ukatonen shook his head. It was all too complicated. It would be so much easier just to make music and forget all about trying to achieve harmony with the humans. He was tired of trying to untangle the whole mess. So much of it made no sense. He longed to be back on Tiangi faced with understandable, solvable problems.

*   *   *

Juna saw the man eyeing her as they got off the train in São Paulo, and smiled to herself. Her figure had returned to her pre-pregnancy slenderness. It was too bad that she didn't have a lover who could appreciate her new figure on a more intimate level. Now that she was away from Mariam, and the demands of breast-feeding, the demands of her own body were making themselves felt. Not, she thought wryly, that there was anything she could do about those demands. Still, it was nice to have someone look at her like she was more than a mobile milk factory.

John Savage, their security escort on this trip, stepped down beside her. The Survey had tried to get her to accept three security guards, but Juna had insisted on only one. John was easier to take than some of the others she'd been saddled with. He managed to be vigilant without the obtrusive nervous paranoia of many previous escorts, some of whom were continually cutting in front of her, or pushing her back in order to inspect a car or a room they were about to enter. John seemed to be content to let her set her own pace, and simply watch the people around them.

Moki stepped down from the train. "I'll go get a porter!" he announced and scampered off toward a group of porters standing near the doors into the station. John tensed and reached to stop Moki, but he was too late. Then Juna saw a man, the same one who had been watching her, move through the crowd toward her bami, his expression grimly intent.

"Moki! Wait!" she called and moved toward him.

There was a sudden loud crack. John grunted and fell, people screamed. Someone grabbed Juna from behind. She tried to pull away and felt something hot pressed against her temple. She could smell the acrid scent of gunpowder.

"Hold still or I'll shoot," a voice growled in her ear.

Juna froze. Moki had turned toward her, his skin a blaze of orange. Just then, the other man grabbed him around the shoulders. Moki struggled, hissing and squalling like an angry cat, his claws extended. He stuck a spur into the throat of the man who'd seized him, and he folded bonelessly to the ground.

"Tell him to stop fighting now. Or I'll shoot you," said the voice in her ear.

"Moki, stop. He's got a gun. Hold still or he'll shoot me."

Moki stood immobile as a statue.

"What should I do, siti?" he asked in skin speech, his skin flaring red with anger. "Should I distract them?"

"Don't try anything, Moki," Juna called, warningly.

"Good," called the man behind her. "This way. You're coming with us." Juna could see several other men wearing hoods and carrying pistols fanning out around them. The crowd backed away. Out of the corner of her eye, she could see their escort, John, lying in a spreading pool of red. There was so much blood! She should have taken the Survey's advice and gotten two more guards. Perhaps John wouldn't have gotten shot.

They were blindfolded with rough black hoods and shoved into a waiting truck. Juna felt the prick of a needle in her arm, and then everything slid into darkness.

She awoke in a small, whitewashed cell with a heavy metal door. There was a battered tin pail in one corner, and a small stack of brown paper squares in a niche beside it. There was a single, unshaded lightbulb and one small, high window. The glass in the window was frosted white, but she could make out the shadows of the bars on the other side. She was alone.

She lay quietly for a few moments, trying to recall every detail of the kidnapping, playing it out slowly, all the way up through the needle and her blackout. Her eyes squeezed shut in pain as she remembered John Savage lying on the ground. She should have agreed to additional security measures.

But would it have helped? Their kidnappers had been frighteningly well-organized. Perhaps even more people would have been killed. Juna shook her head and stood up slowly, still a little logy from the drugs. Where was Moki? What had they done to him? She started pounding on the door, yelling to be let out.

After what seemed like half an hour of pounding and shouting, Juna heard the rattle of keys in the door. She stood back, sudden fear clutching her throat. The door swung open, revealing three guards, two with drawn guns trained on her.

"Where's Moki? I want to see my son!" she demanded.

One of the guards slapped her so hard that she nearly fell. Then he pushed her down onto the bed. Juna's fear turned to terror. She had been raped in the camps. She would die before she let it happen again. She lifted her feet, ready to fight him off, but the guard had already stepped back.

"You'll see him when we're ready for you to see him," he told her. Then he turned and left the cell. The door clanged shut behind him.

Juna shut her eyes and waited while her breathing slowed and her heart stopped hammering. *Mind games,* she told herself. *They're playing mind games. I can't let it get to me.* She used the bucket in the corner, then sat cross-legged on the thin foam mattress, closed her eyes, and lost herself in meditation.

The blurry light that shone through the window had crept down the wall and halfway across the floor before the keys rattled in the door again. Juna opened her eyes. Her mouth was dry, and her stomach was aching and empty.

The guard set a tray on the floor. There was a plate of beans and rice and a plastic cup of water.

"Eat that, and then we will take you to the alien," the guard told her. He was a different guard than before, younger and a little more polite.

He stood, watching her as she ate and drank. The water tasted sweet and pure. It was cold enough that a sweat of condensation beaded the sides of the cup. She had half-finished the beans and rice before it occurred to her to wonder whether they were drugged. She set her fork down and looked up.

"I am done," she said.

"It may be a long time until there is more," the guard cautioned.

She looked away. "I have been hungry before."

The guard shrugged and picked up the plate. "As you wish, senhora," he said. "We will now take you to see the alien."

"My son," Juna corrected him. "Moki is my son."

The guard motioned for her to get up. "Come."

The corridor outside her cell was wide and floored with brown duraplast tile. It looked institutional, as though this place had once been a small clinic or hospital. Behind one of the doors Juna heard a woman weeping. They stopped at a cell across the hall and down several doors from her own. The door opened. Moki was cowering in a corner, the mattress half-pulled over him, bright orange with fear.

Juna crossed the cell and squatted beside him. "Moki, it's me." He did not move. "Bai, please, wake up." He stirred grudgingly. "Link with me, bai," she pleaded. "I need you."

Slowly, painfully, Moki uncurled. He sat up and reached out to her.

"Stop. What are you doing?" the guard asked. Gently Juna rested a reassuring hand on Moki's arm. "He's in shock. He needs to link with me."

"I can't let you do that, senhora."

"If you wanted us dead," Juna said firmly, "you could have shot us at the train station, so I assume you want us alive. If you want Moki to live, you must let him link with me."

"A moment, senhora. I must consult with my superior." He left. A moment later, another guard, this one a woman, joined the other two watching at the door.

About ten minutes later, the first guard returned accompanied by his sergeant.

"I understand that there is something the matter with the alien."

"Moki. Yes," Juna said. "He's in shock. I need to link with him to bring him out of it. If I do not do this, he will die."

"I have heard of this thing. Explain what you will do."

Juna explained what linking entailed. He thought it over for a moment, then nodded. "Go ahead. We will be watching you. If you make any attempt to escape, then you will be shot. Do you understand?"

"Yes," Juna husked grudgingly from a throat that was dry with fear. "I understand. Moki, do you understand?"

Moki nodded.

"Good. We are ready."

Juna took Moki's arms and they plunged into the link. Moki's terror surrounded her, tart and urgent. She breathed deeply and slowly, creating calm within herself, and enfolding Moki in it. Slowly his terror ebbed, and he was able to respond more fully. Gradually she built up a sense of hopefulness within herself, and fed that to Moki, giving him something to grasp and hold when they were apart. They rested for a moment in a tentative, hopeful peace. Then Juna slid out of the link and opened her eyes.

She sat up very slowly, taking a deep breath. Moki's color was a neutral pale green tinged faintly with blue.

"Thank you," she said to the guards. "Moki feels better now. We will need food and water."

Moki opened his eyes. His skin flared orange momentarily, then settled down to a dark, reassuring blue. He was trying to be brave. Juna smiled at him and gently squeezed his hand.

"You must come with us now, senhora," her guard said.

Juna nodded. "It would be helpful if we could link every day. Unless we do, Moki will become hysterical and fearful. He's still very much a child."

Moki, recognizing the cue, grabbed Juna's hand as she stood. "Please, siti, don't go!"

"Shhh, Moki. I have to. I'll be back as soon as I can. Will you be brave for me until then?"

Moki cast a fearful glance at the guards. "I-I'll try. When are we going to go home?"

"I don't know, Moki," Juna told him. "We'll have to be brave for now. Maybe later they'll let us go, and we can see Mariam, and Netta, and *Isukki* again." She felt her own control begin to fail at the thought of her family.

"You must be very proud of yourselves, kidnapping an innocent child," she said, standing up.

"Senhora, that innocent child killed one of our best men," the sergeant told her.

Moki's eyes widened in dismay, his skin clouding over with grey. "I'm sorry. He surprised me. If I'd known what was happening, I would have just put him to sleep."

"Moki reacted instinctively," Juna explained. "His sting is a reflex used to stop predators. He would not do it on purpose."

"I didn't mean to. I'm sorry," Moki repeated.

The guard just shrugged, and held out his hand. "You must come now, senhora."

She turned and looked at Moki. "I will see you as soon as I can, bai."

"Be brave" appeared on his chest in skin speech. Juna wasn't sure whether he was telling her to be brave or reassuring himself.

"If you try to escape, or harm any of my men, we will hurt your"—the sergeant paused as if saying the word was distasteful—"mother. Do you understand that?"

"Yes," Moki said, his skin flaring orange and red with fear and anger. He glanced at Juna. "I will be very careful," he said in skin speech.

The sergeant took Juna's elbow and led her out of the cell, followed by the two guards at the door. Instead of turning left, toward her cell, they turned right.

"Where are we going?" she asked.

"You will see," her guard said. "Come."

They stopped at another locked cell. With a jangle of keys the sergeant opened it. The other two guards stationed themselves beside the door, their pistols drawn.

"Ukatonen!" Juna cried.

He was unconscious. His skin was a strange silvery white, and there were cuts and dark patches on his skin. It took Juna a moment to realize that the dark patches were bruises. He was too far gone to heal the damage they had done.

"What have you done to him?" she demanded.

"He would not cooperate. It was necessary to use force," the guard told her.

Juna squatted next to him. "Ukatonen, it's me, Eerin. Wake up, en."

His eyes slitted open; the pupils were different sizes. "Eerin? Is it really you?" he said in skin speech, the words faint and fuzzy around the edges. "They hit me on the head. Hurts. Can't think. Can't heal. Need help. Moki?"

"He's here too. Shall I bring him?"

Ukatonen started to nod, then stopped. He flickered agreement in skin speech. "Please. Soon."

Juna stood. "He's badly hurt. We need Moki."

"I will send for the doctor," the guard said.

"No," Juna said. "A doctor could kill him. Moki can heal him. But we need him quickly."

The sergeant stepped forward, and caught her chin in a painfully powerful grip. He dragged her to her feet and twisted her head up and around to look at him. "I am in charge here," he told her. "I could hurt you. It would be wise not to forget that."

"Do you want him dead?" Juna asked. "Moki is the only one who can heal him."

The sergeant jerked her up on tip toes, and squeezed her jaw so hard that she thought it was going to break. He let her go with a sudden shove that sent her reeling into the wall. He spoke into a comm unit at his belt. "We will bring him," he told Juna.

"Moki and I will be tired and hungry afterwards. We will need to eat," Juna explained. "This kind of healing takes energy." Her chin felt as though it had been caught in a vise, but she refused to rub it.

The guard nodded grudgingly. "Food will be brought, as well."

Moki was escorted in. "En!" he cried, his skin flaring red and orange. Juna laid a hand on Moki's arm before he alarmed the guards. "He is badly hurt, and needs allu-a."

"I will do what I can, siti," Moki said.

They linked. Ukatonen's normally powerful presence was barely detectable. Juna could feel Moki's anger surging strongly. She contained it before it unbalanced the fragile link. She felt Moki pause, and get control of his anger. It showed a new level of maturity. Juna let her approval of this maturity expand into the link, reinforcing her bami's confidence.

Moki began examining Ukatonen's head injury, and Juna felt his confidence begin to falter. Even without allu, Juna could tell that it was very bad. A pungent coppery aura filled the area around the wound. The damage had affected Ukatonen's ability to repair it. He literally couldn't focus well enough to constrict the necessary blood vessels, and the bleeding had increased the pressure inside his skull.

After putting Ukatonen into a deep, healing coma, Moki constricted the arteries that fed the injury. This helped stop the dangerous buildup of pressure inside the enkar's skull. As the pressure eased, Moki set about repairing the damage. It was delicate, careful work. Monitoring Moki, Juna could feel his fear and frustration build, but it did not affect the care with which he worked. At last, exhausted, he broke the link.

"I've done what I know how to do, siti," he told her in skin speech. "The rest is beyond my skill. There is damage. I don't know how much or how permanent it will be." He glanced down at Ukatonen, lying unconscious on the mat. "I can repair the bruises and cuts, but it would be best if I rested first." He paused, then went on: "I wish Ukatonen were awake. Maybe he could tell me what to do. But I'm afraid to wake him. He would only try to fix the problem, and that would make blood flow to the injury. It's best to keep him unconscious for now."

"You've done well, bai."

Moki just looked at her and shook his head.

"How is he?" the sergeant asked.

"We've done what we can for now. He's stable. We need food and a chance to rest before we do more work."

Food came. Juna ate mechanically, not tasting it, her eyes on Ukatonen. When they were finished, Moki sat, eyes hooded, his skin a muddy roil of turbulent colors.

The door opened, and the two guards at the door visibly stiffened as a short, black-haired man swaggered in. Someone important, Juna concluded.

"How is the injured one?" he demanded.

"The little alien and Dr. Saari have been working on him, Commandante," the sergeant rapped out.

He looked at them. "Well?"

"Moki's doing the best he can," Juna said. "We don't know yet how extensive or permanent the damage to Ukatonen will be. We are resting before we do more healing."

"I see. How long will it be before you know?"

Juna looked thoughtful for a moment. "We're not sure," she said. "At least several days. Possibly a week or more. What do you want with us?" she demanded.

The man frowned. "We will tell you when we are ready to tell you." He glanced at the sergeant. "Carlos, show Professora Saari that we are in charge here."

The sergeant slapped her. Hard. She stumbled back several steps, dizzy, her head ringing. Moki had turned bright red, and started forward.

"Don't hit my mother."

"Again, Carlos."

This time Juna was prepared, and rolled with the blow. It hurt, but it did not stun her.

"No!" Moki cried.

"Again, Carlos. Harder."

This time he slugged her hard enough to knock her down. She hit their dinner trays, and they scattered with a metallic clatter. Moki flew at him claws out, spurs forward.

"Moki, stop!" Juna called through the ringing in her ears.

Two guards wearing thick leather gloves grabbed Moki, pinning his arms down against his sides. He started to struggle.

"Stop!" Juna called again. "Moki, please, stop."

"You can fight, little one, but every time you do, we hurt the professora." He nodded at Carlos, who raised his arm. Juna rolled in time to avoid the worst of the blow, but it still stung.

"Stop," Juna said. "We understand. If you continue to beat me, I will be unable to help heal Ukatonen."

That seemed to stop the commandante. "Enough, Carlos. Do as we say, Professora. And see to it that the sick one gets better quickly. Your lives depend on it." He turned and walked out, not waiting for an answer. Carlos followed him.

The other guard, the kind private who had first brought her food, shook his head philosophically. "Ah, senhora, you should not have spoken so to the commandante. He can be a hard man."

Juna got up slowly, still disoriented by the blows. Each movement made her aware of new aches and bruises. The guard began picking up the utensils. He glanced up at her. "Senhora, why don't you and the little one rest in your cells while we clean up here?"

She shook her head, and winced at the pain the motion caused. "We should look after Ukatonen."

"He's asleep. If he wakes up, we'll send for you. Go on, we can't clean up properly if you are here." It was phrased as a request, but it was clearly an order.

Juna reluctantly agreed, and the guards showed the two of them into Moki's cell. As soon as the door shut, they sat on the floor and did what they could to repair their injuries. They were too exhausted and numb to try to raise each other's spirits. They were too tired to do more than stop the pain and swelling. They broke the link and fell asleep on Moki's thin foam mattress, curled around each other for warmth and reassurance.

Ukatonen felt Moki and Eerin trying to salvage what they could of his bruised and battered brain. They had been working on him for at least two days now, and there was nothing more that they could do. The injured brain tissue could be regrown, but the skills that had been stored there were gone. Still, the two of them kept trying, and he was powerless to stop them.

Ukatonen could no longer control the link. When he reached for the familiar strength of his presence, there was almost nothing there. If he worked slowly and carefully, on a calm patient, he could still heal. But his presence was weaker than that of a new bami. He could no longer calm a frightened person with the force of his will, or hold a dissolving link together. He had lost an ability that had taken a long lifetime to learn. He tried to imagine a village chieftain's reaction to his laughable presence, and darkened with shame.

He was crippled, and a crippled enkar was useless. His injury would cause all the other enkar to lose face. It was time to die, but Moki and Eerin would not let him go.

When Moki and Eerin allowed him to wake up, he explained this to them, as gently as he could.

"Ukatonen, you have a duty to me and to Moki," Eerin said when he was through. "You must live. We need you."

"Why?" Ukatonen asked, not looking at her.

"Because there is something that they"— she motioned with her head to indicate their kidnappers—"want from you. If you die, so do we. I would not want a death that dishonors you so."

Ukatonen sat silent for a while, thinking through her words. He was tired of carrying the crushing load of duty, tired of being an enkar, but she was right. They needed him. Finally, he looked up at her. "You would make a good enkar," he admitted.

"I would not want to carry such a burden as that, en," Juna said. "I am human and we are allowed a few imperfections."

"What do they want?" he asked.

"I don't know, en. I've been afraid to find out. It may not be something that you can do. I will not ask you to violate your honor to save our lives."

Ukatonen looked at her. "Don't be silly, Eerin. You already have."

Eerin looked down. "You're right, en, and I am sorry."

He reached out and brushed her shoulder affectionately. "We will do what we have to do to get out of here."

"It may not be that easy, en," Moki said in skin speech. "These are people without honor. They may not let us go, even when we do what they want."

"Then either they will die, or we will die," Ukatonen replied in skin speech. "If there is a chance to escape, we will take it." He held out his arms, spurs upward. "Let us link. I will not be much help, but it will bring us closer to harmony."

The three of them entered into allu-a. Ukatonen could feel the others' instinctive pause as they waited for his powerful presence to fill the link, and then their grief as they realized that it was no longer there. He struggled to break the link, but Eerin held the link together, blocking his escape. He was surprised at the strength of her presence. Even without allu, she could hold him in the link. He tried to block her as she enfolded him, searching for his pain, but he couldn't stop her. She found the darkness and pain and loneliness inside him, and forced it to the surface. He struggled against it. There was too much pain to face all at once. He tried to make himself go unconscious, but Moki blocked him. Imagine, an enkar of his experience being blocked by a mere bami. He raged angrily, and impotently against them.

Then Eerin and Moki enfolded him, lifting him out of his pain. Exhausted, he let himself drift, surrounded by Eerin and Moki's caring. He was a leaf floating on the river instead of being the river itself. It was like being a bami again. He eddied in the warm currents of their presence, stilled and at peace.

Ukatonen's cell door opened, and he was escorted out. The guards marched him past a row of featureless cell doors and out into the open air. He blinked in the sudden, bright sunlight, flaring his nostrils wide, taking in as many smells as he could. They were surrounded by rain forest, separated only by an expanse of closely mown grass and a barbed-wire fence.

It was odd. Two years ago, such close confinement would have driven him into greensickness. Now, he was too preoccupied with surviving to notice the grim sterility of his cell. Still, the scent of the forest roused a wave of longing so intense that he stumbled and nearly fell. One of the guards jerked him upright and pushed him along the concrete breezeway.

He was led toward a door into another building. A guard opened the door with a stiff salute to his escort. They walked down a long hallway, and into a bright, sunny room. A man lay in a bed, surrounded by guards and subordinates. He was the focus of everyone in the room. Moki and Eerin were waiting. One of the guards had a gun pressed to Eerin's head. Ukatonen fought back a sudden flare of anger. He breathed deeply, forcing himself to be calm.

The man in the bed looked at them. His eyes were pale and cold and hard. Ukatonen knew with a sudden clarity that this was the man who was responsible for their kidnapping. The cold eyes flicked away, back to Eerin.

"Dr. Saari, I am Sefu Tomas."

Eerin's eyes widened at the name. She knew who this man was, and he frightened her.

"I am dying. You are here to heal me. If you do not, you will be killed. If you do, then you will be freed. Your lives for my life. It is that simple."

"How can we trust you?" Eerin asked.

"My people respect me because they know I am a man of my word. I would not jeopardize that trust by violating my word, even to you."

"You understand that I have vowed to stop healing people," Ukatonen said. "It is a matter of honor."

Sefu Tomas looked faintly surprised. "Interesting. A race that eats its own children speaks of honor."

"And a man who kills and kidnaps members of his own species speaks of honor," Ukatonen replied calmly.

Tomas looked at Ukatonen. "I could have you killed."

Amusement flickered over Ukatonen's skin. "But you need me," he replied. "Your life for our lives."

"You could be hurt."

"I could choose to die," Ukatonen said.

"I could hurt the little one, or Dr. Saari."

"They, too, could choose to die. You need us all," he said. "Dr. Saari needs to be in the link. We draw strength from her."

"You could use one of my men," he said. "Any one of them would gladly give his life for our cause."

Ukatonen looked at Tomas's men. They shifted uneasily under his unwavering gaze. "Perhaps if I had not been injured, that would be possible. Now, though, we need someone experienced. Someone who will not panic in the link. I no longer have the strength to control their fear." He looked back at Tomas. "It would be foolish to have done all this, and then die because one of your men didn't know what to do."

There was a long silence. Ukatonen and Tomas regarded each other appraisingly.

Tomas laughed. It was a long, deep laugh that broke the building tension in the room. Even the lines on Eerin's face eased. In that moment, it was obvious what drew men to follow Tomas.

"We will have to trust each other, then," he told Ukatonen. "You will heal me, and you will have your freedom. Yes?"

Ukatonen looked at Eerin and Moki for a long moment, then nodded.

"Good. When do we start?" Tomas asked.

"We can begin now, if you are ready," he replied.

"I am ready," Tomas said.

Ukatonen held out his arms to begin the link. "I have a plan," he told Eerin and Moki in skin speech. "Follow my lead."

Surprised, Eerin hesitated for a moment, then reached out to link with Ukatonen. Moki followed suit.

The link was a roil of emotions. Tomas was a swirl of bloody violence. Moki struggled to keep his fear and anxiety under control, while Eerin fought to suppress her anger and fear. Ukatonen reached into Tomas, and rendered him unconscious, a simple physiological trick. But there was nothing he could do for Eerin and Moki except wait for them to calm themselves. When the link was finally calm enough for him to be heard, Ukatonen sent a flood of reassurance and a sense of anticipation. He was pushing as hard as he could, yet it barely affected the tenor of the link. But it was enough—Eerin and Moki both responded with cautious optimism. He would explain when he emerged from the link.

Then Ukatonen turned his focus to the patient. The cancer was deep and widespread. It was a testament to the strength of Tomas's will that he could appear as healthy as he did. It would be dangerous to underestimate this man.

Ukatonen released the killer cells that would clear away the cancer. With the help and support of Moki and Eerin, he reversed as much of the damage as he was able to, given his own fragile state. When he had done as much as he could, Ukatonen created a temporary pain block. Tomas would wake in pain in the middle of the night.

It was a strange thing to do, and in response to Moki's puzzlement, Ukatonen conveyed anticipation. This was part of his plan. Then he sent a feeling of caution and urgency. He was going to do something. They needed to be ready.

Ukatonen woke Tomas and broke the link, hoping that Eerin and Moki understood him. Moki glanced at Eerin as her eyes opened. She looked at Ukatonen and moved her head in a fractional nod. They were ready to follow his lead. He only hoped that his plan would work.

"How are you feeling, Mr. Tomas?" Ukatonen asked. He felt drained. The link had exhausted him.

Tomas sat up in bed. "Better than I have in months," he said. "It's really amazing."

"The pain block may wear off in a few hours," Ukatonen told him. "If you start to hurt, call us, and we will come and reinstate it. You will heal faster if there is no pain. I have done all that I have the strength to do today. I will do more healing in a couple of days, when I am stronger."

Ukatonen swayed suddenly on his feet, his color paling to a silvery white. "Be ready," he said in skin speech. "Watch my skin." He collapsed, going into convulsions, his skin becoming a riot of color. "I am all right, but pretend I have done too much," he said, the symbols jumbled in amongst the swirls of color. "Get me into another room."

"Ukatonen!" Eerin cried. "What's wrong?" She looked up at the guards, who had their guns drawn and pointed at them.

"He's done too much," Eerin explained. "He needs food. Honey, sugar. Anything sweet. Please! Now! If you don't do this, he will die," she pleaded. "If that happens, he cannot save you," she told Tomas. Ukatonen went suddenly limp, his skin pale silver.

The guards looked at Tomas, who nodded. "Take him out of here, now. Do what they say."

"We'll carry him," Eerin said.

"Let my arm drop," Ukatonen said in skin speech. "I will be dripping something out of my allu."

Ukatonen let one arm droop down toward the floor, and released the first drops of the precursor to a potent sleep drug. It had a faint, acrid odor, but the nose-blind humans didn't seem to notice the smell.

"This way," one of the guards said. "Take them to the cafeteria. Put him on one of the tables."

"Good," Ukatonen said, still in skin speech, "a good place. Everyone goes there."

They laid him on one of the tables, and a guard came running up with a container of sugar from the kitchen.

"Here," he said, handing it to Eerin.

Ukatonen explained what he was doing in skin speech as Eerin opened his mouth and began pouring sugar onto his tongue.

"Tonight, when Tomas has us brought in to relieve the pain, I will release the second part of the drug. They will fall asleep, and will not awake for several hours. Link with me now." He let his skin fade back to a neutral celadon color.

"Thank you," Eerin told the guards. "It's helping. Now we need to link with him."

The guards looked at each other, and then the one in charge nodded. They linked briefly. Ukatonen showed Moki how to synthesize the precursor substance he was producing, then broke the link.

His simulated convulsions over, Ukatonen opened his eyes. He sat up, slowly and painfully. It was not really acting: the link, and then the false convulsions, had drained him. He was exhausted.

"Are you all right?" Eerin asked.

Ukatonen flickered agreement. "Food. I need food," he said aloud.

"So do the rest of us," Moki put in. He began letting some of the clear, synthesized precursor substance ooze from his spurs onto the table, where it evaporated quickly.

Their captors brought plates heaped with food—beans and rice, with fresh fruit and vegetables. They stuffed themselves. And all the while, the precursor oozed from the Tendu's spurs, dripping onto the floor, or spread surreptitiously onto the tabletop. The substance was highly volatile and would evaporate and spread throughout the building, where it would be inhaled and absorbed by every single person inside.

"Could we go to the bathroom before we are put back in our cells?" Ukatonen asked. "I'm afraid there is some urgency."

The guard in charge nodded. Ukatonen left a trail of precursor on his way to the bathroom. He let a small puddle of it accumulate on the floor of the toilet stall, and wiped some on the door handle and faucets. They brought him back to the cafeteria, and then escorted the prisoners back to their cells. Ukatonen stumbled and fell just outside the building, leaving a faint stain of precursor on the walkway. As Moki bent to help the enkar up, he sprayed some on the grass.

"He's still weak," Eerin said. "We should stay with him." The guards hesitated, then one of them conferred with someone on his comm unit.

"Only the little one may stay. There will be a guard outside, in case there is any trouble."

Ukatonen caught a glimpse of Eerins anxious face as they led her off to her cell. He hoped she would be ready to act when the time came.

*   *   *

Ukatonen was asleep when their captors came for them. The guards escorted them to Tomas's room, where he lay sweating and pale in agony.

"Stop the pain," he commanded.

Ukatonen nodded at the others, and they linked with Tomas, putting him under immediately. Ukatonen cleared their systems of all traces of the precursor to the sleep drug he had released earlier in the day. Now the second half of the drug would not affect them. Then, on a prearranged signal, they unlinked. He and Moki began releasing the second half of the drug from their spurs. The light, volatile compound diffused rapidly through the room. It had a peculiar, almost flowery scent. He heard the muffled thud as their guards fell to the heavy carpet.

Ukatonen slipped out of the link and called in the guards waiting outside the room. They were asleep before they took five strides into the room. Ukatonen and Moki crept out into the hallway, releasing the sleep drug from their spurs. Almost immediately the hallway was full of slumped bodies. Ukatonen gingerly opened doors, releasing more activator into every room where he smelled a human. In less than twenty minutes, everyone in the building was asleep except for Moki, Eerin and himself.

"Okay, this building's safe," Ukatonen said.

"I'll call out for help," Eerin said, picking up the comm unit.

"No," Ukatonen told her. "I want to talk to Tomas. I need to understand him. He goes with us."

"Goes where?" Eerin demanded.

"The jungle," Ukatonen said.

"Ukatonen, this compound is surrounded by armed guards. How are we going to get him out of here?"

"I don't know, but we have to."

"We barely have a chance to get out of here with our own skins. It'll be a whole lot harder with a hostage," Eerin pointed out.

"I know," Ukatonen told her, "but it is necessary."

"Siti?" Moki said. "There are trucks here. I heard them come in the other afternoon. Maybe we can use one of them to get out of here."

Eerin looked at him. "That's a good idea, bai. We should move soon, before someone checks the building."

Eerin stripped one of the guards, and put on his uniform. Then she scooped up Tomas's comm, and slipped it down her shirt front, tucking it securely into the waistband of her pants.

They carried the unconscious Tomas to the back door of the building.

"I'll go first, and see if I can find a way to get out of here," Ukatonen said. "You wait here with Tomas."

"Be careful," Eerin cautioned.

Ukatonen slipped out into the night. A few minutes of exploring brought him to a garage filled with trucks and cars. He crept up behind the guard and put him to sleep with a quick sting of his spurs. Then he returned to where Eerin and Moki were waiting.

"I found the garage. Let's go."

They carried Tomas to the garage.

"We'll take that troop transport over there," Eerin said, pointing at the largest truck in the garage. The back was roofed with canvas. Moki searched for the keys while Eerin and Ukatonen loaded Tomas into the back of the truck. Ukatonen climbed into the back of the truck to keep an eye on Tomas. Moki found the keys hanging on a board on the wall. He grabbed them and scurried across the garage toward the truck. Just then a pair of guards walked into the garage.

"Hey!" one of the guards shouted. "Stop, or we'll shoot!"

"Siti!" Moki called. He deftly lobbed the keys through the driver's window with a long-armed toss, and then leaped for the truck. Then Ukatonen saw the canvas truck roof dent as Moki scrabbled up onto the roof . There was a rumble as Eerin started the truck. Moki appeared framed in the opening at the back of the truck as he swung inside. There was a loud, sharp crack and the bami landed in an awkward heap in the back as the vehicle turned, the engine whining loudly in protest. There was the smell of blood, Moki's blood.

Ukatonen moved toward the bami, but just then the truck surged forward, knocking him over. There was a rending crash, and then the garage receded behind them as the truck speeded up. He could hear shouting and more gunshots. There was another crash, and then Ukatonen could see the gate vanishing behind them. He heard more shots, but the bullets whined by without hitting them.

"Are you all right, Moki?" Ukatonen asked, his words glowing in the darkness.

"Something hit me, en. I've stopped the bleeding, but my arm's gone numb."

The truck was bouncing too much for them to link safely. "That's not good. As soon as we're safe, I'll look at it for you."

Moki flickered assent. The truck slowed as they rounded a sharp bend, then swerved sharply and started jouncing over rough ground. Ukatonen could hear branches crash and crackle against the canvas sides of the truck as he and Moki bounced back and forth inside. There was a sudden crunch and a metallic rending, and they slid forward, crashing into the back of the cab as the truck stopped abruptly.

The door of the cab creaked open, and Eerin got out. She climbed up on the back of the truck.

"Come on. We don't have much time."

Ukatonen dragged the still-unconscious Tomas out of the truck as Moki jumped out.

"Siti, I've been hurt," Moki said.

"How bad is it? Do you need me to carry you, bai?"

"No, siti. It's my arm. I can walk."

"Good. Let's go."

Ukatonen swung Tomas onto his shoulder, "This way," he said, guiding Eerin and Moki up a half-fallen tree draped with vines.

They had reached the canopy and were hurrying through the treetops when they heard the whine of approaching vehicles.

The trucks roared past. A moment later they stopped. Ukatonen could hear the grinding of the gears as they turned around.

They swung into the next tree, pausing to convey Tomas across the gap. Behind them, Ukatonen heard the trucks stop. Headlights sent splinters of light into the forest. He could hear the guards calling out orders and crashing through the underbrush toward them.

There was a heavy crack and swish as a branch fell somewhere off to their right, probably snapped as some startled animal turned and fled. The guards shouted and headed toward the noise.

"Go that way," Ukatonen urged, pointing away from the noise. "I'll draw them off. Go until you come to a stream, then head upstream until it branches. Wait for me there. If I'm not there in two days, go on without me."

"Okay, en," Eerin said, "but please, be careful."

"I will be. Now go."

Ukatonen settled Tomas into a secure, vine-draped tree crotch, then moved silently through the trees, moving past the guards and away from Moki and Eerin. When the guards were still a few trees away, he broke off a heavy, waterlogged bromeliad, and dropped it. It crashed noisily through the branches to the ground. The guards headed toward the sound. Ukatonen swung into the next tree, making as much noise as he could. The guards followed him with their torches and guns.

Ukatonen led them through the jungle for over a kilometer before swinging silently back around and retrieving the unconscious Tomas. He managed to carry Tomas about half a kilometer farther into the jungle, and then hid him again. Then he found Moki and Eerin's trail and began tracking them. It was late afternoon before he found them.

"I'm worried about him. He's lost a lot of blood, and there's no feeling in his arm," Eerin told Ukatonen, when he was settled in the nest she had built. There was a pale silvery cast to Moki's skin that worried Ukatonen.

"He doesn't look good," the enkar agreed. "I'll check him as soon as I've eaten."

Eerin handed him a couple of pieces of overripe fruit. "I'm afraid there isn't much to eat," she apologized.

"I didn't find much either," he told her, pulling out a small bundle of wilting fern shoots and two very small fish. "I was too busy getting here to hunt."

"Where is Tomas?" she asked.

"He was too heavy for me to carry the whole way. I left him in a tree. I'll find some more food and check Moki, then go back and get him."

Eerin sighed. There were dark shadows under her eyes. She looked numb with exhaustion. He touched her shoulder reassuringly, then set off to look for food.

The pickings were slim and he was tired, but eventually he came back with some small game, greens, and a few more pieces of fruit. They ate hungrily, wordlessly. Moki had lost a lot of blood. He would also lose his arm. There was little that Ukatonen and Eerin could do to help him. Their reserves had been drawn down to almost nothing. Still, there was a flicker of response. Moki would live through the night. Tomorrow, rested by sleep and restored by food, they could do more.

Ukatonen got up early the next morning and killed a sloth. He and Eerin gorged themselves on the meat. Strengthened by the feast, they were able to work on Moki. It was clear that there was nothing they could do for his arm. Ukatonen took it off, with the help of a machete that Eerin had found in the truck and brought with her. He stopped the bleeding of Moki's stump, and helped it heal over. It would be at least a week before Moki would be strong enough to travel. With patience and careful work, the bami's arm would grow back in less than a year.

Having done what he could for Moki, Ukatonen set off to bring Tomas back. The ants had found Tomas before he did. His body was covered with their bites. Ukatonen healed the bites and woke his captive up enough to make him walk. It was almost as much work as carrying him. He struggled against the fog of sedation that was the only way Ukatonen could control him. It was growing dark by the time they got to camp. He hauled his captive up to the nest, put him back to sleep, then collapsed in exhaustion.

The next day, Ukatonen woke Tomas just enough to feed and clean him. As soon as he was conscious, Tomas began to struggle against the link, battering Ukatonen with his anger and hatred. Ukatonen wasn't strong enough to control the man's emotions. Finally, he rendered him unconscious and pulled out of the link. He sat there, looking down at his captive, his skin roiling with rusty red frustration.

"What's wrong, en?" Eerin asked.

"He's too angry. I can't work with him, but"— he shook his head—"I can't calm him down because of my injury. I have to understand why he's angry, and try to address that."

"Sefu Tomas controlled hundreds of people directly, and millions more indirectly, through violence and fear," Eerin told him. "Now he's alone among enemies in the middle of the jungle. He's angry because he's lost everything. I don't think you can fix that, en."

"But we have something in common."

"What do you mean, en?"

"Coming to Earth, I too have lost everything. But," he said, looking thoughtfully at the unconscious Tomas, "I did it voluntarily. It has been taken from him by force."

He ate and rested, thinking the situation over. Linking with Tomas was like trying to tame a trapped predator.

He sat up. Yes, that was it. He needed to treat Tomas like a wild animal he was trying to tame. It would be much harder because of his injury, but if he proceeded slowly, it just might work.

He linked with Tomas, slowly letting him come to a dreamlike awareness. At first Tomas paced the cage of his mind, searching for a way out, but eventually he became bored and unwary. Then Ukatonen fed calmness into the link. It took hours of painstaking work, instead of the few minutes it would have taken before his injury, but eventually he managed to get Tomas to relax. Gently, slowly, Ukatonen coaxed him into a deep trance. When he was too relaxed to lie, Ukatonen began interrogating him.

Juna half-listened to Ukatonen's interrogation of Tomas. Moki slept deeply, curled against her for warmth. She was hot, sticky, and bored. The insect repellent Ukatonen had synthesized for them was wearing off, and the bugs were starting to bother her. The slim black shape of Tomas's comm unit caught her eye. She flipped it open and turned it on. Once again, the familiar opening screen requesting the password came up.

"Hey, Ukatonen, ask Tomas what the password is for his computer."

Ukatonen did so.

"It's Rimel Moman Jarvi," Tomas droned obligingly. He repeated the words twice more.

Juna's lips pursed in disapproval; two of the words in the password phrase were the names of notorious BirthRight terrorists. But after he had spoken the password, there was a chime and the screen changed to reveal the file finder program. Juna typed in her last name, and did a search on it. There were about two dozen files mentioning her name. But at the end of the list was another file: Mariam Saari Fortunati. Juna swore softly in Amharic. She read through the file, and her eyes grew wider.

"What is it, Eerin?" Ukatonen asked.

"They were considering kidnapping Mariam," Juna told him. "And they were going to use Bruce to do it."

"That's very bad," the enkar said.

Juna continued to scan the file. "Apparently, Bruce contacted the BirthRight movement about taking Mariam. He gave them all kinds of information about us."

"Why, en? Why would he do it?" Juna demanded.

"I don't know, Eerin. Why don't you keep looking, and see if you can find anything else?"

Juna continued searching through the files, while Ukatonen returned to his slow, painstaking questioning of Tomas. She was reading through the files on herself when she came across General Burnham's name. She searched for more information, and found it. Apparently Burnham's office had supplied their kidnappers with vital intelligence about their schedule and security arrangements. They had overridden several attempts by the Survey to increase their security escort. Although none of the information implicated Burnham directly, it was damning enough to end the general's career.

Juna's eyes were sandy with fatigue by the time she reset the password, and shut down the computer. There was enough information on this comp to shut down most of the BirthRight network. There were names, addresses, and organizational charts for the networks on Earth and Mars. She closed the cover with a smile. It had been a most productive afternoon.

Ukatonen sat back and considered what he knew after two days of interrogation. Sefu Tomas grew up in the movement's most radical fringe. His parents took him to BirthRight rallies when he was still a baby. He played under the dining room table with his younger brothers while his father and other leaders of the movement discussed contraceptive reversal techniques, and plotted bombings of Pop Con offices.

He was thirteen when his family were exiled to Mars for population violations. As the eldest, he was allowed to stay behind in the care of relatives. He lived with an uncle for two months, before running away. He was taken in by the leader of the BirthRight movement, and trained as an elite smuggler and spy. By the age of fourteen he was smuggling anticontraceptives and fertility drugs around the world. His youth was the perfect cover. He killed his first man before he turned sixteen.

At seventeen Tomas married the leader's youngest daughter, and became a father before he turned eighteen. By twenty, he commanded several terrorist cells. When he turned thirty, Tomas was designated the leader's official heir. He took over the leadership of the radical wing of the BirthRight movement four years later.

But those were just facts. Ukatonen still didn't understand what moved Tomas. How could he kill so easily, and without apparent thought? What was the source of that anger that Tomas kept bottled up inside himself? Could Ukatonen extinguish that anger, and bring Tomas into harmony with the rest of his world?

Eerin shook her head when Ukatonen asked her this.

"En, we've been trying to find a way to do that for centuries. Every person is different. We carry scars in different places on our hearts. For me, it was the death of my mother. For Tomas? Who knows? His father perhaps. Or the arrest of his parents. Or it could be none of those."

"How do I find out?" Ukatonen said.

"Why don't you just ask him?"

Ukatonen darkened with frustration. "I did. But right now he is angry at us."

"Then ask him to be a child again, and find out what he is angry at when he's a child," Eerin suggested.

Ukatonen stopped and stared at her.

"Thank you, Eerin, I would not have thought of that."

He kept forgetting how crucial a human's childhood was to their eventual development. One chose a bami based on their personality. The willing, honest, and hard-working juvenile tinkas were adopted. Sullen, angry ones were not. Once a tinka became a bami, it was merely a matter of shaping that personality to fit the needs of the village. With humans, a great deal more depended on their childhood.

Patiently, Ukatonen guided Tomas back into his memories of childhood. After several attempts, he managed to make Tomas believe he was a child again. Finally, he was regressed to the age of four; Tomas's whole demeanor and posture changed. The lines left his face; he seemed younger, happier. Ukatonen's eyes flicked to Eerin. She nodded. She had seen the change too.

Slowly, Ukatonen eased him forward in time, until his face began to change. Then he took Tomas back, embedding him in that moment of terror and anger, and plunged into the link.

It was like being tumbled into a rapid at flood time. Ukatonen was caught in a maelstrom of powerful emotions that was much more dangerous than anything intentional that Tomas could have thrown at him. He struggled to maintain his equilibrium in the midst of the turmoil. He was powerless to do anything to calm Tomas. Finally he struggled out of the link.

He sat for a moment, stunned. Then, pulling himself out of his daze, he looked at Eerin and Moki.

"I need your help," he said, holding out his arms, deep brown with shame. "He's too strong for me. I can't calm him."

"Rest and eat, en," Eerin said. "I found some bees; there's honey and honeycomb."

"A moment only," Ukatonen told her. "He is in pain, and we must stop it."

"After all he and his men have done to us, en, I don't really care," Eerin declared.

Ukatonen was shocked. "But, Eerin—"

"Ukatonen, we've been sitting here for eight days while you mess around with him." She gestured contemptuously at Tomas. "My family's got to be worried sick. I want to go home!"

Ukatonen laid a hand on her shoulder. "I'm sorry, Eerin. I've been so absorbed with Tomas that I didn't think about that. We'll leave first thing tomorrow. I promise."

"And him?" she asked, gesturing again at Tomas.

"He will come with us. But you must set aside your anger now, and help me end his pain. Unless we do that we cannot bring him into harmony with us."

Eerin looked down. "I'm not sure that I can, en. I'm too angry about all of the things he has done to us."

Ukatonen touched her shoulder and she looked back up at him. "I did not say that you must forget what he has done, or how angry it has made you, but for now, you must let it go for long enough to help him. Moki and I can help you shed your anger if you will let us."

Eerin was silent for a long moment; then she nodded and held out her arms. "All right, en."

They linked. Moki helped Ukatonen smooth away Eerin's anger. Then they turned to Tomas.

The emotional storm had exhausted Tomas, and they were able to slow the raging turmoil. Ukatonen pulled partway out of the link, and talked Tomas through his pain, monitoring and quietly reinforcing calmness, happiness, peace, and a sense of forgiveness. Tomas slid into a sweet, peaceful dream state. Then Ukatonen reached into Tomas's brain and smoothed away the pathways that led to that anger and violence.

Tomas woke about an hour later. He stretched, and there was a relaxed, almost sweet smile on his face. He opened his eyes, and tensed in fear. It saddened Ukatonen to see the lines reappear in the man's face.

"Good morning," Eerin said. "Or rather, good afternoon."

He looked around. "Where am I?"

"In the middle of the jungle," Eerin told him. "We're not exactly sure *which* jungle, though. Are you hungry?"

Tomas nodded. "What did you do to me?" he asked. "How long have I been asleep?"

"About eight days," Ukatonen replied. "How do you feel?"

"Different," he said. "Better. What happened?"

"We escaped, and took you with us," Ukatonen told him. "I needed to understand you. Your cancer is almost gone, by the way."

"I see. And my men? My wife and family? Where are they?"

"I don't know," Ukatonen replied. "We put everyone to sleep in the building you were in. Unless something else happened, they should be all right."

Tomas hung his head in silence for a few moments, his brow furrowed as though he was puzzled.

"I should be angry with you. No, wait, I am angry with you, but it"— he hesitated—"it's different somehow. What did you do to me?"

"We helped you forget how to be angry," Ukatonen explained.

He sat silent for a few moments, looking inward. "Yes, you have. But it was my anger—Who gave you the right to take it away?" His voice was mild, despite his words.

"Who gave you the right to kidnap us?" Eerin asked.

He shook his head. "You don't understand."

"None of us do," Ukatonen said. "Even after all the work I have done on you, I still don't understand why you have killed so many people."

"I believe that it's wrong to tell me how many children I can have."

"But if we keep having children, humanity itself will die," Eerin told him.

"And if the state had decided that you couldn't have your daughter. What then?" Tomas shot back.

"I don't know," Eerin admitted. "It would have been terrible. I can't imagine life without Mariam now."

"And how is that different from us?" he asked. "We love children. We want to have a lot of them."

"I would have given up having a child," Eerin explained. "But your argument doesn't apply. I was buying a child-right that someone wished to sell. I am not exceeding the population goals. Yes, we restrict the right to have a child, but it is restricted equally for everyone."

"And what about this place?" Ukatonen asked. "Would you have so many children that this forest would be destroyed to feed them? Is it worth the death of a beautiful, living planet to have as many children as you wish?"

"The government has no right to tell us how many children to have," Tomas argued.

"You're right. It isn't fair, but it's necessary. But you have a choice. You can emigrate to Mars, if you want to have more children," Eerin pointed out.

"It's sterile and cold. You have to pay to breathe there."

"At least you have a choice, even if it's a hard one. Someday we'll have Terra Nova, and room to expand."

"In two hundred years' time. What good is that to me? Or to my children and grandchildren and their children?"

"None," Eerin allowed. "But it's possible that the Tendu could help us shorten the terraforming. Or give us the ability to adapt to a living world. You have no idea of what humanity risked losing when you kidnapped us. It was stupid, short-term thinking."

Ukatonen held up his hands. "That's enough," he said. "We will not achieve harmony by arguing."

"Then how will we achieve it?" Moki asked.

"By understanding," Ukatonen told him.

"We understand each other," Tomas said. "We understand each other quite well. But we believe very different things. The two beliefs are diametrically opposed to each other. They do not harmonize. It is impossible."

Ukatonen sat up straight, ears wide, amazed by Tomas's rigidity.

"How can you not want to reach harmony?" he asked. "Is it not the goal of all things to want to reach equilibrium with the world around them?"

"I don't want to accept what is," Tomas said. "I'm fighting to make the world into what I want it to be."

"How can you deny the nature of the world?" Ukatonen asked.

"Perhaps the nature of the world is not as you think it is," Tomas replied. "Perhaps the world you see is an illusion built of your own beliefs. Perhaps belief can alter the nature of the world."

Ukatonen listened in astonishment. "How can you believe this?" he questioned.

"Because humans have always changed the world," Tomas said. "It's what we do."

Ukatonen looked at Eerin, who nodded.

"We have changed our world," Eerin admitted, "but not always wisely or well. Usually we changed the world in response to short-term interests. Greed, if you will. But sometimes we have done so for a greater purpose. We did it to save lives, or to further a religious belief. Many people sacrificed their lives for causes that they believed in. Many others were killed because they would not believe what others wanted them to. Sometimes the attempt worked, lives were saved, wars averted, but just as often people died, or became slaves of one sort or another."

Ukatonen listened in disbelief. Even Eerin felt this way. It was as though he had opened the door to another world. How strange to look at the world as humans did, as a thing to fight against, to alter, as though it were made of clay and could be molded without consequences. This sudden glimpse of human nature frightened him more than the casual brutality his captors had shown them, more than the ravages humans had inflicted on their planet's ecosystem, and even more than the fear he had felt as he saw his planet dwindle into an insignificant speck in an immense and starry sky. He felt as though the world itself had turned upside down, and suddenly nothing made any sense at all.

"I think I shall go hunting," Ukatonen told them. "Will you be all right here?"

Eerin said they would, and the enkar swung off into the trees, lost in thought. Human ideas burned in his head like live coals. What if the Tendu kept trying to change their world? What would Tiangi be like? He paused in mid-swing, and hung swaying from the branch he was on, to think it over. *Would we have cities and streets and huge buildings? Would we live as out of balance as the humans?* The idea made him uneasy. No, not on Tiangi, never. But if he could change Tiangi, what would he change?

Very little, seemed to be the answer at first. But then, as he resumed swinging through the trees, the idea returned, niggling at him like some annoying insect. He thought of the villages, mired in tradition, of how hard it had become to find promising elders who wished to become enkar. He only knew a handful of enkar under seven hundred years old, and most of those were ones he had taught.

More and more villages refused to travel and trade with the sea people, preferring to rely on traders to bring them whatever they needed. And there were fewer and fewer new quarbirri being created and even fewer Tendu willing to perform them. Their world was a stagnant, drying mud puddle compared to humanity's quarrelsome, complex network of cultures.

His people were becoming as stiff and inflexible as a sun-cured hide. This is what he would change, if he could. But at what cost? Change always cost something. His time among the humans had taught him that much, at least. Humans had paid and paid and paid for their ceaseless rush to change their world. If the Tendu changed Tiangi too little, then humans were killing their world with their ceaseless desire for change. If only humans and Tendu could give to each other some of what they lacked. There were the seeds of a new harmony somewhere in that idea. He needed to find them, and plant them in fertile soil.

A flicker of resignation passed over him. Someday, perhaps, but not today. Now it was time to concentrate on finding food. Tomorrow they would start heading out of the forest. The question was, what to do with Tomas. There was nothing more to learn from him. Eerin insisted on bringing him back to the authorities, who would punish him as the humans saw fit. It didn't matter, really. Ukatonen had already punished him. He had made it impossible for Tomas to tell a lie.

CHAPTER

9

Juna sat at the window of their hotel room in Brasilia. It was hard to believe that just two days ago they had emerged from the jungle with Tomas in tow. The trek out had taken a week and a half, mostly because Tomas kept running away, and they had to track him down. Finally, Ukatonen had turned Tomas into something like a zombie, unable to do more than follow them blindly through the forest. It had bothered her, to see him so unmanned, but it had been necessary. After another day's wandering they found a road, which led them to a village where Juna convinced a surprised local policeman to contact the Survey office.

After that things began to happen very quickly. They were flown by helicopter into Brasilia. Tomas was taken into custody. Juna turned his computer over to the authorities. With the information on Tomas's computer, the authorities were able to arrest hundreds of people, some of them extremely well-placed. The BirthRight movement was dealt a blow that would set them back several decades. Most of the people implicated in the terrorist wing of the movement were arrested, and several major illegal contraceptive reversal networks were broken up. General Burnham, faced with the information on the computer, resigned. Bruce was arrested, and charged with conspiracy to commit kidnapping. Word of this had left Juna and the Tendu deeply saddened.

A knock on the door made her flinch. She was still jumpy, despite the security detail outside her door.

She peered through the peephole, cried out in joy, and flung open the door. "*Isä*! Netta! Toivo!" She threw her arms around them, feeling the threads of paranoia part and frizzle away to nothing. "It's so good to see you! How is everyone?" She paused, struck by a sudden horrifying fear that they had come to give her bad news. "Is Mariam okay?"

"She's fine," her father said. "It's you we've been worried about." He paused and looked at her, "For someone who's been through as much as you have, you look good. How are Moki and Ukatonen? I heard that they were hurt."

"You know most of the details already," Juna told him. "Moki's all right, despite his arm. It will grow back. It's Ukatonen that I'm worried about. He was all right while we were getting here, but now . . ." She shrugged helplessly. "Now all he has to think about is his injury. He spends most of his time brooding about what he's lost. I'm worried that he'll decide to die."

"Let me talk to him," Toivo offered. "Maybe I can help."

Ukatonen sat in his darkened room, pondering his situation. At home on Tiangi, he would tie up all the things he had left undone, or pass along whatever he could not complete to the enkar that he had trained. He would then retreat into the forest for several weeks, thinking over his life, and then emerge for a final ceremony of leave-taking with his enkar brethren. Then he would become one with the forest, alive only in the memory of the Tendu.

But he was far from home, and alone. There was no one that could take up his obligations. It might be years before he could go home again. He had to bear the dishonor of living like this. But how?

There was a knock on the door that connected his room to Eerin's. Ukatonen ignored it. He wasn't in the mood for company. The door opened anyway. He looked up, angry, and to his shame, a little afraid.

"Toivo," he said. "I didn't know you were here."

"We just got in," Toivo told him. He paused, "I wish I could heal you the way that you healed me, but—" He spread his hands in a gesture of resignation. "If there's anything I can do to help you, en, please tell me."

Ukatonen sat silent for a few moments, wrestling with his dignity. "How did you manage, living like that? How could you do it?" he said at last.

"It was never easy, en," Toivo told the enkar, sitting on a low stool across from him. "You know I tried to die. My family loved me too much to let me go." He looked down at his hands as they rested on his knees. "At first, I was so angry that I couldn't speak to them. That was when I moved out to the zero-gee satellite, where I could die in peace if I wanted to. And then"— he looked up at Ukatonen—"suddenly I couldn't bring myself to do it. Not there, not so far away from everyone I loved, everyone familiar. Then, a few months later, Juna came home, and I had to see her before I died."

Toivo was silent for a while, his eyes shadowed in the darkened room, clearly remembering that time. "I guess—" he continued, meeting Ukatonen's eyes, "I guess you just take it one day at a time. Don't think of the long run, focus on today, focus on now. If you think of spending the rest of your life as a cripple, well, you'll go crazy."

Ukatonen nodded. "I'll try." Even to his own ears he sounded dubious.

Toivo smiled. "It isn't easy," he said. "But you've got a choice. You can sit here in a dark room and think about your injury, or you can get on with your life. I suggest getting on with your life. You know, it could be much worse. You can walk and talk and even link, even if your skill isn't what it once was."

"You don't understand," Ukatonen protested. "I've lost a skill that took me centuries to learn. My presence was one of the strongest among the enkar. It made me a powerful healer. It helped me resolve differences. Now," he said, a cloud of grey misting his skin, "I'm a cripple. At home my weakness would bring dishonor on all the enkar. I would be expected to die."

Toivo clasped Ukatonen's slender, long-fingered hands in his big, square, work-roughened ones, and met the enkar's gaze. "But you're not on Tiangi, en. You're here in human space. You're doing things none of your people have ever done before. Maybe this is one more thing that you're learning to do differently. Maybe this is a lesson you can take home to your people. You won't know unless you live long enough to find out."

"I suppose," Ukatonen ventured, "I'll have to try. I must live to get back to Tiangi. I need to teach my people what I have learned." *Then I can die*, he thought to himself, but he did not say it aloud.

Toivo held out his hand. "One day at a time, Ukatonen. Let's get started on living through today."

Moki watched Ukatonen struggle with the gap left behind by his injury. He ached to help him, but Ukatonen shrugged off any attempts to reach him through allu-a, though he continued to work with Moki on making his arm grow back. When they returned to Berry Station, Eerin's family did their best to comfort Ukatonen, but that only made him withdraw further into the shell of his dignity and reserve. At least he had reached out to Eerin's brother. Ukatonen would spend hours working beside Toivo, saying nothing, apparently completely absorbed in the task at hand. He came in at the end of the day completely exhausted, but relaxed, his skin a slight bluish green. It was not quite contentment, not quite relief, but it was clear that the hard physical labor had brought the grieving enkar some kind of peace.

There were times when Moki was sure the enkar was going to give up, that they were going to walk into his room one morning and find him dead. But slowly, painfully, Ukatonen began to win against the darkness. At first there were a few moments when the enkar seemed to forget his pain, and then an occasional hour of quiet contentment. Then one evening, right after Eerin had put Mariam to bed, Ukatonen, accompanied by Toivo, knocked on her door and held out his arms for allu-a.

Moki sat up, ears spread wide in surprise, but Eerin laid a cautioning hand on his leg and said, "Of course, en. Please come in."

Moki had never thought he would be relieved by Ukatonen's injury, but after that link, he was. Ukatonen's grief raged through them like a hurricane. He and Eerin waited until the storm passed, and then gently, carefully, enfolded him, soothing away the rest of his grief and pain. Ukatonen opened himself to them like a flower. He had never really fully opened to them before, Moki realized. Before, Ukatonen had always screened a part of himself away. Now, feeling the intensity of loneliness behind the wall of the enkar's reserve, Moki understood why. So much loneliness was a fearsome thing. To Moki, it seemed like it would engulf the world. He started to retreat, afraid that they would be caught in a downward spiral, but Eerin drew him back into the link, and they waited, giving what they could to heal Ukatonen's broken spirit. At last Ukatonen regained a measure of control, and they achieved emotional equilibrium.

Gently, they slid out of the link. Moki was very hungry. Glancing at the window, he realized that the sky was greying toward dawn.

"Let's go get something to eat," he said, looking at the other two. There were dark patches under his sitik's eyes, and Ukatonen was pale with exhaustion. Somehow on the way downstairs the trek to the kitchen turned into a mock hunting expedition. They crept quietly down the steps, peered carefully into the kitchen, and then attacked the refrigerator and pantry. They collapsed on the floor in a rippling, giggling heap, and then, weak with laughter, proceeded to stuff themselves on fruit, honey, bread, and meat.

They were just cleaning up, and getting breakfast set up for the early risers when Danan and Selena came in.

"Hey, Mom and I were in charge of breakfast this morning!" Danan protested.

"Well, we were up," Eerin replied. "It's been kind of a long night." She glanced over at Ukatonen. "But it's over now, and we were going to go upstairs and get some rest as soon as we were done here."

"Well then, shoo!" Selena told them. "You're done. Go get some sleep. You look like you need it."

"Of course, Selena," Eerin said meekly. They trooped up the stairs, passing several sleepy family members on their way down. It felt strange to be going to bed when the rest of the family was just getting up, but Moki fell asleep almost as soon as he had settled himself under the covers.

Ukatonen woke the next morning feeling somehow lighter and more free than he'd felt in several hundred years. He remembered that incredible, harrowing link and slid his nictitating membranes over his eyes and pushed the memory away. He must not allow that kind of pain even a remembered foothold in his mind.

From that day on, it got easier. There were still bad days, filled with the sour coldness of misery, or sour and tight with frustration, but they were only days, or hours, and he could get over them with a link, or sometimes even a joke. Gradually his reserve lifted, and he unfolded like a fragrant girra flower at sunset.

The response from others to this change was remarkable. People opened up to him in ways he never expected. Mariam began solemnly showing him flowers and rocks and bugs. Old Niccolo and his wife Rosa, sat and told him stories of the family and its history. Selena showed him sketches that she had made of the family, and surprisingly, a couple of him, sound asleep. He sat for her while she filled page after page of her sketchbook with drawings of him. She had a real gift for catching a characteristic pose. Suddenly the world was full of warmth and love. How had he missed it before?

He was in the kitchen, washing dishes, enjoying the feel of the warm water on his hands when Moki came bursting in.

"Ukatonen! They're coming! They're coming!"

"Who's coming, Moki?" he asked.

"Anitonen and Naratonen!" he said. "They're coming to Earth on the next supply boat back from Tiangi."

Ukatonen squeezed out the sponge he was using, feeling his happiness ooze out like the water from the sponge. "When?" he asked in sound speech, not trusting his skin to hide the sudden, deep despair he was feeling.

"Eerin says it'll be another six months at least," Moki told him. "The announcement came from a supply ship that just made the jump from Tiangi."

"What about greensickness?" Ukatonen asked. "How are they going to keep them from getting sick?"

"Eerin says that they've specially outfitted the ship to make the Tendu feel more comfortable."

"Good," Ukatonen said. "I'm glad their trip will be easier than ours." He set the sponge down and wandered out of the kitchen, through the fields and up into the forest, where he sat looking out at the enclosed, cylindrical landscape of Berry Station. He was simultaneously anticipating and dreading the thought of seeing the other enkar. What would they think of him now, with his injury, and his lack of a decent enkarish reserve?

He sat there, pondering this until the light began to dim for evening. He got up and swung home with a heavy heart. Eerin was waiting for him on the darkened porch. "Moki thought you might be upset about the enkar coming," she said as he reached the top step.

Ukatonen shrugged. "I'm—so different now. What are they going to think of me, like this?"

"You have much to teach them, en. And not all of it will be about humans."

Ukatonen looked at her for a long moment. "They do not want to learn what I have to teach, Eerin."

"Nevertheless, it's an important lesson and one they should learn. How many wise and intelligent enkar die because a judgment goes awry for reasons they cannot control? How many maimed Tendu feel that they have to die because they are not perfect? The enkar need to learn to forgive themselves, en. Each one that dies is a loss, not just for themselves, but for the Tendu as a species. There are many lessons your people could learn by allowing the disabled to live. Lessons of patience, struggle, and strength."

"Those are human lessons, Eerin," he said. "I don't think the Tendu can learn them."

He turned and went inside, climbed up the stairs to his room, and shut the door. Despite all they'd been through together, Eerin didn't understand, couldn't understand, what he was going through.

Juna drove Ukatonen to the shuttle station two days later. He was heading back down to a research station in Australia, ostensibly to do some restoration work. She had pushed him too far, and he was running away. Not that she could blame him. The news about the upcoming visit from the enkar had nearly unravelled all the progress he had made since his injury.

"You don't have to go, Ukatonen," she said as a member of his security escort opened the door of the truck.

"I have to go," he said. "They need me down there, and besides, it'll give me time to think things over." He brushed her shoulder affectionately. "I know you want to help, but I need to do this my own way."

"All right, en, but remember, if you need us, we're here."

Ukatonen turned a clear pale blue. "I know. And I'm grateful." He enfolded her in a long-armed hug. "Thank you. And please thank Toivo and Moki and the rest of the family for me."

"I will."

He withdrew from Eerin's embrace and picked up his bag; then, accompanied by his guards, he headed down the passageway to catch the shuttle.

Stan Akuka met him at the airport. "How're you doin' mate?" he asked. "We heard you were hurt. You okay?"

"I suppose," Ukatonen allowed.

"They're looking forward to seeing you up at the station. There's a bunch of me mates up there waiting to meet you, as well. You look like you could do with a bit of a party."

Ukatonen nodded.

"C'mon then," Stan said. "Let's go."

He stayed at the research station for a day or two. Then, he moved out into the bush with the Aboriginals, much to the dismay of the researchers and his security escorts. The Aboriginals lived more like the Tendu than any other humans he had encountered. They taught him about the jungle, showing him medicinal plants, and relating stories about the animals—where they lived, and what they ate. They admired his skill at hunting, and his ability to climb trees. He admired the Aboriginals' quiet patience, and their sense of humor.

In the evenings, they told stories, and sang songs, and danced. He would perform a quarbirri, accompanied by the somber drone of the didgeridoo, drums, rattles, and flutes. The Aboriginals watched in silent appreciation.

Sometimes he would link with one or two of the Aboriginals that he especially liked. He found, to his surprise, that his injury made him pay more attention to the others in the link. He learned more about the Aboriginals' internal life than he would have if his presence had dominated the link. Working with them, he learned the advantage of quiet attention and patience. It was a lesson he thought he had learned many centuries ago. He had not expected to have to learn it over again.

Living with these dark, silent people was more like living in a Tendu village than like living among humans. Many of the men and women he talked to were college-educated. Some even had advanced degrees in various disciplines. But at some point they had set down their "white" occupations, as they called them, and returned to the bush, some for a few months or weeks, some for the rest of their lives. He understood, but he didn't think he could explain it to someone who was not an Aboriginal or a Tendu. Eerin might understand, perhaps. She knew what it was like to live this way, but for her, the bush was not really home, not like it was for him, or for these people.

He mentioned this to Stan one night, as the fire died down to embers. Stan nodded. "You either have the spirit in your heart, or you don't. If you don't, it's meaningless."

"Tell me about the whites. I still don't know the story of what they did."

"They came here and drove us off the land," Stan said. "They hunted us like animals, made us slaves. They took children away from their families and sent them to mission schools. They nearly ended the Dreamtime for us."

"Why did they do it?" Ukatonen asked.

"If I understood that, I guess I'd be white too," Stan said. "They wanted our land. We were different. We were in the way. But we survived. Despite all they did to try to change us, we survived. We remembered the old songs, not all of them, but enough. Eventually, they let us alone again, and we were able to rebuild. Sometimes it's still hard. Those of us with degrees, it tore us apart sometimes, the gap between the white world and the real world. Some of us die trying to fill that gap. Others just seem to learn to live with a white soul and a black one. A few, like me, go walkabout and never really return. A lot more stay white. But there's always a new generation of us here in the bush. There's always enough to keep the song lines active."

Ukatonen was silent for a while, then finally asked the question that had been weighing on his spirit since that afternoon on the zeppelin.

"Do you think that humans can do to us what they did to you?"

"If they can, they will," Stan said. "There will always be those who understand, those who care. But there will also be the greedy ones. Both of them are dangerous, because both of them bring change. Those people who built the mission schools cared enough to want to take us out of the bush where we were happy, and try to make us white. You must not let them do the same to your people."

"How do we stop them?" Ukatonen asked.

"If we knew that, this would still be our land. I'm sorry, Ukatonen. That is something your people will have to figure out for yourselves. We'd like to help, but remember, we lost the fight."

"I like them," Ukatonen confessed. "They're so alive. There is so much my people could learn from them. So much we could learn from each other. But—" He shook his head.

"They've made a right mess of the planet, though," Stan noted.

"I don't want that to happen to Tiangi."

"Well, what are you goin' to do to stop it?"

Ukatonen shook his head and stared into the glowing red embers of the fire, lost in thought. After a while he heard Stan get up and walk off to his bark shelter.

Stan's question haunted him for three days. Finally he started gathering his things together.

"You goin', then?" Stan asked.

Ukatonen nodded.

"Have you figured out what you're goin' to do?"

"No," Ukatonen said, "but I do know that I have to stop running away from the problem. I've got a couple of my people coming here to Earth. Maybe they can help me figure out what to do."

Standing in the boarding bay of Broumas Station with Moki and Eerin, Ukatonen watched as the heavy airlock doors swung open. Anitonen and Naratonen were waiting on the other side. It took him a second to recognize them—they seemed strangely long-limbed and fragile. He had a hard time believing they were real.

Anitonen was telling Naratonen how relieved she was to finally be off this ship. It was strange, watching two other Tendu talk to each other in skin speech. He and Moki had fallen into the habit of using a mixture of Standard sound speech and skin speech, and even their skin speech was peppered with human words, unless they wanted to convey something privately. It made the arriving enkar seem like strangers, even though he knew both of them well.

Before he could stop him, Moki rushed forward, and embraced the two surprised enkar. Their ears lifted in surprise, and Ukatonen thought he saw a yellow flicker of irritation on Naratonen's shoulder. He felt a sudden flash of anger. It had been years since Moki had seen another Tendu. Couldn't they understand how much the little bami had missed others of his species?

Then Moki remembered his manners and stepped back, becoming stiff and formal. He put his almost-complete arm behind his back, self-conscious about his stubby, half-formed fingers.

"Welcome, Naratonen and Anitonen. Your presence does us honor," he said both in formal Tendu skin speech and aloud in Human Standard. "Please allow me to lead you to where Ukatonen and Eerin are waiting for you."

Ukatonen stepped forward as they approached. "Welcome, en," he said, doubling the symbol for "en" to indicate that he meant both of them. "We will be staying here overnight, then going to an ecological research station on Earth. It is much like Tiangi there. You'll like it."

"And when will we meet Eerin's family? Moki told us so much about them on the comm," Anitonen said.

"It's midwinter there, and very cold. You would have to wear a warm-suit whenever you went outside. In a few months, when the weather's better, we'll go and visit them. But Eerin's daughter, Mariam, and some of her family will be joining us here on Broumas, so you'll get a chance to meet them. They will be coming down to Earth with us to help look after Mariam."

"I was hoping to see some of the humans' performances," Naratonen told him. "The plays that I saw on Tri-V were very interesting."

"You will," Ukatonen assured him. "After you are recovered from your trip, and are used to speaking aloud, we will visit many different countries around the world, meeting their leaders, and watching their musicians and actors perform."

"I still do not understand the idea of countries," Anitonen said, as they followed their security escorts into the hotel elevator. "Who determines what one is? How do they tell which country a person belongs to? Why are they all so different?"

Ukatonen shook his head. He had forgotten how little he had known when he first came here. They had so much to learn. "It is difficult to explain. Imagine, if you will, if individual villages ran the world. That is what countries are like. Only more so."

Anitonen's ears lifted. "It would be disharmony, and worse. I cannot imagine such a situation."

"It exists here on Earth."

"And have you done nothing to stop it?" Anitonen demanded.

Ukatonen spread his hands. "We have vowed to abide by their rules of noninterference."

"En, it is not his problem to solve. Nor yours," Eerin said. "We humans have been trying to bring peace between our people for millennia. Sometimes the attempts to bring peace only made things worse for everyone."

"I have been studying the problem," Ukatonen said. "Some of the feuds between different groups of humans have been going on for hundreds of generations. It is a very complex tangle, and not easily undone. You loosen one thread and six others tighten. If there is anything that we can do to help bring harmony here, it will require much study before we act."

A blue and green ripple of amusement coursed over Naratonen. "Anitonen is still young, and so much time working with humans has made her hasty."

Anitonen browned with shame. "I am sorry, en," she said as the elevator doors opened.

"You will learn, Anitonen," Naratonen said in gentle, reassuring tones. He brushed her shoulder with his knuckles.

Analin had set up a press conference in the hotel's largest conference room. Eerin, Ukatonen, and Moki took turns translating formal greetings to the people of Earth from the two newly arrived enkar, and answering questions on their behalf. Anitonen and Naratonen watched the goings-on in amazement. At least, Ukatonen thought with a flicker of amusement, they didn't embarrass themselves as much as he and Moki had at their first press conference.

Ukatonen did his best to spin the press conference out as long as he could, but Analin finally brought it to a halt. As soon as they reached their rooms, Ukatonen vanished into the shower, putting off the moment of linking as long as he could. Eventually, the shower timed out and shut itself off, forcing him to face the others. Anitonen and Naratonen were waiting for him in the living room with Moki and Eerin.

"Ukatonen, it has been a long time since we linked, come join us," Anitonen said.

"No, I-I can't," Unatonen said.

Purple clouds of puzzlement flowed over the newcomers' bodies.

"What is the matter?" Naratonen said.

"I was injured."

"Then you need healing. We should link," Naratonen insisted.

"It was my head, the part where my presence lived. Moki did the best he could but— it is beyond healing." he told them, grey with grief. "I would die, but my knowledge is needed. And," he said, gesturing with his chin at Moki and Eerin, "they would not let me die."

"That does not matter. You need linking. Come," Naratonen said, holding out his arms. "We will learn what you have to teach as quickly as we can, that we may not keep you from an honorable death."

Ukatonen knew that once he said the words in his heart, his relationship with the enkar, with the Tendu, and with the universe would change irrevocably. He looked over at Moki and Eerin for a moment, to strengthen his resolve, then spoke:

"Perhaps I no longer seek an honorable death, but an honorable, if imperfect, life."

The two enkar stared at him in amazement. "How can such a thing be?" Naratonen asked. "How can you think this?"

A flicker of ironic amusement flowed over Ukatonen's body. "It is one of the many things I have learned here." He held out his arms. "Link with me, and I will show you."

Naratonen drew back, and Anitonen hesitated visibly. Ukatonen was suddenly amused. They were afraid of him. It was not the response he had expected.

"It is a choice, en, that is all. I realized that despite what happened, I still wanted to live. There is still so much for me to learn. And—" he continued, "I am willing to live with the consequences of that decision."

He held out his arms again. "Link with me, en. It has been a long time."

Anitonen reached out first. Then Naratonen, though a flicker of orange fear passed over him as he did so.

They linked. The strength of their presences washed over him like huge waves. To his surprise, he sensed Moki and Eerin moving to buffer them, but he moved into the enkar's presences, riding the power of their strength. It was good, so good, to feel the presence of other Tendu in the link. He realized how stale allu-a had become. He felt Naratonen examining the scar on his brain. The enkar made a sudden adjustment. Suddenly, like a picture snapping into focus, Ukatonen's presence strengthened. He felt a sudden exultation as he tested his new strength. Then he sensed Naratonen's disappointment, and despair closed on Ukatonen like a giant fist. The improvement was not enough. Not for an enkar.

Ukatonen broke the link and fled, ashamed of his sudden cowardice, but he could feel Anitonen and Naratonen's thoughts coming toward him like a dark line of rain. They were going to offer to help him die, and he was terribly afraid that he would accept their gift.

"Ukatonen, wait!"

It was Eerin. He stopped by the elevator and waited for her to catch up.

"What happened, en?" she asked. "I felt Naratonen do something, but I wasn't sure what happened after that."

Ukatonen darkened in shame as he explained.

"Let's go for a walk," Eerin suggested. "There's a Motoyoshi garden you haven't seen yet."

Ukatonen looked up at her, his skin lightening in anticipation.

"That would be good," he told her.

They went, and he sat in stillness by a small, twisted tree, near a trickling stone fountain letting the peace of the garden seep into him.

"I cannot do this anymore," he told her at last. "I am no longer an enkar."

"But you are something more than an enkar," Eerin told him, "not something less."

"I am a new kind of Tendu," Ukatonen replied. "But I don't know what that means yet. I don't know where I fit into the world."

"You are part of our family, for one thing. There is one place where you belong."

He looked up at her, moved by her words, but saddened also. "Perhaps, for now," he said. "I do not think it will be a long-term solution."

"I know, en," Eerin said, smiling ruefully as she heard herself use the title. "But you need to belong somewhere until you find that solution."

He reached out and took her hand, twining his long green fingers with her shorter brown ones. "Thank you," he said.

Naratonen watched Moki and Ukatonen playing in the trees, marveling at how deceptively normal they seemed. Living among humans had changed them, frighteningly so in Ukatonen's case. It made Naratonen worry about how much he had changed since he and Anitonen had left Tiangi.

Ukatonen's skin flickered in relaxed delight as he chased Moki through the trees. How could an enkar as strong and determined as Ukatonen have changed so much in so short a time? Naratonen had been shocked into stillness when Ukatonen returned after that disastrous first link, and formally renounced being an enkar. Naratonen shook his head. How could Ukatonen renounce his status? It was like renouncing your ears.

But Ukatonen was happy, full of the overflowing joyfulness one normally found in a bami. According to Eerin, it was because he no longer had to strive for the perfection expected of an enkar.

Anitonen touched him on the shoulder. He turned to see what she was going to say.

"Have you spoken to him yet?"

"No," flickered across Naratonen's skin. "I haven't found the right time."

"Then we will have to make the right time," Anitonen declared. "He knows more than any other enkar about humans. We need that knowledge."

"But he is no longer an enkar," Naratonen pointed out. He was still trying to comprehend what that meant.

"So he says," Anitonen replied. "But that does not make it true. Ukatonen is needed, and we must make him understand that."

Naratonen watched Ukatonen playing, green and gold sun dapples sliding across his laughing skin. "I don't see how, en."

"Neither do I, but somehow we must convince him."

Naratonen looked up and felt a faint mist of regret cloud his skin. Ukatonen had come through so much to achieve this fragile happiness, and now he had to destroy it again.

"It will not be easy."

"I can't go back now," Ukatonen said. "Moki needs me. And there's Mariam. I want to stay here and help Mariam grow up."

"And what of your people? They need you too," Naratonen argued.

"I can best serve the Tendu by remaining here and continuing to learn about humans, and by teaching humans and Tendu about each other. You do not need me," Ukatonen said firmly. "You need more enkar who understand humans. Send them here, and I will teach them. But I will not go back to Tiangi until Mariam is old enough to go with us."

"And when will that be?" Anitonen asked.

"Not for several years, at least," Ukatonen said, feeling a twinge of guilt at how far he was stretching the truth.

"You are an enkar!" Naratonen insisted. "Your duty lies with the Tendu!"

"I am no longer an enkar, and I have no duties. I will stay here with Moki and with Eerin and her family."

Naratonen recoiled, his skin roiling with pale orange swirls of horror.

"Other enkar have become hermits, retreating from their duties for a time," Ukatonen told the two enkar. "What I am doing is not too different. As I am, I am not strong enough in the link to be an enkar. Perhaps I will never be. What good can I do on Tiangi, where I would only be a source of shame for the enkar? Here, I am valued. Each day I learn more about humans—who they are, how they think. And most importantly, I have a hand in shaping Moki and Mariam. Those two, raised together, will be a potent force in creating harmony between our people."

"But how can we deal with these humans without you?" Anitonen demanded. "They want so much from us. And some of the villagers are growing impatient. They want the humans' metal tools, and the strong ropes that do not rot."

Amusement rippled over Ukatonen's skin. "This is good. It gives humans and Tendu a reason to listen to each other."

"Perhaps," Anitonen said. "But we have no idea what the next step should be. We are so far from harmony. How can we trade without causing each other harm?"

"If you don't know what the next step should be, then remain still until you know where to go," Ukatonen told them.

"But—" Naratonen began.

"Coming here was a good idea," Ukatonen went on. "I will help you learn and give you advice, but I will not go back with you when you return."

With that, he got up and left them.

When he was gone, Anitonen turned to Naratonen. "Well, what now?"

"I don't know," Naratonen admitted. "Wait, and hope that he changes his mind."

A flicker of ironic amusement ran down Anitonen's torso. "When have you ever known him to change his mind?"

Naratonen's skin was dark and serious. "He has changed so much since he left us. Perhaps that, too, might have changed."

Juna was sitting up and reading when Ukatonen came in, his skin roiling with emotion.

"What's the matter?" she asked.

"Naratonen and Anitonen want me to go back to Tiangi with them."

Juna felt a clutch at her heart. Carefully keeping her face neutral, she set down her book. "And?"

"I said no. I told them that I wasn't leaving until Mariam was old enough to come with us. Moki needs me, Mariam needs me, and you need me. Besides, I want to help you raise both of them."

"Ukatonen," Juna said, deeply moved by his decision. "What about you? What do you need? You've been away from your people for a long time. I worry about what this isolation is doing to you."

"And what about Moki?" he said. "If I leave, he will be the only Tendu in a world of humans."

"Perhaps Anitonen or Naratonen can stay to help."

Ukatonen looked at her for a long moment. His golden eyes gleamed in the dim lamplight. "I don't want to go back to Tiangi. There is no place for me there."

"And here?" Juna asked him.

"Here I have you, Moki, your family, and many friends. There is useful work for me to do, and a whole new world to learn about. On Tiangi, I would be a cripple, and not, as your people call it, 'disabled.' Everyone would wonder why I had not chosen the honorable course and killed myself. I would be shunned and derided as less than honorable. Among the villagers, I would be a laughingstock. Among the enkar, I would be a source of shame."

"Ukatonen, if you return, then you can be an example. You can show your people the lesson that we have learned."

"Perhaps," he said, looking away. "But not yet. I am not ready to go and be an example, Eerin. I am not yet strong enough."

Juna reached out and took his hand. "You will be someday," she said. "You will have to be. You can't spend the rest of your life here. Someday you will have to go home again."

He turned to look at her. "But not now. Anitonen and Naratonen seem to labor under the delusion that somehow I can straighten out all the problems that have arisen between the humans and the Tendu on Tiangi." He shook his head. "I told them that I would stay here and teach other enkar about humanity, but I would not go back. If they accept my offer, I will need the help of you and your family. Are you willing to take on this burden?"

"You know that I will help you all I can, Ukatonen," she said, "I will talk to my family, but I'm sure that they will be happy to do what they can to help."

"We will find what we need when the time comes." Ukatonen said. He stood. "Hopefully, this will benefit Moki as well. He needs more contact with his own people."

"I hope they decide to do it," Juna told him, smiling inwardly. It wasn't just Moki who needed more contact with the Tendu.

*   *   *

Watching the two enkar struggle to comprehend human culture convinced Ukatonen that he had made the right decision. He had Moki teach them to speak human sound speech. Once Moki got over the initial awkwardness of teaching enkar, he proved to be an excellent instructor. It was hard for the enkar to learn from a mere bami. It was especially hard for Anitonen, who had helped Moki through the transformation from tinka to bami.

Ukatonen hid his amusement at the enkar's shame, and watched as they began to appreciate and acknowledge Moki's skill. It was a lesson all enkar badly needed to learn, he thought. If they sent him more enkar, Moki would be one of their teachers.

Despite their initial difficulties, the two enkar learned quickly, and were speaking Standard fluently enough to carry on short conversations in only a few days.

Anitonen and Naratonen came into their own on the diplomatic tour. The diplomats had been briefed on Naratonen's interest in seeing Earth's performing arts, and they were treated to a wide range of performances, ranging from Shakespeare in the original English to the sonorous and majestic Noh theater, the brash and brilliant Chinese operas, as well as atomic-age musicals, and plays and films from every era and age.

In return, the three enkar and Moki performed traditional quarbirri, and improvised with musicians. Naratonen was dazzled by the lights, the sound system, the special effects, and the sheer range and variety of performing arts. He was especially impressed by Chinese opera, and spent hours backstage with the actors and actresses, learning to copy their mask-like makeup. The actors in turn were fascinated by his ability to instantly change from one face to another. By the time Ukatonen bodily hauled him off to a diplomatic reception with the Chinese Minister of Ecology, he had formed a fast friendship with the troupe's director, Li Liu, and they were spinning out ideas for a new opera that would utilize his ability to change his skin color.

Anitonen focused on learning human diplomacy. She spent hours closeted with members of the protocol staff, learning the ins and outs of a diplomat's life. She also spent a lot of time with Analin, trying to comprehend the chaos and violence of human history. Anitonen kept coming to Ukatonen with questions about what motivated humans to do various things. Occasionally, he or Moki could enlighten her, but mostly they all turned to Eerin, whose explanations were often as confusing as the questions they brought to her. But once in a while some revelation would blossom.

The two enkar kept Moki busy, answering their endless questions, and looking after them. Moki blossomed under the enkar's demands. Ukatonen had forgotten how much of a bami's role revolved around serving the elders around him. It was how a bami learned to be a Tendu. He and Eerin were much too self-sufficient to keep Moki occupied.

After the diplomatic tour was over, they returned for a month to Berry Station. The two enkar were fascinated by the Fortunati family, especially Mariam, who was delighted to have two more Tendu to play with.

The enkar spent alternate months on Berry, studying intently; then they would spend a month traveling and meeting people. Naratonen and Li Liu actually managed to create a Chinese/Tendu opera, using both Chinese and Tendu music, though finding a common theme proved difficult. It was a huge success—over a billion people downloaded it. Naratonen's share of the royalties was enough to make him moderately wealthy by Earth standards. Eerin helped him set up a fund to defray the costs of Tendu traveling to Earth. Li Liu gave Naratonen a copy of the score and a chip of the performance to take back to Tiangi. It would require violating the Contact Protocols to show it to any of the Tendu back home, but Naratonen watched the performance so many times that he could reproduce the entire performance on his skin.

As the date for their departure loomed, Anitonen and Naratonen redoubled their efforts to get Ukatonen to come with them. He continued to refuse. At one point, Naratonen even threatened to render a judgment that Ukatonen must go back with them. Before Naratonen could formally phrase his judgment, Anitonen stopped him by rendering a judgment that her life would be forfeit if he created a judgment about this matter. After that, the subject of Ukatonen returning to Tiangi was not spoken of, though it hung in the air like a persistent fragrance.

The enkar's final days in human space were spent in frenetic planning, trying to decide which six enkar would come and study with Ukatonen. They needed to be flexible enough to cope with the humans' radically different culture, and understanding enough to work with Ukatonen, despite his injury.

Then suddenly, it was time for Naratonen and Anitonen to return to Tiangi.

Dread weighed heavily in Ukatonen's stomach on the trip back to Broumas to see them off. It would be more than a year before the next group of enkar arrived. He had grown used to the company of his own people again. It was going to be hard, being only one of two Tendu among all these humans. It was still possible to change his mind and go home, Ukatonen realized. He closed his eyes against the sudden surge of longing as he thought of Tiangi.

Then the shuttle docked, and there were bags to carry, and trains to catch, and then they were standing at the starship gate.

Ukatonen held out his hands, asking for a link. Moki, Eerin, Anitonen and Naratonen found a quiet corner and plunged into a final allu-a. They reached a sad, subdued equilibrium. As the link was breaking apart, Naratonen and Anitonen drew him back into a separate link with just the two of them. They opened themselves completely to Ukatonen. He was startled and touched by the honor they did him. He opened himself to them, sharing his longing for home. He was surprised to see how much this leaving grieved them as well.

Naratonen brushed his shoulder affectionately. "You could still come with us," he offered.

Ukatonen was silent for a moment as he struggled with his longing for Tiangi. "I know, but I am needed here," he replied.

Naratonen nodded. He had not expected Ukatonen to change his mind.

"You have taught us so much. I think we will be better at working with the humans," Anitonen admitted. "But it will be a long time before harmony can be achieved."

"I know," Ukatonen said. "First we must understand each other. Then we can work toward harmony." He looked over at Eerin and Moki. "They are part of the bridge we must build."

Anitonen touched his arm. "As are you, en," she said. "As are you."

The two enkar scooped up their bags and walked through the gate and up the long, spiraling ramp to the starship's passenger airlock. Ukatonen watched until the curve of the ramp blocked them from view. He stood there for a long moment after they were gone, wanting desperately to run after them. Then he turned back to Moki and Eerin.

"Let's go home," he said.

GLOSSARY

Allu *n.* Fleshy red spurs located on the inside of the forearm and their associated organs, used by the Tendu for allu-a.

Allu-a *n. & vb.* The communion between two or more Tendu that involves a deep sharing of physiological state.

Ang-ar-gora *n. & vb.* The art of stealth, of listening without being seen. Usually practiced exclusively by the enkar.

Atwa *n.* The ecological grouping that comes under the care of a Tendu elder.

Bai *n.* Diminutive-informal form of bami, usually used by a sitik to his or her bami.

Bami *n.* A sub-adult who is apprenticed/parented by an elder Tendu. They have the capacity to speak.

Enkar *n.* A class of Tendu who travel from village to village giving advice and settling disputes.

Ganuna *n.* A small lizard with a venomous but rarely fatal bite. It warns off attackers with a loud hissing sound.

Gauware *n.* A rain forest fruit tree.

Girra *n.* A vine bearing extremely fragrant, night-blooming flowers, and edible fruit.

Gudda *n.* An arborial, marsupial lizard, about the size of a medium-sized dog. It is very prolific.

Koirah *n.* Large raptor that preys on animals in the uppermost canopy. One of the most dreaded predators of the Tendu.

Lyali-Tendu *n.* Sea Tendu. Those Tendu who live year-round in coastal waters.

Mitamit *n.* A large predatory insect. The female builds intricately layered webs in which to trap males in order to mate with them. She then lays her eggs inside the male, and the developing young feed on their father.

Na tree *n.* The giant hollow trees that are the preferred living quarters for land dwelling Tendu.

Pika *n.* A starchy fermented dough made from the root of a water plant. It is often flattened and used to wrap around other foods.

Pooo-eet *n.* A fishing bird that lives near the river. During their mating season (also known as the month or "pida" of Pooo-eet) the canopy echoes with their "poooeet" calls, prompting many Tendu to go hunting for a little peace and quiet.

Purra *n.* A mollusc with a thick, hard, difficult-to-open shell. It is prized as a delicacy by the Lyali-Tendu.

Quarbirri *n. & vb.* Traditional Tendu dance/narrative art form, involving music, dance, and skin speech.

Ruwar-a *n.* A system or process in which the elements work together synergetically so that the whole is greater than the sum of its parts. Considered auspicious and harmonious.

Siti *n.* Informal, intimate form of sitik, usually used by a bami to his or her sitik.

Sitik *n.* An elder Tendu who is the mentor/parent of a sub-adult bami.

Tinka *n.* Juvenile form of Tendu, imprinted on a village. Usually six years and older. A tinka can live as long as fifty years before beginning to age and die.

Weedah *n.* A bird that builds a tangled, tightly woven nest. Old nests are often disassembled by the Tendu for the fiber they contain.

Yetilye *n.* A burrowing orange worm roughly equivalent to a Terran earthworm.

NON-TENDU GLOSSARY

Greensickness *n.* A debilitating psychosomatic depression found in the Tendu. It is caused by isolation from a natural ecosystem.

Isi *n.* Finnish for father (informal).

Isoisi *n.* Finnish for grandfather (informal).

Isukki *n.* Finnish: Informal, intimate term for father.

Osento *n.* Japanese term for public baths.

Pikkuinnen *n.* Finnish for little one. Used of children in a family.

Täti *n.* Finnish term for aunt.

Tytär *n.* Finnish for daughter.

Tytärenpoika *n.* Finnish for grandson. Literally means daughter's son.

Veljentytär *n.* Finnish term for niece. Literally means brother's daughter.